Craig Lesley

RIVER SONG

"*River Song* is written in a clear, staccato prose and tells a compelling . . . story. . . . The novel's settings have wonderful authenticity—a reader can smell the forest and the water, the wood smoke and the dusty arenas."
—Michael Dorris, *Newsday*

"A tale of reconciliation between father and son, and of a people with their heritage . . . a skillfully told story that illuminates the plight of American Indians as they battle to keep their way of life alive."
—*The New York Times Book Review*

"Palpable excitement . . . lyrical and dreamlike beauty . . . both an adventure tale and a more subtle story of personal quest and discovery. It is precisely this feeling of archaic time and ancestral communication that Craig Lesley captures with loving simplicity. . . ."
—*Los Angeles Times*

"*Winterkill* was a spell of language I never wanted to end, and blessedly the story now flows on in *River Song*. Craig Lesley has given us another great-hearted book."
—Ivan Doig, author of
Dancing at the Rascal Fair

Also by Craig Lesley

WINTERKILL

RIVER
SONG

CRAIG LESLEY

A LAUREL TRADE PAPERBACK

Published by
Dell Publishing
a division of
Bantam Doubleday Dell Publishing Group, Inc.
666 Fifth Avenue
New York, New York 10103

ISBN: 0-440-50311-6

Reprinted by arrangement with Houghton Mifflin Company

Printed in the United States of America

Published simultaneously in Canada

June 1990

10 9 8 7 6 5 4 3 2 1

BVG

For Katheryn Ann Stavrakis
and our daughters, Elena and Kira

The author wishes to thank the
National Endowment for the Arts
for its generous support.

RIVER SONG

◈ 1 ◈

WARM SPRINGS

Danny Kachiah smelled the burning fires as he watched the Pi-Ume-Sha dancers circle through the hazy air. The Warm Springs Reservation fires had been out of control for three days, and the air was thick with smoke. Cinders settled on the white buckskin dresses of the women dancers and dotted the bright yellow and orange costumes of the Fancy Dancers. Each morning the wind carried the smell of burning pine from the mountains to the town of Warm Springs, but by late afternoon, following the windshift, it smelled of range fires — sage, cheatgrass, and junipers. Danny imagined the resiny trees exploding as the fire raced with the wind.

The dancers paused while Hoot Owl, the powwow announcer, named the Drum change. Some of them brushed away the cinders with their swan and eagle feather fans, and Danny noticed a woman dancing with a small boy. The boy was dressed in full war costume and imitated the older warriors. The dancers reminded him of Loxie, his former wife, and their son, Jack. Danny still found it hard to believe she was dead — killed nine months ago when her car ran into a gravel truck. She was drunk, but even drunk Loxie could always drive, and Danny couldn't figure out how she crashed on those flat Nebraska roads where she and Jack lived with her second husband.

Danny glanced at the plume of dark smoke rising over the high basalt bluffs that surrounded the town of Warm Springs. At one time, he would have eagerly joined the firefighters, seeking adventure and money, but that work no longer held promise. It was only drudgery — boring and hot and then dangerous when the wind changed.

Jack had been eager to go, however, and left the All-Indian rodeo to help build a fireline at Kishwalks, about fifteen miles north. The boy had been staying with Danny since Loxie's death, and although they got along, each guarded his own territory.

The drumming stopped, and as the dancers left the grassy arena, Danny noticed that an eagle feather had fallen from one of the costumes. A dropped feather represented a fallen warrior and required a special ceremony. Hoot Owl called the dancers back. "Just the War Dancers," he announced. "And we ask all you people out there with your cameras and tape recorders to please put them down. There can be no pictures or recording of this ceremony."

Danny hunched forward and tugged on his cap as about twenty men and youths entered the arena, forming two straight lines fifty feet apart. The feather lay between them. All the dancers wore elaborate traditional costumes and eagle feather headdresses; some had streaked their faces with paint, according to their tribes. Danny wished he had paid more attention to traditional dancing when he was younger, but his father, Red Shirt, hadn't taught him. Later, he was too busy rodeoing.

The dancers knelt on one knee, touching mother earth. As the drum started, they stood, shaking their ankle bells to the drumbeats. Dancing toward the feather, they glanced quickly in one direction, then another, as if searching for a fallen comrade. When the drumbeat slowed, they danced backward, away from the feather, until they were once again kneeling. All the while, their shaking ankle bells matched the drumbeat.

A woman with a long blond braid, sitting in the bleachers across from Danny, raised her camera, but before she could take a picture, an Indian girl in a Stanford T-shirt touched the woman's arm and shook her head. Danny smiled, remembering when no one would have dared stop a white woman.

The dancers repeated their approach to the feather three times, but on the fourth approach they formed a circle, and a warrior in a wolfskin cloak scooped up the feather with his eagle fan. Holding the feather aloft for the others to see, the warrior shouted and stamped his feet. Loud drumbeats, shouts, and ringing bells filled the air.

The warrior in the wolfskin cloak, an honored veteran who had been chosen to retrieve the feather, went to the microphone and told of a combat experience. While he spoke haltingly, the other dancers knelt. "I was in the Eighty-second Airborne," he said. "Served in Vietnam. All the time, I kept looking for another Indian to buddy-up with." He paused while the drummer beat the drum and the kneeling dancers shook their ankle bells. "Saw a lot of stuff that's hard to talk about. Halfway through my hitch, a Yakima guy showed up and we were pretty tight. When I was getting out, he still had a year, so we agreed to meet right here. But he never showed. I went up to White Swan, and his folks told me he was missing in action." The warrior paused. "I picked up this feather for him."

When he finished, the dancers stamped their bells and stood in approval. A Fancy Dancer from Montana came forward to claim the lost feather. Two young boys chased in front of the bleachers, throwing firecrackers against the metal seats. The crackers exploded with loud pops, and Danny smelled the sulfur. "Get out of here. Quit acting up, you guys!" he cried.

Danny's mouth tasted like smoke, and he left the bleachers to get something to drink. Small booths and concession stands circled the dancing arena. The vendors sold the usual turquoise jewelry, beaded belt buckles, caps, and T-shirts. Some had furs, hides, and shells for buyers who wanted to make traditional costumes. One artist had painted cattle skulls bright colors and decorated the horns with feathers and beads. Teenagers cruised the area, their T-shirts bearing the names of rock stars, colleges, or other powwows.

Danny paused beside a large display of a black mechanical bull, its rear legs kicking high off the ground. Flashing lights highlighted the display, and a sign read:

GET YOUR PICTURE
TAKEN WITH GUNPOWDER — $5

Two white men in Stetsons smiled at the passersby. One wore a bolo tie with a silver pistol, and his cowboy shirt had blue guitars on the yoke. He grinned at Danny. "Give it a try, Chief. Impress your wife or your girlfriend. You'll get a little respect after riding this rank bull to a standstill."

Danny smiled but shook his head. A one-eyed bull named Cyclops had broken two of his ribs the last time he'd ridden in the Pendleton Round-Up. That had been a dozen years earlier, but his side still ached when the weather changed.

Behind the counter of the frybread stand, a tall man wore a T-shirt with stenciled black letters: MAGPIE ALL-INDIAN BASKET-BALL TOURNAMENT. "What'll it be?" he asked Danny, putting down a cup of ice cubes.

"Coke," Danny said.

The tall man had enormous hands, and Danny figured he had been a good ballplayer. After scooping a cupful of ice from a green cooler, the man added the Coke from the silver spigot, and he waited until Danny took a gulp. "A bad fire, huh?" he said.

"You know it," Danny said, glancing at the smoke cloud. "I keep tasting smoke."

"I was on the line at Mutton Mountain," the man said. "That was the worst."

Danny looked at him more carefully, but the man didn't seem familiar. "I came over from Pendleton just to fight fire that summer. Had to quit rodeoing. The fire tore me down."

The man swirled the ice in his cup and took another mouthful. "Pendleton. Wasn't that guy from there? You know — the one on the dozer?"

"Henry Nine Pipes," Danny said.

"Yeah." The man added some Coke to the ice in his cup. "Wonder what ever happened to him."

Danny shrugged. "He likes to rodeo — probably still on the circuit someplace." Henry had stolen a car and run off to Canada, but Danny didn't feel like talking about it.

"These young punks don't know how to fight fire," the man said. "Take off a few years, toss in Nine Pipes — we'd show them."

"I'd need to take off some pounds, too." Danny patted his stomach where the blue cowboy shirt pulled tight at the snap buttons.

He thought maybe he should have asked for a Diet Coke. Jack was always ribbing him about his weight.

"Some fat's good," the man said. "You got to sweat on the fireline. Keeps you cool. My boy ran off to fight it, but he doesn't know shit. If I could sell him for what he thinks he's worth, I'd make millions."

"I got a boy up there, too," Danny said. "He was rodeoing until they canceled it."

"What event?"

"Saddlebronc," Danny said. "But he kept falling off. Guess he learned it from me."

The man laughed. "After those boys eat smoke awhile, they'll wish they were back here dodging hooves."

"I hear they're building a good firebreak at Kishwalks," Danny said. "That might stop it."

The man squinted at the smoke over Sapa Ridge. The cloud looked bigger than ever. "Wind's coming up," he said.

The wind concerned Danny, because it could be so treacherous. Firefighters cursed the flames, but they cursed the wind more. The wind rested at night while they built the firebreaks, then rose in the morning, fanning the flames. And by late afternoon it roared in from the Deschutes River Canyon, shifting just enough to catch the men off guard and send the flames blazing out of control as it whistled through the draws and across the flats.

He knew how cheatgrass cinders sometimes carried past the firebreaks, starting more fires — too many to douse with the five-gallon, hand-pump extinguishers and too many to turn under with Pulaskis, the half hoes–half axes they carried. Sooner or later, if the fire broke their lines and got behind them, the men would run like hell.

"That fire's going to kick their butts," the man said.

"Those boys are green, but they'll do all right," Danny said, hoping it was true. He hadn't tried to stop Jack from going because he was eager to make money, and Danny knew from experience you couldn't count on rodeo. Besides, the boy was big for seventeen and tough.

Jack could handle himself, but Danny was edgy of the boy's aunt Pudge. After Loxie had been killed, her half sister had made Danny retrieve Jack from his stepfather, and now she kept crowding Danny about the boy. He'd have to face her anger if she found out about Jack's firefighting.

"Probably they'll come out okay," the man said. "It's not like they're in the big timber with the trees crowning like matchtips. On Mutton Mountain I had to douse myself and the other Hotshots, then crawl in a foxhole until the fire blew by and we could lay a cold trail. I just lay there sweating and praying. One guy chewed up his hand to keep from crying."

"I believe it," Danny said.

The man tossed his ice onto the ground and got a fresh cupful. "You know, we should have a reunion — all of us Mutton Mountain vets. I'm going to talk to the Pi-Ume-Sha committee about that for next year. We could get fancy jackets and everything."

"You do that," Danny said. "I'll come."

.   .   .

When Danny left the frybread stand, he started back toward the bleachers, but the fast drumming and high chanting had stopped, signaling the end of the Fancy Dance competition. Over at the far end of the arena, some of the traditional dancers were getting ready.

"Ay gollies, those were the Rocky Boys," Hoot Owl said. "Came all the way from Montana, so let's give them a big Warm Springs round of applause." The whites in the crowd clapped, but most of the Indians just nodded, their way of showing appreciation.

A Warm Springs policeman in a tan uniform climbed onto the announcer's platform and handed something to the announcer. Hoot Owl read it, then turned to the crowd. "Say now. I just got word they can use some fresh firefighters out on the lines, so if any of you young fellows want to learn about hot feet, now's the time. They need some new boys pretty bad. That fire blew by them at Kishwalks and now it's headed for Kah-Nee-Ta Lodge."

There was a murmuring in the crowd, and some of the tourists who were staying at Kah-Nee-Ta Resort started to get up and head for their cars.

"Folks, just sit back down here and enjoy the dancing," Hoot Owl said. "They closed off the road to the resort because of the fire. Everyone's okay up there, so relax. We'll keep you posted."

Danny decided to drive out and check on Jack. Even though they wouldn't let the tourists through, the reservation policemen would probably let him pass, especially since he knew the back roads pretty well. He figured his uncle Billy Que might want to go along for the ride, if he hadn't won at gambling or run across some of his old drinking buddies.

As Danny walked toward the gambling tent, he could hear Hoot Owl over at the arena. "I just want to remind everyone we got the Wanna Be competition coming up later this afternoon. And we're still collecting a few prizes for the Wanna Bes. Got some nice earrings here donated by Ardene Kickup, and a beaded wallet. If anyone else has something, just bring it to the stand."

Danny hoped to be back in time for the Wanna Be Dance, when the announcer had the whites — those who "wanna be" Indians — get into the arena. Danny enjoyed that. Most of the sunburned tourists were reluctant to dance, but they tried to follow the Drum in their shorts and jogging shoes, cameras swaying from their necks.

In the tent, a few of the older gamblers sat crosslegged on blankets, but most of the men and women were on metal folding chairs borrowed from St. Andrew's Catholic Church. Billy Que was sitting on a chair with his arms crossed, so Danny guessed he had lost all his money. Que's stained hat rested on one knee, and he kept nervously moving his other knee, as if he expected something to happen. Danny almost never saw Que with his hat off, and he was surprised at how gray his hair had turned. Although his shirt and pants were old and tattered, he wore a bright blue bandanna around his neck, and Danny remembered hearing how the women had once adored him.

The woman holding the gambling sticks wore purple Nike jogging shoes and a salmon-colored jumpsuit with a large silver zipper up the front. She had on tinted glasses with a rhinestone embedded in each lens. The man next to her, probably her husband, was wearing a long-fringed artificial buckskin shirt with a pearl-gray Stetson. He collected the bets while she sang and threw the sticks. Danny couldn't figure out how the game was played, although he saw they were making lots of money. Some of the Indians were throwing silver dollars onto a bison blanket in front of the couple, and Danny guessed they had been to Reno, because people always came back from Nevada with silver dollars — if they had any money left at all.

After a while, Que spotted Danny, and he put on his hat. As some of the other Indians threw their bets onto the blanket, Que signaled to the man in the buckskin shirt. When the man shook his head, Que pointed at Danny. The man pointed to the blanket and raised an eyebrow, but Danny shook his head vigorously. He wasn't going to let Que rope him into covering bad bets.

Que stood, hitching up his pants. He walked slowly over to Danny. "You're looking cashy," he said.

"Must be because you're wiped out."

"Loan me twenty and I'll win it back. These Yakimas have been cheating, but now I know the angle."

"That's what you said in Reno. We hitchhiked back. Only ate coffee and doughnuts for two days."

Que grinned. "You got a truck this time. Come on, those sticks are getting lucky."

Danny shook his head. "I want to check on Jack. The fire blew by Kishwalks."

"Jack's a big boy. Probably resting up at the lodge, just hanging around the pool with rich Portland women on both arms. They go for firefighters."

Danny started walking toward his truck.

"What makes you think I'm going to tag along?" Que said.

"Might as well, since you're broke."

A new Dodge Caravan had parked beside Danny's faded green Ford shortbed. Que ran his fingers over the Dodge's shimmering paint job and glanced at the price sticker on the window. "These Warm Springs do all right," he said.

"You bet," Danny said.

When Danny started his pickup's engine, the gas gauge read below a quarter tank.

"Better fill up," Que said. "You don't want a tankful of fumes around that fire."

"I just filled it yesterday," Danny said. He tapped at the gauge with his finger.

"Some kid probably siphoned it. Reservation credit card."

When Danny got out to check, he saw the gas cap lying on the ground where somebody had run over it. He tried to screw the cap back on, but it didn't fit. Disgusted, he sailed the cap sidearm into the brush at the edge of the parking lot. "I hope the little bastard rolls his car," he said, climbing back in.

When he pulled into the service station, he thought they had jacked up their prices. "Discount for cash?" he asked, but the attendant shook his head.

"Beats driving all the way to Madras," Que said.

The attendant tried three different gas caps, but none of them fit. "You'll have to try the Ford dealership in Madras, or send up to Bend."

"No time right now," Danny said. He took one of the pink rags they used to smear the windshield and stuffed it into the neck of the gas tank.

"Seventeen-fifty for the gas," the attendant said. "Make it eighteen-fifty with the rag."

Danny handed him a twenty. "Glad I didn't need a sheet." He bought a couple of Cokes from the machine with his change and climbed back into the truck, handing a can to Que.

"Should've let me win with that twenty," Que said. "It takes money to make money."

"I wouldn't know," Danny said.

The markers on Highway 3 to Kah-Nee-Ta Resort were shaped like arrowheads. Que tossed his empty Coke can out the window at one, but missed. When they reached the top of Sapa Ridge, they had a good view of the fire in the distance, and Que let out a low whistle. Danny pulled the pickup onto the shoulder.

After the fire had jumped the line at Kishwalks, it had blackened Schoolie Flat. A few junipers were still burning like yellow tongues, and patches of gray ash showed where the sagebrush had once grown. Thick black smoke rose from the cheatgrass and gray smoke from the sage. The front edge of the fire, perhaps a half mile wide, was racing toward Hell Gate.

Several miles in front of the fire, the crews were building a fire-break along Whitehorse Road. Danny was too far away to see the men, but he could make out the gray tank trucks and yellow bull-dozers, like toy cars in the distance. Danny guessed that if the racing fire got past the line at Whitehorse, nothing could save the lodge.

The wind blew tumbleweeds past the pickup. "Kicking up strong today," Danny said.

"They might need Hotshots for this one," Que said.

"It's too late," Danny said. "Anyway, they're busy fighting timber fires in Montana."

"That lodge has some big timbers," Que said. "A couple million dollars' worth."

They drove for a while in silence, both watching the fire until they were close enough to see the burning cheatgrass and hear the explosions of the junipers as they ignited.

"You remember Virgil One Wound?" Que said.

"Yeah. Henry Nine Pipes's cousin."

"He tried to be a Hotshot, but he didn't pass the parachute exam."

"How's that?"

"It never opened. All the way down he kept yelling, 'Bury me in Salt Lake!'"

Danny shook his head.

"He went and joined the Mormon church right before he left the reservation."

"Henry never told me anything about it," Danny said. "Seems to me Virgil's still in the army."

"Henry had already hightailed to Canada," Que said. "Anyway, I saw the silver dollar Virgil had in his pocket when he hit. Bent it into a U, like Superman squeezed it between his thumb and finger."

"I'm sure I'd hear about it," Danny said. "There wasn't a dressing or anything."

"They had it at his wife's folks, back in South Dakota, because Virgil looked awful and she didn't want any of his old friends to see." Que paused. "When he hit, his legbones jammed clear up through his shoulders. He looked just like the top half of a spider.

Perry Pretty Mink was telling me about it. Said he hardly recognized Virgil, because it made his face so short. Pushed his mouth up by his eyes."

"Virgil's still in the army," Danny said.

Que shook his head. "I'll bet you twenty bucks. Vincent's the one that's in the army."

At the junction of Kah-Nee-Ta, a white and blue Warm Springs tribal police car blocked the road. Danny stopped the truck and a policeman climbed out of the car. He had on dark glasses and a nametag above the badge: Slickpoo.

"How you doing?" Danny said.

Slickpoo stood by Danny's window. "Can't let you through," he said.

"They going to evacuate the lodge?" Danny asked.

"I don't think it'll come to that," Slickpoo said. "But they're bringing over some big choppers from the Army National Guard base in Portland — just in case. Taking precautions. They'll stop it at Whitehorse."

"Maybe," Danny said. "But I hope you guys kept the fire insurance paid up on the lodge."

"Not my department," Slickpoo said. "I'm from Lapwai."

"Nez Perce?" Danny said, and when Slickpoo nodded, he said, "Me too. Danny Kachiah. This is my uncle Billy Que."

Slickpoo took off his dark glasses. "I don't know you," he said.

"I live around Pendleton," Danny said. "Tell you what. My boy's up there fighting fire. I just want to check on him."

"Pretty risky," Slickpoo said. "Lots of smoke across the lower road, and that fire's coming fast."

"He's just seventeen," Danny said. "I got a little worried —"

"Look here," Billy Que broke in. "This guy fought fire on Mutton Mountain while you were still tugging at your mother's tit. He knows more about fires than a goddamn Dalmatian dog."

Slickpoo grinned at Danny. "The old man's got a way with words. You know these roads?"

Danny nodded.

"It's your neck. If you get cooked, I can always say you snuck in the back way." Slickpoo returned to his police car and backed it up a little so Danny could squeeze by in the pickup.

After Danny had driven down the road a quarter mile, he said to Que, "I guess maybe Jack gets his smart streak from you."

"Most cops need to hear things explained right out," Que said.

Half a mile east, the gray-black smoke obscured the road and Danny stopped the pickup, waiting to see if it would clear.

"Getting worse," Que said after a few minutes. "What do you want to do?"

"Start driving, I guess. Maybe it gets better."

"Beats walking. Roll up the damn windows."

Danny eased the pickup ahead and turned on the lights, even though he knew they wouldn't do any good. "Take a deep breath," he said, pretending not to notice the smoke rising through the floorboards.

"Getting dark," Que said. When he tried to breathe, he started coughing.

Danny's eyes stung and his chest ached. He put his shirtsleeve over his nose and took a shallow breath, but then he started to cough too. The right front wheel slid into the soft shoulder and Danny twisted the steering wheel, bringing the pickup into the middle of the road. He didn't want to roll into the barrow pit.

Suddenly the smoke was gone and they were on hard dirt road. He and Que rolled down the windows to clear the cab. When they came to the Whitehorse Road turnoff, Danny passed it and headed for the resort. "Let's just take a quick look to see if Jack's hanging around the pool," he said.

The fire reminded Danny of a TV movie he had seen about a group of tourists trapped on a South Seas resort island when a volcano erupted. Paul Newman played a construction supervisor who helped some of the tourists escape. Those who didn't follow Newman were killed by flying lava bombs or swallowed by the molten lava.

But no one at Kah-Nee-Ta Resort was panicking. At the Tipi Village and Hot Springs, tourists sunbathed and swam or bought ice cream and hamburgers from the Snack Shop. Danny slowed the pickup to watch a girl in a sun visor and bikini spread lotion on her long bronzed legs. Her languid motions showed she was used to an audience.

Que pointed to the smoke cloud billowing behind the main

lodge, which overlooked the golf course. "Hope that smoke doesn't block the sun. Might spoil her tan."

Three large green helicopters had landed at the edge of the golf course in case they needed to start evacuating tourists, but the golfers weren't paying any attention. Shaded by blue and white umbrellas, they drove golf carts from tee to tee or putted on manicured greens. Yellow flags marking the cups snapped in the wind. Danny stopped the pickup in front of the Pepsi sign that read:

> THANK YOU FOR SELECTING KAH-NEE-TA
> FOR YOUR GOLFING HOLIDAY
> HOPE YOU RETURN SOON

He glanced at his wrist, pretending he had a watch. "Isn't it time to tee off?"

Que looked at the golfers in their bright clothes and hats. "Golf," he said, shaking his head. "You're too young to remember that fat priest at Mission who played golf all the time. Kept bragging about his score and nudging his ball into the hole. That one lied like a rug, even for a priest. He made the boarding school kids build him a putting green behind the church.

"Red Shirt kept stewing about those kids working so hard, and one afternoon he started turning over rocks, hunting scorpions. He never bothered wearing gloves — just snatched three big ones by the stingers and plopped them in a jar. For a week, he kept shaking and rattling that jar, tormenting those scorpions.

"One foggy morning, he warmed them in the toaster-oven, so they'd be wide awake. Then he snuck out and dropped them into the cup on that putting green.

"Red Shirt watched from the puckerbrush until the priest came out and tried a practice putt. It was short, so after sneaking a look around, he nudged the ball in with his foot. But when he reached in the cup, he started screaming and running toward the church, sucking that stung hand with his fat lips.

"That hand swelled like he had blackleg. His arm too. I guess it was poor circulation because of the fat. All summer, he kept going to the doctors to get it drained," Que paused.

"Red Shirt kept the putter," Danny said. He had heard his father tell the story dozens of times.

Que chuckled. "That priest ran off and left it. Red Shirt claimed it was a coup stick."

Kah-Nee-Ta Lodge dominated the dry hillside above the golf course. It was a light cedar color, with orange trim and red doors. Wooden sculptures of salmon, bear, and eagle adorned the entrance. When the Army Corps of Engineers had put in The Dalles Dam, drowning Celilo Falls, the Warm Springs, Yakimas, Umatillas, and Nez Perce had all received settlements. The Warm Springs had built the lodge after receiving their settlement for the loss of their fishing sites along the Columbia River. Kah-Nee-Ta had been a good investment for the Warm Springs and had become a popular tourist resort.

Four young Indian boys had carried hoses up to the roof of the lodge and were wetting it down to keep it from being ignited by the wind-carried cinders.

Below the boys, tourists stood on the balconies outside their rooms, sipping drinks and watching the fire. The boys played the hose over the side of the roof for a few moments, dousing several tourists. One man in a yellow terrycloth robe shook his fist. The boys sprayed water on him until he ducked inside his room. Then they scurried to the far side of the roof.

"Are you planning on buying me a drink?" Que asked.

"Not just yet," Danny said.

"Maybe we better check on Jack, then."

Danny turned the pickup around and headed toward Whitehorse Road.

"I know what it is," Que said, a sly look coming over his face. "You wanted to drive up here just to see if these white dudes were sweating."

"Maybe," Danny said, surprised Que could read him that well.

They were building a wide fireline at Whitehorse, and Danny thought, for the first time, that they might be able to turn back the fire. Men with propane torches were setting backfires off the side of the road closest to the fire. They were burning away as much of the cheatgrass and sage as they could, hoping to slow the main blaze once it reached the blackened land. Another crew was using chain saws to cut down the junipers for fifty yards on both sides of the road, while a big diesel cat with a brush chain dragged the cut trees some distance from the fire's path.

Two reservation tank trucks pumped water onto the grass on the side nearest the lodge, while crews of sweating men cleared another strip beyond that with their shovels and Pulaskis.

Danny drove along the road searching for Jack. There was a first-aid tent near the end of the firebreak, and a Bureau of Land Management ranger in a light khaki shirt came out. When he saw Danny, he waved at him to stop.

"How the hell did you get through?" the ranger said.

"Officer Slickpoo told me to come on up," Danny said. "My boy's a brush-ape on the line somewhere, but I don't see him."

"He's got to be here," the ranger said. "We pulled all the crews off the He He Butte fire, and the Kishwalks people are here too. If the fire gets by now, they'll have to evacuate the lodge."

"Jack was on the line at Kishwalks," Danny said.

The man jerked his thumb in the direction of the tent. "Some of the Kishwalks boys got banged up a little."

If anything happened to Jack, Danny thought, he would never forgive himself. And Pudge would never let him hear the end of it, either. "Better stay here," he told Que. "They might need to move the truck."

Inside the tent, he found Jack sitting on a folding cot and holding a green plastic oxygen mask over his face. He was barechested and his boots were scorched black. So were his jeans up to the knees. When he saw Danny, he gave him a half wave and took the mask from his face. "I'm okay," he said. "Swallowed some smoke."

Jack turned his head slightly, and Danny could see that the hair on the right side had been singed. "What the hell," Danny said. But he was relieved the boy could talk and patted his bare shoulder.

"Your son?" the medic asked.

Danny nodded.

"You've raised one gutsy kid," the medic said. "When the fire swept past the line at Kishwalks, your boy and three others were trapped. No one knew exactly where they were, so they didn't want to risk a rescue team. Figured these boys to be crispy critters by then, anyway."

"On the line, you're supposed to keep track of each man all the time," Danny said, interrupting.

The medic spread his hands. "Somebody screwed up, I guess. All of a sudden your boy came running through the flames and smoke, packing a kid that broke his ankle. The other two were right behind. They were a little toasty around the edges — I don't think any of them would win a hairy legs contest — but I've seen a lot worse."

Jack seemed embarrassed by the praise. "I did like you said," he told Danny. "Doused my clothes and boots with water and pulled the shirt over my head, then ran like hell. That's all."

"Carrying another guy," Danny said. "Don't forget that. I guess you're smarter than you look." He turned to the medic. "Smart enough to listen to his old man."

"One thing bothers me," Jack said. "I saw a little guy out there, strange-looking. He wasn't part of the crew, but he was hanging around."

"Probably someone from the lodge went out to rubberneck," Danny said.

"But no one saw him after we came out, and I'm thinking maybe he was trapped." Jack looked at Danny. "I wish you'd go see, because I owe him one."

"How's that?" Danny asked.

"After the fire surrounded us, I got confused. Nothing but smoke and flames any way I turned. Diggy had a busted ankle. Everyone was shook, starting to panic. Run the wrong way and we were dead."

"So you lucked out," Danny said.

"No," Jack said. "There was this whistle, real loud, like a signal. I could hear it over the flames."

"One of the crew, probably," Danny said.

Jack shook his head. "They were honking horns, but too far away to hear. I figure it had to be that guy. When I heard the whistle again, I doused all of us good, hoisted Diggy up on my back, and headed out — praying like hell we were going the right way."

Danny didn't say anything for a while. He was remembering the fire on Mutton Mountain, but that had been a long time back. "You sure it wasn't yelling?" he asked.

"Maybe he yelled, too," Jack said, "but I didn't hear it. That whistling was what saved the day. I just hope that guy made it out himself."

"If it'll make you feel better, I'll go take a look," Danny said. "Where was it?"

"Right where the Kishwalks road meets Schoolie Flat."

"All right," Danny said. "You take it easy awhile."

"Don't worry," the medic said. "He's off the line. We'll drive him up to the lodge shortly."

Danny stood a minute, wanting to say something more to Jack, but he didn't want to embarrass the boy. "You did good," he mumbled as he ducked out of the tent.

The wall of fire was clearly visible from two miles away. Flames shot thirty feet into the air and pushed the hot wind into Danny's face. Grass fires were tricky. You saw low grass on the rangeland and forgot how high the flames could build.

The BLM ranger stood with his hands on his hips, not taking his gaze off the moving fire. "I hope we're ready," he said. "It's heating up like hell's kitchen."

"Maybe the wind will shift," Danny said. "Give you a break."

"We could use one," the ranger said.

Danny explained about the little guy Jack had seen and told the ranger he wanted to check the Schoolie Flat area. Maybe the man was stuck someplace. With water and a blanket, he might have lasted through the fast-moving fire.

"I can't tell you what to do," the ranger said. "But I don't think there's much chance." He shrugged. "We counted our people. Everybody's out."

"My boy saw someone," Danny said.

"How well do you know these roads?" the ranger asked.

"Good enough," Danny said. "I can follow Whitehorse to where it meets the Mutton Mountain Road, then cut back. That should take me around the fire okay."

The ranger nodded. "If it gets by us here, don't try to drive back. Head straight on over to Simnasho. We'll all be riding helicopters, taking the scenic route."

"Mind if I borrow a couple extinguishers and some blankets — just in case?"

"Help yourself."

Danny lifted a couple of the five-gallon, hand-pump extinguishers to make certain they were full, then carried them to the pickup. He threw them in back along with a couple of heavy wool blankets.

"What's all that stuff?" Que had the door open and was fanning himself with his hat.

"I'm driving out to Schoolie Flat, checking on a guy Jack saw. Maybe he got stuck. You want to ride shotgun?"

"I might explode if I go," Que said. "Much as I've been drinking all these years."

"Maybe that's what we need," Danny said. "Like an oil fire. They drop explosives right down the shaft."

"You been watching too much TV."

Danny climbed in the cab and shut his door. "You coming or staying? If that fire slips by here, you'll have to dogtrot back to the lodge or get the hotfoot."

"I don't see why two dumbasses should go out to the flat," Que said.

"Suit yourself." Danny started the engine.

Que closed the door slowly and put on his hat. "I guess I can help you look. Somebody might have to save your neck."

"Thanks," Danny said.

"I always pick a hard place over a rock," Que said.

At Mutton Mountain Road, Danny turned left and headed toward Kishwalks, planning to drive as far as the old firebreak, then go two miles past. If they didn't find anyone, he would head back.

Schoolie Flat was partially blackened. Ash-gray patches of sage smoldered and a few juniper skeletons still smoked, but some sage clumps were burned only in patches. The fire had swept by so quickly it left some brushy areas just singed. The timbered round butte in the middle of Schoolie Flat was burning on the south side, but the trees in the north draws seemed untouched. A little two-track road rose toward the butte, and Danny decided to check it coming back.

Burned jackrabbits littered the road; Danny knew they had been too slow to outrun the windswept fire. The cottontails had deeper burrows and could wait out the fire if it didn't suck the oxygen from their holes. Danny was glad it wasn't grasshopper season. He remembered the sickening smell of burning grasshoppers at Mutton Mountain.

"See anything?" Danny asked Que every so often. "Car or anything?"

Que shook his head. "Wild goose chase."

A mile past the Kishwalks break, Danny saw a burned-out car and he stopped. He gouged the blackened metal with his pocketknife and dug out rust; it was an old wreck. He drove another mile, then turned the truck around.

"Let's head on over to Simnasho," Que said. "We can buy a six-pack. All this burning makes me thirsty."

"Your memory's shot. Except for Kah-Nee-Ta, this reservation is dry." Danny jerked his thumb at the extinguishers. "Ten gallons of water there in back."

"I'm not that thirsty yet," Que said.

"I'll give the flat another look."

"It's a waste of time," Que said. "We'll have to head out this way anyhow. They won't stop that fire and it'll cut the road."

"You're probably right, but I promised Jack," Danny said. He hoped they had taken Jack to the lodge by now.

Que slumped down further in his seat.

When they reached the two-track, Danny turned off and headed for the butte. The tracks had deep holes in places and the two men bounced in the cab.

"Jesus," Que said. "Some shortcut."

"A little spring comes off the north side of that butte," Danny said. "Or used to. If a guy got stuck, he might head for water."

"You'd have to know the country," Que said. "And it's too damn far from the fireline. No one could outrun that fire, and we haven't seen a car."

"Just taking a squint," Danny said. "With the smoke and all, somebody might mistake this two-track for the main road."

"Don't get too close," Que said as they neared the butte. "That fire's on the move."

The road dead-ended at a gulley and Danny stopped. He studied the timbered butte. Que was right. The fire was crowning, burning from treetop to treetop, sweeping around the hillside to the north. Once ignited, the trees burned from the tops down, like matchsticks.

"The wind's changed," Danny said.

"From bad to worse, maybe," Que said.

Danny got out of the truck and scooped a handful of ash. He tossed it into the air and watched the wind carry it north.

"So you're right," Que said. "But there's nobody here. Let's go."

"In a minute," Danny said. He was trying to remember which draw was the source of the spring. He decided it was the middle one on the north side and he studied it carefully. On top, the yellow pines were burning, and the fire was moving lower into the jack pine thickets and scattered junipers. As he stared through the smoky haze, Danny thought he saw something standing beside one of the junipers.

"Look there," he said, pointing to a dark patch where the trees were most dense. "Sort of in the middle of those thick junipers. Something's there."

"I don't see anything," Que said after a while. "Did it move?"

"No," Danny said. "I see it right there."

"Must be a snag, then. Or a tall stump. Anything else would be running like hell."

Danny stared at the spot, but the heat waves were making strange undulations. "Probably a snag, after all," he said.

One of the yellow pines exploded about halfway down the butte. Danny heard the sudden roar followed by the snapping of burning twigs. Fiery needles rose in the wind like sparks up a chimney. A whistle — one high, wavering note — drifted from the hillside in the momentary calm before another tree exploded.

Danny turned to Que. "You hear that?"

"Sure," Que said. "They always blow like that when they're dry and pitchy. One time your father didn't get around to taking down the Christmas tree till damn near Easter. He jammed most of it up the fireplace and touched it off. Now, that was a roar. It got his eyebrows, most of the carpet, and half the paneling in the trailer's front room."

"Not the trees," Danny said. "I heard something else." When Que didn't answer, Danny took an extinguisher from the pickup bed and strapped it on his back. He used water from the second extinguisher to soak the blanket, his boots, and his pantlegs. "I heard something coming from that draw," he said.

"Trees are blazing like crazy," Que said. "And when those junipers explode, there'll be pitchbombs burning everywhere."

"I'll be back in ten minutes," Danny said.

"If you're not," Que said, "can I have the truck?"

"Fight Jack for it." Danny walked quickly to the base of the hill, then moved through a fringe of junipers. A blanket of long reddish-brown needles covered the ground, and he knew it would burn fiercely, once started, making it impossible to cross. He draped the wet blanket over his head and shoulders to keep any flying sparks off his shirt and out of his hair.

The fire had moved down the hill and was burning in the thick jack pines. The draw angled to the left, then curved. The sides were steeper and broken with clumps of junipers. Glancing back, Danny could no longer see the pickup. The extinguisher felt too heavy, so he wriggled out of the straps and left it lying beside a rock outcropping.

A trickle of water came down the draw, and Danny knew the spring had to be nearby, but it was getting too hot to move much closer to the fire. Pausing for a moment, he tried to decide which stand of junipers he had seen from below, but at this angle he couldn't tell.

Then he heard the whistle again, clear and high. Danny felt a chill in spite of the fire's heat. He hurried on. The water was thick and dark from the burning. Where the draw straightened, Danny stopped. Perhaps fifty yards ahead, a small, dark-skinned man stood beside the blackened water. His face was turned toward Danny with his head cocked at an odd angle, as if he were listening. In his hands, he held a shiny plate.

"This way!" Danny shouted. "The fire's moving downhill. Run this way!" He waved at the man.

A stand of brushy junipers covered the steep bank above the man, and their tops formed a kind of canopy over him. As Danny watched, the junipers began to burn, their long needles dropping like fiery rain.

"Quick. This way!" Danny yelled and started up the hill.

The man stared past Danny, his head still cocked, a surprised look on his face. Maybe he was hurt, Danny thought, or scared witless. The man threw his arms up, dropping the plate, then lurched back a couple of steps and lowered his hands to his stomach. His face twisted and the mouth opened as if to scream.

A juniper beside the man exploded, and Danny twisted to protect himself from the heatflash, throwing his right arm in front of his eyes. He tried moving ahead, but the other trees had ignited, forming a fireball on the hillside. A pitchbomb whistled past, and Danny felt burning twigs falling on his blanket.

"This way!" he yelled. "Come down the hill!" He retreated a few steps. Staring at the place where the man had stood, Danny saw nothing but smoke and fire.

It was almost too hot now to breathe and the blanket was dry. Danny smelled the smoldering wool and felt the heat from large coals dropping on his back and shoulders. He turned, making his way downhill quickly but carefully. He didn't want to break an ankle. The fire raced along the ridge above him, then started burning down into the draw. When he came around the curve, Danny was amazed to see some of the trees ahead of him, downslope, already crowning. At the outcrop of rock, he grabbed the extinguisher and whipped off his blanket, trying to ignore the silver-dollar-size smoldering patches. He soaked the blanket and his clothes again.

Danny dropped the extinguisher and draped the blanket over his head and shoulders. He dashed downhill, ducking under the burning branches and stumbling over the tree roots. Patches of needles burst into flame, and Danny prayed that the entire carpet wouldn't ignite until he made his way through the juniper fringe.

The acrid smoke was choking him, and he pressed the wet blanket against his mouth and nose, cursing himself for not doing it sooner. When he tried taking shallow breaths, he gagged, so he ran without breathing until his lungs burned and he doubled over with cramps.

Stumbling ahead, he finally cleared the last scattered junipers and pitched forward onto the blackened earth. He rolled clear of the smoldering blanket and came to his hands and knees, retching and choking to clear the smoke from his lungs.

Que ran toward him from the truck, dragging the second extinguisher. He stood over Danny, pumping water onto his hair, back, and legs. Que was panting from the exertion. His eyes bulged and he had lost his hat.

Danny rolled onto his back and let Que spray water on his chest and face. Then he propped himself on his elbows, opening his mouth a little to drink some of the stale water. The wetness cooled his burning throat.

Finally, he sat up and shook his head to clear the water from his ears.

Que let go of the extinguisher. "You gonna live, then?" he asked.

Danny coughed when he tried to speak, so he just nodded.

Que kicked over the extinguisher and started back after his hat. "You and Smokey, the goddamn bear," he said.

After he had regained his breath, Danny stood and tried to brush off some of the wet soot and cinders, but all he did was smear the black ooze around. He picked up the extinguisher, and suddenly it felt very heavy. Danny dropped it and sat down, closing his eyes.

"Didn't you hear me honking?" Que said.

Danny opened his eyes. Que's hat had a black smudge near the crown.

"Those trees were popping all around. And you kept heading up that hill."

"I couldn't get to him," Danny said. "I kept yelling for him to come down, but he stood there like a rock, just staring past me."

"Who?"

"That guy, up by the spring. He was standing right under some junipers. When those trees went . . ." Danny shuddered.

Que slowly shook his head. "I can't read the newspaper up close or see Miss April's tits without my cheaters. But way off — like that hillside — I see things pretty damn good. I never saw nobody up there but you." Que stood. "Maybe you took a bead on a tall stump. Those heat waves might make a stump look lively."

Danny studied the blazing hillside. It was all fire and thick black smoke, and he couldn't pick out one tree from another. "You had a bad angle," Danny said. There was the other part too — the whistling — but Que would just say that was from the fire, maybe a damp stump singing.

"What do you think somebody would be doing way out here," Que asked, "stuck in the boonies with no car?"

"I don't know. Maybe he hiked out from the lodge," Danny said, but it didn't sound very convincing. "Anyway, there's nothing to do but tell Slickpoo. When that hillside cools, they can come out and get the body."

"You can tell him," Que said. "I never saw anything."

Danny knew it didn't make any sense, but he had seen the man with the plate and heard the whistle. Why wouldn't the man come down the hill, unless he was hurt? And why had he thrown his arms up like that and staggered backward?

At the lodge the guests were celebrating. Once the manager had received word that the fire was sweeping north, he had ordered free drinks for everyone.

Que left Danny in the parking lot and headed for the bar. "Maybe you should clean up some before you come around," Que told him. "Don't need you cramping my style. I'll be right there inside, letting some wealthy widow-woman pour whiskey down my throat."

Danny dug through a pile of stuff he had thrown behind the pickup's seat until he found a fairly clean shirt and a pair of jeans. He carried them into the men's room, just off the main lobby, where he stripped to his underwear and spent twenty minutes scrubbing with wadded wet paper towels. Two golfers came in to pee. When they saw Danny they quit talking, stood quietly at the white urinals until they finished, then ducked out. Danny kept scrubbing until the towel dispenser was empty and then checked himself in the mirror. Streaks of soot remained around his neck and forehead, just under the hairline, but it would have to do. He wrapped his dirty clothes in a tight bundle and put on the clean ones.

He found Jack at the pool wearing white swim trunks and a matching Kah-Nee-Ta shirt. Danny guessed he had bought them at the gift shop.

The boy was surrounded by four girls in brightly colored bikinis as he talked to a man with a notebook and a woman carrying a camera bag. The woman was taking pictures of Jack, having him face one way, then the other. He spotted Danny, but quickly glanced away.

For a moment, Danny had an urge to walk over to the pool, introduce himself as Jack's father, then strip and dive in, but he didn't. Tomorrow they would leave for Hood River and do orchard work to make Jack's rodeo entry fees. That would spoil the boy's fun soon enough.

When the woman finished taking pictures and the man closed his notebook, one of the girls brought out a Polaroid and started taking more pictures of Jack. One by one, the other girls posed with him. He turned his head this way and that, like a young peacock. Danny left.

He found Slickpoo at the edge of the golf course talking to the last of the helicopter pilots from the Army National Guard base. The pilot and Slickpoo shook hands; then the pilot climbed in the copter and took off, the blades stirring the dust until Slickpoo had to grab for his hat. As the pilot flew north of the lodge, Danny guessed he was going to take a look at the fire before he returned to Portland.

Slickpoo watched the helicopter disappear, then turned toward his police car. He saw Danny. "What happened to you?"

"I got mixed up with the fire," Danny said. "You should have seen me before."

Slickpoo shook his head. "Find your boy? I hear he's a damn hero."

"He did all right," Danny said. Although he was proud of Jack, he didn't want to brag.

"A lot of boys would lose control," Slickpoo said.

"Right now, he's losing it by the pool. A bunch of girls have him twisted. And he's talking to some newsguy."

"I'd swap places with him in a minute," Slickpoo said. "Wouldn't you?"

"Damn right." Danny grinned.

"Maybe he'll need an agent. I hear they made a movie out here."

"*Tonka*," Danny said. "That was a while ago. Sal Mineo starred and Tonka was his horse. Sal had a hell of a time learning to ride Indian style."

"Were you in it?"

"Sure," Danny said. "Everybody was. I came over from Pendleton to be an extra. Twenty dollars a day just for hanging around. Sometimes we'd put on paint and ride across the hills. Those days we got fifty."

"Easy money," Slickpoo said.

"And women," Danny said. "Those California girls liked the real thing." Afterward, when he returned to Pendleton, Danny had started combing his hair like Sal Mineo's and had told his friends he had a part in the movie. But when they went to see *Tonka* no one could spot Danny. After that he'd got a crew cut and quit flashing Sal's autograph. Years later, his sister-in-law Pudge told Danny that Sal had gone queer and been stabbed by one of his buddies. She read about it in a gossip magazine at the beauty shop. The news made Danny feel sad, somehow, and old.

"I'll be watching for your boy, then. Sounds like you still have big connections." Slickpoo moved toward the car.

"Wait," Danny said. "There's something else. Jack saw somebody hanging around the fireline at Kishwalks. He was worried that the guy never got out, so I went to take a look."

"See anything?"

"You know that butte by LaClaire Springs?"

"Sure," Slickpoo said. "But that's pretty far from Kishwalks."

Danny nodded. "That's where he was, though. Up that middle draw, right by the springs. I tried to get to him, but it was burning all around. He must have been scared because he just stood there in the flames."

Slickpoo shook his head. "People get funny around a fire. Right now, we got a lot of folks reported missing. Later, most of them will show up. After that hill cools, I'll send someone out." He took a pencil and a small notepad out of his shirt pocket and flipped some pages. "You got a general description? I figure he'll be fried crisp."

"He was small," Danny said. "And he had something shiny in his hands — a big plate, maybe."

"That's it?" Slickpoo kinked his eyebrow.

"It was burning like hell up there."

"How about a car or pickup. You spot anything?"

Danny shook his head. "Just check the middle draw. You'll find what's left."

Slickpoo closed the pad and put it back in his pocket. "You sticking around? I'll let you know what turns up."

"We're leaving for Hood River tomorrow," Danny said. "Stephenson Orchards. They're old friends." He had started to tell Slickpoo General Delivery, but then he would have guessed that Danny was about broke and doing orchard work.

"You spell 'Stephenson' with a V?"

"The other way," Danny said.

"I'll remember," Slickpoo said. "Glad your boy's okay."

As soon as Danny walked into the Appaloosa Lounge, he noticed the bartender and waiters were wearing light blue ribbon shirts with fancy gold ribbons. Bone and turquoise chokers adorned their necks. The ribbon shirts bothered Danny a little. They were valued gifts, treasured for life, and were supposed to be saved for ceremonies or special occasions.

Que was sitting at a window table that overlooked the swimming pool. He was with a man in a yellow knit shirt and a white cap that read: OLD GOLFERS NEVER DIE. THEY JUST LOSE THEIR BALLS.

"Here comes Smokey now," Que said when he saw Danny. "I was just telling Bud about the priest." Que went back to his story. "Then I told Red Shirt," he said, "'Let's roll over a few rocks, find us some big scorpions.'"

"Jesus!" the man said. "You hear this one?"

Danny nodded. He sipped a beer and stared out the window.

Every so often the man would laugh and throw back his head, showing his teeth, and Que would say, "That's right, isn't it, Danny?"

Danny nodded, but he wasn't listening to the stories or watching the golfers. He was thinking back years ago to the fire on Mutton Mountain.

A troop of Explorer Scouts from Madras had tipped over their boat in Whitehorse Rapids and come ashore on the reservation side of the Deschutes, near Mutton Mountain. In order to dry out their clothes and warm themselves, they built a fire on the riverbank. They circled the fire with stones, but never bothered to clear away the dry cheatgrass, so the fire smoldered in the grass under the stones. That afternoon, the wind breathed life into the fire and sent it racing through the dry grass and sage along the riverbank. The scouts tried to stomp out the flames or douse them with water, but the fire was already out of control.

Rather than chase the fire, the scouts jumped back in their boat and drifted downriver. They tried to call in an alarm from Whiskey Dick's, at the mouth of Oak Canyon, but Whiskey Dick didn't have a phone, so he drove the scout leader and one of the older boys to the nearest farmhouse, fifteen miles away.

Danny and Henry Nine Pipes were on the All-Indian Rodeo circuit when they heard about the fire. They had finished out of the money at Toppenish, and Henry figured they could make more money fighting fire than they were getting by splitting an occasional rodeo purse.

Henry drove from Toppenish to Warm Springs in just under three hours — Danny thought that still had to be some kind of record. He knew it was a big fire when he saw busloads of Mexican fieldworkers brought in from Boise. He and Henry got on one of the green buses and rode to the main camp the Fire Management Unit had set up.

They lined up to receive equipment: duckcloth coveralls, long-sleeve shirts, asbestos gloves. Each man was given a five-gallon, hand-pump extinguisher and a Pulaski as well as a disposal sleeping bag for rest periods. The night crews had miner's lights run by six-volt batteries strapped to their belts. Henry and Danny helped the Mexicans get into their equipment, and Nathan Charley decided to put each of them in charge of a twenty-one-man fire crew.

"Look at this," Henry said. "I didn't have to join the army to be a leader of men. I got damn near two dozen beaners following every order."

"They don't understand you," Danny said.

"If I shout, they do," Henry said.

They built a firebreak along an old logging road between Oak Canyon and Skookum Creek, working through the night by the light of their miner's helmets; some of the Mexicans grew so hot, they took off their coveralls and worked in just their underwear and boots.

Henry walked the line, shouting orders to his crew: "Keep working, brush-apes. Assholes and elbows. That's all I want to see!" Shortly after midnight, they took a break and gobbled the C rations they carried on the line. The Mexicans loved the canned meat and chocolate but wouldn't eat the hardtack biscuits, so they left a little pile of them under one of the junipers.

"Think we'll stop it?" Henry asked.

Danny shrugged. At night, when the wind died, it seemed they might control the fire. But it blew up again late each afternoon. "Ask me about suppertime tomorrow afternoon," he said.

Henry stared a few minutes at the red glowing. The sky was smudged with dark smoke. "If it blows by us here, the Warm Springs are going to lose all their reservation timber," he said.

"You know it," Danny said.

Henry shrugged. "Well, they're paying us by the hour, so we can't lose, cuz."

The crews worked a double shift through the night and built another fireline half a mile beyond the first, then prepared to backfire. By noon the next day the wind started, and the fire was sweeping toward them. Kanum Kena, one of the dozer drivers, got cinders in his eyes, and they took him to the hospital. When Nathan Charley asked if anyone else could drive the big dozer, Henry raised his hand. Nathan told him to take his crew and extend the first fireline, stretch it out toward Eagle Springs.

"You sure you can work that dozer?" Danny asked Henry.

"Hell, if Kanum can do it, how tough can it be?" Henry said He drove off in the big yellow dozer, his crew of brush-apes walking alongside. A couple of the more adventurous ones climbed onto the raised dozer blade for a free ride.

As the fire moved closer, frightened deer bounded ahead, their gentle brown eyes wide, their tails flared. The deer paused when they saw the lines of men working the firelines, but they broke on by, panicked by the fire raging behind. Jackrabbits came next, a few of them burned. Then clouds of grasshoppers whirred ahead of the fire. Their singed bodies smelled like old wheat.

Just before dark, the fire blew by the Skookum Creek line and the men retreated to the second fireline. They waited, hoping for the wind to die, so they could light their backfires with Fusees. The crews worked feverishly to douse any sparkfires sputtering in the dry grass beyond the second break.

When the wind died, they lit backfires along the lower half of the second fireline, praying for calm, to avoid trapping Henry and his crew. But the wind rose suddenly, shifted, and the backfire joined the main fire — the two raging uphill between the firelines.

Nathan Charley drove up in his shortbed Dodge pickup. "Hop in," he told Danny. When Danny got in the cab, he could see the tension on Nathan's face. "Son-of-a-bitching wind," Nathan said.

They drove uphill until they ran out of road; Nathan stopped the truck. The spreading fire still raced ahead. "Do you think Henry finished that line?" Nathan asked.

Danny didn't say anything. He just watched the fire.

"Maybe he got his crew safely to Eagle Springs." Nathan was almost whispering.

Danny shook his head. "Not much chance."

They climbed out of the truck and ran to the top of a smoldering knoll. The ground was still hot, and Danny's feet felt uncomfortable in his boots. Looking off toward Eagle Butte, he saw nothing except smoke and flames.

Nathan clenched his fists. "That fire blew all around them. Poor bastards wouldn't know which way to go."

Danny stared toward the butte, hoping to see some sign of Henry.

They watched in silence for fifteen minutes. Finally Nathan said, "I think we held it down below, but I've got to go back and check."

"Then go," Danny said.

"The wind's dying a little." Nathan touched Danny's shoulder. "We won't find much until after things cool."

"You go ahead," Danny said. "I'm just going to keep watch a while."

"All right." Nathan toed a rock, flipping it with his boot. The underside wasn't black. "But keep your eye on that fire. I don't think it'll blow back this way, but it's fooled us before."

After Nathan drove off, Danny walked a little closer to the fire. His eyes stung and he wiped them with his shirtsleeve. Singed grasshoppers still whirred out of the burned grass. Some of them had partially burned legs and wings, and they flew in crazy patterns. When they landed on Danny, spitting brown juice, he knocked them away.

Once he thought he saw a gray rock move, but it was a burned rabbit. As he got closer, he saw it didn't look much like a rabbit anymore. He killed it with a stick and scuffed some dirt over it.

Danny was taking deep breaths now, and he felt as if he were going to throw up. The billowing smoke looked greasy, and he could imagine the men burning. He was ready to give up and leave the knoll when he heard a noise above the roaring of the fire, a metallic banging like a shovel hitting rock. When he heard it strike again, he stared toward the sound.

All at once, like a huge, scorched bug crawling from a campfire, the blackened dozer came into view. Its blade was down, pushing the fiery grass to both sides and turning up fresh earth. A blanket over his head like a shawl, Henry gripped the wheel. As the blade clanged against another large rock, he turned the dozer slightly, angling the blade away from the rock, steering out of the fire.

Henry had dropped the brush chain, so it was dragging behind the dozer. The Mexicans were strung out along the chain like beads on a rosary. Clinging to it with one hand, they shielded their singed faces with the other.

Danny held his breath as he counted the men: twenty-one. He counted again. Twenty-one! Then he began shouting and running toward Henry.

Clear of the smoke, Henry saw Danny and raised an arm in salute. The Mexicans dragged Henry off the dozer's seat and lifted him to their shoulders, shouting something Danny didn't understand, but later he learned it meant "Firechief."

As soon as they put him down, Henry grabbed Danny and they danced like crazy men. Henry slugged Danny's arm a few times, and Danny shook him until he collapsed.

After a while, when he'd caught his breath, Henry told Danny what had happened. "We finished the line and set backfires," he said, "but when we tried to get out, the whole thing blew up again. Goddamn, I was scared. Then I heard you whistle."

Danny shook his head. "I didn't whistle."

"Come on," Henry said. "You're the only guy around. When you whistled, I headed this way. Followed the calls until I was clear."

"Not me," Danny said.

Neither of them said anything for a few moments. The sound Henry heard could have come from a damp stump singing in the flames, but Danny knew it hadn't.

"Steah-hah," Henry said finally. "Stick Indians."

"Maybe," Danny said. He wished Henry hadn't spoken their name, because he knew that sometimes made them angry.

Later, after the fire had cooled and Henry had received an award from the Warm Springs Tribal Council, he and Danny drove out to Little Skookum Creek. They scattered boxes of matches for the Steah-hah. Stick Indians usually stayed in the darkness, so they were very fond of matches. Danny hoped they accepted the gift.

2

HOOD RIVER

"I HATE THIS job," Jack said to Danny. "My back hurts and my legs feel like rubber."

"If you want to pay entry fees, keep thinning," Danny said. He drew in his shoulders a couple of times and stretched his neck to take out some of the soreness. His legs felt numb. He wasn't used to ladder work, so he put his weight on one foot, then the other, until he could feel his feet — steady on the ladder rung.

"Seems to me my firefighting money should have lasted a little longer," Jack said. "At least through White Swan rodeo."

"Remember, you like to eat three square ones," Danny said.

"I wasn't counting on buying pickup tires."

"You're not walking, are you? Anyway, money never lasts. That's why they put the rodeos so close together."

The money never had lasted, even during those few years when Danny had won an occasional large rodeo purse. At first, he hoped rodeoing would lead to national championships and big-time endorsements, but his ambitions were soon crowded out by younger cowboys with thick bankrolls, some of whom had attended professional rodeo schools taught by former champions.

As the years passed, he tried the smaller rodeos in towns like Joseph and Heppner, pretending he could gradually climb back to the big circuit. Finally, he went on the All-Indian circuit, competing in places like White Swan and Warm Springs. He continued riding, because he had nothing better to do, until he picked up Jack from his stepfather Hanson.

The last few years, when old-timers approached Danny for beer or cigarettes, their stories had started to sound familiar. Each explained his crippled hands or twisted back, and Danny gave them money freely, almost as if he were paying for his own good health.

"Que should be helping us out here," Jack said. "I bet he fell off the ladder on purpose. He said this was Mexican work."

"You might be right, at that," Danny said. Two days earlier, Que had complained of dizziness and taken a fall. A short one. He had just shifted his ladder and was starting back up when he crumpled to the side, landing on his shoulder.

Danny had wanted to take him to the hospital for X rays, but Que insisted his shoulder wasn't broken. He kept rubbing it with liniment until their picker's cabin smelled of wintergreen, and he swore he couldn't lift that arm above his head.

Danny moved up another rung. The green pears hung in twos and threes on the branches around him. They were about the size of walnuts, and he had to pick off the ones that were too small or too close together, allowing the remaining ones to develop into top-grade fruit.

"How many acres in this place, anyway?" Jack asked.

"Forty or fifty."

"Thank God that rodeo's next week."

"You better win something," Danny said, "or we'll spend the rest of the summer right here."

Jack shook his head. "Too many trees for us to thin all by ourselves."

Four empty ladders stood two rows over. The Immigration and Naturalization Service officers had made a sweep early that morning, and the illegal Mexicans working for Stephenson had run off to hide. About fifteen minutes before the authorities showed up, an old Mexican in a white pickup drove by, laying on the horn. Gonzales and the others had leaped off their ladders and dashed into the woods at the orchard's edge.

When the INS people showed up, they thought they had bagged a couple of illegals until they figured out Danny and Jack were Indians. The Hood River county sheriff was with them and seemed to enjoy their disappointment.

"Indians, for Christ's sake," one INS man said. "Why don't you stay on the reservation?"

"Somebody's got to thin these pears," Danny said.

The man looked at the four empty ladders. "Those wetbacks sure cleared out fast."

"The Taco Telegraph," Danny said, and chuckled, because people were always saying Indians got word of things by the Moccasin Telegraph.

Now, as he thinned, Danny was careful to leave the pears six to eight inches apart. "A dick's length," Red Shirt had always said. "Your dick, not mine, or there'd be just one pear on a branch." He had laughed when he said it, then repeated it, laughing harder.

"Picking pears is worse than thinning," Danny said, making conversation to pass the time. "You strap a big canvas bag around your neck, sort of like a paperboy. Only the bag loads from the front, so the weight always pulls you forward. All day long, you strain against that weight. Thirty or forty pounds, sometimes."

"You call that hard work, I suppose," Jack said. "Not like this easy stuff."

"You hate pears," Danny said. "But you have to treat them gentle. Bruise a few and the field boss rides your ass, docks your check. I've seen those pears wrapped in foil, tucked in fake grass. Grade A. Fancy-assed. No one thinks about the picker's sweat."

Jack half turned on the ladder. "Look. At Hanson's place, I did all kinds of shit. Picked rocks, shoveled ditches, ran the propane burners. The harvest was a super bitch." He pressed his lips together and knocked off a couple of green pears with his fist. "I thought I'd do a little better out here with you."

"Don't put my saddle on Hanson's horse," Danny said.

Jack climbed off his ladder and shifted it so he was turned away from Danny.

Danny glared at the boy's backside, his stiff neck. All the bad times with Hanson sure hadn't knocked out his sass, he thought. Maybe Loxie got credit for that. You had to give her something.

Danny remembered his last harvest with Red Shirt. In those days drifters, not illegals, worked the harvests. They were gaunt men with big-knuckled hands and chafed wrists. Their battered cars and hollow eyes told about hard times.

Reno Slape wasn't like the rest. He had shiny black hair, the color of fresh oil on a back road, and he wore it long, curling behind his ears. In spite of working outdoors, Reno had pale skin, the color of fish-belly, and while he talked, he tugged at the long dark hairs on his arms. Black T-shirts made his skin look paler, and he rolled the sleeves to the shoulder. He tucked a pack of Pall Malls on his left shoulder; a king of hearts was tattooed on his right.

Red Shirt and Reno became drinking buddies, although Reno was only a few years older than Danny. Sometimes, after supper, they drank wine on the stoop of Reno's cabin and swapped lies about jobs and women.

In the long evenings, Danny hunted blue jays on the orchard's fringe with a BB gun old man Stephenson loaned him. The gun had a weak spring, so Danny could follow each shot's copper arc and make adjustments before sneaking up on the next jay. Stephenson set a nickel bounty per bird, and on a good night, Danny might make fifty cents before it became too dark.

One night, when Danny returned with seven jays in a flour sack, Red Shirt and Reno were flipping through a stack of comic books, pointing and laughing.

"What've you got there?" Danny asked.

"California comics," Reno said. "Take a look." He held out one of the books, but Red Shirt slapped his wrist. "Want him to go blind?" he said, and both men laughed. Red Shirt shoved the pile of books behind him.

Reno laughed again; his lips pursed and his eyes danced. Maybe it was the farmyard light, but at that moment Danny thought Reno looked like Elvis, at least a little.

When Danny returned with his thirty-five cents from Stephenson, Reno and his father had left in Reno's Buick for town. Reno hadn't padlocked the door to his cabin, so Danny went inside.

Under the cot, he found a brown cardboard suitcase with the dirty comic books. Reno had Li'l Abner and Daisy Mae, Jiggs and Maggie, even Sergeant Preston of the Yukon. The drawings on each page varied slightly, so when Danny flipped through the books quickly, the characters seemed to perform all kinds of sex acts.

When Danny left the cabin, his mouth was dry and his heart was racing. He got a drink from the faucet outside and stared at the night sky. He kept seeing Daisy Mae doing those things with Li'l Abner. Going inside his own cabin, Danny lay down on his cot, but he couldn't fall asleep.

When the lights of Reno's Buick flashed in the cabin window, Danny suddenly became worried about the suitcase. He couldn't remember if he had snapped the latches closed. He heard car doors slam and the rustling of a paper sack. Occasionally he heard his father's deep laugh and Reno's softer one.

Sometime later in the night, Danny felt his cot jiggle; then a hand touched his leg. "Hey," he said. "Your cot's across the room."

"Shhh. It's all right." It was Reno's voice, but it didn't sound right.

The hand moved up Danny's leg, and he felt Reno climb on top of him, the weight pressing him into the cot.

"Get off."

Reno's breath, warm and sweetened by wine, was in his face. "I've been watching you."

Danny struck out hard with his fist and felt something crack — Reno's nose.

"Christ on a crutch!" Reno squealed. "You little bastard!"

The weight was off, and Danny heard Reno stagger toward the door. In a few moments, the faucet outside began to run. Danny found his jeans in the dark and took out his pocketknife. He opened the blade with fumbling hands, then sat quietly in the darkness, biting his lip whenever he got sleepy.

About an hour later, Red Shirt came in and switched on the light. He leaned to one side, like a man walking in a stiff wind.

"Where the hell have you been?" Danny said.

"Fell asleep out there." Red Shirt rubbed his face and neck. "Damn mosquitoes ate me alive." He took a couple of steps toward Danny. "Son of a bitch," he said. "You cut yourself."

The sheet was stained with blood, and Danny kicked it off the bed. They both stared at the sheet lying on the floor. "Nosebleed, I guess," Danny said finally.

"Quit picking the damn thing," Red Shirt said and switched off the light.

The next morning, Reno didn't show up to pick. Red Shirt tried picking for an hour but gave up; he was too shaky on the ladder.

Swarming yellow jackets were blowing the fallen fruit under the trees. Some buzzed Red Shirt, attracted by the wine he had spilled. When he took off the shirt and snapped it at them, one of the yellow jackets stung him. He threw the shirt over the ladder rung and walked to the edge of the orchard, then lay down to sleep it off.

About eleven, Danny saw Reno's loaded Buick drive up the lane and pull onto the blacktop. A few minutes later, old man Stephenson came out of the orchard. He paused when he saw Red Shirt lying in the grass and put his hands on his hips. Then he shook his head and walked out to where Danny was picking.

"Reno's not such a pretty boy anymore," Stephenson said. "That's a bad nose." He glanced at Red Shirt. "Your father looks pretty wilted, too. They must have had some fight."

Danny stared down at Red Shirt. From his position, high on the ladder, his father seemed shrunken and pitiful. The pears around Danny's neck felt incredibly heavy, and he clutched the ladder with both hands to keep from falling.

Now Danny watched Jack working. Jack's quick hands reminded him of Red Shirt's. That stubborn streak was also in his father's blood. And Loxie's. So the boy got his stiff neck from both families. Well, Danny thought, I can be stubborn, too. Maybe I'm no bargain as a father, but I'm giving it a shot.

Stephenson stood beside Danny's ladder and studied the branches. He wore a blue baseball cap with a yellow diamond on the crown and yellow letters spelling DIAMOND FRUITS. "Good thinning," he said.

Danny nodded. Red Shirt's measuring stick.

Stephenson picked some small green pears off the ground and rolled them between his thumb and forefinger. Glancing at the trees, he said, "The pears are getting too big. I hope those boys can come out of the woods soon, so we can speed up this thinning."

"We're working hard," Jack said.

"Sure." Stephenson smiled. "Until the next rodeo. Your grandfather was the same. He'd work here awhile when his luck was bad, but run off after he made enough money for entry fees and gas."

Danny laughed. "That's him, all right."

"Runs in the family," Stephenson said. "Steady workers. Steady by jerks."

"How long will those greasers hide in the woods?" Danny asked.

"Three or four days," Stephenson said. "Damn politics. Somebody in California complains about illegals taking jobs, so Immigration raids here. They grab a couple of old people and some kids and make like it's a big whoopee. After they're shipped south to Mexico, the illegals scrape together more money and sneak back. It doesn't make any sense, and losing workers pisses me off."

"I believe it," Danny said.

Stephenson tugged at his cap. "Got to get back to the house. The wife's making lunches and I'm sneaking them into the woods. If my boys run off, I'll never get this orchard thinned."

"Wait a second." Danny stepped off his ladder. "We've been working five days, and I've been thinking about an advance."

"Rodeo fees?" Stephenson folded his arms.

Danny nodded at Jack. "He's going to White Swan in a couple days."

Stephenson toed a dirt clod. "Come over to the house right after lunch."

After Stephenson left, Jack said, "He seems okay."

"Just like his old man," Danny said, climbing up the ladder. "Whenever Red Shirt bottomed out, Stephenson found him some work and a place to bunk. If rodeo money ran dry, we'd pick pears and apples."

"Not me," Jack said. "School's better than that." He turned toward Danny. "I been meaning to tell you. After White Swan, I thought I might go down my own road awhile."

Danny looked at him steadily. He hadn't figured on Jack's running off and leaving him. "You mean follow the rodeos?"

Jack squared his shoulders. "Some of the guys were talking at Pi-Ume-Sha. A few are going on the circuit. Vinny Pinto said he had room if I wanted to share gas."

Danny climbed off his ladder. Under his feet, the ground seemed uneven. He knew Vinny's father and didn't like the smirk on his face. The old man's black baseball cap had red letters across the crown that read SMILE IF YOU'RE NOT WEARING PANTIES, and a lot of passing women smiled. "Gas can get pricey," he said.

Jack took off his gloves and came down the ladder until he was standing with one foot on the ground, the other on the first rung. "I've got money coming from this orchard work."

"You don't think you'll miss my company too much?"

"I'll try not to," Jack said after a few moments. "Anyway, I'll be back when school starts, more or less."

"Maybe I should come along. Show you a few tricks."

When Jack didn't say anything, Danny pretended he had been kidding. "I'm getting too old to wrestle stock. Darned lucky my head's still above my shoulders."

"You and Henry went on the circuit when you were sixteen. You told me dozens of times."

"Maybe we were seventeen," Danny said. "I can't quite remember." They hadn't had a car, but Henry sweet-talked an older woman he knew into loaning him hers for a weekend while she visited her sister. Two months later they returned, broke, with a smoking engine and bald tires. Henry had sold the radio and spare tire for gas. Although the woman tried to have them jailed, the cops just grinned and shrugged because they were all Indians.

"I'll be eighteen pretty soon," Jack said.

"Whatever you say." Danny tried to hide his disappointment. He had wanted to show Jack where he had rodeoed and other places that had been important in his youth. He had just started being a father, but perhaps it was already too late. Maybe he should cut Jack a little slack. That would give them both more breathing room. Although Loxie had been dead almost a year, she seemed to stand between them, and Danny realized the boy sided with his mother. Every story had two versions, but Loxie was dead, and that gave her version the edge.

Danny remembered how Red Shirt had been pleased to get him out of his trailer because it allowed the old man more time to carouse with his girlfriends. Before Danny left, his father jammed his second best straw cowboy hat on Danny's head and tucked a ten-dollar bill in his pocket. "Buy some rubbers," he said. "Don't spoil good times by getting clapped up."

"Your aunt Pudge isn't going to like it much," Danny said to Jack.

"Don't tell her," Jack said. "I won't if you won't." He held out his hand. "Shake."

Danny took Jack's hand. "While we're at it, don't say anything about the fire," Danny said. He was afraid Pudge would figure things out, though. She was like a bloodhound where Jack was concerned.

"One more thing," Jack said, holding on to Danny's hand. "I want Stephenson's check in my name."

"What the hell!" Danny started pulling his hand away, but Jack squeezed it. Danny squeezed back hard and Jack gripped tighter. Surprised at the boy's strength, Danny grinned, clenching his teeth as he felt his wrist constrict. Just for a second, he was afraid he wouldn't be able to break Jack's grip, then he did. "In your name?" he said, still grinning and pretending his hand didn't hurt. "Don't you trust me?"

Jack smiled as he rubbed his red hand against his jeans. "I trust you, but I still watch you. Especially with money."

"I trust you, too," Danny said. "But just barely." He examined his hand. "I think something's busted."

"Good," Jack said. "No more thinning."

Both relaxed a little, as though an understanding had passed between them, a momentary truce.

Neither said anything for a minute. Jack started some shoulder twists to relieve the stiffness. "Some of the guys are on weight training programs for the rodeo," he said. "Vinny carries weights in his pickup. He can bench press three hundred pounds." Jack lifted an imaginary bar over his head. "I'm thinking about starting."

"You can't outmuscle a horse," Danny said. "It's timing and reflexes. Not to mention luck."

Jack lowered the bar and rubbed his belly. "What do you think Que fixed for lunch?"

"Bologna cups," Danny said, after trying to recall what food remained in the cabin. "One of his specials." Que threw slices of bologna in a hot frying pan until their sides curled. Then he spooned scrambled eggs into the cups.

Jack kicked the ground with his tennis shoe. "Maybe I can find those greasers and share their lunch. I'll bet Stephenson's old lady fixed them a regular picnic."

On the walk back to the picker's cabin, they paused at an orchard clearing where Stephenson had pulled out old trees and replanted seedlings. The grassy hillside sloped toward the blue Columbia. Across the river, bright green orchards contrasted with snow-topped Mount Adams. Sailboards skimmed the whitecapped Columbia, their bright sails resembling summer butterflies.

"Looks like fun," Jack said.

Danny took off his cap and wiped his forehead. "That's for rich guys." Replacing his cap, he stood, hands on hips, studying the scenery. "Damn nice place." He wondered what it would be like to own land, run an orchard with your family. Maybe he could even get some work out of Que if they had a place.

"What's that?" Jack pointed to a small grassy island in the river. A rock cairn with a white marker stood on the upriver end.

"Lower Memaloose," Danny said. "Klickitats were buried there. And one white guy. That's his marker. He thought when the resurrection came, only the Indians were going to heaven, so he decided to take his chances with them."

"That's a switch," Jack said. "He really believed it?"

"I guess so."

"There's a fool born every minute," Jack said. "And only one dies a day."

"No bologna cups," Jack announced to Danny. "Que fixed salmon." He had taken off his shirt and was washing up at the green pump in front of the cabin. While Danny worked the pump handle, Jack splashed water onto his face and neck. He was getting broad shoulders, like Red Shirt's, Danny noticed, and he had his grandfather's clean jawline, too, although beer and fatigue had finally caused Red Shirt's to sag.

Que tossed Jack a towel. "Nothing but the best for a couple of hard-working men."

"Where'd you get the fish?" Danny asked. He kept the pickup keys in his pocket, but he knew Que could hot-wire it and drive to town, especially if he got thirsty.

"Some Yakima fellows showed up in a brown Plymouth beater. That car was old enough to vote. I thought they was leaking gas, but when they popped open the trunk, it was chockablock full of silvers, all iced down. The trunk was rusted through and leaking, but those were choice fish. I picked the best. It had blood-red gills and still thought it was swimming upstream. Five dollars, that fish cost me."

"You drove a stiff bargain," Danny said.

"Betcha!" Que said, and a crafty look came into his eyes. "Those boys are over a barrel. The feds threw a bunch of them in jail for selling fish out of season. It used to be they'd sell them right off the platforms. Or you could buy a fish in the alley behind most bars if you hung around a little, asked the right people. But like I said, the feds put the squeeze on.

"So they're peddling them out of town, calling on the farmers and greasers." Que chuckled. "No way a greaser's going to turn in anybody. Half of them don't even have green cards. And those farmers love to dodge store prices. Everybody comes out sweet." He turned toward the cabin. "Finish up now. Soup's on."

Jack pumped while Danny washed. As he splashed the cool water onto his face and smelled the delicious fish, Danny remembered Celilo Falls.

Red Shirt had taken Danny to Celilo Village before The Dalles Dam flooded the falls. More than five thousand Indians came that year for the salmon fishing and the feast. They took turns dipnetting from the flimsy wooden platforms that extended over the churning whitewater. Most wore raingear to keep the mists from soaking their clothing, and they smoked their pipes upside down to keep the tobacco dry.

Danny and Red Shirt were Sammy Salwish's guests at the celebration. Danny was surprised to see Sammy feed his dog raw salmon because he thought salmon poisoning would kill her. Sammy grinned, explaining that Celilo dogs had developed an immunity over the years.

Red Shirt tried fishing from Sammy's platform, but he had been drinking and was too unsteady. Danny had no raingear and was soon shivering from fright and cold. The platform shuddered with the water's force, and the treacherous wind nearly blew him from the scaffold. When his father forced him to eat a salmon eye, Danny vomited and left the platform.

As the sun was setting, fishermen came off the platforms carrying their dipnets and gunnysacks filled with salmon. They cast dark shadows against the fiery mists, and it seemed to Danny they were walking out of campfires.

After supper, his belly stretched with salmon, roots, and strawberry pop, Danny listened to his father tease Sammy about going elk hunting in the Wallowa Mountains after the fishing sites had been destroyed. Sammy just shook his head.

One morning, Sammy drove them near Spedish on the Washington side and showed them the petroglyphs along the river. One canyon was full of carved figures, and others adorned the steep basalt rimrocks. Danny had been fascinated by the rock carvings of antelope, elk, and figure people. The fierce Water Devils frightened him. "Who made these?" he asked.

"The Old Ones," Sammy said.

In some places the surface rock had been torn away, revealing the lighter, unweathered basalt. "What happened here?" Danny asked.

Sammy wiped his face with his denim shirtsleeve. "Museum people. Collectors."

"You ask too many questions," Red Shirt said. Motioning for Danny to follow, he walked a short distance from Sammy. He lit a cigarette and ground the match into the dirt with his heel so it wouldn't ignite the cheatgrass. "Sammy thinks this is a religious place," he said. "Like the Wallowas are for our people. Pretty soon most of this will be under water." Red Shirt pointed to a large face high in the rimrock. "Not that one, I guess."

Danny looked up at the face. It had large eyes circled by thick double lines and round ears, like a bear's.

"She-Who-Watches," Red Shirt said.

The eyes stared out across the Columbia, and the mouth was open in the shape of a square, as if she wanted to speak, but no sound came.

Glancing back, Danny saw Sammy take a ceremonial arrowhead from his pocket and lay it below one of the carved figures.

Remembering that morning with Sammy, Danny decided he should take Jack to see the old paintings that remained above the water. After he had dried his arms and face, Danny draped the towel across his shoulder and turned to Jack. "If you want to run off rodeoing, that's your business. But there are some places along the river you should see first."

Jack squinted. "What places?"

"Red Shirt showed me some things years ago when he took me to the Celilo Salmon Festival."

"You're talking ancient history," Jack said. "Besides, I've got to get up to White Swan and pay my rodeo fees."

"Tomorrow's Sunday. We'll skip work. You can go after that."

Jack shrugged. "Could be poking around beats working. I can't cash the check until Monday, anyway."

When they had finished eating, Que pushed himself away from the table. "All that needed was some Walla Walla Sweets. In a couple of weeks, those onions will hit the market."

Jack took the last bite of his salmon. "Delicious, Que. But next time try serving a delicate white wine, perhaps a Chardonnay or Chenin Blanc." He grinned. "We had a teacher last year who told us all about wines instead of social studies."

Que fumbled through his pockets. "I can't figure where I put the key to the wine cellar."

Danny poked his fork at the empty fish platter, picking scraps. "Damn good, Que. No kidding, you outdid yourself."

"Living is easy around here," Que said. "You can long-arm apples and pears over the fences, catch a few fish. This is milk and honey compared with the rez. Tonight I'll be serving tender rabbit in a light cream sauce. Campbell's Cream of Mushroom."

"Rabbit?" Danny asked, trying to remember if rabbit was okay.

"I spotted some rabbit hutches straight down the road. Those bunnies were mighty cramped, so I plan on thinning them out a little this afternoon. Got my eye on this plump doe."

No. Rabbit wasn't okay, Danny decided. Red Shirt had always said you ate rabbit only during months with an R. "This is July."

"You're fussing about *wild* rabbits," Que said. "Tularemia. Remember, old Marvin Kishwalks got that. Cut himself skinning a cottontail and turned yellow as a chink. His eyes, too. They looked like old eggs. Of course, his liver was shot anyway, but that rabbit fever finished him quick."

Jack pushed his chair away from the table. "I can't eat rabbit."

"These are *tame,* damn it," Que said. "Perfect timing, too. If anyone misses a rabbit, they got to figure a wetback made rabbit stew in the woods." He leaned back in his chair. "Now let's see. What wine goes with rabbit?"

"I just won't eat it," Jack said. "Sorry."

"Every bite reminds him of the Easter bunny," Que teased.

But Danny saw the expression on Jack's face. "What's wrong?"

"Mom brought me a rabbit once, as a pet. I guess I was nine or ten. I planned to breed the rabbit, maybe make some money. Hanson didn't think I took good enough care of her — cleaning the cage and all that. One day, after Mom picked me up at school, we went back to the place and found Hanson in the kitchen. He had butchered the rabbit and was going to fry it up like a chicken. The guts, hide, and head were on some newspaper in the corner. When he saw us come in, he said to Mom, 'You're just in time to fix supper.'"

Danny shook his head. "She let him get away with that?"

"Not exactly," Jack said. "She told him she had to hang up her coat, and when she came back she had Hanson's pump shotgun. 'Eat it raw,' she told him. When you looked at her face, you knew she meant business. She had me get a glass and a bottle of gin out of the cupboard for her. 'You pour,' she said to me, and I did. She'd take one hand off that gun for just a second whenever she tossed down a drink. But her finger always stayed on the trigger.

"She made Hanson eat every bit of that raw rabbit. When he finished, he looked sick, but he was still sort of smiling.

"'Now eat that,' she said, and she pointed to the stuff on the paper. He quit smiling and leaned toward her. It was then she fired the gun. The whole front of the woodbox was blown away.

"'Plenty left,' Mom said, and when she started to pump the gun, I thought we'd be picking pieces of Hanson off the wall. But he went over to the corner and actually ate a few bites of the guts before he started puking. 'Get out of my kitchen,' she said then, 'and take that with you.'

"He scooped up the guts and ran out the back door, and you could see him on the porch, heaving over the railing. Mom threw his coat out after him and locked the door. Half an hour later, he was pounding on the door to get in, but she wouldn't let him. Finally he started up the tractor and drove to town. Stayed away for three days before he tried coming back."

"I'll bet he slept with one eye open after that," Que said.

Danny didn't say anything.

"I guess rabbit is definitely scratched off the menu for this evening," Que said. He looked at the salmon's skeleton. "Bologna cups tonight, unless Pudge has a better idea."

"Pudge?" Danny said.

Que took a crumpled postcard from his pocket. It showed the Grand Entry at the Pendleton Round-Up. Jack read the card while Danny stared at the mounted flag bearers carrying the flags of the United States, Canada, Oregon, and the Umatilla Nation.

Jack handed Danny the card. "She's going to a softball tournament in Toppenish and coming here first. Looks like she'll be here tonight."

"Surprise, surprise," Que said. "She's taking the long way around, don't you think?"

"She probably wants to check on Jack," Danny said.

"This one came, too," Que said. "You forget to pay a ticket?"

It was a business envelope from the Warm Springs Tribal Police. The note was direct:

> That was some snipe hunt. We combed the
> butte twice and came up blank. Thanks for wasting
> my time.   Sgt. Slickpoo

"They couldn't find an elephant's ass," Danny said, tossing aside the note. Maybe a tree fell on the body. Most likely, they never went up there at all. Lazy cops."

Que kinked his eyebrow as if to say "Told you so."

"I know what I saw," Danny said.

Stephenson's house was a quarter mile from the pickers' cabins. When Danny was a boy, it had been a modest, two-story clapboard farmhouse, but the family had completely redone it after old man Stephenson died. A new addition served as a greenhouse, and there were skylights in the roof.

A weatherbeaten utility building held the old John Deere tractor, mower, and rake that Stephenson used to cut the orchard grass. A sprayer rig that ran off the tractor's engine was also housed there.

An open-sided shed held a couple of dozen three-pointed aluminum ladders and a few of the old wooden ladders. Canvas fruit bags hung from the ceiling so they wouldn't mildew, and there were stacks of old apple boxes. Some still had the blue and yellow Diamond label even though the fruit packing plant now belonged to a California co-op.

An orchard required relatively little equipment compared with a wheat or cattle ranch. If he won the lottery or married a rich woman, Danny had always thought he'd buy a cattle ranch, but now he wondered if it wouldn't be less trouble to manage an orchard.

The fronts of both the utility building and the sheds were covered with bleached deer and elk antlers. Some of the elk racks were nearly trophy size.

Danny stepped onto the porch of the main house and started to knock, but Stephenson saw him through the kitchen window and waved him in. Danny hesitated in the entryway because his boots had Vibram soles that picked up the dirt.

"What the hell," Stephenson said. "It's indoor-outdoor carpeting. A man's got to wear boots in the house. All this fixing up — that's my wife's idea."

The interior had been freshly painted and wallpapered. The kitchen had a Jenn-Air range and microwave wall oven. Stephenson was heating water on the range. "Making coffee," he said. "You want a cup? It's just instant."

"Sure thing," Danny said.

"Go on in the front room. Look around. I'll be there in a jiff. You take anything in it?"

"Some cream and sugar if you got it," Danny said.

The front room had a beige sofa and matching chairs and a glass coffee table. An old oak roll-top desk occupied one corner. Planters seemed to hang everywhere.

"You got a regular garden here," Danny said as Stephenson joined him.

"Those belong to the wife. I work hard enough fooling with that damn orchard." He handed Danny his coffee.

The men sat down and Stephenson said, "So Jack's the next rodeo star."

"All I ever got in White Swan was bruises," Danny said. "Maybe he'll have better luck. He hasn't learned all my ways of falling off yet."

Stephenson chuckled and sipped his coffee. "Que's shoulder doing okay, is it?"

"Sure," Danny said. "He only fell about five rungs."

"Kids won't do orchard work. They're all at McDonald's or the pizza joints, hanging out."

"I know it," Danny said. "Jack runs into town every chance he gets."

"That leaves the Mexicans. They're pretty good workers, and they can't sue. That's one good thing about hiring illegals. I don't carry half the insurance I used to." Stephenson stood and walked to the window. "Look how the limbs are hanging. I got to get those trees thinned. Hell, we've had illegals around here for years. All those Chinese cannery workers were illegal."

Danny put his coffee cup on the table. "When Red Shirt took me around The Dalles, the only Chinese I saw were in restaurants."

"I'm talking years ago, when the salmon canneries were in full swing. The Chinese did all the butchering and packing. Twice a year, just before the big salmon runs, a trainload came up from Portland. My old man called it the Chinkee Choo-Choo. Most of those workers were illegal — came down from Canada originally."

"Cheap labor, I guess," Danny said.

"No, not really. The China Boss organized the workers so they got good wages — of course, he took his cut." Stephenson sat down again and took a sip of his coffee. "Damn good workers. Those Chinese had small hands, like a woman's, but their wrists and fingers were strong. They had to butcher and pack twelve hours straight.

"When I was a kid, some weekends I'd spear suckers and sell them in the China camps. I'd get hard candy and some pennies. Once they gave me a mah-jongg set, but I couldn't figure how it worked."

"I never saw those camps," Danny said.

"Indians never went near them because they thought the Chinese cast spells."

"Everyone kept to his own, I guess," Danny said.

"White men never went near those camps, either, unless there was mischief — liquor or women. You can bet they didn't demand green cards or work permits, not back then, and everything worked fine. People made good money. The Indians caught the fish, the Chinese canned it, and the owners showed a good profit."

"It's all gone now," Danny said.

Stephenson settled back on the couch. "The Iron Chink got rid of some workers. You know, the butchering machine. But it couldn't handle the fancy packing of the big Chinooks. When they build the dams, everybody lost. The salmon runs stopped and the canneries closed. The Chinese went back to Portland or wherever."

"The Indians scattered, too," Danny said.

"That's right, now that you mention it." Stephenson stirred his coffee. "My father took me to Celilo a few times when the fish were running. Indians came from all over in buckboards and broken-down cars. The way they fished from platforms — that's something I'll never forget." He put down his cup. "It was a shame when the dam flooded the falls."

Danny couldn't say anything.

"Any of your people fish there?"

Danny spread his hands. "My great-grandfather Left Hand fished there with his wife's people after his band was run out of the Wallowa Mountains. And my grandfather Medicine Bird tried fishing but got crowded out by in-laws most of the time." He chuckled. "My grandmother had lots of brothers and cousins."

Stephenson laughed. "Relatives are the same all over."

"Maybe so." Danny could have told Stephenson more — what he'd learned from his grandfather.

Danny's great-grandfather Left Hand had been a Dreamer Warrior and fought beside Chief Joseph, after the Nez Perce had been driven from their Wallowa Mountain homeland. The Dreamers refused to accept Christianity and believed that by practicing the old ceremonies, they could drive the white men from their lands.

During the Nez Perce War, Left Hand's wife and child had been killed at Big Hole. After the Nez Perce surrendered in the Bear

Paws, Left Hand had made his way back to the Umatilla Reservation, where he married for a second time and pretended to be a Christian Indian.

During the salmon runs, Left Hand travelled to the Columbia River and fished with his wife's people. The Indian Agents were fooled by his disguises and never believed he had been a Dreamer Warrior, even though he practiced the Washat Seven Drum religion at secret places on the reservation.

Every spring, Left Hand would return to the Wallowas to rendezvous with other Dreamer Warriors who had seen battle. After years of performing the old mountain ceremonies, one spring he disappeared. Medicine Bird never carried the story beyond that, although Danny suspected he was holding something back.

Stephenson finished his coffee and stood. "That's all in the past," he said. "What's now is this damn orchard. You want to draw wages?"

"We got five days put in," Danny said. "I want to get a hundred advance. My boys wants a hundred, too, in his name."

Stephenson took out the large checkbook from the oak desk. He opened it and started to write on one of the pale green checks.

"Can you make mine a hundred and fifty? Give me the fifty in cash?"

"Do I look like a bank?"

"Jack's aunt is coming, and we can't cash those checks until Monday."

"You taking tomorrow off?" Stephenson put down the pen. "The Mexicans never work Sundays because they're Catholic. Me, I don't get any holidays. That's a fact."

"I'll be coming back Monday," Danny said. "Tomorrow, I thought I'd take Jack above The Dalles. A few of the old River Indians still fish there."

"I guess I'll have to thin pears tomorrow myself," Stephenson grumbled. He took fifty dollars from his billfold and had Danny sign a receipt. After he finished writing out the two checks, he handed them to Danny. Then he put the checkbook back in the drawer.

"Funny thing," he said. "Years ago, my father probably sat at this same desk and wrote out checks to Red Shirt. Lots of them, I suppose. Come to think of it, there's a picture around here we ran across in an old shoebox. My dad and Red Shirt. They were a lot younger then."

He shuffled through the papers in one of the cubbyholes until he found the old photograph. It was Red Shirt, all right, and he looked thin, so Danny guessed it was before he had gone to Korea. Both Red Shirt and old man Stephenson were kneeling. In front of them were two large elk racks, and the two men had placed their rifles across the horns as if they were yardsticks. Red Shirt wore his old yellow crusher hat and Stephenson had on a plaid cap. A fifth of whiskey sat on the ground in front of them.

"Each year they bet who'd kill the biggest elk," Stephenson said.

"I remember that," Danny said as he tried to read the label on the bottle.

"My dad hunted up there in Tygh Valley and yours went over to eastern Oregon."

"The Wallowas," Danny said. "He said the biggest elk were over there."

"I guess he proved it," Stephenson said, looking at the photograph.

"If nothing else, Red Shirt was a good hunter." Some of his father's friends had claimed Red Shirt knew the Elk Chant, one of the old Dreamer ceremonies. But Danny didn't know for sure that was true. He wished Red Shirt had passed the Elk Chant along, as fathers were supposed to, but he had died before he had the chance. Or maybe he hadn't known it, after all.

"Those two guys were characters," Stephenson said. "Genuine characters." He handed Danny the photo. "You keep this and show it to your boy. I had another made up from the print."

"Thanks," Danny said. He looked at the photo again before he tucked it into his pocket along with the checks.

．　．　．

When he and Jack got back from the orchard that evening, Danny saw a yellow Vega with a black stripe parked in front of the cabin. The window on the passenger's side was broken out, and Danny figured someone had looted the glove compartment.

"Pudge got a new beater," Jack said. "Air-conditioned."

Danny glanced in through the broken window. The lock in the glove box had been forced, so it hung open. The tape deck had been ripped out, too. Pudge's red and white Bravettes uniform was in the back seat along with a couple of softball gloves. Canvas bags jammed with bats covered the floor.

Inside the cabin, Pudge and Billy Que were sharing a twelve-pack. When Danny and Jack walked in, Pudge put down her bottle and stood. Her grape-colored blouse separated from her black polyester pants, showing a strip of skin lined with stretch marks. She gave Jack a big hug and kissed his forehead. "How's my favorite nephew?"

"Doing great," Jack said and did his best to return her hug.

She gripped his shoulders, studying him at arm's length. "What a handsome dog! If I didn't want to keep you all to myself, I'd fix you up with a couple girls on the team."

"Come on, Pudge," Jack said.

"Say, what happened to your hair?" She touched the singed patch.

Jack glanced toward Danny. "I got careless lighting the wood-stove."

"No wonder. Living like wetbacks crammed in a picker's shack. If Loxie were still around — God bless her — she'd think that took first place." She glared at Danny and Que. "If you get tired of these lowlifes, come stay with me. You got a standing invitation."

"Thanks," Jack said. "I'll keep it in mind."

"Toss me a beer, would you?" Danny said, and Pudge tossed one a little harder than he'd expected. He was relieved that Jack hadn't said anything about the Warm Springs fire. Later on, Danny might tell her about it himself if the mood hit him. He opened the beer, gulping quickly to catch the foam. "We can't all live in fancy BIA places," he said to Pudge. She had a new house from a makework government contract, but he expected it to fall apart quickly, like most reservation projects. He'd stick with Red Shirt's trailer.

"You have to show a little gumption," she said. "And draw a steady paycheck."

Danny counted the empties. Sometimes, after she'd had a few, Pudge nagged about his lack of ambition. "We're making pocket money. Over a hundred bucks a day until Que got hurt."

"Don't trust him with your banking," Pudge told Jack, thrusting her chin at Danny.

"I figured that out on my own." Jack took the check out of his billfold and waved it slowly back and forth. "White Swan is waiting. The saddlebronc and steer wrestling purses have my name written all over them."

"Easy money," Danny said, catching Jack's mood. "He made entry fees and has money to burn."

"Don't spend it all yet," Pudge said. "Every year, your father went bust at White Swan. Always claimed the locals rigged it." She laughed at Danny. "Isn't that right, Easy Money?"

That darned Pudge had a memory like an elephant. "The straight truth is I drew bad horses," Danny said. He sipped his beer and grinned. "Seems I'm always getting stuck with old nags."

Pudge snorted and Que laughed, leaning back in his chair so only two legs touched the floor. Jack coughed, covering his mouth with his hand. "Thanks for the postcard," he said, trying to change the subject.

"That softball tournament starts real early tomorrow, does it?" Danny asked.

"Don't try the bum's rush," Pudge said. "It starts whenever I get there, because all the equipment's in my car."

Danny spread his arms. "Stay as long as you like. My *casa* is your *casa*."

A bug crawled across the floor and Pudge squashed it with her tennis shoe. "I hope I don't catch cooties from your *casa*."

"I been bit a time or two myself," Que said.

"Good. Then they'll all die or wind up in detox." She examined the squashed bug. "Earwig. You should buy some Lysol or rent a flamethrower." She sniffed the air. "Que's liniment sure stinks!"

"You get used to it," Danny said.

"I need fresh air," Pudge said.

"Lose some weight?" Danny couldn't really tell, but it was the kind of thing Pudge liked to hear. He knew Pudge was touchy about her weight, especially since Loxie had always been naturally thin — the kind of woman who ate salad without dressing just because she liked it that way. Looking good had come easy to Loxie, Danny thought. But then, so had everything else, at least in the beginning.

Pudge rubbed her stomach. "I'm down a size, thanks to softball." She slapped her thighs. "Hard to keep it off here." Her tone softened, and she seemed pleased Danny had noticed.

"What position?" Jack asked.

"Mostly missionary," she said, then added "ayyy" to show she was kidding. "Catcher. I can burn one to second from a crouch. They call me Slingshot and I'm doubletough." She put Jack's hand on her biceps. "Feel this."

"From a crouch, huh?" Jack whistled softly as he squeezed her arm. "I believe it."

"Want to toss the ball around? There's an extra glove in the car."

"Sounds good," Jack said. "I need to limber up after standing on that ladder."

Pudge started for the door, then paused. "Stomach's starting to growl. You fixing supper?"

Que shrugged. "I was planning some rabbit stew, but these guys won't touch it."

"Who can blame them?" she said. "This is July."

"We'll go to town after a bit," Danny said. "I want to talk with you, anyway."

Pudge tugged her blouse. "I'm not fixed up."

"You look okay," Danny said.

"Who's buying? Don't pull out an empty wallet after you've licked the plate."

"I'm cashy," Danny said. "Stephenson just gave me an advance."

"All right," she said. "Give us fifteen minutes. I want to show Jack my arm."

"I'll be right along," Jack said as Pudge went out to the Vega. Jack turned to Danny and pointed to the singed spot on his head.

"What do you want?" Danny asked.

"Cash," Jack said, holding out his hand. "Fifty-fifty. You guys take Pudge's car and let me drive the truck. There's a waitress at the pizza parlor I want to check out."

"Hey, somebody's got to drop me off," Que said. "I'm getting cabin fever."

"Jeez," Danny said. He took out his wallet, opening it carefully so Jack couldn't see the money. "I thought we had a deal." He handed Jack a twenty.

"Deals were made to be broken," Jack said, pocketing the money and going outside.

"This is worse than White Swan," Danny said.

"Who knows," Que said. "Maybe you'll get a re-ride."

Danny took Pudge to the Riverview Café. He had heard it was the best in town, not counting the real fancy places. The food looked good, too. The apple pie in the stainless steel case was at least three inches thick. "Save me a piece of that pie," Danny told the waitress, and she winked.

When they had left Jack and Que back at the cabin, Jack had been cleaning up for town and Que was grumbling about his taking so long. "You be good," Pudge had said to Jack. "If you can't be good, be careful." She also mentioned that there were some cute girls on the team who wanted to meet him, and Jack said maybe he'd catch a ride over to Toppenish after the White Swan rodeo.

Danny and Pudge sat at a booth with a view of the Columbia River and Mount Adams. Pudge looked out the window for a few minutes before opening her menu. "It's a nice place," she said. She pursed her lips and concentrated on the day's offerings. Danny checked out the prices.

"That Special looks good," Pudge said and closed her menu. "I like Swiss steak, but it's usually too much trouble just cooking for one. I mostly heat and eat."

"That's why they make TV dinners," Danny said. He wondered if "cooking for one" was a hint.

The waitress came to take their orders. Danny asked for the T-bone, medium rare.

"So what's on your mind?" Pudge asked.

"You were giving me a pretty hard time back there," Danny said.

Pudge sipped her water. "At first, the picker's shack bothered me some. And I wish you'd stick closer to Pendleton so I could see more of Jack."

"We need pocket money," Danny said. "Jack wants to rodeo, and there's no work around Pendleton." The Grain Growers used to hire Indians for part-time help, but after the pine mill closed, those jobs went to laid-off millworkers.

Pudge nodded. "Right now, it's tight most places. But thanks to car wrecks and drunk cowboys, the hospital's in clover."

Danny leaned back in the booth. "How's the program?" Pudge was in her second year of nurse's training, and he was a little envious of her opportunity for a steady paycheck, but he didn't want to let on.

"It's okay, except for chemistry. I need special tutoring. After work, I study a few hours every night."

"Sounds tough."

Pudge nodded. "I remember my mother. God, she worked hard getting her nurse's training and keeping me and Loxie fed. Four o'clock in the morning, we'd hear her banging around the kitchen, making coffee and clearing a space on the table so she could study."

"That's about the time my old man stumbled home," Danny said.

"If we tried to get up, too, she'd slap us back to bed." Pudge opened a container of sugar and dabbed at the crystals with her forefinger. "Relocation finished her."

"Loxie told me about it," Danny said. "That was some crazy idea, sending reservation people into big cities."

Pudge nodded. "The relocation people gave her a one-way ticket to Denver. She'd never even been to Portland, let alone Denver. But when they came around the reservation to sign people up, she was one of the first in line. Figured she'd start over, I guess. A new life and all that."

Danny remembered what Loxie had said. When her mother was sent to take blood samples at the hospital, some of the patients refused to be treated by an Indian, so she pretended to be Italian.

"She should have just gone home," Pudge continued. "She wasn't happy in the big city — didn't know anybody and never could figure out how to use the buses. Hated the cold." Pudge thought for a moment. "She must've missed her family, too. But Mom didn't want to be a quitter."

Danny knew the rest of the story. When Pudge's mother was assigned to the pharmacy, she started taking drugs. After that, it was one downhill slide. "Anyway, you're doing okay."

"Thanks," Pudge said. Reaching across the table, she took Danny's hand in both of hers and gave a little squeeze. When she looked right at him, Pudge's eyes reminded Danny of Loxie's before she crawled into the bottle. But Pudge's were kinder. Maybe she should be tougher, Danny thought. It was too easy to take advantage.

"Loxie battled with her every day," Pudge said. "She told everyone Mom was crazy. I'd hear her mumbling to herself and think so too. When we went out, Loxie always walked a few feet apart from us. What did I know? Six years old."

"Your sister had a way of stirring trouble with a short stick," Danny said. "And poking at old wounds. I remember how she used to say I'd make a lousy father. Just like my old man."

"She used to say lots of things," Pudge said. "I'm an expert, because I listened to her for a long time. I thought she was so smart and beautiful, she must be right." Pudge stared out the window at the mountain. "That's not to speak ill, but let's change the subject. What about Jack? Think he's got a chance with rodeo?"

"Slim," Danny said. "At least I got Corky Freeman to give him some pointers about riding horses. Not that they worked."

"Why?"

"Jack keeps falling off."

Pudge laughed and Danny did, too. It was good to have a woman laughing at his jokes, not just because she was waiting for another drink or working to forget a lousy marriage. He liked how Pudge looked when she laughed, and sometimes he wanted to care about her more than he did. If Loxie hadn't been her half sister, it might have made a difference.

When Danny went to pay the bill, he noticed two punchboards half hidden behind the counter. "What's on the boards?" he asked the cashier.

"Shotgun on one," the woman said, "little color TV on the other. Lots of candy still on both. It's two chances for a buck."

He handed her a five. "I'll go with the color TV," he said. After she gave him the board, Danny punched out ten numbers and started unfolding the papers. He won a box of chocolate-covered cherries with the fourth and another with the ninth.

"Must be your lucky day," the cashier said.

"I can't wait for tomorrow." Danny took the boxes back to the table and set them in front of Pudge. He thought her birthday was close, but couldn't remember. "A guy ran off and left these," he said.

"I'll bet." She opened one of the boxes and bit into a candy. The liquid cordial ran onto her fingers. "Fresh," she said, licking them clean. She held out the box.

Danny shook his head. "Pie was just right."

"Go on," she said. "Try it."

When he took one, it tasted pretty good.

They stepped outside the restaurant and Danny started for the car.

"Let's walk a little," Pudge said. "Let the meal settle. But I don't want to carry these." She set the candy inside her car on the front seat.

They started down the hill toward the town, and Danny put his arm around Pudge. The ground was uneven, making the walking awkward, so he decided just to hold her hand.

The setting sun cast long shadows on the river, and the hills on the Washington side glowed crimson. "Look at that," Pudge said. "Pretty."

Across the road, a small motel's neon sign blinked and hummed in the twilight.

Some young Mexicans came by in a low-rider Plymouth with a shaker hood and undersize tires. They were smoking cigarettes and laughing. The driver gripped the small chain-link steering wheel.

"You know why they have those tiny steering wheels?" Danny asked.

"No," Pudge said.

"So they can drive with handcuffs."

Pudge laughed hard, and it sounded good to Danny.

She turned, glancing back toward her car. "I don't want anybody stealing that softball stuff. I bet it was wetbacks got that tape deck."

"They look like trouble," Danny said. He wondered if they had green cards. "How far you planning on walking, anyway?" He wasn't big on after-dinner walks.

"Maybe just across the street," she said.

Danny glanced at the motel sign. "I'll see about a room."

"I'll get the car," she said. "I want to park it close by." Pudge started uphill toward the café.

When Danny opened the motel's office door, a little bell rang, and he could smell fish cooking.

After a minute, a woman in an apron came out of the back room. "*Yo habla Español,*" she said.

"I'm not Mexican," Danny said.

"Oh," the woman said. "Can I help you?"

"I want a room — just tonight."

"How many people?"

"Two," he said.

Pudge pulled up in the Vega and the woman glanced out the window. "Number eight has a double bed," she said. "I'm sure you and your wife will be comfortable." She handed him a registration card. "Just fill this out. It's twenty-two dollars. That's the cash discount price. We don't take credit cards or checks."

Danny looked at the registration form. "Just a second," he said. "I've got to check the license number." He went outside. "I'm a little short," he told Pudge. "You got ten dollars?"

She dug in her purse and handed him two fives. "I guess we're going Dutch," she said.

The room was small and smelled of disinfectant, but it had a good view of the river and Mount Adams.

Danny turned on the TV set, just to see how it worked. He got a sharp picture. *Hee Haw* was on, and he watched Buck Owens and Roy Clark for a moment before switching it off.

Pudge put the opened box of candy on the nightstand and sat on the bed. She started unlacing her tennis shoes.

When they had both undressed, Pudge lay back on the bed. Her large breasts flattened. Turning on her side, she took one of the candies out of the box and crushed it, then dripped some of the liquid around her nipples. Danny took one of her nipples in his mouth, and under the chocolate and cherry flavors, he tasted salt.

After they were finished, Pudge said, "I'm going to take a shower. Get the sticky off." She paused by the shower door. "You want to come in?"

Danny rolled over onto his elbow and looked at her. "Not right now, I guess."

Pudge turned on the shower, and after a while the bathroom filled with steam. Danny could hear her humming.

He got out of bed and went over to the window. It was almost dark, and he saw car lights crossing the bridge into Oregon. Maybe the cars were filled with young people going to a movie or having pizza. He remembered the fun he'd had with Loxie.

Pudge came out of the bathroom with a towel wrapped around

her head, another draped across her front. She smelled like motel soap.

She stood beside Danny. "When Loxie and I were young," she said, gazing out the window, "our grandparents used to take us huckleberrying on Mount Adams. They picked and we ate. Later, the old man drove around The Dalles and we sold quarts of berries door-to-door. We were cute kids — even smeared with berries — and no one could resist us." She laughed softly. "Later, he'd give us money for candy and strawberry pop while Gram shook her head. Loxie always got sick, but it never bothered me." Pudge patted her stomach. "Cast iron."

Danny nodded. He squinted and tried to think of the two young girls, but he kept seeing only Loxie.

"After the season was over, some of the old women set fire to the berry fields to burn away the vines and scrub brush. Next year those berries would be back, bigger and sweeter than ever. The ash made a kind of fertilizer, I guess."

"I heard that," Danny said.

"The wind had to be just right, so the fire couldn't get into the trees. I remember the red glowing at night and the warm wind rustling through the leaves."

"If that wind kicks up too much, watch out," Danny said. "There at Warm Springs, it blew the fire right by Jack and his crew —" He stopped suddenly, but Pudge hadn't missed it.

"You let Jack fight that fire?" Her eyes widened. "You know how dangerous it is!"

"He wanted to," Danny said. "And it's good money."

"Don't you have any sense?"

"It's not that dangerous," Danny said.

"How'd his hair get singed, then?" Pudge stepped back from the window. "You're careless," she said. "Damn careless."

Danny stared at the blue-black shadow of Mount Adams outlined against the night sky. He wanted to tell Pudge she was wrong, but she could always bring up Loxie. He was wondering if Loxie had felt anything when she hit the gravel truck. "Let's just drop it."

"Danny, he's all you've got," Pudge said after a while. "He's all we've got left." She touched his arm. "You're cold," she said. "You're shivering."

He turned from the window, but didn't say anything.

They crawled under the blankets this time, and even when they made love, Danny was thinking of Loxie. Pudge went to sleep, but Danny lay beside her a long time, watching the covers move with her steady breathing.

Sometime in the night he awakened; Pudge was sobbing. "What is it?" Danny asked.

"Loxie," she said. "She was talking to me. She was here."

"It was a dream. Go back to sleep."

"No, I can't. I don't know what's going to happen."

"It'll be all right," he said, hoping that it was true. She turned her back to him, and Danny held her long into the night, glad for the warmth.

3

SPEARFISH

"EAT IT!" Red Shirt had shouted over the roar of whitewater.

Danny stared at the salmon eye his father held. Wide as a dime, it had a black pupil the size of a matchtip. A dark bloody patch partially obscured the yellow iris.

Red Shirt swayed slightly on the flimsy fishing platform, and Danny didn't know whether his unsteadiness was from his drinking or the force of the water rushing beneath them. Red Shirt had taken off his safety rope, and the thick line trembled slightly on the wood, like a freshly killed snake.

At the end of the platform, beyond his father's bulk, Danny saw Sammy Salwish sitting on an apple box. The dipnet's handle braced against his shoulder, Sammy waited for another large Chinook to enter the hoop.

Danny wished that he had never told his father he wanted to try platform fishing with the Celilos. A sly look had come over Red Shirt's face and he said, "If you want to see like a Fish Indian, you got to eat salmon eyes."

Red Shirt took a second salmon eye from the front pocket of his snapbutton shirt and rolled the two eyes in his palm like dice. He took one between his thumb and forefinger, tossing it in the air. Tipping his head back and opening his mouth wide, he caught the salmon eye as it fell, then swallowed.

Red Shirt winked at Sammy, then grabbed Danny's head, squeezing his cheeks until the boy opened his mouth to shout. At that moment, Red Shirt shoved in the salmon eye, clamping Danny's jaws tight.

The fish eye slid in Danny's mouth like an oily grape and the strong taste made him gag, so he swallowed quickly.

"Salmon Boy!" Red Shirt seized Danny around the waist and held him over the roaring whitewater. He let go and Danny dropped toward the water, sucking a deep breath. The safety rope jerked his middle, and he grunted from shock and pain, vomiting the salmon eye.

Dangling above the whitewater, Danny closed his eyes, fearful that the rope would snap or the trembling platform tear loose from the basalt anchor. After a while, he felt the rope being tugged up, and once he was on the platform, he smelled pipe smoke. Opening his eyes, he saw that Sammy had rescued him.

"He's been drinking," Sammy said. He walked off the platform, two large Chinooks hanging over his shoulder.

Danny sat on the wet wood, afraid to stand because his legs might buckle. Fresh slime covered the platform near the apple box, and Danny saw a rainbow in the sheen. A few salmon scales glittered like sequins. Near a couple of the crushed Rainier cans beside the apple box lay the salmon eye Red Shirt had pretended to swallow.

Danny crawled over to the eye and was about to flick it into the water when he remembered how the Fish Indians claimed that by eating salmon eyes, one could see like the salmon. Studying this eye carefully, Danny had the sense that the eye watched him, even though he had seen his father gouge it from the socket with his thumb that afternoon.

He put the eye into his mouth and this time he did not gag. After swallowing it, he untied the safety rope and followed Sammy off the platform.

Now the Indian fishermen had built wooden fishing platforms and open-sided shacks on the basalt rocks half a mile below The Dalles Dam, just upstream from the bridge that crossed into Washington. With Celilo Falls drowned by the dam, the Indians fished the whitewater from the spillways. They still called this fishing site Lone

Pine, but the pine tree was gone. Inside the Portage Inn, people dressed in Sunday clothes were sitting at the window tables ordering the champagne brunch. Occasionally, they glanced out at the river and the Indians fishing.

After they finished eating, some of the people walked to the edge of the parking lot for a closer look. The women stayed on the asphalt because they were wearing high heels and light dresses, but a few of the men and children scrambled down the dirt embankment and ventured a short distance out onto the basalt rocks. The midday sun was hot, so the men took off their jackets and folded them over their arms as they watched.

The fishing shacks contained cheap Styrofoam coolers, Fritos, sacks of cookies and candy bars, radios. One had a TV set, but there was no picture. The Indians, dressed in jeans and cowboy shirts, sat on apple boxes or on the bare platforms, holding the long dipnets in the water. Two of the younger men were listening to Walkmans and keeping time with their feet. Now and then, they would take cans of beer from a red and white Playmate cooler. After drinking the beer, they glanced over their shoulders at the people on the rocks, then threw the empty cans into the river and grinned.

Every so often one of the white men would see if he could buy a salmon, but an old Indian man in a denim shirt would come to the edge of the platform and spread his hands. "No fish today," he would say. "No fish for sale."

Danny and Jack had been sitting on the rocks and talking about fishing for an hour, but they hadn't seen anyone catch a salmon. There were a couple of large Igloo coolers on the scaffold, and Danny knew that's where the netters would put any fish they caught.

After a while, all the white people had left and the old man came out again. "No fish," he said to Danny.

"Just watching," Danny said. As the man started to turn back, Danny called, "Huk-choot," a river greeting that meant "good luck."

The man came off the platform and onto the rocks. He squinted at Danny. "Do I know you, grandson? You're not from around here."

"We live up on the Umatilla Reservation," Danny said. "Danny Kachiah and my son, Jack. My father, Red Shirt, took me to Celilo Falls to see the fishing. He knew Sammy Salwish."

The man sat down beside them and pulled makings from his shirt pocket. He started rolling a cigarette. "Sammy left the river, a long time back."

"I know," Danny said. "He kept a sheep camp near us. After the backwaters from the dam drowned Celilo Falls, Sammy left, because it made him sick to see the river ways disappear."

The old man shook his head. "Sammy and sheep. That didn't make sense." He put the cigarette in his mouth and lit it. "Sammy had that dog."

"Judy," Danny said. He had shot the dog after Sammy died and Judy started running sheep.

The man smoked quietly for a few moments. "That's right," he said. "Judy. You knew Sammy."

Danny realized he had been tested.

"Willis Salwish." The old man gave Danny his hand and they shook lightly, the Indian way. Then he shook hands with Jack. "Sammy was my cousin," he said. "He always liked your father."

He stood and looked around. "Some of the river people are in jail for selling fish," he said. "Undercover cops set up a fish-buying shack at Celilo Village and even sent Indian policemen out here to trap us. They got my son Orville, but not me. I'm like Speel-y-ai, Old Coyote. I been around a long time."

"You can sell fish," Jack said. "It's in the treaty."

"Lots of laws been passed since that treaty," Willis said. "Commercial season doesn't start for a while. Now it's just sustenance fishing. Family only."

"We're all one big family," Danny said. "How much you selling them for, anyway?"

Willis finished his cigarette and flipped the butt into the water. Then he laughed at Danny's trickery. "Not selling them at all, grandson. Just catching the fish for my family. You come over to Cloudville tonight. We'll have salmon. You know where it is?"

"Just across the river, then up toward Spearfish."

"Spedish." Willis corrected him, and Danny was sorry he hadn't used the old name.

On the way back to the truck, Jack shook his head. "They used Indian policemen. That's disgusting."

Danny nodded. "That's the government." He remembered how the cavalry had recruited Nez Perce to fight Yakimas during the Yakima wars after the government kept reducing the size of the reservation it had promised. At the time, Old Joseph of the Nez Perce wanted peace. Later, after the government's broken promises to the Nez Perce, young Joseph showed them the rifle. When Danny asked his grandfather Medicine Bird about the Nez Perce fighting their Yakima cousins, Medicine Bird's eyes had filled with tears. "At least they didn't get Willis," Danny said.

"Old guys like that are barely hanging on," Jack said. "The sad thing is, you know they're going to lose — one way or the other."

Danny and Jack crossed the bridge into Washington, and Danny stopped the pickup at the Wish-Ham Cemetery, about half a mile from the river. The cemetery was surrounded by a ten-foot chain-link fence topped by three strands of barbed wire. There were five-pronged barbs instead of the usual three found on rangeland cattle fences.

When Danny got out of the truck, he was surprised at how much the wind had picked up. The grass was low and he hadn't noticed it blowing, but in this country the wind always blew. He and Jack walked over to the fence and looked in. Flowers and other mementoes had been placed on the graves. Plastic statues of deer and horses were popular. A small statue of a German shepherd adorned one grave; another had a sculpted head of a man with braids and feathers. An orange toy car caught Danny's interest, and he wondered if it was the grave of a child or just someone who liked cars.

"That's a pretty heavy-duty fence," Jack said, picking the thistles out of his jeans.

"They want to keep out the grave robbers and looters."

"Seems funny to steal old bones." Jack walked over to the locked gate and looked at the faded white and black wooden sign. "Wish-Ham," he read. "Hey, I know about this place. One of the kids at school told me they moved all the bones here from a burial island in the river."

"Two islands," Danny said. "Grave and Memaloose. They were

flooded by the dam's backwaters, so the Army Corps of Engineers moved all the bones here. Took them out by helicopter. Those are the treaty chiefs over there." He pointed to three white headstones. "Five hundred or more skeletons are buried in that mass grave with the large concrete slab and marker."

"Why not just let the backwaters cover the islands?" Jack asked. "That should keep away the grave robbers and everyone else."

"The bodies weren't really buried," Danny said. "Those islands were basalt. Mostly they were in shallow pits or in wooden houses. And the newer bodies were stacked in their caskets on the rocks. If the dead hadn't been moved before the flood, they would have washed away."

"I didn't know they left them out like that."

"It used to work," Danny said. "The dead were in the middle of the river, away from the dogs and coyotes. Their relatives left them with anything they might need in the spirit world — pots and kettles, skins and firearms. And money. That's what the looters wanted mostly. They found a twenty-dollar gold piece clenched in one skull's teeth. After that, the hunt was on. Boats landed on the islands, and the white guys went around smashing the skulls with rifle butts and rocks, looking for more gold. They took the other things, too, and when they were finished, they scattered the bones or threw them into the river."

"I wouldn't think anybody'd get much up here now," Jack said. "That's a wicked fence."

"They had to put it up. Even after the bones were moved, people came out here with metal detectors and started digging. But the gold was gone. They found only copper beads, some trinkets. Now it's against the law."

Jack laughed. "They're really helping out those dead Indians."

Danny nodded. He knew it was terrible to disturb the bodies, but it was far worse not to prepare a dead person for a proper burial. In that case, the soul had no rest. However, he didn't want to say that and take a chance of reminding Jack about Loxie. The boy was touchy enough.

After Celilo Falls had been drowned, the backwaters were called Celilo Lake. On the hill overlooking the lake was another small gravesite with more recent tombstones. Miniature American flags snapped in the wind over the gravestones of veterans; bright pin-wheels spun beside some of the others. One of the stone markers had been painted with reddish-brown figures that resembled the old pictographs.

"More Wishrams?" Jack asked.

"We can ask Willis tonight," Danny said. "These are probably Cloudville people."

They passed a small day camp area with picnic tables, then drove across a set of railroad tracks to a boat ramp. A lone birch at the water's edge was completely covered with the carved names of lovers.

"Look at that tree," Jack said. "Not enough room to carve one more name."

"Teenagers drive over from The Dalles, I guess," Danny said. "Come here to look at the lake."

"That's not all they come for, I bet," Jack said.

"Wakemap Mound used to be out there." Danny pointed toward the middle of Celilo Lake. "Wakemap was a campsite for thousands of years. People came for the fish and to trade."

"Funny name," Jack said. "Like Wake-em-up in the morning."

"Right. It means Ogress. She was sort of like a witch, but her specialty was killing young men. Actually, she was an old hag, but she had a trick to make herself beautiful and attract them. The legend says her vagina was filled with sharp stones." He paused to see if he had Jack's attention. "The men who slept with her, they died a pretty terrible death, I guess. And she always changed back, too, so they could see how ugly she was, right before the end."

"You made that up," Jack said.

"No I didn't. Ask Willis, if you want. Come on." As they followed the tracks, Danny explained, "Thousands of people used to come to Wishram to trade. They brought canoes, seashells, and baskets from the coast. Furs and slaves from Montana. Copper from Michigan. All kinds of stuff."

After a quarter mile, the railroad track cut through a low hill, running parallel to a basalt bluff where the rocks formed palisades. Danny noticed a game trail following the base of the bluff, and he stepped off the railroad bed. "We've got to climb a little. It's snaky sometimes, so be careful where you put your hands."

When they had climbed partway up the bluff, Danny pointed to the figures carved on rock, then outlined in dark reddish-brown stain. The round-eyed Spedish Owls, unique to this part of the river, seemed to stare curiously at Danny. The Water Devils appeared ominous: their wide mouths had pointed teeth and their narrowed eyes seemed evil. The frightening faces peered out from a series of wavy lines that warned about dangerous sections of the old river channel, where whirlpools or treacherous floodwaters might drown the unsuspecting.

"There were signs for lots of things around here," Danny explained. "The Water Devils meant, stay away from this stretch of river. No one quite knows what those owls meant."

Jack rubbed at the rockface with his thumb. "Nothing comes off."

"The old ones had special stains," Danny said. "That carving is a couple thousand years old, then they stained over it."

"No way," Jack said. "With the heat and wind, a stain would never last that long."

"I said they were special stains. They used roots and berries."

Jack climbed down from the shelf and stood by Danny. "The rock's all busted up from freezing and cooling. I could break that loose with a crowbar. It's not going to make another thousand years."

"I won't be around to worry about it," Danny said. "But leave your crowbar at home. It's a federal case if you take any of these. Of course, they took a bunch out when they figured the water would cover them."

"Who?"

"Scientists, museum people, all those guys. Red Shirt and Sammy showed me a little canyon covered with old carved paintings like this. But they're all gone now — or flooded."

Danny and Jack climbed to another level of the bluff where a basalt column held the largest figure. The eyes, nose, and mouth made a distinct face, which overlooked the placid waters of the lake.

"Tsa-gal-al. She-Who-Watches," Danny said.

"A protector, like the Wéyekin," Jack said.

"A little like that," Danny said. "The Wéyekin protects a person. She watched over the whole village."

"Not counting the ones the Ogress got."

"I guess not."

Jack looked again at the dam and the lake. "If She-Who-Watches was supposed to take care of things, I'd say she fouled up."

Danny didn't say anything; he just started climbing toward the top of the bluff. He wondered if Loxie had ever talked with Jack about the Wéyekins. He didn't know what she believed because they had never talked about the spirit world when they were married. But Red Shirt knew his Wéyekin appeared as Hímiin, the sacred wolf. Hímiin protected Danny, too. As a boy, he had seen the wolf high in the Wallowas. He still recalled the yellow flicker of its eyes.

When they reached the top of the bluff, Danny and Jack stood side by side for a moment. Across the Columbia, the bare hills glowed in the sunlight and dipped into shadow, smooth as sculpted stone. "I wanted to show you this," Danny said, "because Sammy and Red Shirt showed me." He thought of She-Who-Watches, thousands of years old, and all she must have seen as she stared silently from this spot. He tried to imagine the canyon of ancient carvings at the bottom of the river, faces peering into the murky water. Maybe, somewhere far below the placid surface, the falls still sang. "The old places are vanishing. Even now it's different than I remember."

Jack looked over the flat waters of Celilo Lake toward The Dalles Dam. "I'll bet that used to be some wild river."

"It roared through the old channel," Danny said, "and it was always dangerous. Currents and eddies everywhere. You saw the Water Devils. Even with those warnings, so many people drowned. Sammy said that when he was a kid, he had to keep away from the river at night. His parents warned him the dead might pull him down."

"That's old men's superstitions," Jack said.

"Maybe. But when they built the dam, a dump truck carrying rockfill slid into that fast water. Divers went down to locate the truck, but they couldn't. After the first dive, they refused to go again, because they saw white monsters down there."

"Sturgeon. White sturgeon grow over fifteen feet long."

"That truck's still down there someplace."

Jack picked up a rock and threw it toward the river. It arced off the bluff and made a small splash as it hit the blue water. He threw another, a little farther than the first. Then he sat on a flat basalt rock. "All day something's been bothering me."

"You look a little off your feed." Danny sat on a rock across from him.

"Don't think I'm spilling my guts."

"All right."

Jack stuck a long piece of dry grass between his teeth. "A strange thing happened last night while I was at the pizza place. I was done eating and ready to leave when the door banged open and I felt a cold wind at my back. This woman was standing outside the door, staring straight at me."

"Like Pudge said, you're a handsome dog. Maybe she wanted to pick you up."

Jack spit the grass from his mouth. "Knock it off. This wasn't just any woman. She looked exactly like Mom. From what I could see. It was dusk and her face was in a shadow, but everything else was like her, even the way she dressed. You remember that blue shawl?"

"I remember," Danny said. He put his hand on the warm ground and dug his fingers into the sandy soil. When he picked up some of the dirt, it trickled away.

"I know it sounds crazy," Jack said, "but she stood there a long time. Everyone else was talking or eating. No one seemed to notice. Then she motioned at me, like, come here."

Danny closed his eyes. "Did you?"

Jack shook his head. "No."

Danny looked at Jack. "And she left?"

"Somebody dropped a tray of drinks, breaking glass all over the tile floor, so I turned toward the noise. When I looked again, the door was closed. I started outside, but when I touched the door handle, I couldn't open it."

"Stuck?"

"I don't think so. My knees gave out. After that, I tried ordering a beer, but the bartender laughed and called me Sonny Boy."

Danny wiped a line of sweat from the back of his neck. "Have you seen anything else like that?"

Jack shook his head. "Lots of times I dream about her." He stood and looked past the river at The Dalles Dam. "I wasn't going to say anything, but all this talk about digging graves made me jumpy."

Danny got off the rock and wiped his hands on his pants. Jack's face was turned so he couldn't see it. "You've been thinking about Night Ghosts. Tsikaatpama Tsau-tsau," he said.

"No one really believes that stuff anymore. Everyone's Catholic or Methodist."

"Maybe. But a lot of priests and ministers won't go near an Indian graveyard at night."

"I don't know." Jack turned around to face Danny. "It was spooky."

"Don't look snakebit. Who did Loxie's service?"

"Some guy Hanson knew. A Lutheran minister."

"But she had a dressing earlier?"

"Sure," Jack said. "And the old women came to sprinkle the house with rosewater. Hanson kicked up a fuss and called us heathens."

"I wouldn't worry," Danny said. "You did all you could. Anyway, lots of times you see someone who looks like someone else. I remember one high school game when Baker had a basketball player that looked exactly like me. Well, maybe a little uglier. If we didn't have different uniforms, no one could tell us apart."

"No kidding, huh?"

"After I changed into my street clothes, his girlfriend threw herself at me. She was a Baker cheerleader built for breeding, so I didn't let on for a while." Danny chuckled. "I heard that guy became a movie star someplace. Italy, maybe."

Danny kept on about the Baker cheerleader as they walked back to the truck. But he was concerned. If it was a Night Ghost, something was wrong, and she would be back.

At dusk, Danny and Jack drove into Cloudville. The town consisted of five weatherbeaten houses fringed by broken-down cars and fishing boats. A grove of cherry trees grew beside the settlement. A flat-tired Bronco was parked under one of the trees and two children were on the Bronco's roof, picking cherries from the lower branches. A white cross on a basalt knoll overlooked the settlement.

Willis met them at the door. He had taken off his fishing clothes and now wore old deerskin pants and red Converse hightops.

"Smells good," Danny said when they stepped inside. "I love fresh salmon."

"We've been getting some pretty good silvers," Willis said. "Kind of slow, though. Summer runs were big before the dams." He motioned toward a couch covered with a worn Pendleton blanket. "Park it there."

"You got a nice place here," Jack said after sitting down. "Who made that?" He pointed to the brown and orange God's Eye hanging on the wall.

"My granddaughter Velrae. That's her stirring around in the kitchen. She takes art classes there in The Dalles at Treaty Oak Community College."

"Sounds all right," Danny said, wondering what Velrae was like. Red Shirt had always told him to steer away from college women.

"My son Orville kept pestering her to finish that God's Eye so he could hang it above the fireplace, right next to Jimmy's picture. That's my grandson. Jimmy made the all-state team two years running." In the photo, the boy was grinning and holding a basketball.

"This is Orville's place, then?" Danny asked.

Willis nodded. "I'm usually down at my Wind River fish camp. But now that Orville's in prison, I stick around here more, keeping an eye on things. When commercial season starts in a couple weeks, I'll head back."

"I probably saw your place when I drove by," Danny said. Wind River was one of the in lieu sites the government had designated for Indian fishing when Bonneville Dam had flooded the traditional fishing sites. Only a few people stayed at Wind River year-round, and during the fishing season set by the tribes, visiting fishermen camped there in trailers and tents or lived out of their cars. According to the agreement, white sportfishermen also used the facilities to launch their boats.

"Orville and I been fishing there a long time," Willis said. "But this year my grandson Jimmy has to help out. He hates fishing because he says fish stink, but he loves that rodeo. I guess he thinks horseshit smells like daisies." Willis stood and flexed his back. "Damn platform fishing makes my back kink. I'm going to see how that fish and the General are coming along. Got it cooking the old way."

Danny remembered the salmon feasts at Celilo with the salmon planked over alder coals. "The General? He's your brother?"

"General Electric." Willis grinned. "Stove's damn near thirty. An old man."

"When you said 'the old way,' I thought you meant planked."

Willis shook his head. "Baked. Microwave is new. We keep up." He shouted toward the kitchen doorway. "My belly thinks my throat's been cut. When do we eat?"

Velrae appeared wearing dark green camouflage pants and a red T-shirt with three leaping salmon that said SACRED RITES. Her black hair was almost a crew-cut, except for a ridge of jutting spikes. Danny thought Velrae resembled a porcupine that had tangled with a thresher and come out second best.

"This here's Danny Kachiah and his boy, Jack," Willis said. "Orville's daughter, Velrae, chief cook and bottle washer."

Danny and Jack stood as they said hello and she nodded at each of them, smiling slightly to show small white teeth. "Willis tells me you knew Uncle Sammy."

"We visited him at sheep camp," Danny said. "My father and me."

She folded her arms. "He should have stayed on the river. Too many people left after the dams flooded the old sites."

"They're still leaving," Willis said. "Or getting pushed off. I got an eviction notice tacked to my fish camp right now."

"What's that about?" Jack asked.

"The BIA claims those sites were never meant for year-round living," Willis said. "Hell, people lived year-round at all those places they flooded, but now they say we're breaking the law just by staying there and fishing."

"Sounds stupid to me," Jack said.

"It's high time we started pushing back," Velrae said, her eyes narrowing. "Hard." She stepped back into the kitchen. "You guys can wash up in here. The bathroom sink is shot."

Danny and Jack used Lava soap to scour away the rock-climbing grit, and Danny ran the water long enough to carry the dirt down the drain. Jack splashed water on his face and smoothed back his hair. "I'll bet she goes for handsome dogs," he whispered, grinning at Danny.

"The hell." Put sunglasses on Velrae and she could hijack a plane. What was it Henry used to say? At seventeen, he'd screw a snake.

"Take the blue chairs," Velrae said. "The brown ones wobble."

"Thanks," Jack said, scraping back the chair. "I worked up some appetite climbing around this afternoon."

As Velrae prepared to serve the salmon, Willis picked up one of the thin white plates, tapping it with his fingernail to make a slight ping. "Company Corningware. Don't think we eat like this every day and twice on Sunday."

Danny chuckled, but Velrae scowled.

"He'll just keep it up if you encourage him," she said. "Now pass your plates over."

As Velrae put the salmon on his plate, Danny noticed that her fingers were short and blunt. Across the knuckles of her right hand, the letters R-U-D-Y were tattooed in black ballpoint. She had L-O-V-E across her left knuckles and a rough diamond tattoo on her ring finger. The letters in RUDY were a little blurred, and Danny guessed she had tried bleaching them with Clorox.

Velrae had garnished the salmon with sliced onions and lemon circles. The flesh was moist but flaky enough to fall apart at the fork's touch.

"Delicious," Danny said.

"Thanks," she said. "I cook enough of it. Sometimes I get tired of fish."

Willis put down his fork. "Our Creator sends us the salmon. That's no way to think."

"It's how I feel," she said, not looking at him. "Anyway, thanks to the dams, He only sends about a tenth of the salmon He used to."

It was silent for a few moments. Then Willis picked up his fork to resume eating. "Velrae's not one to mince words."

Jack swallowed the last of his helping and held out his plate. "How about a little more?" As Velrae served him another portion, he said, "This sure beats what we ate on the firelines."

Velrae put down the spatula and concentrated on Jack, as if she were interested in him for the first time. "You don't look like a firefighter."

"I was rodeoing at Warm Springs, but they pulled all the cowboys to fight fire. The Kishwalks fire damn near burned down the lodge."

"Wish it had," she said. "They used river money to build that place."

Jack shrugged. "Anyway, I hurt my knee carrying a guy out of a flare-up. Maybe you noticed me limping."

"You been sitting down," she said. "How could I see that? So what happened?"

Jack leaned back in his chair. He was enjoying this. "Another firefighter broke his ankle and I had to lug him out. There was a wall of flames and I thought we were goners, but I chose the right way." He tapped his head. "Instinct."

Danny wondered if Jack was going to mention the whistling, but he didn't. "He damn near saved the reservation all by himself," Danny said to Willis, but so everyone could hear. Then he added "ayyyy," to show he was kidding. "If I bought him for what he was worth and sold him for what he thinks he's worth, I'd be in clover."

"I used to go with a smoke jumper," Velrae said, ignoring Danny. "He went to Hotshot school in Missoula and everything. You should have seen the calluses on his hands from using a shovel. Those Hotshots parachute into the most dangerous places, too."

Jack glanced at his own uncallused hands. "I was thinking about Hotshot school myself, soon as I finish high school. Just one more year. How about you?"

She shook her head. "Goldendale High was a bad hit. I took my GED in The Dalles."

"I haven't been to Goldendale since the eclipse," Danny said. "The second one, I mean. The first one was before my time." He gave Velrae his best smile and she seemed to soften a little.

"Everyone came for that eclipse," she said. "Goldendale never saw so many people. They opened up the high school gym and cafeteria for all the hitchhikers."

"Henry Nine Pipes and I drove over in Henry's truck," Danny said. "We ate in this place that served special burgers — Eclipse-burgers, they called them. It was a hamburger with an egg on top, sunny side up. They had a slice of tomato partially covering the egg and served it open-faced."

Velrae smiled. "The Sunset Grill and Lounge," she said. "My aunt Louise worked there then, and they must have served a thousand of those things. They got so busy, I helped out after school. Maybe I even served you."

"I ate mine in the bar," Danny said.

"You got Louise, then. I was too young for the bar. But I snuck in late when the band took a break and that crazy drunk got onstage. Did you see him?"

"I don't remember it," Danny said, but he knew she meant Henry.

"This Indian guy — he wasn't from around here — he got on the stage and whooped and recited some kind of crazy poem. Called himself Chief Little Sun. I was shamed out."

Danny took a sip of his coffee. "Sounds pretty silly," he said. "There were a lot of crazies. Druids from California hanging around that Stonehenge replica on the Columbia. I remember them."

Henry had wanted to go to the eclipse because he thought they could find easy women there. "It's the moon that does the trick," he had said, "by pulling on their reproductive systems."

On the drive to Goldendale, they had tried picking up backpackers several times, but they either already had boyfriends or were afraid to ride with two Indians. After Henry had drunk too much in the Sunset, he decided to go onstage. "Women are nuts for performers," he told Danny. "Those guys in the band always have somebody waiting."

Henry's act bothered Danny some, too, but it worked. A couple of girls came over to their table afterward and made a big fuss over Henry. The girls had looked enough alike to be sisters, but they weren't. Each was wearing a dark blue T-shirt with a bright yellow sunburst that said IN THE PATH OF TOTALITY. Later, the one who slept with Danny told him she was glad he was an Indian and confided she had been a Seminole in a former life. Danny said he knew they had something in common.

After the excitement over the eclipse passed, Henry drove all four of them to The Dalles. They ate a big meal in Woo Lung's and the girls caught the bus south to Modesto, promising to return that summer so Henry and Danny could show them around. They never did return, although Henry said maybe they did but missed him because he was out rodeoing.

"We ought to go look them up," Henry would say to Danny every so often.

"They're probably married, anyway," Danny said.

"Fat. Carrying kids, maybe." Henry laughed. Each time they shared a bottle of Gallo, Henry would mention those women again because the Gallo was bottled in Modesto. "Here's to California girls," he'd say.

"Goldendale was the very center," Velrae said. "Who'd ever think a dumb little place would be the center twice."

"It all comes back," Willis said.

He didn't seem to be talking to anyone in particular, but they all stopped to listen.

"Everything that happens comes round again," he said.

Danny wanted him to say more, but he didn't.

Velrae pushed back her chair and started clearing the table. "I cooked," she said. "You guys can do the dishes." She turned to Willis. "Where'd you put the car keys?"

"Another damn meeting?" he asked.

"The lawyer's coming up from Portland," she said. "He's reviewing the whole case."

Willis shook his head. "Check my jacket pockets. And put some gas in it. You brought it back empty last time, and I drove on fumes to the station." He turned to Danny. "So you showed Jack the old paintings?"

"Those that are left," Danny said.

"You warn him about Wakemap?" Willis asked, winking at Velrae, who pretended not to see him.

"What I can't figure out is the color on the rocks," Jack said. "If those paintings are two thousand years old, why does that color still look sharp? I thought the wind and sun would wear it away."

"Somebody has to go down there every few years and touch

them up a little," Willis said. "I've been doing it a long time, but now I'm too stiff to climb those rocks. So my boy Orville does it when he's around. Maybe it's Velrae's turn."

She shook her head. "Fooling with that old stuff is a waste of time. You should be helping the River People get organized." She put the last of the dishes in the sink. "Those keys better be around. You know you're starting to drop things everywhere." She left the kitchen.

"You really doctor up those paintings?" Danny asked Willis. He couldn't believe anyone would touch them.

Willis smiled. "All the teachers and dudes come to take pictures. Those old markings in the rock don't have much color anymore, so I touch them up. The best pictures aren't down there, anyway."

"I know," Danny said. "They took a bunch of them into Portland before the dam flooded them."

"And back East," Willis said. "That Smith-place museum. When they lock those pictures up in glass boxes, it cramps the spirits. But they still didn't get the best ones." Willis leaned over a little toward Danny. "We went ahead and helped ourselves. Hid some away before the museum looters could get them all."

Danny was amazed. "I knew some of them disappeared, but I thought the white guys got them."

"They're still trying to get them," Willis said. "Some son of a bitch from The Dalles is coming out with scuba gear and trying to steal the old carvings from the underwater canyon. And pothunters are still digging between here and the river. We find their sifting screens and shovels all over the place."

When Velrae returned, she was wearing a black and yellow letterman's jacket with RUDY stitched above the breast pocket. "I can't find those keys anywhere."

Willis checked his pants pockets, then shrugged. "Stay home. We got company."

She crossed her arms. "Everybody's counting on me. We're planning strategy to get them retried in tribal court." She paused. "I'll walk if I have to."

"I'll drive you," Jack said. He looked at Danny. "Anyway, I'd like to find out what's going on."

"Thanks," Velrae said. "Stick around for the meeting. We need fresh ideas."

"You aren't fishing," Danny said to Jack. "Keep your nose out of it."

"They want to take away everyone's rights," Velrae said. "All our people need to get involved."

"What you need is long hair and a rifle," Danny told Jack. "I'll bet they've got a few trigger-happy vets that are itching for another Wounded Knee."

"Don't give him that," Velrae said. "We've got one rowdy who had Agent Orange sprayed on him. You can bet he loves the feds."

"Come on," Jack said to Danny. "You're the one who wanted me to learn about this stretch of river. Wakemap and Celilo Falls are history. Besides, I'll be going to White Swan tomorrow."

"I can't wait," Danny said. He took the truck keys from his pocket and slowly handed them to Jack. "Don't stay too late."

"Thanks." Jack tossed the keys and caught them. On the way out, he asked Velrae, "Who's Rudy, anyhow?"

"He's old news, but I kept his jacket." Velrae paused at the door. "Hey, I'll bring him back early."

"Whatever," Danny said. Velrae reminded him of the AIM women who tried to stir things up on the reservations, but he couldn't blame her for wanting to free her old man.

Willis took two beers from the refrigerator, and after opening them, he handed one to Danny. "Wash or dry?"

Danny checked the dishes piled in the sink. The salmon oil had congealed. "Dry, I guess."

"I shouldn't ask," Willis said. He ran hot water into the sink, squirting streams of pink dish soap to make piles of suds. "Velrae's been a little skitterish since they took her dad away."

"She seemed edgy." Danny picked a towel from the cabinet. "What did he do, exactly?"

"Sold salmon out of season. Only a couple hundred, but they gave him three years." Willis handed Danny a plate.

"That's a long stretch."

"Put those in the cupboard above your head." Willis rinsed another plate and handed it to him. "They're setting an example, I guess. Velrae's got this big-shot treaty lawyer working on a loophole or at least a trial in Yakima Tribal Court. Whatever happens, they twist words around and we lose."

"Maybe he shouldn't have sold the fish. He probably knew the law."

"Oh, he knows it all right," Willis said. "But he's descended from Smowhalla, the prophet, and lives according to the old ways. He fishes when our Creator sends fish so our Creator will be pleased and send more. New laws and restrictions mean nothing to him."

Danny remembered Smowhalla had prophesied that if the Indian people were faithful and followed the Washat religion, the white people would disappear from the earth and leave them alone. But more white people kept coming, pushing the Indians off the river until only a few clung stubbornly to the old ways. "Sometimes you have to take what's yours."

"Sure. That's why I grabbed those carvings. Just helped myself before they got dragged off to museums."

"I'd like to see them again," Danny said.

"Later on, maybe, when I get to know you better." Willis handed Danny the last pot and let the water out of the sink. "Funny thing. A lot of tribes sent young men to study with Smowhalla. One named Red Shirt came from the Nez Perce."

"He wasn't related to my father," Danny said. He remembered how Red Shirt used to mock the Dreamers by spinning in drunken circles and saying he was a Spinner. But sometimes he'd sit through a Washat service at the salmon feasts. "You know, I saw a lot of those carvings with Red Shirt and Sammy. Can you tell me what you have, at least?"

Willis stared out the kitchen window into the twilight, as if he were either remembering or deciding whether to tell Danny. "I've got Star Boy and the Sheep with Hunters." He turned from the window and looked at Danny. "Weýuukye."

Danny couldn't believe Willis had the elk; his father had said it was one of the oldest and most important carvings along the river. Danny expected the museum people would have taken it for certain. "But how did you move the carvings without special equipment?"

"Pretty hard work," Willis said. "If they were close enough to the water, we got them on rafts and floated them downstream to load on flatbeds. If they were near the tracks, we used a handcar. Sammy borrowed one from the railroad yard in Wishram. Indian discount, he called it. But he had to keep close watch on the trains."

"You got Weýuukye," Danny said. He was thinking about the Elk Chant. When his father had seen the elk carving along the river, he had touched Danny's shoulder and spoken of the chant. Danny had believed then that his father knew several chants for power and curing, but he had not passed them down.

"Do you know anything about the Elk Chant?" Danny asked.

Willis shook his head. "That's probably old Nez Perce. Along the river, we've got our own." He squinted at Danny. "I'll bet you've got some Yakima blood."

Danny nodded. "My grandmother was part Yakima. Mostly, I'm Nez Perce. Maybe my father knew some of the old songs, but he never taught me."

"Too bad," Willis said. "They're probably gone, then, unless you've got an uncle or someone."

"No," Danny said, thinking of Que. "I was hoping to teach Jack."

"So much has been lost," Willis said. "But you still can earn your own songs or get them from Wéyekins."

"My great-grandfather came here after the Nez Perce War," Danny said. "He was trying to gain strength and attract more Wéyekins."

Willis nodded. "A lot of the warriors came to the river because the River People still had power then. Now we're just hanging on."

Danny wanted to say something encouraging, but he couldn't.

"Your father came, too, when he was young. He and Sammy sang in the sweathouse. They taught their power songs to one another, but each held something back so the other couldn't steal it. You know how it is."

Danny shook his head. "He never told me . . ."

Willis shrugged. "Red Shirt even fished along the river for a while, but he let Sammy keep the salmon. And every year, your father traded elk meat for dried fish and salmon pemmican."

"I remember that," Danny said. "He always griped about the sand in Sammy's pemmican, and claimed that Sammy dried that fish in the windiest places along the river. But I never knew he fished." Danny wondered how Red Shirt had inherited the fishing sites. Maybe some of them had been passed down from Left Hand's wife's people.

"After your mother died, he just quit coming," Willis said.

"Other people took his places, and then the dams wiped them out."

"I was only two," Danny said. His father had never mentioned the songs or the sites, and it stung Danny to think that Red Shirt had turned his back on the old ways. Maybe it was out of grief.

"We been gabbing like old crows," Willis said. "I was going to have a pipe. You'll join me?"

Danny knew Willis offered the pipe in friendship.

Willis went into the bedroom, and Danny heard him open a drawer. After a few minutes, he returned with a black velvet cloth. He kept the pipe in darkness in order not to confuse the spirits. As Willis carefully unwrapped the cloth, Danny saw cigarettes and small animal fetishes that were used to appease the spirits. The bloodstone bowl was decorated with carved salmon.

"That's a fine pipe."

"My grandfather's," Willis said. "Minnesota bloodstone." He took a smooth river pebble from the cloth and dropped it into the bowl. The pebble prevented them from drawing burning tobacco shreds into their mouths. Willis began stuffing the pipe with dark green tobacco.

"I haven't seen tobacco like that," Danny said.

Willis smiled, "Velrae grows this stuff along the river. She keeps the place secret."

When Danny awakened, he didn't know at first what had caused him to stir. Then he heard a long, wavering note, the shrill whistle of a night bird. He got out of bed and slipped on his shirt and pants. He carried his boots into the kitchen and, without turning on a light, peered out the window at the tableland. Fog had come in off the water, and mists swirled around the basalt mounds so they looked like islands.

Danny thought he saw something move in the fog. Then he looked at the clock: it was almost four. He checked the sofa and saw that Jack was asleep, his bare feet sticking out of the blanket.

Danny stepped outside and took a few deep breaths of night air, trying to clear his head of the fuzziness caused by the medicine pipe. When he opened the door of his pickup, he half expected to rouse the village dogs, but they must have been asleep. Reaching behind the seat, he found the big Sportsman flashlight he kept there and turned it on. The bright light carried a good distance onto the flat, but he didn't see anything but fog and rocks.

He walked half a mile toward the river, moving in and out of swirling patches of mist. It was a low-lying fog, and if he looked up, he could see the stars clearly.

When the ground began sloping away, Danny realized he was moving into a little gully. It was completely shrouded by fog, but the fog seemed to clear on the other side. He gripped the flashlight and started across.

Moisture formed on his face and hands, and his heartbeat increased just a little. The flashlight felt wet and slick. He played it to both sides, then straight ahead, but the thick fog absorbed the light. Danny moved forward cautiously. Off to his left, a form loomed out of the fog and Danny stopped, stiffening. Then he relaxed. It was just an old car body. As he passed by he patted the hood, brushing away a few beads of the fog. There was something reassuring about the solid feel of the cold metal.

Then he heard the whistle again, closer this time and higher pitched. Danny whirled, the flashlight sweeping the fog. He moved quickly to the other side of the gully and climbed to the top, then crossed a small flat. The ground underfoot became hard and rocky, and he realized he had reached the low basalt bluffs that overlooked Celilo Lake. Carefully, he worked his way along the bluff, trying to find a way down in the fog. Although it wasn't a high bluff, a fall could hurt him, and he didn't want to wind up on the railroad tracks, run over in the night by a Burlington Northern. Another drunken Indian picked the wrong place to sleep, they'd say.

A whistle came from beneath him, near the river, and Danny tried to get down the bluff. He found a break with several outcroppings, like stairsteps set wide apart. He listened. The fog swallowed every noise now, even the lapping waves. He needed two free hands, so he stuck the flashlight in his jacket pocket, then lowered himself over the side, feeling with his feet for the first outcropping. He tested his weight, gradually putting more onto the rock, until his arms just maintained balance, but when he straightened his knees, part of the rock suddenly crumbled beneath him and he slipped. When his right arm caught and held, he thought it was wedged somehow in a rock crevasse. One foot remained planted on the outcropping, but there was no room for the other, so he poked with his foot at the bluff face for a moment until he found a toehold. He tugged at his right arm, trying to free it, and a few pebbles knocked loose above.

As Danny glanced up, a large head thrust over the bluff directly above his right arm. He froze. The oval face was white with dark, slitted eyes. The head was hairless. But three feathered plumes rose from the glistening scalp. The deformed mouth had fleshy lips protruding into a pursed O. It whistled, high and frantic.

Danny jerked his hand free and fell backward off the bluff. He heard a cry above the shrill whistling and realized that it was his own wild shout.

Danny heard flowing water and the mists cleared. Below him, cutting through a steep basalt canyon, was a river, high and roily with springmelt. A dark gray sandbar stretched along the river's near side for a hundred yards. Light green trees bordering the riverbanks were leafing out. Away from the river, tan bunchgrass covered the rocky sideslopes.

A man in a blue shirt walked downstream along the sandbar. He had dark skin, and his hair was black as tar. He rolled his pantlegs up and squatted in the gravel at the water's edge. He scooped some gravel and water with a pan, and Danny thought at first he was washing out a greasy dish, but the way the man swirled the pan, then poked at its contents, showed he was panning for gold.

More dark men came onto the sandbar from the upstream end, and Danny realized there was a cabin snugged against the rocky hillside. Three walls were rock; the hillside served as the fourth. He hadn't seen the cabin at first because the mossy roof and rock walls blended with the surroundings. Looking closer, he saw fresh diggings near the cabin and a small sluicebox. One of the men untied a skiff and two others climbed in. Danny guessed they were going to cross the river to mine the other side. Some of the men joined the first one, the sun glancing off their swirling gold pans. Two took off their clothes and bathed quickly in the cold water. Returning to the sandbar, they briskly rubbed themselves, drying off in the morning sun.

The man in the blue shirt cocked his head, and when he stood up, Danny thought he recognized him. Suddenly the man threw his hands above his head, dropping the pan into the water. He clutched his stomach, as if in sudden pain, then fell backward into deeper water. The current caught him, and he began floating along the sandbar's edge. A couple of the men chased after him, but others turned toward the hillside, their faces twisted with fear. One spun crazily, then pitched face first onto the dark sand. Another folded slowly, like an old cot.

Horrified, Danny realized they were being shot.

He screamed for them to take cover, but no sound came from his mouth.

The three men in the skiff paddled furiously for the river's far side, but one by one they jerked and slumped, dropping their paddles. The skiff spun crazily downstream, slammed against a rock, and flipped.

Danny stared at the men on the sandbar. Only one was moving, crawling crablike toward the cabin. Then part of his head blew away and he stopped crawling. The man in the blue shirt had drifted to the sandbar's low end and caught on some debris. His body bobbed in the current.

Smoke rose from the hut, and red flames burst through the wooden roof. Danny tried to see more, but there was smoke everywhere. Then he heard a whistling so loud it seemed to split his head.

The earth trembled beneath Danny, and the loud whistling grew closer, then subsided. He opened his eyes.

He was lying on his back beside the railroad bed, and he saw the dark caboose of a Burlington Northern train about a quarter mile away, its red light blinking. Danny cautiously moved his arms and legs to see if anything was broken. Something was poking into his back, and he curled into a sitting position. He had fallen into a sageclump, and one of the wiry trunks had been jabbing him.

The flashlight was a few yards away, closer to the bluff's base. It was still shining in the dim light. Danny crawled over to it, and as he reached to switch it off, he saw that his jacket sleeve was torn and there were long red scratches on his right forearm and wrist.

He put the flashlight in his pocket and stood, feeling as if he had been beat up. He took some deep breaths to clear the pain, then climbed slowly up the railroad bed until he was standing on the tracks.

From there he studied the dark waters of Celilo Lake for a while, then turned on the light and shone it along the bank. He half expected to see bodies, but there were only white rocks and floating logs. From high on the bluff, She-Who-Watches stared out impassively. Across the lake the headlights of the cars and trucks swept along I-84.

Danny heard something above him on the bluff and he whirled. But it was only Willis, holding a flashlight.

"Hey, grandson? Are you all right?"

"Just barely," Danny said after a few moments. "Some rock gave way."

"You shouldn't wander out here at night," Willis said. "Too dangerous." He was quiet for a few moments, as if waiting for Danny to reply, but when he didn't Willis said, "There's a break in the bluff fifty yards or so upstream. Come on, I'll show you."

Danny followed the railroad track until he found the place Willis meant, and he started climbing the game trail. When he reached the top of the bluff, he saw that the old man held something in addition to the flashlight: a box of kitchen matches. It was almost empty.

Willis shook the few remaining matches in the box. "You weren't in bed, so I followed your tracks across the top. Over there" — Willis nodded to the place where Danny had fallen — "I scattered a lot. Come back later this morning, when it's full light, you won't find any matches. Steah-hah seem to like Ohio Blue Tips best."

"You heard them, too?" Danny asked.

Willis nodded.

Danny wanted to say something more, but he wondered if the old man had played some kind of trick on him. He stared at the ripped jacket, the red slashes on his arm. No, he decided. It would be too dangerous to wear a Steah-hah mask.

Willis rolled a cigarette and lit it with one of the remaining kitchen matches. He held the cigarette out, but Danny shook his head. His hands were trembling, and he kept them in his pockets.

Both men watched the lake and the moving traffic while Willis smoked his cigarette. When he was finished, he said quietly, "Some of our people are locked away in the white man's hospitals. They don't speak to any of us now, and their eyes are empty. They just listen for Steah-hah. Year after year they listen, and that is their punishment, because they didn't listen before."

Danny decided to tell Willis what he had seen.

When Danny finished talking, Willis stood and pointed upstream. "Grave Island and Memaloose used to be over there," he said. "One spring, there was terrible high water, a big flood, and many of the bodies floated downriver. Could you be remembering that?"

Danny had studied the lake and the canyon walls for a long time, but the trees were wrong and the other river had been in a steeper canyon. "No," he said. "It was a different place. And so were the men. At first I thought they might be Indians, but now I think they were Chinese."

Willis nodded. "The Chinese were here a long time back," he said. "When everything was different. They came each spring to work the salmon canneries. The China Boss always hired members of the same tong so they wouldn't fight. They all rode up from Portland on a special train car. We used to watch them get off. They carried everything they needed in tin buckets — no suitcases. Later, they used the buckets to wash clothes and take baths. When the Chinese fought, it was over gambling or an old quarrel. They used hatchets or long butcher knives from the cannery. No rifles. We found one dead man a year, maybe two. But never more. The China Boss saw to that."

"I saw at least twenty," Danny said. "And they were shot."

Willis raised his hand. "Don't tell me any more," he said. "I don't know this trouble. Maybe part of it is here, but the rest is someplace else. You saw another river."

Danny nodded. He closed his eyes and tried to remember more details about the river, but he just kept seeing the dead men on the dark gray sandbar.

Opening his eyes, he saw that Willis had drawn a straight line in the earth with a stick. On top of the straight line was a circle that touched the line in just one place. "Everything that happens, it will come back," Willis said. "Steah-hah have warned you."

"I don't know what to do," Danny said.

"I know a Medicine Woman in Lapwai," Willis said. "You better see her."

❖ 4 ❖

MEDICINE
WOMAN

TRAVELING TOWARD LAPWAI, Danny felt uneasy. His father and grandfather had always avoided Lapwai, the center of the shrunken reservation, and the treaty Nez Perce who settled there. Danny wondered if he was doing the right thing, seeing this Medicine Woman.

Willis had drawn a map on brown butcher paper. After leaving Lewiston, Danny followed the twisting Clearwater until he got to the place Willis had marked with a heavy black X, and then he stopped the pickup. A glint of sun reflected off a small travel-trailer's aluminum side. Danny hadn't seen it at first because it was snugged behind the small gray house. Pieces of the house's composition roof had been torn off and were strewn across the yard. Danny figured somebody must be trying to fix up the roof before the heavy autumn rains. Some fence posts circled the house, but there was no wire. On one of the posts hung a sign: KEEP OUT. NO HUNTING. NO TRESPASSING.

Watching for dogs, Danny slowly opened the door. When none came, he got out and crossed the little grassy patch of lawn, being careful to avoid the pieces of roof and shingle nails. The trailer door was half open and Danny poked his head in, but no one was there.

He knocked on the main door of the house. The front window was broken out and someone had put up a blanket as a curtain.

He stood on the cement stoop, waiting, and a scrawny cat brushed his leg. The cat's bowl held some food, but it had been rained on and he doubted the cat would eat it. He knocked again, harder this time, and thought he heard someone rustling about inside.

The door opened — first a crack, then wider. An old woman wearing a green bandanna over waist-length gray braids thrust out her head and glanced toward Danny's feet.

"Rattlesnake!" she said.

Danny quickly jumped back, tipping over the cat's dish. After he had retreated a safe distance, he looked for a snake slithering through the tall grass beside the house, but he didn't see one.

The old woman pointed at Danny and waggled her forefinger. "That was you put them snakes on my stoop. Two of them, wasn't it?"

Danny shook his head. "I don't know anything about snakes."

"A live one and a dead one," she said. "The live one was for me, or maybe Wauna. But I came in the back door when I saw you already busted out the window." Her eyes glinted with anger. "Tricked you."

Danny half spread his arms, his hands open. "I don't know anything about it," he said.

"After you put them snakes there to protect you, then you busted on in here and took stuff. Ate all the cheese and sausage from the refrigerator. Didn't you? Then went sneaking away."

"I've never even been here before," Danny said. "I'm from Pendleton."

"Bad ones there, too," she said. "I know all about you bad ones."

"I just came up to see Wauna," Danny said. "Willis Salwish sent me. See." He reached into his pocket and took out the map. "Willis drew this. Like I said, I've never been over here before."

The old woman didn't even look at the map. "Wauna's in Lewiston," she said. "Or maybe Moscow. She just takes off days at a time. Leaves me all alone. I never know when she'll be back. Maybe two or three days."

It had been a long ride for a wild goose chase. The old woman had no phone, so he couldn't call. And if he came back in three days, that was still no guarantee.

"Maybe I can leave her a note," he said. "Do you have any paper?"

She seemed to think it over for a moment. "Why don't you use the other side of that map?"

"Okay," Danny said, "but I still need a pen."

"You sure you didn't fool around with those snakes?"

"Cross my heart."

"I'll look," the old woman said, and left Danny on the stoop. After a few moments she returned, opening the door enough for him to squeeze in. "You can use the table in the kitchen."

As Danny passed through the living room, he saw a sofa, chair, and TV. The walls were covered with pictures, some of people wearing full ceremonial costumes, probably on their way to pow-wows. A large portrait of a young woman holding a brightly decorated shawl hung on one wall. Her hair and makeup suggested that the picture had been taken about the same time Danny went to high school. Her lips were colored too red, matching the shawl. The picture had been tinted by a photographer.

The kitchen had cracked blue tiles and a pale blue Formica table with matching chairs. A big woodstove dominated the room, and Danny guessed they used it for heating as well as cooking. After removing some magazines from a chair, he sat down.

Overall, the place looked like a lot of others he'd been in. Danny hadn't known what to expect, but he felt as if something were missing. He thought he'd find stuff he hadn't seen before in a healer's home.

In a few minutes, the old woman came in with a pen. When she handed it to Danny, he noticed a plastic band on her wrist, the kind used in hospitals. "You been sick?" he asked.

"Diabetes," she said. "First the doctors about killed me. Then the hospital cooks tried with their aluminum pans. Now Wauna's taking care of me. I have to drink this damn herbal tea she makes four times a day. It tastes terrible."

"I believe it," Danny said. Another cat appeared from behind the stove and rubbed against his leg as he began to write:

> Wauna. I have some trouble. Willis Salwish
> sent me to see you. You weren't here, but I'll
> come back in three days. Danny Kachiah

When he finished signing his name he felt a breeze, as if someone had opened the door. Glancing up, he saw a very tall woman standing in the entryway. She had on a pair of black jeans and a bulky red sweater. Her coppery hair was twisted in a single braid down her back. The green-framed glasses she wore were oversize; her eyes seemed magnified behind them.

"I'm Wauna," she said.

Danny scraped back his chair and stood. "You spooked me!" He held out the note. "I'm Danny Kachiah. Your mother told me you were in Moscow."

"She gets mixed up," Wauna said. "I was just over in Lapwai. Sit down. I didn't mean to startle you."

She took the note from Danny, and he sat while she read. "What kind of trouble?" she asked.

"Kind of hard to explain." Now that she was here, he didn't know quite what to say, and he didn't want to seem foolish. Another problem was that Wauna seemed too young to be a medicine woman. He had expected someone much older.

"It's a nice afternoon," she said, glancing out the window. "Let's sit under those trees and talk. I've got some lawn chairs."

They went outside and she stepped into the trailer. In a moment she came back out with two green folding aluminum chairs. She handed one to Danny and motioned for him to sit.

He placed the chair where the sun was behind his shoulder because he wanted to study her face. It was midafternoon, and he knew the sun would go behind the canyon rim before long. But now it was warm. He took off his jacket and hung it over the back of the chair.

"The last of summer," she said. "But it stays warm some afternoons."

"I've got a few beers in the truck," Danny said. "You want one?"

She shook her head. "I don't drink, but you go ahead."

"Maybe I'll have one after a while," he said. As he sat, he noticed a blue pickup about a hundred feet up the road. It hadn't been there when he drove in. Two young men were hauling junk out of a root cellar dug into the hillside. It struck him suddenly that there were no other cars in the yard, so Wauna must have come with the boys in the pickup — unless she walked or hitched all that way.

Wauna leaned back in the chair. "That sun feels good," she said. "I'm like an old cat out here. The wind's coming soon, so we better enjoy this warmth now."

"It feels good all right," Danny said. He studied the upper branches of the trees. The cottonwoods' leaves were quiet, so he though she was wrong about the wind.

"You've had a pretty long trip," she said.

"Willis told me I should see you."

"About the trouble?"

Neither one of them said anything else for a while. He was reluctant to tell her too much at first, until he found out something about her and decided if she knew what she was doing.

"I had a long morning, and I'm a little tired," Wauna said after a while. "One of my cousins was killed in a car wreck a couple months back. The tribe's setting up a memorial scholarship in his name."

"I'm sorry to hear that," Danny said. "About the wreck, I mean."

She nodded. "He drove too fast, and he wouldn't wear a seat belt. It's easier to protect someone if they help out a little."

"I see what you mean," Danny said.

"You wonder about me, don't you," she asked. But before Danny could answer, she turned her head slightly. "Listen . . . The wind. It's coming."

Above them, the cottonwood leaves rustled.

"I was living in San Francisco when I first learned about my power." She laughed quietly, back in her throat. "My radical stage. Alcatraz."

"Alcatraz?" Danny asked.

"During the takeover. Red Power and all. You remember."

"I heard something about it," Danny said.

"A Navajo medicine man took charge of me for a while because he said he could feel my power. One day, after we meditated, we walked out along the island. Grasshoppers flew around us, and I thought that was odd until it struck me that he got his power from the grasshopper. He had conjured them all up somehow."

Danny knew Navajos put more faith in insects than Nez Perce did, and there was something about grasshoppers in one of their creation myths. He couldn't remember what.

Wauna continued. "'Now you try,' the Navajo man said. One of those tourboats was going by, with the guide talking about Alcatraz. That broke my concentration a little. As soon as it passed, I concentrated harder and a waterspout came up. Then another. And another. One came right toward us, and when it reached land it swirled dust all around us, picking up a bunch of those grasshoppers. Suddenly it stopped, dropping them all, and they hopped every which way. Confused.

"After that, he never talked to me again. But a friend of mine told me he was jealous. I was just starting to learn my power then."

Danny put his head back and ran his fingers through his hair. Clouds were moving across the sky and the cottonwoods' leaves were rustling harder. The winds of autumn, he thought. Wauna wanted him to believe she had called them up, but he wasn't so sure.

One of the boys came running out of the root cellar. The second chased after him, holding a big snake. It must have been three feet long, and it twisted and writhed in his hand. Dropping the snake to the ground, he picked up a rock.

Wauna stood up, cupping her hands to her mouth. "Leave it alone!"

Danny jumped, startled by the loudness of her voice.

The boy dropped the rock and ducked back into the root cellar. His friend followed.

"I used to be a cheerleader for Kamiah," Wauna said. "They called me Foghorn."

"You made me sit up and take notice." Danny shifted in his chair. "How old is he?"

"My nephew? Sixteen. Old enough to behave. This winter I'm taking him to the Medicine Dances. He'll learn a few things."

"Jack's seventeen," Danny said. "So he thinks he knows it all."

She laughed. "They sure do at that age. But sometimes, underneath, they're very fragile."

"You know it," Danny said. "Speaking of age, I thought you'd be older."

Leaning back in her chair, she closed her eyes. "You come from Pendleton, right?"

"Mission," Danny said. "That's close enough."

"You remember the man from the reservation who murdered his girlfriend last year?"

"Blinky Two Blankets. He was a year behind me." Danny remembered the taped black glasses Blinky had worn in high school. He heard that Blinky had bad dreams and hung himself in the Pendleton jail just before the trial.

"That girl's family is still having trouble."

Danny studied Wauna's face. He knew the family kept bringing the minister out to the house because he had seen his Ford parked in front. But they remained tight-lipped about the reason. "Maybe so."

Wauna nodded, her eyes still closed. "When those people come home at night, they still see her through the window, just sitting on the La-Z-Boy, watching TV like old times."

"Maybe so," Danny said again. His head felt strange.

"They hurry in the door and turn on the lights, but she's gone. The TV is still on."

Danny stared at her. Was this a trick?

Wauna held up a finger. "And when they're inside — maybe the mother is canning fruit in the kitchen or drying dishes — she sees the girl outside, just glimpses her before she's gone."

Danny shook his head. How could she know? "They smudged the house with *p-tass-way*, alpine fir, and they scrubbed the floors and woodwork with rosewater. What else can they do?"

"It's her hair," Wauna said. "They overlooked something. Maybe a comb she used is under the bed or a twist of her hair is hidden behind her dresser. Something like that. They need to take care of it."

"I'll tell them," Danny said.

A smile tugged the corners of her mouth. She seemed pleased. "Now, what about you?"

"There've been Stick Indians," Danny said. "And the boy's seen Night Ghosts."

Wauna opened her eyes and her smile vanished.

After he finished telling her about the figure Jack had seen, Wauna leaned far back in her chair and gazed high into the rustling leaves. "Stick Indians and Night Ghosts can be difficult, sometimes dangerous." She tilted her head forward until she was looking directly at Danny. "Some precautions and a healing usually help. You understand?"

"Yes."

"Good. Does he keep her picture around?"

"Right by his bed." Danny didn't like the picture because it was taken shortly before Loxie died. She had cropped her hair, and her staring eyes were dark as bruises. "He won't let it go."

"Try to get rid of it. If you can't, at least sprinkle some rosewater on it. What about clothes? Anything that might have her hair or sweat?"

"I don't think so."

"Wait a minute." Danny remembered something. "She made him a ribbon shirt for ceremonies."

Wauna frowned. "He shouldn't wear that. Take it away."

Danny could imagine the fight he'd have with Jack over the shirt. "Is it important?"

"All this is important," she said firmly. "That's why you came."

He glanced away, feeling a little foolish.

"You've had warnings." She leaned closer to him. "Now listen to me. Down the road a little there used to be a farmhouse. You can still see where the foundation was. A young family moved in there and they had a little boy, about five years old, who played outside and liked to explore the hill.

"There were a few graves on top of the hill, and the dead had never been buried right, although a Catholic priest had said services and sprinkled water. Everyone around here knew that wasn't enough, but these people had just moved from Seattle.

"One night, the mother was inside fixing supper when she heard the boy talking with someone outside. Later, she said she thought he was just talking to himself — it sounded like gibberish, so she didn't pay much attention.

"He wouldn't eat supper, just wanted to go back outside. He said there was a young woman who had played with him there. She was wearing a white doeskin dress with a beautiful necklace, and she told him there were more beautiful things way up the hill.

"He kept insisting he wanted to go outside, and they finally let him, but told him to stay close to the house. The mother put a dark blue sweatshirt on him because it was getting cold.

"In about an hour, they called for him to come in, but he didn't answer. It was dark by then, and they were worried. They went looking around, searching that hillside, and a big owl flew right out of a tree close by. You know what an owl means. That really scared them. The father started running up the hill and the mother jumped in the car and came after me.

"When I got there, the boy was already in a trance. The father had found him way up the hillside, and he'd seen the woman in the white dress, just for a second.

"The boy's eyes were open, but he wouldn't say anything. His breathing was very shallow. I started working on him — touching him, talking to him in the old tongue — and after a while, he started talking back. His parents were still very frightened — they'd never heard anyone speak that old language before.

"I took off all his clothes and rubbed him with some sweet grass and kaus I took from my bundle. He stayed in the trance — rigid, like a board — and never even flinched when I dropped him in the freezing water. I made sure the water was moving swiftly — no slow currents — so he was really cleansed. All the time, I talked over him, then carried him back to the house. We dried him off and dressed him in all new clothes.

"I carried his old clothes up the hillside. The wind blew hard, bending the trees. I probably could never have found those graves in the dark, but I saw the woman standing under a clump of pines. Singing my song quietly, I started moving toward her, and she drifted away. 'Shame on you,' I called to her in the old tongue. 'Leave these people alone.' She came after me, then. Her eyes were white and fierce, and when she reached for me, her hands snatched like claws. The others were around me, too, but she was the only one I actually saw and she couldn't touch me. I sang louder, and the wind carried her off a little ways. She stayed there, keeping a distance, because she knew my power. I buried the boy's clothes the best I could, covering them with dirt, with sticks and rock.

"That night, I stayed with the family — just in case — and by the next morning the boy was fine. He got right up and ate a good breakfast. Whatever happened the night before, he didn't remember anything. I tried talking to him in the old language, and he just stared at me like I was talking crazy.

"Later that morning, I got a couple of old men, and we headed up that hill to do things right. They held a proper burial service, and that took care of it. The parents moved away — went back to

Seattle, I think — and soon after that the house burned to the ground. Of course, there's no fire department way out here.

"The glowing fire woke me one night, so I put on my glasses and went outside. I stood there for a long time watching the house burn, and I saw the shadows moving up on that hillside.

"Some of the people around here claim it was faulty wiring that burned the house, or maybe a hobo lighting a fire." Wauna laughed. "I know what it was."

Danny stood. The clouds covered the sun and the wind chilled his sweat. He put on his jacket. "Whenever you talk about ghosts, it gets cold real fast."

"Come inside," Wauna said. "Some tea will warm you. Probably you're a coffee drinker, but this tea is better for you."

Danny had heard that in the old days, when a child became sick suddenly or quit breathing, the people believed one of the dead spirits had clamped his hand over the child's mouth to suffocate him. The medicine man tried to find out which spirit, then placate him. But usually by the time he found the right spirit, the child was already dead. If Wauna's story was true, she had more power than any of the other medicine people Danny had heard about.

After Danny drank some of the tea, he felt too warm, so he took off his jacket again. Wauna poured a cup of tea for her mother and took it into the back room. "She's watching her favorite soaps," Wauna said when she returned. "TV's hard on her eyes because our reception's bad out here, but she'll watch *The Guiding Light* until she goes blind."

"My grandfather was the same," Danny said, "except with him it was *The FBI*. You try tinfoil on the antenna? Sometimes that helps."

"Coathangers, too."

"My father, Red Shirt, used to dangle salmon lures from ours. He never caught many fish that way, so he got some good out of hanging them on that TV." Danny sipped some more tea. "I think I taste cinnamon and cloves. Something else, too." Danny thought the tea might be part of the healing. Maybe Wauna gathered the ingredients from the woods.

"Ginger root. Cardamom. Just a pinch of pepper."

"You make this up special, then?"

She shook her head. "It's Yogi tea. I buy it at the health food store in Lewiston. They make it somewhere in California. Santa Monica, I think."

"Hippies, I'll bet," Danny said. "They make everything like that now."

"Maybe. All the old hippies are wearing coats and ties now. Left the beads and headbands for us." She laughed. "I saw too many of those phonies in San Francisco." She stood and poured Danny another cup, then refilled her own. "This is pretty easy on Mom's stomach. No caffeine."

Danny held his cup with both hands and looked at the swirling tea leaves. He felt comfortable with Wauna, he decided. The tea tasted good, although he never worried about caffeine, even when he got the jitters. Red Shirt had always said you could smooth out the coffee shakes with booze, and it usually seemed to work pretty well. Even so, Danny figured that by the time his father died, the alcohol was so far ahead, it would have taken another lifetime for the caffeine to catch up.

"You haven't told me everything," Wauna said. She sipped her tea, staring at him over the top of her cup.

Danny put down his cup and glanced away. "Why do you think that?"

"You drove a long way to talk about Stick Indians and Night Ghosts. Everyone has problems with them sooner or later, and the Feather people at Umatilla could probably handle them. I wonder if Willis sent you here for something more."

Danny took a gulp of tea, choking it down as he felt the heat course through him. Wauna was almost too clever, and he felt as if she were studying his guts. Even so, he needed help. "All right."

When he finished telling her about his visions of the dead men along the river, he felt better, as if some dark corner of his mind had become gray instead of black.

"Chinese?" she asked.

"I'm pretty sure. Maybe Indians."

"And you didn't recognize the river?"

He shook his head. "I've seen it so often — there in my mind — that I'm starting to imagine I know it. Still, I can't place it or figure out what it has to do with me." He looked at Wauna, hoping for an answer.

"A healing will take care of Night Ghosts, like I said. The Stick Indians keep bothering you because the vision is important." She tapped her cup with her forefinger. "These things are probably connected, but sometimes we can't see the pattern."

Danny spread his hands on the table. "Willis said maybe it was something from way back." Although he knew Willis meant something different, Danny was sometimes afraid his own past would catch up. He had wasted his youth and squandered the marriage with Loxie. Now he hoped to salvage something with Jack.

"Just wait here a minute." Wauna left the kitchen, and Danny heard her rummaging through drawers in the bedroom. He was becoming impatient with all the talk, and he suddenly felt tired. After adding more sugar to his tea, he tasted it. Too damn sweet.

Wauna returned with an old photograph. "Here." She handed it to him.

The picture showed about forty men in front of a building. Some were sitting, others standing. Their features reminded Danny of the Coast Indians', but these men had rounder faces, narrower eyes. Their hat brims were level, not turned down, and some wore long buttoned shirts that hung loose on their bodies, almost like blouses. Danny stared at the photo. Some of the men could be those in his vision. His eyes blurred, and he was unable to hold the picture steady, so he put it on the table.

Wauna touched the photo with her forefinger. "Chinese."

When Danny felt he could hold his cup without spilling, he took it in both hands and drank. "They resemble the men I saw."

"That's a start." Wauna seemed pleased. "The Chinese had a large joss house in Lewiston, sort of like a lodge. This picture shows the members shortly after the Nez Perce War."

"A joss house?" Danny hadn't heard the term before. He was still trying to control his hands.

"The Chinese came to work on the railroads. Later they mined or ran small businesses. Many settled around Lewiston and formed a lodge. A very few were taken in by Nez Perce. Do you think any of your ancestors married Chinese?"

"No," Danny said after thinking a moment. He had seen old

photos of Indians with Asian features, but they were not from his family.

"You're sure? Go way back."

"Yes, I'm sure. My great-grandfather Left Hand was one of the Dreamers who fought with Joseph. Left Hand married a young woman from his own band, the Wallowas, and they had a child. His wife and daughter were killed at Big Hole. After the war, he married a Umatilla, and she had my grandfather Medicine Bird."

"Just one child?"

Danny nodded. "My grandfather. He told me how Left Hand pretended to be a reservation Indian. He cut his hair short and traveled with his wife's people to the Columbia during the fish runs. Sometimes he practiced the old Dreamer ceremonies in the Wallowas. You know the ways they tried to dance and sing away the white men?"

Wauna nodded slowly.

"Finally he disappeared."

"Disappeared?" She raised her eyebrow.

"No one knows what happened, although there were lots of stories about Left Hand. Eventually, his son Medicine Bird grew up and married a Nez Perce–Yakima woman. They had my father, Red Shirt, who married a Nez Perce." And slept with a hundred others, Danny didn't add. "Oh, Billy Que — my uncle. I almost forgot him."

Wauna sipped her tea for a few moments. Then she spoke in a voice so soft, it was almost a whisper. "If Left Hand was a warrior, maybe he went bad and killed Chinese."

"No!" Danny was surprised she would even suggest such a thing. Even though Medicine Bird had said Left Hand became a fierce warrior after the deaths of his wife and daughter, Danny knew he had no quarrel with the Chinese.

"A lot of people hated the Chinese," Wauna said. "Claimjumpers shot them for their gold, and some Indians hunted them like rabbits."

"Bannocks and Snakes, maybe. Not Nez Perce." Danny banged his cup on the table. "I told you Left Hand wouldn't kill Chinese."

"All right," she said, her voice as smooth as river stones. "I need to know, because it might explain the visions."

"It has to be something else," Danny said. He was beginning to believe that coming to Lapwai was a mistake. All his relatives had been nontreaty, and they distrusted the treaty Nez Perce, who had settled here with Reverend Spaulding after signing away their Wallowa homeland and cutting their hair. Spaulding burned all their traditional clothing and religious articles, except for the trunkloads he sent to museums in the East. Danny's people claimed that the treaty Nez Perce were traitors who had sold their ancestors' bones. Now he tried to hold his anger in check, but it was difficult. "You just say that because Left Hand kept his hair long and fought with Joseph for his homeland."

Wauna stayed unruffled. "I like to help all my people," she said quietly. "Clearwater, Grande Ronde, Wallowa. Even the old fierce Dreamers and their descendants." She smiled slightly. "We are all Nimipu, People Who Walked out of the Mountain. But we bicker with our cousins like coyotes quarreling, and that makes us weak."

"Maybe so." Danny disliked lecturing, especially by a woman. Why hadn't Willis sent him to an *ithlata*, a medicine man. Most of them skipped all this talk and got right on with the healing. "Look," he finally said, "I don't want to argue, but I need to know what to do."

Wauna held up her right hand, palm toward him. "Show a little patience."

Danny scraped back his chair and pointed his finger at her. "You're the one who warned me about the ghosts coming after the boy. All this talk won't settle anything."

"You're worried about Jack," she said. "But I know what I'm doing. " She stood and poured herself more tea. "Refill?"

Danny put his hand over the top of his cup. "I've got to get going."

"Relax. The wind wears down the mountain, but slowly, slowly." She sat, studying Danny. "I'm almost finished. Tell me, did you attend Loxie's dressing?"

Danny shifted in his chair and glanced away; she had touched a raw nerve. "I was off rodeoing. I didn't even know she was dead until after the funeral. When her sister, Pudge, told me, I went to pick up Jack."

"Then you should gather some soil from the Wallowas and

sprinkle it over her grave. We need to do this whenever our people die a long way from home."

"I can handle that." Danny started to get up, but she placed her hand on his arm.

"It can wait. The most important thing is to get rid of Loxie's things. Have you ever been to Big Hole?"

Danny shook his head. "My father wouldn't go near it."

"His mistake," she said. "Because sadness is a part of your past. Stay away too long and you die slowly, like a coal lying away from the fire. Go now and see the place where Left Hand lost his wife and daughter. Maybe you'll learn something about the visions. Take Jack's shirt and hang it on the Medicine Tree. It's important to get rid of Loxie's things. You know about that tree?"

"I know," Danny said. "But what about the healings — sweats and all that?"

She sipped her tea. "This is part of your healing. After Big Hole, come back here. And remember this." She was staring at him. "Tsikaatpama Tsau-tsau could be very strong near her grave. You need to build your strength with sweats and smudging. The boy, too."

"He's off rodeoing and it'll take a while to get hold of him." Danny felt very foolish suddenly for letting Jack take off after he'd seen Night Ghosts.

"Don't look so worried." She touched his hand. "I've seen these kinds of troubles before. Worse even, and it's turned out okay. But I do want to give you something for a safe journey."

She went out of the room and Danny gripped his cup. Maybe he had drunk too much, because beads of sweat were popping out on his forehead. "If anything happens to that boy . . ."

Wauna returned, carrying an *ilpahoke,* an elkhide medicine bundle tied shut with a thin leather thong. "This will protect you and bring you back safely." She repeated her instructions as she tied the bundle loosely around Danny's neck. "Remember. Big Hole and the Medicine Tree first. Then bring the boy back here for a healing. After that, you can go to the Wallowas and gather the dirt for Loxie's grave."

"Maybe I should write all this down." Danny smiled. He touched the pouch with his fingers. Medicine Bird had worn one, and when they buried the old man, it was still intact. Sometimes, at a dressing, an elder cut open the bundle to see what charms had given the dead man power during his life. Usually, the Wéyekin told the wearer what items belonged in the bundle.

Danny had been curious to see Medicine Bird's and imagined it held wolf claws, some pebbles from the Columbia River, and elk teeth, because the old man knew the Dreamer elk ceremonies. Whatever it held remained secret, since Red Shirt wouldn't let anyone touch it. And later, when Billy Que and Danny had buried Red Shirt, they didn't disturb his bundle, either.

Now he touched the bundle Wauna had given him and thanked her.

Taking him by both shoulders, she held him at arm's length and said something in the old tongue. Her strength amazed him, and he felt something else — a kind of attraction. Embarrassed, he pulled away when she finished speaking.

As he stood awkwardly, she asked, "You plan on camping out?"

"I usually sleep in the truck, especially if it's snaky." Occasionally, if he picked up a woman, he rented a motel room.

"Don't camp at Big Hole. When it gets dark, go into town."

"What's the deal?"

"No one should camp there." Her brow furrowed. "A medicine man was shot there and sometimes, at night, you can still hear the battle."

Danny nodded. "My grandfather mentioned it. He never went to Big Hole unless he felt strong. I won't camp."

"Good," she said, crossing her arms. "Your healing will be in a week. I'll be ready by then."

A week. That would give him time to get some dentalia, corn husks, and elk teeth as tokens of appreciation. Healers didn't like to use the word *payment*. That was for white medicine. But he knew she expected some gifts for her help.

"And bring the boy," she said.

After leaving Wauna, Danny wondered if he'd said too much. She had power — no question about that — and he wanted to trust her, although he wished she wasn't from Lapwai.

As he drove, Danny thought about gathering his gifts for appreciation. There was a coffee can of beads and dentalia shells around the trailer. They had belonged to Danny's mother, and even though Red Shirt could have sold them to go on a toot, he never did. But he had come close.

Years after his mother died, Danny once came home from a movie to find his father sitting at the kitchen table, the open can in front of him, the dentalia spread out on the blue Formica like poker chips.

It took a while for Red Shirt to realize that Danny was in the room, and when he did, a sheepish look came over his face. He put the shells back in the can and made a show of snapping on the lid. "They're still here," he announced. "Every last one of them. I was just counting them to make sure."

A couple had rolled under the table, so Danny realized his father hadn't really counted them.

"You know about her dress?" Red Shirt asked. "She worked on it for six years."

Danny knew it had been eight.

Red Shirt handed the can to Danny, placing it firmly in his hands. Then he waggled his finger under Danny's nose. "You hide these real careful-like, just in case Billy Que comes sneaking around. I thought maybe he was already dipping into her shells. Sometimes I don't quite trust that guy — my own brother. It's a terrible thing."

"Don't worry," Danny said. "I'll take care of it."

Before Red Shirt went out, he took the .30-.30 from the closet, so Danny figured he was going to hock the rifle for whiskey instead of selling the dentalia. He wanted to believe his father had taken the shells out for another purpose, but he couldn't think of any. After Red Shirt left, Danny hid the can behind the large family Bible on the bookshelf. It made the Bible stick out a little farther than usual, but Red Shirt never noticed. Danny knew the shells were safe because Red Shirt would never touch the Bible. Billy Que would also steer a safe distance from the book.

Now, Danny had some doubts about giving his mother's dentalia to Wauna, but that was how appreciation was given, and he believed his mother would approve, under the circumstances.

When he got to North Lewiston, Danny stopped for coffee and a piece of pie. He was so tired, his knees ached, and he had a difficult time climbing onto the truckstop stool.

"Long time on the road?" the man in the apron asked as he filled Danny's cup.

"Sure feels like it," Danny said. "I'll try that apple pie, I guess."

He poured sugar and cream into the coffee, then stirred it. He wondered how to ask Pudge for the elk teeth. She kept an old necklace and was fond of saying if you wore elk teeth, you'd never sleep alone. It was an old joke. Of course, she usually slept alone, anyway, unless Danny was around. At least he thought so.

The man set Danny's pie in front of him and warmed the coffee. Danny stirred in more sugar. He could tell Pudge right out why he wanted the teeth. But she would expect something in return. If she knew he wanted those teeth bad enough, he'd have to pay through the nose. The straight truth didn't seem like such a hot idea if he could think of another way. The pie tasted like sawdust, but Danny finished it anyway. He wondered how they managed to make apples taste that bad.

Orange and green neon lights reflected on the wall. He squeezed his eyes shut and tried to remember the stories his relatives had told about the Chinese.

Red Shirt had told Danny they ate dogs and stole children and that the women's pussies were slanted. But that was Red Shirt's bluster. He claimed to be an expert because he had fought in Korea, although he could never tell one Asian from another. The Chinese had good doctors, Danny knew.

Medicine Bird had once been very ill, and for weeks he had vomited everything he tried to eat. The elders performed the Feather Ceremony, but it didn't help, and the white doctors planned to cut most of his stomach out, then feed him through a tube in his side. Finally, Medicine Bird sought help from an old Chinese doctor. And he recovered. Danny was positive that if Left Hand had ever killed Chinese, Medicine Bird wouldn't have gone near one of their doctors.

◈ 5 ◈

PENDLETON

"You're looking a little peaked," Pudge said. She handed Danny a plate with two fried eggs and several slices of bacon. "Road food's going to be your death." She paused, the spatula half raised. "You guys quit on the Hood River job, huh? Que slunk back three days ago."

Danny broke one of the egg yolks with his fork. Too runny. The bacon looked undercooked. He like his crispy so there could be no chance of trichinosis. But his refrigerator was empty, so he'd stopped by Pudge's when he saw her car.

"I said you must have run out on that easy Hood River money." Pudge loaded the food onto her own plate and sat across from Danny.

"You writing a book or what?" He didn't feel like telling Pudge everything. Spill your guts to a woman and she takes advantage. He felt he had told Wauna too much.

"Jack must be sleeping in, huh? After working orchards and rodeoing, he needs a good rest."

"I guess so," Danny said, glancing away, because he didn't want to tell her Jack was on the rodeo circuit. "Those windows look shot." All the windows were steamed up from the cooking, but a few were permanently opaque.

"It's as bad as having cataracts," Pudge said. "That Thermopane fogged up and the BIA's supposed to have someone replace it."

"Don't hold your breath," Danny said. He had Visquene over his trailer windows, so his view wasn't much better.

"It's pretty cozy, all in all. Beats a picker's shack."

"You had to get that in." He looked around the front room, but he didn't see any new softball trophies. "You guys get beat at Toppenish or what?"

"Those umpires threw the game. They called me out on a long fly, but I'm sure that fielder trapped it. Missed the championship by one run."

Danny leaned back in his chair and smiled as if to say I told you so. "They rigged that White Swan Rodeo, too."

"Trudy was sure disappointed Jack never showed up. She's dying to meet him. Say, we've got practice tomorrow night. Send him over."

Trudy Two Sleeps was one of the best-looking young women around Mission, and she never wore a bra. Danny liked watching her pitch. "Jack might be busy, but maybe I'll stop by." He had to get on the road if he wanted to do all Wauna had laid out for him, but a day's wait couldn't hurt.

"The way you hang around drooling embarrasses me, so keep your tongue in." Pudge cleared the table and put the dishes in the sink.

"Why don't you put them in the dishwasher?"

"I can't. It leaks all over the floor." Pudge looked at the calendar above the stove. It was from Saint Anthony's Hospital and showed an old doctor and a young girl. She was holding out her doll and he was listening to its heart with his stethoscope. "School starts in three weeks. Have you checked over Jack's schedule to make sure he's got the right courses?"

"Just getting around to it," Danny said.

"This year is real important. If he does okay, maybe he can go to college. There's government money for scholarships, you know."

"Sure." Pudge should know about money, Danny thought. She had cozied her way into this BIA house and was working a steady job at the hospital.

"The health care profession is wide open for men. He could be a physical therapist or a nurse. Maybe even a nurse practitioner. That's almost as good as a doctor. But he's got to take science."

"I said I'd check into it." Danny couldn't see Jack being a nurse. The men all seemed swishy, padding around in their thick-soled shoes.

"Somebody better." She put her hands on her hips and seemed ready to say more about it, but she didn't. Glancing at the clock, she took off her apron. "Time for work. Actually, I'm kind of glad you stopped by, because that car's been hard starting. A couple times, I flagged down people so they could jump it. Yesterday, I had to call Que."

"Maybe it's the battery," Danny said. "Hey, you know how to tell the best man at a Mexican wedding?" He grinned.

"Sure. He's the one with the jumper cables."

Danny was a little disappointed. "I just heard that one in Hood River."

"Jokes make the rounds." She grinned. "Here's one. Do you know why there's a Mexican restaurant in Pendleton?"

Danny shook his head.

"That's where their car broke down." Pudge laughed. "Now look at my car, would you? I don't have time to clown around." She took her car keys off a hook by the back door.

"It's probably the battery."

"Don't give me that. When I was growing up, my mother's clunkers were always breaking down, and those slicks at the service stations sold her a new battery every time. They saw her coming, and two hungry kids to feed didn't mean a damn."

"I'll take a look." Danny got up from the table. He went outside and tried to start her car, but when he turned the key, it just clicked. Opening the hood, he saw that the battery looked shot. Both terminals were corroded, and one cable was so frayed, all the copper wires were exposed.

He knew Que had borrowed his jumper cables and never returned them, but he dug around in the junk behind the seat of his pickup, putting on a show for Pudge. He wanted to soften her up a little, because he needed those elk teeth. He spilled empty beer cans and fast-food containers out onto the ground. His fishing rod had been slammed in the door, breaking the tip, and he made a note to buy a new one. Rope, tow chain, short-handled shovel. He found a full beer can and set it on the front seat.

"I hope you're planning to clean up this mess. I know you throw trash around your trailer, but this is my place," Pudge said. She wore her Bravettes jacket over the nurse's uniform.

"No jumper cables. That darned Que must have run off with them." Danny frowned. "You called him yesterday?"

"Maybe those were your jumper cables," Pudge said. "Que was grumbling and mumbling because I woke him. Every night he's been closing up the Outlaw Club toward Hermiston, pestering the dancers out there. No fool like an old fool."

"Get in the truck," Danny said. "I'll take you to work. Later on, I'll come back and jerk that battery, run it into town for a quick charge. When did you buy it?"

"Who keeps receipts?"

"They can try to charge it, but I think you'll need a new one. Don't worry. By the time you're off work, you'll be set. And they won't try to take advantage of me. They figure women don't know cars."

Pudge gripped her purse in both hands and stood beside the pickup. "What's this going to cost me?"

Danny chuckled. "Jeez, you're suspicious. Well, how about supper tonight, as long as you mentioned it?"

Pudge relaxed a little. "I guess so. You'd probably be over here mooching off me anyway. I'll fix something for you and Jack."

"Just me. I think he's got plans."

As he drove Pudge to the hospital, Danny was almost pleased things were working out this way. If Pudge owed him, she couldn't complain too much about Jack's being on the rodeo circuit. And she might even part with the elk teeth. "Of course, you'll need to pay me for the battery and cables, now that I think of it."

"I want to see the receipts."

Danny stopped at Milo's Pioneer Auto to fill the pickup with gas and check on batteries. While Milo pumped the gas, Danny examined the used batteries Milo stored under the workbench. A couple looked pretty clean, and Danny thought he could convince Pudge they were new. Milo frequently sold new batteries to drivers who didn't need them. He'd knock ten bucks off the price of a new battery for trade, then turn around and sell the old one for a good profit. Danny felt a little uneasy about shorting Pudge, but he figured his time was worth something. And going on the road, he might need extra cash.

"Danny, what else can I do you for?" Milo asked, rubbing his hands on his green coveralls.

"Just poking around," Danny said. If he seemed too eager, Milo would gouge him.

"Truck giving you any trouble? I got some good used batteries for forty. Your pick."

Danny shook his head. "She runs like a top. Starts good, too. I was just looking for Jack, my boy. He's got his mind set on this used car — nice little Mustang — but I thought it started slow. Just a little sluggish. Well, if he decides to buy it, I'll have the dealer charge it up good." Danny unbuttoned his shirt pocket. "How much do I owe you?"

"Twelve bucks."

Danny handed him a twenty.

While Milo went inside the office to the cash register, Danny pocketed a few receipts from the book on the bench. He took them from the back so Milo wouldn't miss them for a while.

Milo returned with eight dollars in his hand, but he didn't give it to Danny. "You know, a fellow's first car is pretty important. He'll be wanting to take his girlfriends for a ride. You don't want him calling you from hell and gone with road trouble."

"You got a point," Danny said.

"Damn betcha." Milo nodded, then lowered his voice. "Look, I don't want to badmouth fellow associates in the auto business, but those dealers usually put bad batteries in used cars, then sell the good ones."

"No kidding," Danny said.

"I used to work the lots myself — there in Portland along Eighty-second Avenue. Even if you charge up those batteries, they'll fizzle out. Tell you what, Danny. I just took in a good battery on trade — that little Delco on the end. This woman is a widow, see, and I've known her for years. She buys a new battery every year — calls it cheap insurance — because she lives way up the Umatilla River, almost to the Bar-M Dude Ranch. I could let you have it for thirty." Milo toed the battery with his boot. "Maintenance free. As long as that little bubble stays green, she's got more juice than a Texas whore."

"I don't know," Danny said, pretending to think it over.

"To tell you the truth, I was saving it for a guy — salesman who's a preferred customer — but what the heck. I want your boy to get fixed up right."

"Only a year old, huh?"

"More like eight months. As I recall, she got it around Thanksgiving." Milo rubbed his chin, pretending to think. "That's right. I remember now, she had a big old turkey from Safeway, and I did a quick exchange for her because she didn't want that bird to thaw before she got home."

"Maybe twenty-five," Danny said. "Cash."

Milo set his jaw. "Danny, that's food out of my mouth." He folded his arms. "Thirty's about the bargain basement."

When Danny didn't say anything, Milo hoisted himself up so he was sitting on the workbench. "I got a funny battery story to tell you, long as I'm between customers. You know Bill Strong — lives up in Cayuse?"

"I know his place."

"Well, he came in a few weeks back because someone had ripped off a battery from his pickup. He's got that little shortbed Dodge he uses for the farm."

"I've seen it," Danny said. Strong had a big blue Olds Toronado he liked to drive into town for show. The pickup stayed home.

"Anyway, the battery got ripped off while he was gone, and old Bill was in here cussing up one side and down the other. Then, a few days after that, he came back wanting to return the battery I sold him. But a deal's a deal, I said. Even so, I took it back at discount."

"You sold him a bum battery, huh?"

Milo shook his head and seemed disappointed. "Danny, I *guarantee* my merchandise. What happened was, somebody dropped off a brand-new battery at Bill's place plus two tickets to the Trailblazer exhibition game they had at the armory."

"The hell." Danny had wanted to go to the game himself, but it had sold out.

"And they left a note with the tickets. It was from this doctor, who wrote he was over scouting the country before deer season when his battery conked out. It seems he had to hurry back to Portland for a scheduled heart surgery, so he took Bill's battery. When he returned the next week, he brought the new battery and those tickets."

"I wonder why he didn't leave some money the first time or maybe write a note then."

"Exactly. You're a smart man, Danny. Of course, he could have been low on cash — even if he was a doctor." Milo picked up the wrench and tapped it against the workbench. "Bill and the wife got all gussied up. Had a great meal at Cimiyotti's, and saw the Blazers bounce Seattle. Bill's always been a fan of theirs, even though he never forgave them for trading those three guys to Denver. So Bill got home from the game and found his place was ripped off." Milo laughed and slapped his knee. "The whole fucking place, while they were at the game. The thieves brought in a big truck and hauled off everything that wasn't bolted. Goddamn, but those were smart characters."

"They take the new battery?"

"Sure. Cut the cables and yanked it out. So Bill had to buy that used battery for another go-round. Those turned out to be the priciest tickets old Bill will ever see."

A motor home pulled into the station and Milo stood up, grinning. "Here goes fifty or sixty gallons."

Danny knelt down to take another look at the battery. The case looked solid and the terminals hadn't been broken.

"Fucking tourists." Milo returned. "All they wanted was directions and a map. Does this look like a goddamn Triple-A office?"

Danny stood. "Well, I'm supposed to meet Jack. He's underage so I got to cosign. By the way, you're still holding my eight dollars." When Milo's mouth opened, Danny added, "Change from the twenty. It's right there in your front pocket."

Milo pulled out the five and three ones and looked at them in feigned surprise. He slapped his palm to his forehead. "I plumb forgot. We got to jawing about this battery deal. Twenty-five cash. Was that what you said?"

"Better give me a receipt," Danny said. "Just in case."

"That's a darned good battery, but I have to sell them as is. Just so there's no misunderstanding." He handed Danny a scrawled receipt.

Danny gave Milo another twenty and kept his hand out until Milo returned his three ones.

"Be sure to tell your boy about my work," Milo said. "Tuneups, brakes, whatever. Mustangs are kind of a specialty with me. Used to have two of them myself."

"I'll let him know," Danny said. He carried the battery to the pickup and set it in the bed on some cardboard. "By the way, what's that battery go for new?"

"Sixty-five. Maybe seventy. If I make any more deals like that one, I'll hold a going-out-of-business sale. Probably need one anyway. You heard the mill's closing?"

"You're kidding," Danny said.

Milo shook his head. "This town's going to hell in a handbasket."

The Pendleton Grain Growers sold battery cables at bargain prices, compared with Milo's, so Danny bought new ones there. To his surprise, a new battery was sixty-five dollars, exactly what Milo had said, and after he traced Milo's signature onto the blank receipt, Danny stood to gain forty dollars. Feeling good at the profit, he stopped at Safeway and bought six Swanson Hungry-Man TV dinners instead of the usual Banquet discounts.

The morning's business had tired him, so he decided to fix lunch before installing Pudge's replacement battery. Over the years, he had cooked thousands of TV dinners, and the stove's dial was grooved at 350. He could have set the correct temperature blindfolded by listening for the slight click.

While waiting for the oven to heat up, he took the can filled with beads and shells from behind the Bible. The Bible hadn't been moved since Red Shirt's death, although Pudge probably dusted it before Jack came to live with Danny.

Danny sat at the kitchen table and opened the can. The dentalia were in little leather pouches. Dumping them onto the table, he counted twenty-five shells in the first pouch. That didn't look like very many, so he counted twenty-five more. The dentalia came from the Makahs, who harvested them from the sea. It seemed odd to Danny that he was using them now to pay Wauna.

His mother had died when Danny was too young to remember, but Red Shirt had told him that she worked on her dress for eight years, adding shells and beadwork every winter. When Danny was growing up, Red Shirt had a picture of her wearing the dress just outside the entrance to Happy Canyon. She was facing the sun, and even though she was smiling, her narrowed eyes made it seem more like a grimace. Red Shirt posed with her in another picture, but he was wearing a storebought cowboy shirt and beaded bolo tie, in contrast with her traditional clothes. Someone had broken into his truck and stolen his ceremonial outfit. For years he watched for it at every powwow, but it never turned up, and he figured a collector had it, or maybe a museum. No other dancer would dare wear ceremonial gear to a place where it might be reclaimed by the rightful owner. Whenever Red Shirt mentioned losing his gear, his voice thickened, and once or twice Danny had seen him quickly wipe his eyes with his shirtsleeve. His father carried the picture of Danny's mother for years, but that was lost, too, along with his wallet when he was mugged on Burnside Avenue in Portland.

Outside the trailer, a car door slammed, and after a few moments Que opened the door and yelled, "Hey! Welcome back!"

"Don't wake the dead," Danny said, a little surprised Que was so glad to see him.

Que looked at the TV dinner wrapper on the counter. "Cooking chicken, huh? That's funny. You don't look like Colonel Sanders."

"I can buy you lunch. Chicken or turkey?"

Que shook his head. "My stomach's fritzy." He sat at the table across from Danny. "Bad ice."

"Pudge told me you've been closing down the Outlaw Club."

"She's on my trail like a bloodhound." Que mimicked Pudge: "'Where's Danny? When's Jack getting back?' I told her I'm not your keeper." Que took off his cap and scratched his head. "Where do you figure that boy is, about now?"

Danny counted the days since White Swan. "Maybe Omak for the Stampede and Suicide Race."

"We figure alike. Jesus. You don't think he'd try that?"

Danny got up and put his dinner in the oven. "I did once. Just once." The race required riders to take wild horses down a slick suicide hill at breakneck speed, then swim their mounts across a river. Omak bordered a reservation, and most of the participants were Indians. Over the years, a lot of riders had taken bad spills.

Que fiddled with some of the shells. "These your mother's?"

"That's right," Danny said. "Don't go mixing them up."

"I thought Red Shirt drank these away years back."

"He tried, but I guess he had a moment of weakness."

"You must have found a good place to hide them."

"That's my business." Danny wished Que hadn't seen them. Now, whenever he left the trailer, he'd have to padlock the door.

"Speaking about business, I was just heading for the Outlaw Club when I saw your truck. Figured you might like to come along. The dancers start at one. Continuous showing until midnight."

"I don't think so." Danny figured Que just wanted him along for bait to attract the younger women.

"They've got Nevada girls now, not those local hangdogs. Some used to be showgirls and they're on the dance circuit. One comes right to the edge of the stage and bends over backward so far you can see her tonsils from the bottom up. 'Here's a close-up of Winnemucca, boys!' That's what she shouts." Que chuckled. "Pretty nice stretch of real estate."

Danny wondered if they were under new management. The last time he'd been to the club with Que, they'd featured a tough looker with tattoos and stringy hair who called herself Bull's-eye.

"Come on. Save that dinner for later. They got heat-up sandwiches."

"I'm tired," Danny said. "I drove in late last night."

Que got a crafty look. "Pudge roped you into fixing her car." When Danny didn't say anything, he added, "I knew it when I saw the battery in your truck." Que shook his head. "I thought Loxie kicked some sense into you about women. There was misery in high heels. Nothing but trouble from her beehive to her butt. And now you're off humping her sister."

"I'm just changing a battery for her. She's in a jam."

"Marry her, so she can give you orders all the time. Believe me, the battery's just the beginning. After you overhaul her car, you can start on the house. Those BIA jimcracks are falling apart. Roofs leak like sieves. Appliances shot to hell —"

"I'm sticking with this trailer," Danny said, trying to get off the subject of women. Que took a stubborn pride in his bachelorhood, as if it had been his choice to remain single.

"A trailer's built to last. Got to be, since it was designed to be hauled all over hell. Take a long look at any house they move for a freeway or bridge construction. Shot to shit after one move. But trailers take a beating."

Danny nodded. Red Shirt's trailer had held up pretty well, all things considered. And driving down the road, Danny saw places where people owned several trailers, each a little bigger and better than the last. They kept the old ones for extra storage, pets, maybe downluck relatives. People must like them, he figured, or they wouldn't keep buying more.

Que stood. "Well, I'd like to hang around and chew the fat, but I don't want to disappoint those girls. Anyhow, their fat's more fun." He hesitated. "Say, how about loaning me twenty. I've hit a dry spell."

"You spent all that orchard money?"

"I bought drinks for old pals. Can I help it if I'm generous?"

"If you bought drinks, they marked it on the calendar as a wild card holiday."

"I've been keeping my lips closed around Pudge. She thinks Jack's with you. Twenty bucks would lock it tight." Que eyed the dentalia. "There's money in the bank."

Danny scooped the dentalia back into the can. It didn't seem as full as before and he wondered if Que had pocketed some. "When you planning on paying me back?"

"I might have a line on a job. Word is, the tribe's putting in some fish ponds on the Umatilla. Figure they should be eager to hire a vet."

"You're really going to work?" It didn't sound like Que.

"I figure it's a goldbrick. Throw some pellets to the fish every so often. Play cards. At night, I'll sneak back and run a net through the ponds, sell a few fish to restaurants."

"You'd get jailed."

"Who's counting fish? Besides, look at all those guys on the Columbia selling them door-to-door. Anyway, I think the treaty says I can do anything I want with the fish, and the point is, I'll pay you back soon."

Danny handed Que two tens, and his morning's profit was diminished by half.

"Thanks, Danny." Que tucked the money in his pocket. "I'll tell those girls to keep the burners warm, just in case you come out."

After Que left, Danny ate his TV dinner. He wasn't looking forward to working on Pudge's car. And he was going to have to tell her Jack was on the rodeo circuit. If he didn't, Que would keep coming back for more money until he was tapped.

Pudge frowned, squinting at the receipts in front of her. Danny had waited until after supper to pull them out, because he wanted her to be well fed and a little drowsy. She had taken out her contacts and was wearing a pair of oversize glasses with bright orange frames. On each lens was an orange *P* with a rhinestone inside.

"Milo always rips you off," she said. "I can't understand why you bought a battery from him." She poured each of them a cup of decaffeinated coffee.

"Milo's an independent," Danny said. "I like giving some business to the little guy. Anyway, the battery was exactly the same price at the Grain Growers. I checked before I spent a penny. But the cables were cheaper there." Danny leaned back in his chair and folded his arms. "All the way around, I got you a square deal."

"There's eighty-five dollars out the window. If this keeps up, I can't afford to keep working."

"You got reliable transportation now." Danny drank some of his coffee. It tasted pretty good. "Besides, think how much a new car would set you back."

"I don't even want to think about it." She went over the receipts again. "Eighty-five dollars."

"A check will be fine," Danny said. "No charge for labor."

Pudge took her checkbook out of her purse and started making out the check. It was from the Inland Empire Bank and had a picture of cattle and wheat fields. At one time, Danny and Que had some fancy checks printed up that said D AND Q CATTLE COMPANY. For a while they had actually owned ten or twelve head of cattle, but they had sold them off for drinking and traveling money.

Pudge ripped the check out of the book and handed it to Danny.

"I'm a little cranky — it was a tough day at work. Got to put my feet up."

"No problem," Danny said. "What are friends for?"

When they finished the coffee, they went into the living room and Pudge sat on the couch. She took one of the satin pillows and put it on the coffee table. The pillow had BEWARE OF SOFT SHOULDERS stitched across the front and a strip of gray that resembled a highway.

After putting her feet up on the pillow, Pudge leaned back, wiggling her toes. "I must have walked a hundred miles today. It was like being a waitress all over again. Maybe even worse. Meals, juice, snacks. But there aren't any tips." Taking off her glasses, she set them on the coffee table beside the pillow.

"They better appreciate you," Danny said.

"I hope so. In a month, I've got an important exam. If I pass, I'll be an LPN."

"It'll come out okay."

"Let's see what's on TV," Pudge said. She picked up the *TV Guide* and put on her glasses, squinting so her nose wrinkled. "I'm not quite used to these yet."

Danny wondered how much glasses cost. Pudge's vision must be getting worse, because the lenses magnified her eyes so that she looked like she was staring even if she wasn't. "Those glasses look like Hollywood."

Pudge tapped the side of one lens, near the *P.* "How about the rhinestones. They're high style now."

"I've seen Dolly Parton wear those."

"Sure." Pudge laughed. "But you weren't looking around her eyes." She studied the page for a moment. "There's a good movie on later. Maybe Jack wants to come over and watch it in color. Too bad he missed out on dinner. One of the nurses gave me that recipe."

"I never had chicken fixed like that before," Danny said. Pudge's chicken had been swimming in a strange red sauce.

"Mine turned out different from hers, though. Maybe because I'm not Hungarian." Pudge chuckled, but Danny didn't get it. She tossed the *TV Guide* onto the sofa. "I'm bored with reruns. That's the worst thing about summer TV."

Danny wished she'd turn on the set because he wanted to see how good the color was.

"I think there's some ice cream and chocolate sauce out there. Maybe I should fix sundaes."

"Sounds good."

"Come out to the kitchen. I don't want stuff spilled on this new upholstery."

Danny sat at the table and watched Pudge put scoops of vanilla ice cream into two large red bowls — three scoops per bowl. She poured Hershey's chocolate sauce over the ice cream until each bowl had sauce two fingers deep. After piling Cool-Whip on each scoop, she pushed one of the sundaes at Danny.

He started eating while she picked up the phone. "Maybe Jack wants to come over." She let it ring a long time while Danny concentrated on his ice cream.

"Out catting around, I guess," she said. Sitting down at the table, she started eating her own sundae. "Who's he hanging out with these days?"

"Different guys," Danny said around a spoonful of sundae. "Ice cream tastes good. If the hospital goes bust, you can work at Dairy Queen. You already got a white uniform."

He chuckled, but she didn't, and he realized she was staring at him. He tried another bite but had difficulty. "You watching every swallow, or what?"

"No. I was just wondering when you were going to tell me about Jack."

She said it so calmly, Danny blinked a couple times before he was positive he'd heard her right. "That goddamn Que," he said. He nudged the ice cream away and sighed. "Now before you go flying off the handle, just remember Henry and I were sixteen when we went. Jack was crowding me, so I said take off. It'll probably be good for him." Danny hunched his shoulders and stiffened his neck, waiting for Pudge to light into him, but she just kept eating her ice cream.

"Things were different then," she said after a while. "Now it's just crazy. You should see the drug cases we get — twelve-year-olds all strung out."

"He's traveling with friends."

"Vinny Pinto? Don't make me laugh."

Danny stiffened in his chair. "Wait a minute." Que didn't know Jack was traveling with Vinny Pinto.

Her arm flashed and the slap knocked Danny sideways in his chair, his elbow bumping his sundae onto the floor. The bowl skittered right side up across the tile and rested against the refrigerator. He watched, amazed the ice cream didn't slide out. Then he felt the stinging in his cheek.

He half rose from his chair, his jaw set and his neck tight. But he didn't hit her. Instead, he walked across the room and picked up the sundae. After he returned to the table, he said, "I hope you feel better."

"I'd like to beat you near to death," she said. "But that's been simmering, so I do feel a little better."

Danny touched his cheek. "That was a pretty good slug, for sitting in a chair." He tried to laugh it off.

"Listen to me." Her voice was low but insistent. "Jack called here two nights ago — somebody stole his wallet in Omak. First he called your place, but you were God-knows-where and Que was out. I sent him two hundred dollars. You can pay me back later. That's not the point." She took off her glasses, revealing red-rimmed eyes. "Why work so hard to deceive me? He's your boy. But he's all that's left of Loxie, so I try to watch out for him. And it makes me feel small when you go sneaking around, trying to hide things." She took a tissue from the table and started cleaning her glasses, but she kept her eyes fixed on Danny.

"That's why you kept mentioning Jack," he said quietly. "You wondered when I'd say something."

"Here's something else. You don't fool me anymore, Danny. One time you did, but now I see through your two-bit cheating. Who cares about you, except for me and that boy. If you don't watch it, you'll wind up like Que — a mumbling old man."

Danny's ears burned and his stomach twisted. Pushing back his chair, he went over to the window and tried to look out, but he had picked one of the opaque ones, and all he saw was a fuzzy reflection of his face. He decided he wouldn't cash her check.

She cleared the table and put the dishes in the sink, turning on the water full force.

"I'm sorry, Pudge." The water was so loud, he didn't know if she'd heard.

"That's right," she said. "You're one sorry son of a bitch."

"Maybe I should tell you where I was."

"I could care less." She wouldn't look at him. "Shacked up, I suppose."

He shook his head. "Lapwai."

"Lapwai?" She shut off the water and turned toward him. "What were you doing there?"

Danny felt weary suddenly, as if his knees would buckle, and the blood seemed to drain from his face. Mentioning Lapwai brought back the visions. Here in Mission, on familiar ground, he had felt safe with the old places and routines, but he knew that was just a cover, like a new blanket thrown over a rotten couch. "Sit down. This is going to take a while."

"Wait." Pudge opened a cupboard door above the sink and took out a bottle of Seagram's Seven. Putting it on the table, she said, "You look snakebit."

"I thought you quit this stuff."

"I keep some for Code Blue emergencies."

Danny took a stiff drink and set the bottle down, then changed his mind and took another long pull. Pudge listened while he told her about the Stick Indians and the dreams. He avoided mentioning Loxie's Night Ghost because he knew that would upset her. When he finished, Pudge stared at her hands.

"You're sure about this?"

"There's even more, but I don't need to go into it all right now."

"Maybe I should go with you or go look for Jack. Who knows where he is? But I can't take off from work now, with those examinations coming up. I just can't."

"Wauna said we'd be okay," Danny said. "She even gave me this bundle." He unbuttoned his shirt so Pudge could see it. "Anyway, don't worry about Jack. He'll call again. Just tell him to meet me in Lewiston a week from today. I'll pick him up at the bus station."

"A week from today," Pudge repeated. "I'm going to write it on the calendar so there's no mistake." She took a pen from the drawer and put down the date. "What if he needs money for a ticket?"

"You can pay for it here. They'll give him the ticket on that end."

"What if he doesn't call? Maybe he'll win a big purse."

"Don't worry about it," Danny said. "I've seen him ride."

Pudge relaxed a little. "So have I."

"There's something you can do. I need elk teeth for the medicine woman. You know — the appreciation."

She got up and stirred around the kitchen a little, clattering dishes, wiping the stove, trying to look busy. "I've had those elk teeth a long time. They were my grandfather's . . . And you know what they say about elk teeth?"

"And not sleeping alone?"

"You're leaving tomorrow?" she asked. When Danny nodded, she said, "Well, I better go hunt them up."

Danny took another couple drinks of the Seagram's. Pudge was pretty agitated, keeping just under control, and that made him feel more uneasy. After a few moments, he heard sounds coming from the bedroom and he tiptoed to the doorway.

Pudge sat on the edge of the bed, her face in her hands. He switched on the light and saw the elktooth necklace beside her. Her glasses were on the nightstand.

Danny picked up the necklace and carefully laid it beside the glasses. Sitting on the bed, he put his arm around Pudge. "I'll get elk teeth someplace else."

She dug her fists into her eyes. "I'm worried sick. When Mom got bad, people kept telling her she needed a healing, but she refused. Said it was an old superstition. She just kept bringing home more pills, and after a while, she even stopped telling us they were for her back."

Pudge took a tissue from the nightstand and blew her nose. "The apartment was a mess. Loxie tried to fix it up some. She got a box of old postcards, and she'd tack the cards on the walls, then tell me about all the places she was going. I believed her because she was different. Loxie could make things happen. Me, I just keep my head down and work.

"I remember one night when Mom got home late from work and Loxie hadn't started supper yet. They had a terrible fight. Loxie called Mom an addict and a loser, and we both expected Mom to hit her. But she didn't. She just looked at us, like we were strangers, then went into the bedroom. That scared me more than anything."

Pudge turned to Danny. "Later, she tried to see a blackface healer up the coast, but he was gone, so she brought us back two pounds of saltwater taffy. If she'd had a healing, maybe things would have turned out different. What do you think?"

Danny couldn't look at Pudge's eyes. "I don't know."

"Maybe we missed something." She gripped his arm, squeezing until it hurt. "I keep thinking we missed a chance."

"You were just a kid." Danny tried freeing his arm, but Pudge had too strong a grip. "What could you do?" It had been the same with Loxie, but he didn't want to think about lost chances.

"Nothing better happen. Promise me." Pudge squeezed tighter.

"All right."

"Your fingers aren't crossed?"

"No, but you're tearing off my arm."

Pudge relaxed her grip and tried smiling. She picked up the elk teeth and examined them under the lamplight. "You know what they say."

"I know."

She let them drop on the nightstand. "You'll stay?"

Danny nodded. He didn't want to be alone, either.

6

BIG HOLE BATTLEFIELD

THE MEDICINE TREE WAS a tall Ponderosa pine that grew along the Bitterroot River in Montana. According to the Salish legend, Coyote tricked a giant Bighorn sheep into butting the tree until its horns became stuck. Coyote planned to eat the trapped sheep. But while he worked up his appetite traveling around the country, some Indian people freed the sheep. One of its horns remained embedded in the tree, and the sheep promised the people good luck and freedom from evil spirits if they hung bright strips of cloth, wampum beads, or other adornments from the horn. Eventually, the tree grew large enough to bury the horn in its trunk, but the people still paid tribute to it because of the powers it held.

Danny parked the pickup and got out. He knew Left Hand had stopped there with the other Nez Perce on their retreat through the Bitterroot Valley.

The Medicine Tree was decorated with brightly colored ribbons, beads, and strips of cloth. Because the ram's horn was no longer exposed, people had pounded nails into the tree and adorned them with personal objects and tokens for curing and luck.

Coins were pounded into the thick yellow bark of the tree or wedged into cracks. Danny counted several quarters, a couple half dollars, and one Susan B. Anthony dollar. A silver tag hung from one of the nails. On one side was a red cross. When Danny turned it over, he read, BEARCOAT. LAPWAI, IDAHO. BUREAU OF

CATHOLIC MISSIONS. A hospital wristband with the name Smith, C., hung from one of the other nails. A folded piece of paper was skewered on another nail. He removed it and slowly opened the paper. Someone had made a crude pencil drawing of a man with a crewcut and twisted face. The eyes were uneven and the nose pushed to one side. Underneath was scrawled, "Please help this soul."

Danny wanted to see the objects people had thrown into the branches, but the tree was so tall, even the lowest branches were twenty feet above him, and the angle of the sun made it difficult to see anything clearly. He strained his neck, trying to look at the branches, until he got a crick.

A faint trail scuffed into the hillside indicated where people had scrambled up in order to throw things into the lower branches. Danny followed the trail, digging in his bootheels to keep from sliding back and grabbing onto brush to help pull himself along. The trail ended in a bitterbrush thicket. It was still a pretty fair toss to the branches. Danny saw several eagle feathers twisted on rawhide thongs, bright neckerchief bundles, even a woman's purse. He wondered what tokens they contained. A pair of skimpy women's underpants dangled from a far branch.

Returning to the pickup, he removed a paper sack from behind the seat. Inside were Jack's green ribbon shirt and the photo of Loxie. He had sewn some dentalia shells and bear grass into the shirt pockets and sprinkled the photo with rosewater, as Wauna had instructed.

Trying not to think about how angry Jack would be, Danny hung the photo on the tree, twisting a piece of baling wire to connect the photo's frame with a nail. In the bright midday light, he read the sorrow in Loxie's staring eyes. He had scrawled, "I'm sorry. DK," on the back of the photo. He had considered writing his full name, but he was afraid someone stopping by would know him. Loxie looked so different from her Pendleton days that he doubted anyone would recognize her.

Scrambling up the hillside again, he found a place where he could toss Jack's shirt into the lower branches. It was a beautiful shirt, and if he left it on the trunk, he was afraid someone would steal it. After placing a few small rocks on the shirt, he folded it into a bundle, tying it closed with the sleeves. He tested the weight, then hurled it high into the tree. It arced soft green against a hard blue sky until it dropped to one of the upper branches, causing the limb to bob as if a bird had landed from overhead.

The Big Hole National Battlefield was divided into two areas, the Nez Perce Camp and the Siege Trail. The camp lay on the broad camas meadow east of the Big Hole River, just under the shadow of Battle Mountain. On this meadow, the National Park Service had reconstructed the Nez Perce village by putting up eighty-nine tipi frames laid out in a V shape. The tipi poles were bare, not covered by the buffalo hides the Nez Perce had used. Over the years, they had weathered gray, a color that resembled the faded wood on the buildings in abandoned towns. The stark poles contrasted with the lush camas meadow and the thick red willow swales along the river. Even casual visitors sensed the sadness that lingered more than a century after the battle.

After leaving Idaho and traveling through the Bitterroot Valley, the Nez Perce had felt safe because they had enjoyed a peaceful history with Montana's settlers. Runners informed Chief Looking Glass that General Howard was days behind, and the chief was so confident of his people's safety that he failed to post sentries the night before the attack. He also stopped the fierce warrior Five Wounds from backscouting the trail because he was afraid Five Wounds might kill some of the neutral settlers or otherwise turn them against the Nez Perce.

During their journey along the Bitterroot River, the Nez Perce had stopped at the Medicine Tree and paid homage by hanging ribbons and wampum. In that hallowed place, some of the old men became worried and complained of ominous forebodings. One warned Looking Glass that death was following them, but the chief laughed at the old man's superstitious nature.

They established camp along the Big Hole River, because the water was good and pine trees were nearby. Looking Glass instructed the people to cut and strip lodgepoles for their tipis and travois. The sun was warm that August afternoon, so the children fished and swam or played the bone game along the river. That evening, several boys saw two men wearing gray blankets observing the camp from across the river, but the boys assumed the men were friendly settlers and never reported the sighting. The women spent the day digging camas bulbs on the broad meadow, and they put them in the ground to bake overnight. Before retiring, every family tethered their best horses near their lodgings.

On the morning of August 9, 1877, Colonel John Gibbons and his soldiers attacked the sleeping camp. They had come from Fort Missoula, on a forced march over several days, and traveled the last five miles in silence in order to catch the Nez Perce off guard.

The soldiers waded across the Big Hole River just before dawn and attacked the sleeping village. They killed the tethered horses and tried to set fire to the tipis. The buffalo hides were heavy with morning dew and only a few ignited, but the alarmed Nez Perce ran from their tipis into the soldiers' gunfire.

Eventually, the warriors rallied and drove the soldiers back across the river into the woods. Some of the burning tipis had collapsed on the fallen horses, and the pungent odor of burning horse-flesh mingled with the sounds of gunfire and the loud wailing for the dead.

A wooden box held blue brochures that described the features of the Nez Perce camp. Danny was supposed to leave a quarter for a brochure, but he pretended he had no change. "Indian discount," he said. He took a second one in case he lost the first.

A broad trail led to the camp. Brown grasshoppers jumped ahead of him, spreading their yellow wings and sailing into the tan bunchgrass. As he neared the camp, the bird songs seemed quieter, as if the birds respected the sacredness of the place. The bare tipis reminded him of skeletons, but the bones of the dead had been uncovered and reburied elsewhere.

Markers indicating where the dead had fallen had been placed throughout the tipi village and along the riverbank. Wooden "eagle feather" markers, gray with black tips, showed where the Indians had died. Blue hats marked the fallen soldiers and tan hats the Volunteers. Danny quickly scanned the camp and realized there were not enough eagle feathers. More than seventy Nez Perce had died here.

The chiefs' tipis were indicated by red-lettered wooden signs. Danny saw signs for Looking Glass, Lean Elk — whom the whites called Poker Joe because he loved the game — White Bird, Ollokot, and Joseph. After the battle here, the people lost faith in

Looking Glass's leadership, so the other chiefs gained more respect.

One tipi, not marked as a chief's, had five feathers within the circle of poles, and Danny realized an entire family had been killed, perhaps when the soldiers rushed inside, firing their weapons point-blank.

Danny studied the camp, trying to determine where Left Hand's tipi had stood. Medicine Bird had told him it was at the camp's lower end, where the Volunteers had failed to establish control, thereby giving the warriors a chance to regroup. Left Hand had climbed a tree near the riverbank and fired on the soldiers until a bullet struck his right shoulder, knocking him to the ground.

Near the riverbank, Danny saw a slight mound and depression marked by two eagle feathers. One of the feathers had fallen over. Danny knelt and tried to stick the feather back in the ground, but the pointed end was broken. He took out his pocketknife and dug a small hole. When it was deep enough, he put the feather in and tamped dirt around it. After he finished he stood, staring at his hands. He half expected to see blood or camas roots, but there was nothing except the yellowish clay soil of the riverbank.

Consulting the blue brochure, Danny learned that this was the place where Wahlitits and his wife had died. Wahlitits — Shore Crossing — was one of the first young warriors to charge the soldiers at White Bird, the first battle of the war. Along with Strong Eagle and Red Moccasin Tops, Shore Crossing had worn a red blanket coat to flaunt his bravery and had blown his eagle wing whistle to turn the bullets magically. A medicine man had promised him that no bullet could kill him when the sun was high because his power made him thin, no wider than a blade of grass. But his magic failed at Big Hole, where a bullet found him in the early dawn twilight. Danny shook his head. He hoped Wauna was more powerful than that old medicine man.

Making his way down the riverbank, he squatted by the water, rinsing the dirt from his hands. The water made him uneasy. After the attack, the Nez Perce were forced to bury their dead quickly and break camp. When General Howard arrived a few days later, his Bannock scouts dug up the dead and scalped them, rinsing the bloody scalps in the river. By desecrating the dead, the Bannocks made it more difficult for the people to enter their spirit world.

The brochure said nothing of Left Hand, but Danny knew his

story. After falling from the tree, wounded, he crept back to the wrecked camp. He raced to his tipi but found only an old woman huddled in a corner, crooning to herself. Outside, a small boy cried for his lost blanket. The old woman seemed not to hear him when Left Hand shouted questions at her.

Then Left Hand ran to the river. A number of women and children had tried to escape that way, and there he found Swan Lighting. Later he learned that she had been trying to dig a hiding place for their baby in the riverbank but had been shot in the breast. She had pitched into the water, struggling, and floated downstream until another woman caught her and pulled her to the side. The woman placed Swan Lighting's head on a gravel bar just out of the water. She died soon after, her blood turning the water red. On the riverbank upstream, Left Hand found his infant daughter, her head crushed, as if by a rifle butt.

After patching his wound, Left Hand returned to the battle. That afternoon, he killed two soldiers, and that night, when a Volunteer snuck to the riverbank to get water for the desperate soldiers, Left Hand stalked him. After stunning the man with his stone warclub, Left Hand held his head underwater until he stopped struggling and bubbles no longer broke the surface.

"Rainbow and Five Wounds were fierce warriors," Medicine Bird had told Danny, "but my father was their warmate. He had to sing their death chants because they had been killed too quickly to sing them."

Danny knew that long after the war, Left Hand had returned to Big Hole to honor his fallen comrades and his family. Sometimes he took Medicine Bird with him. As far as Danny knew, Red Shirt had never gone.

Now, Danny hung three ribbons from the red willows along the river. The next time he came, he would try to bring Jack, because the boy should know this place, too. Looking carefully at the camp, the river, and the hillside, Danny thought about the vision of the men dying on the sandbar. This had been a terrible slaughter. But it was not the same place he had seen in his vision.

The Siege Trail led Danny through a yellow pine thicket on the east side of Battle Mountain, about a quarter mile south of the camp. After Gibbons's initial attack on the camp, the warriors had man-

aged to regroup and chase the soldiers back across the Big Hole
and into the woods. Here, Gibbons's men found their escape route
cut off by Nez Perce sharpshooters. The soldiers dug shallow fox-
holes with their trowel bayonets, and the Nez Perce, anxious for
revenge, climbed trees farther up the mountain and sniped at the
pinned soldiers. Some of the soldiers formed a siege line toward
the camp side of their position to defend against other warriors,
who fired on them from the willow thickets along the river. From
time to time, one of the Nez Perce would try to charge the en-
trenched soldiers.

The fighting lasted throughout the day and the long hours of the
night. The wounded soldiers were racked with thirst because the
Nez Perce had cut off their access to the river. Unable to get med-
ical supplies, the soldiers spit tobacco onto their wounds. Some cut
open their cartridges and shook out the black powder, then ignited
it to sear their wounds and stop the bleeding. While many of the
warriors kept the soldiers pinned down, others helped the women
and old men bury their dead in shallow graves or conceal them in
willow thickets along the river.

Danny felt a grim satisfaction when he saw that only a few
feather markers rose from the lush green grass under the pines. But
there were many blue hats, and from a distance they resembled
clusters of lupine dotting the undergrowth. After the way the soldiers had attacked the sleeping camp, they deserved to die on the
hill, Danny thought.

It was cool in the trees. Danny had been sweating in the sunlight
at the camp, but now the sweat chilled in the slight wind that rustled the pines.

He paused at the top of Battle Gulch, a brushy gash in the hillside thick with red willows. The feather marker here showed the
place Five Wounds had died. The warmate of Rainbow, Five
Wounds vowed he would die on the same day as his friend, who
had been killed in camp. After drinking a little whiskey from a dead
soldier's canteen, Five Wounds charged the soldiers on the hillside.
He had gotten so close to the soldiers, the other Nez Perce were
unable to retrieve his body for burial. Danny imagined the Bannocks had scalped his corpse later. It seemed as if he had died fool-
ishly. Even so, Danny knew, many came to decorate the place
where he had been killed. However, there were no ribbons now, so

Danny guessed no one had come lately. Or maybe souvenir hunters had stripped them.

Farther up the hill was the marker for Red Moccasin Tops. His death interested Danny because he had a wolf Wéyekin, just as Danny did. He had worn a wolfskin cloak into battle and believed himself invincible, so he crawled very close to the soldiers, wounding several, before he was killed. An old medicine man had told Red Moccasin Tops his body was bulletproof. After the battle at White Bird, he had taken off his red blanket coat and shaken out the deformed bullets that had blunted against his skin. He had seemed almost bulletproof here, too, protected by a special power. He fought with the wolf cloak draped around him, the wolf's head pulled over his own.

But his throat was bare, and a soldier's bullet went through his neck, severing his wampum necklace. Several young warriors had been wounded trying to retrieve the body and the cloak, for Yellow Bull shouted that anyone who saved his son's body could have the cloak and the power it possessed. Later, he went back on his word, but they were glad to save their friend's body anyway, because they didn't want him disgraced by being cut into pieces by the whites or the Bannock scouts.

A concrete marker paid tribute to the soldiers who had fallen at Big Hole. Twenty-nine soldiers and Volunteers had been killed, more than forty wounded. Danny thought of the five feathers inside the tipi frame and nodded.

The trees thinned and the trail led through a sagebrush flat that overlooked the Indian camp. There was a small pine bench and Danny sat. He was tired from walking and it felt good to rest. The sun warmed his knees.

He stretched his legs in front of him and leaned back, closing his eyes. In spite of the sadness of the place, he felt good being there, and Medicine Bird's stories rang true. Danny recalled how his grandfather's voice had cracked as he described the Bannocks scalping the dead, disgracing the Nez Perce bodies for their own shabby dignity.

Danny awakened, stretching and squinting his eyes against the bright afternoon sunlight. The broad camas meadow and the river

winding through the red willows resembled a picture postcard. It
seemed so peaceful . . . until his eye rested on the gray tipi frames.

After taking another look at the camp and terrain from this vantage, Danny was certain this was not the place he had seen in his
vision. There had been another slaughter, somewhere.

Heading back along the trail, he had walked halfway across the
sagebrush hillside when he stopped, frozen to the place.

Two duck heads were lying in the trail a few feet away. They
were brown mallard hens; the necks were still attached, the raw
meat and white bone curving under the brown feathers of the
heads. Dark wet spots by the heads looked like blood soaked into
the dirt, and Danny guessed the heads had been wrung off. The
bright orange beaks were wrapped with a thin strip of rawhide, so
the ducks had been unable to squawk.

"What the hell!" Danny said, stepping back to avoid touching
them. He looked around quickly but saw nothing, no movement
in the willows or along the sagebrush hillside. Ahead of and above
him, the dark forest seemed ominous.

He studied the trees, starting at the place where the trail entered
the woods and slowly working his way up. The shadows and
stumps appeared as dark figures. He blinked his eyes, remembering
what Red Shirt had told him about looking for game. Don't look
straight ahead but glance off to the side a little, because your vision
is better that way, especially if something is moving.

He tried it, and it worked. A hundred yards above, just where
the sagebrush met the treeline, something flickered. He blinked a
couple of times to make certain he hadn't imagined it, that it wasn't
a leaf turning or an odd ray of light angling off a lightning strike.
But something strange was definitely twisting below the bottom of
a tree branch.

Running up the hillside, Danny dodged sagebrush clumps and
rocks. He moved clumsily in his boots and doubled over with a
cramp in his side halfway up the hill. "Damn altitude." He forced
his breath in sharp pants and tried to straighten. "Can't get my
wind." His throat was dry, and he vowed to quit eating so much
pie at truckstops.

After he regained his breath, he moved more cautiously, stopping
ten yards from the treeline. Two eagle feathers hung from a low

pine branch by a piece of dark blue ribbon. The feathers were upside down, black tips toward the ground. Beneath them was a ceremonial arrowhead.

Danny knelt, touching the arrowhead with his forefinger. It was
made of black obsidian and felt cool. He smiled a little. Someone
had been paying tribute to his ancestors. He had come in through
the forest to avoid being seen by the rangers at the tourist center.
Maybe he had put the duck heads along the trail, too, although
Danny didn't know what they meant.

Deciding to respect the privacy of the person who placed the
feathers, Danny stood, ready to leave. And then he saw her standing beside a broken Ponderosa.

Lightning had scarred the bark down the tree's sides, peeling it
away to reveal the crusty yellow wood. Although a canopy of
branches shadowed the ground, enough sunlight filtered through
to create a kind of twilight.

She wore fine traditional clothes, a velvet print dress with beaded
moccasins and a cornhusk sidepurse. She draped her blue shawl,
the one she wore for dancing, over her right arm, and she appeared
ready to attend a celebration.

"I was off rodeoing," he said, "or I'd have come."

As he spoke, she turned to face him. The wind ruffled her hair
and lifted the corners of her shawl. She didn't look like her picture.
Her smooth dark hair was long and held back with a beaded comb
that had been her mother's. Her eyes were bright, the way he liked
to remember them. When her lips moved, he thought she was saying his name, although he couldn't hear any sound.

Taking several steps toward her, he saw a small gully between
them, and before he could cross, she stretched out her arm, and he
felt an overpowering fatigue. He stood, unable to cross.

She unfolded her shawl carefully, draping it over her head and
shoulders. Turning her back to him, she began walking into the
woods.

"Loxie!" he called, but she continued walking. The shawl's
fringe swayed with her steps.

When his strength returned, he crossed the gully, scrambling
quickly up the other side. He searched under the tree, but the soft
ground held no impression of her footprint. He half expected the
scent of her perfume to linger, but there was no trace, only the

smells of pine and moss. Overhead, jays scolded in the high branches. Sitting beneath the tree, he leaned back against its rough bark and dug his fingers into the carpet of pine needles.

When he came out of the woods, Danny was surprised to see a National Park Service pickup. A ranger in a gray uniform was sitting at a little picnic table peeling an apple. He cored it with his knife, then cut some slices. He picked up one slice with the point of his knife and stuck it into his mouth. As Danny got closer, the ranger half raised his hand in greeting.

"You see the deer?" the ranger asked.

Danny shook his head.

"They were in the willows. A nice little doe and fawn. They spooked into the woods when I got out. Looked like they were headed your way."

The ranger stuck another apple slice and held it out. Danny could see the point of the knifeblade through the apple's flesh. "No thanks."

The ranger put it into his own mouth and chewed. "After work tonight, I was thinking about fishing." He nodded toward the water. "Good trout stream."

"I believe it," Danny said, although he wouldn't fish where the Bannocks had washed scalps.

"Lots of good water around here," the ranger said. "I'm from Iowa originally, so you can imagine how great this is." He closed his knife and put it in his pocket. "I drive down here on my breaks. Gets me away from the tourists at the visitors center. Only a few people walk the trails like you did. That's how to really know the place. I've been over every inch myself — first thing I did when I transferred out.

"You haven't seen the center yet. We've got a pretty nice exhibit. Joseph's war coat is there and Wounded Head's drinking gourd. It's made of buffalo horn — bison, I should say. Yellow Wolf's war club, too."

"Sounds like quite a collection." Danny imagined the gawking tourists snapping photos of the sealed objects.

"You'd like the Howitzer. It's the original. The army dragged it all the way here, but fired only one shot before the Indians chased them off." He gave Danny a sidelong look. "You come here often?"

"This is my first trip."

The ranger nodded. "We find things all the time — ribbons, little fetishes, parts of animals. Some of the rangers claim they hear voices, like singing, but we never see anyone." He shrugged. "Maybe it's the wind. Anyway, when I saw you hanging ribbons from the willows, I got curious . . ."

"I lost some people here," Danny said. He doubted if the rangers ever stayed the night. They'd hear some terrible things then, according to Wauna.

"Sorry. I didn't mean to intrude." He wiped the knifeblade on his pants and, closing it, slipped the knife into his pocket. "By the way, I saw you running up the hillside. What was it?"

Danny looked at the visitors center, perched on a knoll across the camas meadow. Although it stood a long way off, the center afforded an excellent view of the camp and hillside. "You saw me, huh?"

"Yeah. We keep tabs when people walk the paths. Everybody wants souvenirs. We've replaced a couple hundred of those feather markers this season. It keeps the guys in the shop busy."

"It was a big farm dog," Danny said after a while. "At first I thought it was a wolf."

The ranger seemed puzzled. "Wolves usually come in winter." When Danny didn't answer, the man glanced at his watch. "I'm way overdue — my supervisor will skin me." He got in his truck and started it. "Like I say, stop by. I'd be glad to show you around."

"Sure thing," Danny said, almost under his breath. He watched the truck drive away until it looked like a toy. A few cars were parked near the center, and they looked like toys, too.

Danny didn't want to see the artifacts in their cases. Out here, in the open, the spirits could still move. Before nightfall, he'd drive on to Wisdom and get something to eat, then look for a motel.

The sun had dipped behind the mountains and already he felt chilly. Surveying the empty campground, he wondered if anyone stayed. He imagined frightened tourists, roused by gunfire and the shouts of warriors, throwing tents and sleeping bags into their cars. As the fallen medicine man's spirit conjured and reconjured the battle, they would race toward the lights of Wisdom while the wailing of the women and children receded in the distance.

Danny stood and surveyed the battlefield. It was evening now, all grays and shadows. A few wisps of fog rose from the river near the tipi village. He remembered.

On the morning of the soldiers' attack, the medicine man had been dreaming by the river. As the soldiers charged, the holy man began singing his power song. When a bullet struck him, smoke poured from the wound. As other bullets struck him, smoke came from those wounds, too, and from his mouth and nose.

He kept singing as the smoke gathered into a low ground cover, like fog. Some of the women and children escaping from the burning tipis hid in the smoke until the warriors rallied and chased the soldiers back across the river. They came out of hiding then, amazed that the medicine man still sang.

Now Danny touched the medicine bundle around his neck and was reassured as his fingers felt the small, hard objects inside the elkskin. In a way, he envied Wauna's power and regretted that his family had lost theirs. Left Hand and Medicine Bird had known old ceremonies and songs, but whatever was left, Red Shirt had wasted. He had passed nothing on. Danny felt weakened by that loss and by the deaths of his mother and father. Loxie, too.

He stared at the bare tipi skeletons along the river and tried to imagine the holy man singing, the smoke pouring from his flesh and covering the ground. But he couldn't do it. Straining to remember a few notes of his grandfather's songs, he felt confused. A sound started low in his throat but seemed to be snatched away when he opened his mouth.

THE HEALING

DANNY USED HIS HANDS to dip water from the bucket and sprinkle it onto the heated stones. "One for you," he said, nodding to Jack. "One for me. And one for the Old Man." Here the Old Man meant the sweathouse. It was made of treated canvas stretched over a bent willow frame with green sticks angled into the ground, helping the steamy air to circulate so it wouldn't burn their shoulders.

Wauna had spread red cedar and fir boughs in the sweathouse. The boughs were fragrant, and the *kaus kaus* root in the water bucket filled the air with a celery aroma each time Danny sprinkled water on the stones. Since this sweat was for spiritual cleansing, Wauna had instructed them to sweat seven times and plunge into the river between sweats.

"Getting hot," Danny said, backing out of the sweathouse into the cool evening air.

"I'll be along soon," Jack said. "That water's cold and the wind cuts through you."

"Summer's over," Danny said. "Not on the calendar, maybe, but it's over."

Twenty yards downhill from the sweathouse, the Clearwater formed a deep eddy. Danny ran the distance and dove in. The cold water made his teeth snap. He closed his mind to the cold until he started to feel a warming in his numbed fingers and toes.

It was nearly dark, but a few rays of evening light reflected from the river's surface. Darting swallows chased insects, a late mosquito hatch. Their hum was barely audible over the water's song. Occasionally, headlights flickered along the willow thickets, but Danny knew the cars' occupants couldn't see him or Jack when they emerged naked from the sweat.

Now Jack hobbled down the hill, pressing his left palm against his deeply bruised thigh where a horse had kicked him during the Omak Stampede's Suicide Race. He tried smiling, but it was more of a grimace.

"You'll remember Omak." Danny chuckled.

"That makes two of us. Mom told me you about turned white riding down that hill."

Danny slapped at a mosquito hovering over the water. "Close. In those days, I thought I could ride into hell with a bucket of water. But that Stampede showed me."

"Me too," Jack said. "When I broke over the top, I saw those fancy dudes behind the ropes shrink away from the horses." He chopped at the water with his hands. "So I whipped mine harder, just to show those fatasses in their kangaroo boots and turquoise rings. If my horse hadn't fallen . . ."

"Those dudes used to chew at my guts, too," Danny said. "It's just sport for them to watch some crazy Indian kids ride wild horses. I'd say you were lucky to escape with only that bruise."

"Lucky? Don't forget somebody swiped my wallet. Damn near two hundred bucks."

"Vinny Pinto'd kill for that much."

Jack shook his head. "He was riding with me, and somebody broke into his truck during the race. I was afraid of losing my wallet when the horses plunged into the river, so I'd left it behind."

"Vinny's got buddies," Danny said. "It's an old trick."

A swallow flashed between them, and Jack looked startled. "Now that you mention it, Vinny threw money around all night long. I thought he was just trying to impress the buckle bunnies. And he kept buying me drinks. As he got drunker, he put his arm around my shoulder and cursed any dirty dog that'd rip off his good buddy."

Danny shook his head. "Two-faced — just like his old man."

Inside the house, Wauna was singing and beating her drum. The kitchen window was open and they could hear her clearly, even when they were inside the sweat. Earlier, she had vomited, and Danny knew she had used the emetic sticks to purify herself. Later she would smudge the house with *p-tass-way,* the special alpine fir that grew high in the mountains, and she would bring them inside to cleanse the impurities and chase away menacing spirits.

"You think all this is necessary?" Jack asked.

Before replying, Danny listened for a few moments to the singing and the drumming. Although Wauna was singing her power songs, the rhythm resembled one of the Washat's religious songs.

"When you start seeing Steah-hah and Night Ghosts, you'd better take care of things."

"Whatever you say." Jack stirred the dark water with his fingers. "I never thought I'd get mixed up in any witch business."

"She's a medicine woman," Danny said.

"Not much difference. It can get pretty creepy. At school, one of the Bella Coolas told about a witch they had in the village. After she lost her lover to another woman, she took out her bitterness with witchcraft. Once she gained her power, anyone who seemed happy became her victim."

"I know that type," Danny said.

"She'd take some hair from the young men or women in the village, then wait for the spawning salmon. At night, she'd fish away from the village, using a lantern and a net. After she caught a dying salmon — the darker the better — she'd tie her victim's hair around its gills, then release it to go upstream and die.

"Strong, happy people would sicken in a day or two and become gloomy and sorrowful as that salmon thrashed upstream, farther and farther from the village. Of course, she was working spells, too, back in her hut on the edge of the village."

"So you believed her witchcraft worked?" Danny said.

Jack shrugged. "Maybe. But it happened way up in Canada. Those people are still kind of backward."

Danny knew that when the problem was physical, like a wound or disease, a medicine woman used plants and herbs. At one time, special healers had been trained to help warriors with poultices from blue violets, *kaus kaus,* and camas. A different healing was needed for spirit problems. You could be having trouble with drinking, gambling, or something else in your personal life. Someone might be practicing bad medicine on you, making a spell. Perhaps they had gathered some things that belonged to you — hair, nails, pieces of food — and wrapped them in a bundle with bad objects or pieces of a corpse. These were serious problems, and you needed a powerful *ithlata* such as Wauna to help counteract the spells.

Once Medicine Bird had told Danny of a witch who made sick people die by putting a cloth soaked with her menstrual blood under their beds. Sometimes she wrapped her victim's hair in the cloth.

A powerful medicine woman finally reached into one of the witch's victims to see what bad thing the witch had created. Exposed to light, it resembled a writhing white worm with a bloody head. Chanting over it, the medicine woman threw the worm into the fire.

Some distance away, village women were baking camas roots in a deep firepit. Suddenly, the one who turned out to be a witch shrieked and leaped into the fire before any of the others could stop her. Until then, no one had suspected her of wrongdoing. "You must always be careful," Medicine Bird had warned.

They had sweated and plunged five times — talking about rodeos and witches, fishing and sports. The sixth time in the sweat, Jack laughed quietly.

"What?" Danny asked.

"Just thinking about Hanson. He never bathed in winter."

"You're kidding," Danny said. Even though he hated hearing Hanson's name, this struck him as funny, because he remembered that Loxie spent half her life in the bathtub — whenever she was upset or depressed.

"He'd put his smelly boots by the woodstove to dry, and pretty soon the whole place stunk like sour silage."

Danny shook his head.

"She warned him to leave those boots on the porch, but he ignored her. One morning they were gone, except for a blackened hunk of lace."

Danny chuckled. "Cross her once and she'd never back off."

"Hanson tried to get even by holding back grocery money — claimed he needed it to buy a new pair. I had to scrounge change for lunch and Mom ran out of makeup. So she took a job waitressing at Red's Cornhusker Café." Jack rested his chin on his hands and looked past Danny as if he could see the entire scene. "What a dump! But it was the only job in town — at least for a woman.

"Even those weary-eyed farmers dug good tips out of their coveralls. It made Hanson boil."

"I can see it," Danny said. He imagined the slow-talking men gripping mugs of steaming coffee with chapped hands and smiling at Loxie's back talk.

"Finally, she got real sassy with Red, so he came out from the kitchen one day and flung his apron at her. 'See if you can cook any better,' he said. She was so good, he hired her regular."

When Danny knew her, Loxie could do almost anything she set her mind to, if she wasn't soaking off a hurt. "Your mother learned the restaurant trade at Shorty's," he said. "You know, Shorty's Short-Stop, there on the east side of Pendleton. His Grand-Slam burger might have weighed two ounces, if you skimmed the fat. And he wanted the tomatoes sliced thin. Whenever she sliced the tomatoes, he'd complain, 'If you can still see red, they're too damn thick!'"

Jack laughed again. "I'll bet she sliced them thick on purpose."

"You bet. Out of sheer spite."

Jack shifted. After a long pause he said, "So what do you remember about her?"

"Lots of things, I guess." Danny wasn't sure what to tell Jack because he never knew what would make the boy flare up. He squeezed his eyes tight and tried to think about something good.

"Well, once we drove to the Lloyd Center, that first big mall they had in Portland. Half the reservation went that year to look at the stores and watch the skaters. We bought matching sweaters at Meier and Frank and ate in a little restaurant over the skating rink. Fancy. Then we tried ice skating. I was worse than a calf on a frozen pond — all over the place. Your mother was pretty good, though. After a while, I just hung on to the rail and watched her.

She made some picture out there, with her long hair swishing behind."

"I wish I could have seen that," Jack said quictly.

Danny nodded and smiled. "We had a good time." He decided not to tell Jack the rest. Loxie had borrowed her aunt's car for the trip. It had power windows, and when they left Portland it was warm, so they left them down, catching the breeze along the Columbia. At Cascade Locks it started raining, but the windows stuck. Because they didn't want to ruin the upholstery, Loxie held her coat over her window, and Danny drove with one hand, jamming his Levi jacket against his. The wind blew hard at Hood River, whipping rain into the car. By the time they reached The Dalles, it had stopped raining but they were soaked, and Danny worried about pneumonia. Loxie's thin blouse clung to her skin, revealing her dark nipples. Her wet hair seemed darker, and drops of water ran down her face.

They looked at each other, laughing so hard Danny had to pull the car over. Loxie jumped out, running across the railroad tracks, and Danny followed. They made love in the wet brush along the river. After they finished, they heard the rumble of a train in the distance, and Danny jumped up to grab his clothes. But Loxie lay in the grass, her breasts still bare and her slacks pulled down around her ankles, laughing as the round engine light came closer. Danny could still remember the surprised look on the fireman's face as the train roared by, several feet away.

"Sometimes, I know she was thinking about you," Jack said.

Danny started. He couldn't believe how it made him ache, just remembering the sleek wetness of her thighs. No other woman had stirred him as Loxie had.

"She had a way of looking at me, a real special kind of way, and I think she was remembering you."

Danny didn't say anything, but he thought of times when his telephone had rung, usually late at night, and he was sure Loxie was on the other end, even though she never spoke. He'd just listen awhile to the sound of the empty distance, then hang up.

Danny closed his eyes. The heat and the steam caused him to relax a little. Inside the sweat, it was almost too dark to see, but he sensed Jack's presence and heard the boy breathing. He had sweated with his father and grandfather in the willow sweathouse they had built up the Umatilla. How old had he been then? Eleven or twelve? But he had gotten away from sweating during all those years on the rodeo circuit. A few times he had thought about going back, but something always seemed to get in his way.

Jack was whispering, and Danny opened his eyes. The boy squatted over the fir boughs, his face shining in the gloom. His lips moved but little sound came out, and Danny had to hold his breath in order to hear the whisper "Tsikaatpama Tsau-tsau."

"Don't worry," Danny said. "Wauna has things under control. She wants me to gather some dirt from the Wallowas to sprinkle on your mother's grave."

Jack focused on Danny as if he hadn't seen him before. "When are you going?"

"Pretty soon, I guess." Danny wanted to return in time for the Pendleton Round-Up. "I did something else Wauna told me," he said, "and you're not going to like it."

Jack didn't say anything but cocked his head, listening to Wauna's singing as it pitched higher and more insistent.

"I hung your ribbon shirt on the Medicine Tree — back there in Montana."

"You did what?"

"It's right near Big Hole —"

"I know where it is." Jack pushed past Danny and dipped his hand into the water bucket. "One for him." He splashed another handful of water and refused to look at Danny. "One for me."

"There's something else you should know." It was getting too hot in the sweat, and Danny almost choked on the strong *kaus kaus* smell. "Not long after I left that shirt, I saw her. You understand? I saw her, too."

Jack had dipped another handful of water, but it trickled through his fingers before he could splash it on the rocks. "I don't believe you."

Danny nodded. "She was in the timber, high above the Big Hole Battlefield." He closed his eyes. "She was beautiful again, like I remember."

"You don't know anything. Nothing." Jack edged forward, his

voice odd. "Whatever you saw wasn't what I saw, because you never even knew her."

"I knew her," Danny said, surprised at Jack's reaction.

Jack shook his head. "Fifteen years she was with me, not you. A lot happened that you can't pretend to know about. When I saw her ghost, I missed her so much, I wanted to go away with her, no matter what."

"That's crazy talk." Danny tried to grab Jack's arm, but the boy lurched backward, out of reach. He started dipping water. "One for you, one for me, one for the Old Man." It had become a chant. Jack's lips trembled as he spoke and his hands dipped with quick, jerky movements.

Beads of sweat broke out on Danny's skin and he felt a burning across his neck and shoulders. He imagined himself as a hot coal glowing in the dark. Scrambling out the doorway, he gulped at the cool air before running downhill and plunging into the water. Green lights flashed behind his eyes and his teeth snapped with the cold. Surfacing, he struck the water with his fists. He was angry at himself for all his false hopes.

The drumming had stopped, and Danny wondered if Wauna was listening to them. What would she think?

After a few minutes Jack burst from the sweat, his face grim as he limped downhill.

Both men remained quiet in the water, avoiding each other like circling boxers. Jack's face tempted Danny to strike, but although he clenched his fists underwater, he didn't lash out, because he know that would ruin the healing.

"Remember one thing," Jack said when the silence had become unbearable. "She's always going to stand between us. You should grab on to that, because it's never going to change."

Danny pressed his fists against the sides of his legs until his wrists ached. "Whatever you say, Hotshot."

The drum started again, a different song, and Wauna's penetrating voice carried on the night air. It was one of her power songs.

"Let's get the healing over with. This fucking water's freezing," Jack said. After listening a minute, he left the river and limped stiff-legged up the hill.

Danny was so cold he was numb, except for his aching wrists.

He opened his hands and flexed his fingers. "Feels good," he muttered. After Jack's words, the river's cold couldn't touch him, and he remembered how Whip Man had rounded up the frightened children in February's blue-black mornings and chased them toward the icy Umatilla. He had slashed at the children with green willow switches, the quick panting of his breath coming in small white clouds. When he had them on the riverbank, shivering from cold and fear, Whip Man made the children strip, then break through the shore ice and dive naked into the water. Those who hesitated or cried out were lashed harder. Danny did not cry out, and he stood on the riverbank laughing at Whip Man, even as the fierce old man grunted savagely, striking him time and again until his whip hand fell limp and the snow was spotted with blood. Then Danny turned his back and plunged into the water.

Medicine Bird had covered Danny's wounds with special salve and they seemed to heal almost overnight. When Whip Man came to collect his pay for teaching discipline, he told Medicine Bird that Danny was the toughest. Danny had been listening from his trailer bedroom and overheard.

Now, Danny opened his mouth and laughed, but it came out twisted. He wasn't certain if Whip Man had been right or dead wrong. He floated on his back, staring into the night sky. Overhead, he saw the Bear and the Hunter. To the north he saw the Windwalker. Danny wondered if Wauna now sensed something about him, the way Whip Man had. Once Danny had been tough, but he wasn't certain how much toughness remained.

When they emerged from their seventh sweat, Wauna draped heavy wool blankets over their shoulders and led them into the house. She had heated *p-tass-way* boughs on the woodstove, so the rooms were filled with the pungent odor of fir. In a darkened corner of the front room, they changed into the new clothes they had bought at J. C. Penney's before leaving Lewiston. Danny had selected Big Mac work clothes, but Jack chose newer styles. Glancing into the little bedroom off the front room, Danny saw a flickering light and guessed that Wauna's mother was watching television.

Once dressed, they sat at the kitchen table, and Wauna gave them hot drinks in mugs. Danny thought it might taste like the Yogi tea she had given him earlier, but this was different, stronger and more bitter. On the table were fans made from swan and eagle feathers, clumps of bear grass, a fawnskin pouch.

Wauna wore a long docskin dress with a beaded sash, and a bear claw necklace adorned her throat. Taking one of the smoking fir boughs from the stovetop, she slowly waved it through the air, like incense. Replacing the bough, she motioned for them to stand, and when they did, she sang and moved her hands through the air around them, tracing their outlines. She did this again with the fans and bear grass, changing songs each time she selected a new object. When she brushed them lightly on the backs, chests, arms, and legs, for the moment, Danny's fears and doubts disappeared.

Opening the fawnskin pouch, she took out a pinch of brown powder and sprinkled it over Jack's head. Then she cupped her hands, as if carrying water, and appeared to pour something into the top of Jack's skull. After she finished with the pouring, Wauna moved her hands as if sewing up a wound. She chanted softly, stopping only to speak in the old tongue.

When she finished with Jack, his eyes remained open and unblinking, but he didn't move.

She turned to Danny and sprinkled powder on his head. Although he knew the powder was cool, he felt his scalp warming and then the heat penetrating his skull. When it became almost too hot, he felt the coolness of running water. He closed his eyes.

Wauna sang, and at first the voice seemed distant but clear, like music across a lake, but then the singing grew closer and closer, filling the room. Opening his eyes, he saw her mouth moving and the song entered his mind. He felt incredibly tired, but he could not close his eyes, and then he felt he was in the center of things, exactly where he belonged.

When Danny came out of his trance, the pungent *p-tass-way* smell flared his nostrils. The healing. He could almost believe he was just a boy again, waking up from a night of dancing with his grandfather and father, comfortable after sleeping under the robes between the two men.

Then he heard Wauna's voice and closed his eyes again, pretending to sleep. "You can't go placing blame," she was saying. "No one can bring her back."

"Not even you?" Jack taunted.

"I can give people strength."

The only sound was Wauna sipping tea. Then Jack whispered, "Maybe I should have gone with the Night Ghost."

"I know about that," Wauna said firmly. "The authorities call me when they find our people's bodies floating in the river or smashed in cars. The worst ones don't die but scream and scream in white rooms while Tsikaatpama Tsau-tsau shreds their minds."

Danny heard her get up to fix more tea.

"I can give people strength. Sometimes I can keep them from making mistakes. I know, at times, it doesn't seem like much." She wasn't apologizing, just stating facts.

"Maybe it's better than nothing." Jack's chair scraped back. "I'm going outside for a while. Clear my head."

After he heard the door close, Danny waited a few minutes, then pretended to awaken. He watched Wauna take the teapot off the stove. She had moved the smoking *p-tass-way* branches to one side.

Wauna sat at the table, facing Danny. "When someone dies, it weakens us. That's when Night Ghosts show up."

Danny figured she was referring to Loxie. "It's been almost a year," he said.

She shook her head. "Time passing doesn't mean anything if you've ignored the old ways. Did you wait a year before you went hunting or fishing?"

Danny spread his hands.

"You're supposed to wait a year, then hold a giveaway and a feast."

"Hardly anybody practices those old ways anymore," Danny said. But he was sorry for his words.

"And look at the shape we're in," Wauna said. "This was probably your first sweat in a long time."

"Okay, it was," Danny admitted, suddenly feeling foolish. All the elders harped on keeping old traditions, but Danny felt he had driven too far to settle for those tired words. "Now that we've done this, will Loxie keep bothering us? Not her, I mean, but the ghosts?"

"I'd say that's up to you," Wauna said. "By taking her things to the Medicine Tree, you have protected yourself and Jack from the Night Ghost. Probably it can't harm you. But . . ."

"But what?"

"Loxie's soul is still wandering because you didn't give her a proper burial. She can't harm you now, but it would be a kind thing to put her soul to rest. You must get dirt from the Wallowas — where her people came from — and sprinkle it on her grave."

"But there's still something else," Danny said. "What about the visions I had?"

Wauna shook her head. "I think your dreams of the men along the river are something different. The healing should help, but this trouble goes back to your ancestors." She seemed puzzled, as if she had thought about it a long time. Sensing Danny's disappointment, she added, "I can't give you all the answers. I can only show you a way to go. If you begin at the Nimipu Trail, you might learn something."

Danny nodded. Joseph and the nontreaty Nez Perce had taken the Nimipu Trail when General Howard removed them from their Wallowa homeland. The trail started on the lower Imnaha River, crossing Summit Ridge to Dug Bar on the Snake, where the people forded high water into Idaho. He could see that trail when he gathered dirt for Loxie's grave; both places were in the Wallowas.

Wauna folded her arms and glanced toward the bedroom door. The television no longer flickered. Danny realized it was time to offer her the items for appreciation.

Taking a large blue bundle from a paper bag near the stove, he untied the neckerchief and spread the contents across the table: corn husks, bear grass, Pudge's elktooth necklace, and the dentalia. "I know I can't offer you enough," he said. "This is just a little token."

She examined the items one by one. Touching the necklace first, she ran her long fingers over the yellowed ivory. "This is very old. Maybe your grandfather shot these big bulls."

"Not mine. A friend gave me those teeth when I told her we needed a healing."

"Anyone who'd part with this is a good friend." Wauna untied the leather pouch that held the dentalia. Pouring them onto the table, she said, "These are old, too. Early trade. I've been decorating a dress and these should work very nicely."

"They were my mother's," Danny said. "She was working on a new dress, too, but she died before she finished it."

"Sometimes, when I see old dresses in museums or for sale in secondhand stores, I wonder what sadness made the people let them go."

Danny knew that Spaulding had wrenched the traditional clothes from the people and either burned them or sent them to his friends in the East, then forced the people to wear ill-fitting missionary garb. "I don't know what happened to my mother's dress." He wondered if Red Shirt had sold it.

After Wauna finished examining the items, she moved the bear grass and corn husks to her side of the table. "Your appreciation is very strong. Keep the necklace or the shells."

Danny stared at the dentalia and the elk teeth. He imagined his mother sewing the dress, the long hours she spent decorating it with beads and shells. Part of him hungered for the shells because so little remained of his mother. But Pudge had given him the elk teeth — her sacrifice. His hand hesitated over the shells, then he touched the teeth.

Smiling, Wauna nudged the necklace toward him. "You know what they say about elk teeth?"

"I know, I know." He put the teeth back in the bag. "Thank you."

She put her hand to her mouth and Danny realized how tired she must be. "We should head back to Lewiston," he said.

"Danny?" she said as he turned toward the door. "I was waiting until the healing was over, so it wouldn't interfere. But I want to ask your help."

Danny felt awkward. For a moment Wauna looked uncertain, and he wasn't used to seeing her that way.

"Sure," he said. "What is it?"

"There's been trouble along the Columbia, and there'll be more. Will you go see about it?"

Danny tugged on his hat.

"Willis called me at work." She paused, and Danny could see the worry in her face. Then she said gently, "It's his grandson. His grandson Jimmy drowned."

As soon as they checked into a Lewiston motel that night, Jack fell asleep, but Danny stayed awake watching HBO. *The Road Warrior* was on, and he was fascinated by the vehicles and violence. He remembered going to the Pendleton Drive-In with Loxie, especially after Jack was born, because it was cheap entertainment and close to Mission. If they wanted to be alone, they drove to Milton Freewater's drive-in, and they always parked in the darkened back rows, even after they were married. Sometimes Danny could hardly concentrate on driving home. Back in the trailer, Loxie'd tuck Jack into his crib, then pretend to be too tired, so Danny had to drag her toward their bedroom while she laughed and struggled, pummeling him with her fists. A couple of times, their lovemaking wakened Jack.

Now Danny turned toward the boy sleeping in the next bed. Thinking of Jimmy, he leaned closer to make sure Jack was still breathing; then he pushed the thought out of his mind. Jack's dark hair spread on the white pillow, and his lips parted slightly. He looks like Loxie, Danny thought, the way she was when they first married.

In those days, the little money he made they spent like water. Danny collected benefits from Red Shirt's veteran insurance and he hunted odd jobs, mostly ranchwork. They ate commodities: condensed milk, Karo, canned meat, beans, rice, peanut butter. Potatoes were cheap. And Danny always had a venison quarter hanging in the Port-A-Shed. No one minded poaching on the reservation.

Danny rodeoed awhile, although entry fees kept him broke, and he had to bum drinks from his single buddies. He also played summer softball for the Umatilla Coyotes, writing a bad check at Oscar's Sporting Goods to cover a new glove and cleated shoes.

Six months after Jack was born, Madame Aurora opened a dance studio over the Stockmen's Bar and drummed up business by telling local girls they had talent. Sometimes while Danny and his friends drank, they could hear the dancers overhead.

Through the heat of July and August, Loxie practiced in the cramped studio or on the dirt bib in front of the trailer. The soles of her bare feet were black, and the sweat curled her hair into ringlets around her face. She played the records loud enough to drown out Jack's crying and ignored Wilson Windyboy's leering face thrust out his broken kitchen window.

"I don't know what the hell's going on," Danny said one time after the Toppenish softball tournament. "You're too damn old to be a cheerleader."

If either of them had given an inch, they might have gotten

along, but they were both stubborn. Eventually Loxie refused to make love, so Danny slept on the couch, even though the Naugahyde made him sweat.

When he drove to Que's for advice, he found his uncle sitting on a folding lawn chair outside his trailer, clad only in his underwear to beat the heat. Aluminum foil covered the windows to keep out the sun. "I can see you're packing trouble," Que had said, and poured him a tumbler of Old Grand-Dad.

He drank the whiskey, then asked Que what to do. His uncle's eyes narrowed and he made a fist.

Danny didn't hit Loxie then, but he broke the record player and refused her money for a new one. She started taking off with Jack while Danny was away at softball tournaments. He checked a couple of times at Madame Aurora's, but she wasn't there. He hung around anyway, watching the supple dancers, pretending he expected her to show up.

During a home game with Warm Springs, someone mentioned seeing her at the Outlaw Club near Hermiston, and Danny left before batting. He topped ninety on the interstate, the cleats of his shoes digging into the gas pedal, because he knew about the women who danced and cozied up to the cowboys and long-haul truckers, keeping a percentage of the high-priced, watered drinks. Some used the rooms in the back, but he tried not to think about that.

The Outlaw's parking lot held only one truck, a flatbed Ford with warped cattleracks. It was loaded with striped Hermiston watermelons. Inside, the driver sat near the bare stage, watching Loxie dance to the juke. She wore a red G-string, pasties, and high heels.

Her eyes were seductively half closed, but they widened in surprise as Danny's cleats clicked on the linoleum. The trucker watched her a second too long and had only half risen and turned when Danny's sucker punch caught him. He hit the floor like a wet bale of hay and never twitched.

Danny jerked Loxie off the stage and nearly pulled her arm from its socket as he dragged her to the pickup. Then he went back in after Jack. The bartender just said, "Pack it up, Chief," and Danny figured he had already dropped the dime for the cops.

After handing Jack to Loxie, he stripped off his softball jersey and tossed it at her. Then he vaulted into the flatbed and cleated watermelons until his shoes were soaked with juice and his white athletic socks turned pink. When he heard sirens on the interstate, he started driving his pickup slowly toward Hermiston. At the Inland Empire Bank, he turned right and continued toward the Columbia. After that, he took back roads to the reservation.

In the pickup, Loxie lay Jack on the seat between them and held him with one hand. Danny watched her from the corner of his eye. She sat stone-faced, and neither of them spoke until they were inside the trailer, Jack tucked in bed. When she took off the jersey, he saw the pasties.

"Slut!" He backhanded her just once, and she staggered across the kitchen floor. He half expected her to scream or reach for a knife, but she didn't. And she didn't cry, even though a welt marked her cheek.

"The next time I leave, you won't find me," she said, making each word ring with hate. And he knew it was true. Then she went into the bathroom and locked the door.

He didn't try to break in, even though he could have. The water was running, and after a while he heard her crying. Satisfied that she was ashamed, he went out, his own face flushed with anger.

Now he touched his cheek and discovered it was wet. Surprised, he saw his fingers glistening with tears, and when he felt his cheek again, it was smeared. What the hell, he thought. He sat on the edge of the bed, his face buried in his hands, crying quietly so he wouldn't disturb the boy.

◈ 8 ◈

WIND RIVER

AFTER DRIVING ALL morning, Danny crossed the Columbia at Umatilla and took Highway 14 along the Washington side. He knew it would be slower than the freeway, but he wanted to see the river from that side. The sparse traffic gave him time to think about Willis's loss and about fishing along the river. The day was warm, and the dry cheatgrass had turned honey-color. Danny kept the pickup window down — the air had the dry smell of autumn mingled with the scent of the river. Jack slept while they passed the settlements of Paterson, Alderdale, and Roosevelt. During one winter snowstorm, Danny remembered, a Burlington Northern train had been stranded in Roosevelt, and the townspeople took care of several hundred passengers for days, keeping them warm in the schoolhouse and feeding them in their own homes.

Today, the intense sun made the school's yellow pumice blocks resemble adobe. New playground equipment decorated the side yard. A flashing sprinkler system kept the grass so green it seemed artificial. Roosevelt had only a few scattered houses, many of them sandblasted bare of paint by the wind. Danny wondered if the teacher lived there, in one of the painted houses with a patch of lawn, or drove over an hour from one of the bigger towns — The Dalles or Goldendale.

From Roosevelt, a narrow county road with broken black asphalt twisted up the dry hillside. On the basalt plateau above the

Columbia, golden wheatfields stretched for miles toward Bickle-
ton, and he imagined the heavy heads of wheat nodding in the sun.

He had driven that road once to visit a wild ranch girl and
counted the bluebird houses on the fenceposts. There were thousands of them in Klickitat County. The girl was short, with hair
like cornsilk, and they made love with his Levi jacket spread beneath her hips. She hugged him tight with arms that could build
fence, and her laughing eyes were quick and restless.

Across the Columbia from Roosevelt, sunlight glinted off the tall
grain elevators at Arlington. At one time a ferry had connected
Arlington with Roosevelt on a sporadic basis, but it didn't run anymore. Doc Severinsen, the trumpet player on *The Tonight Show*,
was from Arlington originally. Sometimes Johnny Carson kidded
him about it on TV.

Danny glanced quickly at the river, because the blue was so
bright it hurt his eyes, making them sting. Commercial nets formed
long curves on the water, their white float lines gleaming like polished teeth. He doubted if the Indians who owned them were
catching many salmon. In this heat, the fish would lie close to the
bottom, resting in cool water before traveling farther upstream.

Danny was hungry. He remembered that sometimes Red Shirt
had taken him to a café across from the Union Pacific station at
Pendleton. His father was usually sobering up with coffee and
didn't eat, but he always ordered a short stack and sausages for
Danny. The short stack had four thick buttermilk pancakes, and
Danny could never eat all of them. When the railroaders clomped
in with their bib overalls and striped caps, Danny admired the way
they polished off tall stacks of golden brown cakes and sides of
ham and sausage. They were gruff, big-stomached men who
smelled of diesel and creosote, and they usually stopped by Danny's
stool to tousle his hair and ask him if they could eat his leftovers.
He had always been partial to the railroad cafés.

Now Danny remembered a good café in Wishram, and he was
almost at the Wishram cutoff. But when he saw Stonehenge
perched on the basalt bluff overlooking the Columbia, he decided
that Jack should see it, and he pulled off onto the Stonehenge road.
Danny drove past the broken concrete weathervane that reminded
him of a large birdbath and stopped in front of Stonehenge mon-

ument. It was a concrete replica of England's Stonehenge, as the designer figured it must have looked originally. Danny had wanted to take Loxie there, but he never got around to it.

Jack woke up. "Where are we?"

Danny told him.

Jack shook his head. "The hell. We had to study about Stonehenge. It's over in England and all busted up."

"This is how it used to look," Danny said, getting out of the pickup.

Jack got out, too, and they walked inside the first circle of concrete columns.

"Weird." Jack rubbed his arms briskly with his hands. "I'd hate to be stranded out here at night."

"Ooooooowww." Danny made a sound like a ghost. "Maybe the sacrifices start wandering around."

Jack sat on the large flat slab. "Sort of like the healing."

"What do you mean?"

Jack shrugged. "I didn't feel much different. Did you?" He started digging a pebble out of the concrete with his fingernail.

"You were in a trance. I saw you."

Jack squinted at him and flicked the pebble toward one of the columns. "Mom took me to a revival once back in Nebraska. It was a big tent with benches and folding chairs inside. Hanson scoffed at it. Even he could smell a ripoff."

"She must have been desperate."

"She tried everything for a while. I hated that minister. He strutted around the stage tent like a rooster and called out for all the sinners to come forward. She was the first, and the way he hugged her, I wanted to punch him."

Danny shook his head because he didn't want to know Loxie has been desperate enough to go to a revival. She had always been able to stand and spit in your face. Then he remembered her chopped hair and bruised eyes.

Jack stood and brushed off his pants. "The next week the tent was gone and she was back on the bottle. Some cure."

"Wauna's different," Danny said.

Jack tilted his head so he could read the plaques on the columns. "Whatever you say."

Danny read the names of the Klickitat County war dead inscribed on the tall cement pillars designed to resemble stone. None of the names sounded like Indians, and he wondered if they had been allowed to fight in World War One. Plenty of them had died in later wars, he knew.

On the river side of Stonehenge, a trail wound down to a granite gravestone for Sam Hill, the man who had decided to erect the war memorial. A small sign warned walkers to beware of snakes.

Danny was surprised to see all the fruit orchards and buildings in the settlement below him. Peach, apple, apricot, and pear trees dotted the stretch along the river. The state park and boat landing had been improved and expanded, too. He saw several windsurfers launching their crafts.

"That used to be an Indian settlement down there," he told Jack. "Rock Creek band, I think. They moved them all out when they put in The Dalles Dam. Told them to get out before it flooded."

"Looks pretty good now," Jack said. "Those orchards must be worth a small fortune."

Danny nodded. "I don't know where those people went. Maybe up around Goldendale someplace. They're sure not around here anymore."

The dry hillsides east of Wishram were scorched black, and the burn pattern showed that the firefighters hadn't held the fire before it reached the highway. Sparks had blown across the highway in places, but those blackened patches were smaller, ranging from room size to the size of a basketball court. The brush no longer smelled scorched, so Danny figured the fire was a few weeks old.

He put the pickup in second and used compression to slow the steep descent into Wishram. It had once been an important railroad town, first for the SP&S, later for the Burlington Northern. Danny had visited there when he was in high school. The town had taken its name from the Wishram Indians, but that band had settled downriver about eight miles, and their site had been covered by the dam's backwaters.

"Our freshman team played a ball game here — just once," Danny said. "They weren't on our regular schedule, but the coaches were friends. We barely beat them. They still had those old-time backboards, and I swear one basket was about a foot lower than the other, so we had to adjust our shots after the half. Some of the spectators pelted us with rocks as we were leaving the gym, and others blocked the road with rocks and railroad ties. When we got out to move them, they rolled boulders down the hillside. That was the only time I ever wished we'd lost."

Jack laughed. "Think about the refs. They were probably tarred and feathered."

"I don't know," Danny said. "Maybe they grabbed the first train out or snuck across that railroad bridge in the dead of night."

They reached the bottom of the steep grade and started passing the small houses. One had a front lawn crowded by statuary. Although the yard couldn't have measured more than twenty by twenty, it contained more flamingos, birdhouses, deer, frogs, Mexicans, and burros than Danny had ever seen before. He imagined that an older couple lived there. The house next door had a Harley-Davidson and a dark gray German shepherd in the yard. As the pickup passed, the dog bared its fangs and strained against the chain. Danny wound through the narrow main street, ticking off the little businesses he remembered. Gas station, Pastime Bar, and a little store that now claimed to have deli foods.

He drove by the small post office and across the tracks. A large wooden building painted green and white was the first Burlington Northern place, and the café had been in the building just beyond. But when Danny drove past the first building, he stopped in amazement. The café was gone.

The earth showed the fresh marks of a dozer blade that had piled the rubble closer to town. The pile had been burned, but a few charred wooden snags showed from the concrete debris. A couple of kids were poking at the rubble with long sticks. They had a rusty wagon half filled with salvage they planned to cart off.

Danny stared at the rubble and shook his head. His vision of a chicken-fried steak with mashed potatoes and green beans followed by Marionberry pie suddenly vanished. "I can't believe they tore down the Wishram Lunch," he said. "Why would they do a thing like that?"

"I should know there'd be a screw-up," Jack said. "How could there be a good place to eat in this dump?"

An old man wearing suspenders over his faded blue shirt came out of the first building. He had almost walked past them when Danny called, "Why'd they tear that building down?"

The man approached the pickup. He was older than Danny had first thought, and he had missed some patches of long, yellowish-white whiskers when he shaved. He fiddled with a hearing aid.

"Why'd they do it?" Danny asked. He pointed to the rubble.

The old man shrugged. "You tell me. You got to go to the deli now if you want something to eat. I hate deli sandwiches. They all taste the same."

"How'd the hillside get burned off?"

"Cinders from the trains used to do it in the old days," the man said. "But this was Fourth of July nonsense. You fellows Indians?"

Danny nodded, even though he was surprised by the question.

"One of your people is selling fireworks up there along the road. Crazy Charley. Illegal stuff, but he claims it's Indian land, so he sells whatever he wants and they can't touch him. About two weeks before the Fourth, the deputy here figures it's a good idea to show the young people how to use fireworks safe and sane, so he rounds them all up for a demonstration. That's how the fire got started. One of Charley's Saturn rockets blasted off course and blew sparks across half the hillside. It took the whole town to stop the fire at the road. I'll bet Crazy Charley laughed himself sick."

As the old man continued walking, Danny and Jack stepped out of the pickup. Looking downriver, Danny saw the SP&S railroad bridge that spanned the Columbia and more or less connected Wishram with Celilo Village. In the old days, he knew, the braver Indian kids dared to cross that bridge from settlement to settlement. But you needed to know exactly when the trains were coming. Directly across from Wishram was Celilo Park, put in by the Army Corps of Engineers when they flooded Celilo Falls. Windsurfers were launching from the park. Their sailboards danced like bright butterflies on the water.

"I told you about Celilo," Danny said.

Jack groaned. "Dozens of times. That's history. Look at those windsurfers!" His voice was tinged with envy.

A woman steered her sailboard close to their side. She wore a bright green wetsuit, and her hair streamed out behind as the sailboard knifed through the water.

Jack waved, and she returned the wave, her bronze arm flashing in the sun. "I hear *Sports Illustrated* is doing its swimsuit issue on the Columbia," Jack said.

"Is that so?" Danny was only half listening. A lot of the women who windsurfed were knockouts, but he figured they were unattainable. Jack would learn that, too, after he'd kicked around a little more.

Gazing across the shimmering Columbia, Danny saw the cedar shake longhouse at Celilo Village. Red Shirt had taken him there for the salmon festival. Ignoring the warnings of their elders, children had climbed the steep bluffs behind the longhouse, then slid downhill until their clothes were black with sandy dirt. Later that winter, the frightened children had tried to scale the slick, frosty bluffs when Whip Man herded them toward the icy river. Those who nearly escaped, he lashed the hardest.

The Wind River in lieu site was one of several promised to the River People in 1937, when Bonneville Dam flooded the traditional fishing places guaranteed by the Treaty of 1855. Although the Army Corps of Engineers intended to rebuild the fishing villages on lands purchased by the government, World War Two delayed its plans. For a number of years, the displaced people lived close to the river, anywhere they could find shelter, until the government finally purchased forty acres of in lieu sites instead of the four hundred originally agreed upon. The control of these sites was eventually turned over to the BIA, which insisted that no permanent residences be constructed on them.

However, Willis and the other River People clung to the in lieu sites rather than moving onto the reservations. He and his son Orville built shanties along the river and occupied them year-round. They also rebuilt the fish drying shacks the government had replaced; the government workers had made them from tin, which cooked the fish, instead of the proper materials — plywood and mesh screen. By living on the sites, Willis believed they were exercising ancestral claims and preventing the land from being taken away again, perhaps sold to make parks catering to windsurfers or expanded facilities for the white sportfishermen.

The Wind River site consisted of Willis's two-room plywood house cobbled against the basalt hillside, an improved boat landing for both sport and Indian fishermen, restroom facilities that were kept permanently padlocked, a plywood and mesh screen fish-drying shack, numerous small trailers, some of which remained there year-round, and fishing boats in various stages of disrepair. During fishing season, the fish buyers from Astoria and Port-land established stations and pulled in large refrigerator trucks to hold the catch before they took it to distributors in Portland and Seattle.

When Danny arrived at Willis's fish camp, the River People and their supporters were holding a salmon festival to raise funds for Orville Salwish and the other Indian fishermen arrested for selling salmon to undercover agents. Friends and relatives were gathering to show support.

The small parking area near Willis's place was crowded with ve-hicles, and at first Danny thought hundreds of supporters had come. Then he realized that a lot of the cars and vans had racks for carrying windsurfing equipment. The sailboarders were using the parking lot, too.

The Indians had constructed a temporary shelter of plywood and blue plastic tarp between the fish-drying shacks and a row of beached, broken boats. Picnic tables and benches cluttered the shel-ter's center, and aluminum folding chairs formed a fringe. Old men wearing bright ribbon shirts occupied some of the chairs while women in calico dresses or buckskin rested in others.

A fire pit had been dug near Willis's net-drying racks. Two young men were adding briquets to the alderwood fire while several cooks wearing pink caps with pompoms pointed directions. Children straggled back and forth between the windsurfers' beach and the salmon bake, carrying cans of Pepsi and Nehi sodas. They had chased a large gray goose beneath one of the refrigerator trucks and threw stones while the goose thrust its neck between the wheels and hissed.

"Let me out," Jack said as Danny turned into the lot.

"What for?" Danny slowed but didn't stop.

"I got to check out these surfing women." Jack opened the door, and he looked as if he would jump.

"Don't go breaking a leg." As Danny stopped the truck, Jack hopped out, but kept the door open. Danny leaned forward. "Wil-lis will want to see you."

Jack slammed the door and thumped it. "I'll be around later."

With all the visitors, it took Danny some time to find a parking space. Getting out of the pickup, he walked slowly along the line of boats and studied the old men in the chairs. He didn't see Willis, and he wasn't certain what he would say when he did see him. He stopped by one of the fishing boats, a red Fiber Form shaped like a dory.

Danny stared at the left side, where a big chunk was missing, ripped away as if by a giant shark. His mouth went dry as he imagined the driver hitting a jagged rock or snag at full throttle. It was a wonder the boat had made it to shore at all.

Several Pepsi cans and an Orange Crush bottle littered the bottom of the boat. Ants had found their way into the bottle and were eating the sticky residue. Other ants gathered on some scattered chicken bones. Colonel Sanders, Danny guessed.

He ran his fingers over the shreds of cross-hatched fiberglass as if he could read the boat's history in braille. He dug his thumb into the reddish-brown stain on the gunwale. Fish blood, he thought.

"You can't afford that boat."

Danny would have recognized her sarcastic voice anywhere. "Hello, Velrae," he said.

She was standing with her legs slightly spread, her hands jammed into the pockets of black jeans. Although her eyes were dry, the puffiness around them showed she had been crying.

Danny made a fist and rapped the side of the boat. "Your brother?"

She nodded, biting her lower lip.

"I'm sorry." He reached out to touch her, but she dipped her shoulder, so his hand fell away. "What happened?"

"A state fisheries boat rammed them in the dead of night." She made "state fisheries" sound like a curse.

"Who the hell was driving?"

"Willis. Not that it matters. That boat came out of nowhere."

"Was he running with lights?"

"Hell yes. But the state boat had every light hooded. It was jammed with wardens looking for illegal sets."

"Didn't they see him?"

"You figure it out." She spit onto the ground and toed some gravel over the white gob. "The tribal chairman has filed a protest and we're going to sue — not that it means shit. Cops always cover their ass." Her voice cracked and she turned away from Danny, facing the river.

He figured she was crying and didn't want him to see, so he watched the water. It was a thin blue, reflecting the high, cottony clouds. Sailboards skimmed the surface, and several sportfishing boats trolled lazily, the sun winking off their aluminum hulls. On one of the boats, a father netted a salmon for a small girl in a bright red T-shirt. The fish broke the water, shaking diamond drops from its tail.

When the fish was in the boat, Danny shook his head, as if to conjure another scene — a night collision with a boy pitched from a boat, his lungs filling with black water and gasoline. One image faded into another, and Danny saw a different river. A dark-haired man bobbed face down at the lower end of a long gray sandbar. Feeling unsteady, Danny leaned against the boat and took a couple of deep breaths.

Velrae still faced the river, away from Danny. "Seventeen," she said. "Just two years younger than me, and he couldn't swim a stroke. Anyway, his gum boots dragged him down, and it took him three days to float to the surface." Her shoulders trembled slightly. "They wouldn't even let my father out of jail for his service. They treat Orville like public enemy number one."

"I'm damn sorry." Danny shifted from foot to foot while he waited for her to say something else, but she was finished. "Maybe I better go talk with Willis. Where is he, anyway?"

"Check the house," Velrae said, and jerked her thumb toward the ramshackle building. "All he does now is sleep."

"I'll see you later, then."

Velrae shrugged, but as Danny started walking away she asked, "Hey, where's Jack?"

"Looking at the windsurfers. He was on the rodeo circuit but he slunk back, all beat up and broke."

"Rodeo." A smile played across Velrae's lips. "I wish my brother was still out there riding broncs."

"That's right," Danny said, but he knew how unsafe the rodeo life could be. Walking toward the house, he remembered Ormond Nine Pipes, Henry's cousin, who had left the Wolf Point Stampede cashy with rodeo winnings, only to head-on with a grain truck on the highline. He had wound up just as dead as if he'd been sucked underwater for a week.

Glad that, at least for this moment, Jack was where he could keep an eye on him, Danny bolted up the steps.

Waiting for Willis to wake up, Danny sat quietly in a metal folding chair. He liked the inside of Willis's place. Two large pictures of Christ hung on the wall, and a little table held a large open Bible. Christ's words were in red; the rest of the text was black.

Swan and eagle feathers were laid out on a worktable, and a big ceremonial drum dominated one corner of the room. Willis was sleeping on a cot covered by a five-point Hudson's Bay blanket, white with green and red stripes.

Willis's army picture hung on the wall along with a picture of Sla-kish, the Klickitat chief who had signed the Treaty of 1855. That treaty had guaranteed the Indians' rights to fish in all the usual and accustomed places. Below the pictures was a construction paper poster with a large red heart and a flower. A child's hand had lettered: FREE ORVILLE.

A black vase shaped like a cowboy boot held dried wildflowers from along the river. Scotch tape, rubber bands, and strings of assorted beads hung from hooks screwed into the wall.

"Jimmy?" the old man cried, sitting straight up in bed. When he recognized Danny, he slumped back. "For a minute there, I thought you were Jimmy."

Danny shook his head. "I was sorry to hear about your grandson."

"You know about the accident?"

Danny nodded. "Velrae came by while I was looking at the broken boat."

Willis sat on the side of the cot. He took a cigarette from a pack on the floor and lit it. "The Old Man — he got another good boy. Those gum boots . . ." Willis shook his head. "He stayed down almost three days. Finally, I went back near the place we got hit and I threw in some shells and beads. Chanted a little to tell the Old Man we wanted that boy back. They found him down near Cooks the next day, snagged on a log."

Danny didn't know what to say.

"I paid that river before." Willis knocked ashes from his cigarette, then began putting on his shoes. "Paid him too much this time, maybe. I'm getting old. Keep losing things."

"It's a tough break," Danny said. "What happened?'

"Jimmy planned to leave for Toppenish early the next morning. Wanted to go back cashy — impress his girlfriend, you know. Sometimes the Neptune fish buyer comes up at six, and Jimmy wanted all his money before he took off, so we went out at night to check the nets. Those fish were moving good then. We filled the bottom of the boat with Chinooks and a few sturgeons.

"We didn't even bother with the nets at Preacher's Point — that's how many fish we already had. So I just headed back, sticking to the middle of the river because I didn't want to foul anyone else's net. Jimmy was feeling good, thinking about the fish money. I heard him singing.

"All of a sudden, I sense something wrong, and when I look up, there's a big blackness right in the middle of the channel. Then searchlights come on. I'm blinded for a minute. I yank the wheel, but it's too late. My boat's sluggish from the weight of all those fish. The next thing — bang! The side of my boat explodes and I'm in the water — stunned. I stay down awhile to miss the props, and some fish bump against me. Our salmon are lost, too. My lungs go pretty fast — these damn cigarettes — so I come up choking on water and gasoline. The searchlights are all over the water. I see an empty gas can and grab it. Than a game warden jumps in with a life jacket and they haul me out, put a couple of blankets over me. We stay out there a long time and the Inter-Tribal boats come out, too. They crisscross that place, but no Jimmy."

Willis tied his shoes and went over to the window. "Later on, when I got back here, I had to call his mother. After I told her, that's when I felt the cold, like it was me lying on the riverbottom." He folded the blanket and put it at the foot of the cot. "Still can't get warm, and I keep taking these naps. Seems like I'm always tired now."

Danny stood and walked over to the table where Willis was making fans. He ran his fingertips across the beaded handle of a swan fan.

"I always wear tennis shoes," Willis said, "even though my feet get wet and cold. You can kick off tennis shoes. But that boy wore his gum boots. Anyway, he was probably knocked out cold from the impact." Willis lit another cigarette. "I can't go on that river for a year, now that I lost that boy. If you don't treat that river right, nothing comes back, even the fish. That's why the salmon runs were down so long. Young people, they never followed the old ways. I've got to stay away a year now out of respect. After that, I'll sweat and get out the impurities. Then have a big give-away and a feast."

"That should do it," Danny said.

Willis went over to the window again. His lips moved, and Danny thought he was counting cars in the parking lot. "How many showed up today?" he asked.

"Eighty people. Maybe ninety." There had to be twice that many windsurfing.

"I got to get down there. Say some words. Damn, but it's hard." Willis's expression changed, and for a moment, Danny thought the old man was going to cry. "Sometimes I think if I had kept payment in my pocket, the boy might still be here. You ever hear about that fisherman they called the Duck?"

"I don't think so."

"Some say he was almost as old as the river. When I was a boy, he was the oldest man I had ever seen — long white braids — but he could still fish with the best of them, there at Celilo. When his eyes turned milky and his legs went bad, he carried wampum in his shirt pocket. Said if he ever fell in, he'd pay the river off quick and get right back out."

"Indian insurance," Danny said, and Willis laughed.

"Sure enough, one day a big Chinook — one of those June Hogs — swam into his hoopnet. He was thrown off balance and plunged into the water, right there at the Horseshoe where the falls churned back under itself.

"Someone ran quick to get his wife. She was Yakima, younger than him, with firm legs, and she hurried to the platform and threw a bundle into the water.

"He still had good lungs, that old man, and he had taken a deep breath when he fell." Willis crushed out his cigarette. "Later he said that the water swept him way back under the falls, where the churning calmed and things were almost quiet. Some light still came through and he opened his eyes. Everything was shades of gray under there, he said. What do you think he saw?"

"I don't know," Danny said. "Salmon, maybe."

Willis nodded. "Thousands of them. June Hogs. Those big Chinooks that used to go a hundred pounds. They swam right by him, like they were curious about him, what he was doing there.

"Then he heard a high chanting — not the deep booming of water crashing over the falls but another sound, like the falls were singing. He opened his mouth to sing, too, but the water rushed in, nearly drowning him.

"Right then, he remembered the wampum, so he ripped open his shirt pocket and held out the shells. Old Man snatched them away, and the current swept him out from under the falls. He banged against the rocks, but they were worn smooth by the boiling water, so he just pushed away from them as the river carried him farther downstream.

"He felt like a hand carried him through the foam and sent him swirling in a little back eddy. Two dipnetters on the rocks went popeyed when he surfaced, but they put their nets out for him and brought him ashore."

"He must have been pretty powerful," Danny said.

"You bet he was powerful. He swore it was the payment he kept in his pocket, but his wife said he was too ornery for the river to keep. Claimed she got stuck with him. You know, the funny thing is, he fell in that water twice and survived."

"Do you think what he said about the salmon and the singing was true?"

Willis shrugged. "Nobody else was ever under there to say yes or no. But everyone believed him because that old man had respect."

"Jack's watching the windsurfers. When he gets back, you've got to tell him about the Duck."

"Okay. These young people need to learn the old stories." Willis took an orange ribbon shirt from the closet and started putting it on. "Velrae, she doesn't care much for the old stories, but Jimmy, he'd listen. Of course, stuck with me way out in the boat, he didn't have much choice."

"So what are you planning to do now?"

Willis put on a beaded blue cap that said YAKIMA NATION. "Times are going to be pretty thin. I was counting on fishing — still got that old green tri-hull they made on the reservation. It's not pretty, but it floats." He shook his head. "But I can't go on that river for a year. Velrae — she'd go — but I won't let her."

"You're right," Danny said. He knew that after Red Shirt and Loxie died, he should have followed the old customs. Now, he could at least help Willis out. "Maybe I should look at that tri-hull."

"You know anything about fishing?"

Danny grinned. "Wear tennis shoes."

"That's a good start," Willis said. "If you want to help out, I can show you the basic stuff pretty fast. The fish are running real good, so you have to catch something. But you need at least two people to handle the motor and the nets."

"There's Jack, if I can convince him. He'll do about anything for money."

Willis clapped his hands on his knees. "This is sounding pretty good. Hey, you know why a fish buyer puts a metal tray under the scales?"

Danny nodded. "So if you stick railroad spikes or rocks down the salmon's throat, he'll hear the clang. I thought everyone knew that old trick."

Willis grinned. "In the old days we used to wrap those spikes with burlap. Sometimes we fooled them. But when the Chinese butchers ruined their knives belly-cutting fish, they shouted louder than the cannery machinery."

After he and Willis worked out plans for fishing, Danny found Jack over by the broken boat. The boy was running his lean brown hands over it, pausing to feel the shredded fiberglass as if he were touching a wound. He picked a fiberglass shred off his finger. Glancing up, he saw Danny. "Velrae told me how it happened."

"I don't see her around."

Jack nodded toward the beach. "She said she was going for a long walk. Wants to be alone for a while."

"She seemed anxious to see you."

Jack wiped his hands on his pants. "I tried talking with her a little, but she didn't have much to say. Still busted up, I guess."

"Willis, too." Danny took a step closer to the boy. "He won't go near the water, now that he lost his grandson."

"He doesn't have a boat, anyway. Look at this thing." Jack tapped the broken hull with his knuckles. "It's a miracle anybody survived. Think he's got insurance?"

"Are you kidding? Nobody insures Indians." Danny pointed to the drab green reservation tri-hull tied to the floating dock. It was an odd-looking boat with a blunt nose and blocky shape. "Willis says it floats."

"That boat's been hit by the ugly stick. I've seen better-looking garbage cans, but if Willis wants to fish with it, that's his business."

"I already told you — Willis is respecting the old ways and won't go fishing for a year, until after Jimmy's memorial."

"Tough luck," Jack said, his eyes narrowing a little. "The runs are good, I hear. Maybe he can get one of his relatives to help out."

Danny shook his head slowly. "They're all busy. But Willis and I were talking."

Jack threw up his hands. "Wait a minute. I read you like a book. You want to drag me into fishing. No way, José."

"Hold on," Danny said. "We'd be helping Willis out and making a little money for ourselves. It beats orchard work."

Jack took a quick look around the camp. "Anyway, where would we stay? We can't move our trailer down here because the tires are flat."

"Willis said we could bunk in that little travel trailer. There's even a stove." The way Jack's eyes shifted away from the trailer, Danny knew he thought it looked pretty rough. Sections of the rust-colored paint had chipped away, revealing scabby patches that resembled a dog with mange.

"I don't think so," Jack said quietly. "Just take a good look around."

The Indian fishing boats were all covered with dried mud and slime, so in spite of their original color, they had a brownish-green hue, the color of bad teeth. Trash filled the unusable boats, derelict cars, and Neptune fish totes. The garbage consisted primarily of fast-food wrappers, soft drink cans, and motor oil containers, although there was also an assortment of discarded clothes and two smashed television sets.

"Get Que to help you," Jack said. "He'd take to this place."

"Que's not reliable," Danny said. "Come on and give it a try. In two weeks, you'll be bucks up and go back to school with fancy clothes." Another idea came into his head. "Maybe you can buy a good used car," he suggested. "Tell people you hit a couple late rodeos in the Dakotas, and everybody will think you came back a big winner. No one cares where the money came from once it's in your pocket."

Jack looked out at the river. The float lines from several nets were in view, their inner-tube and Clorox-bottle buoys shifting with the wind. "What do you figure I'd make?"

"Lots and lots," Danny said, exaggerating. "Willis gets seventy percent and we split the rest. That's fifteen percent each."

Jack chewed his lower lip. "Doesn't seem like much."

"It's pure profit," Danny said. "We already got a place to stay, and maybe we can talk Velrae into cooking a little, since we're kind of helping her out, too."

Jack rubbed his chin. "I could sure use a good car, and there's no way to scratch a payment together around Pendleton."

"That's right," Danny said. "We're not talking McDonald's wages here. Four thousand Chinooks are going over Bonneville each day, and Willis says three quarters are upriver brights. They're bringing in about two dollars a pound, and I figure we can catch a half ton a day. Now you figure fifteen percent."

Jack smiled as he did the calculations. "I could buy a car."

"Sure thing," Danny said. "Three hundred bucks a day for a couple of weeks. That beats lunchmeat." He felt a little bad not telling Jack that inferior tules or "dogfish" — spawning salmon, which brought a much lower price than brights — would make up a larger amount of the catch soon. Nor did he tell him that prices might drop drastically when the white gillnetters below Bonneville Dam put in their nets, sweeping the lower river clean of fish and glutting the markets. What he claimed was true just for now, but that was good enough, he figured.

Looking directly at Danny, Jack folded his arms. "How do I know you won't gouge me?"

Danny scooped up a handful of gravel and started tossing the pieces, one by one, into the water. "Just check the fish tickets. It's easy enough to keep track." He never saw anyone so fussy about money, except perhaps Pudge. Jack must take after his aunt, Danny thought.

"So you think Velrae will be sticking around, too, huh?"

"Trouble never takes the first bus," Danny said.

Split lengthwise, two fifty-five-gallon barrels made four grills. Each grill was filled with alder coals and briquets. Salmon steaks sizzled on the racks. Larger pieces of salmon were wrapped in aluminum foil. The women turned the larger pieces from time to time, revealing the brown underside of the foil. The wonderful smell reminded Danny of the Celilo longhouse feasts. This wasn't as big an operation, but it was a good one.

Large jars of potato salad cooled in washtubs filled with cracked ice. Smaller jars held blue-black huckleberries. Danny couldn't imagine how anyone saved enough huckleberries for a feast like this. As a child he had tried picking, but he managed to cover only the bottom of the wooden hallocks because he kept stuffing the delicious berries into his mouth. The other children ate the berries, too, and when they laughed, their teeth and gums were stained. It had taken Danny several days to wash the sweet-smelling stains off his hands.

Plywood sheets placed on sawhorses functioned as serving tables. They held pans of cornbread covered with Saran Wrap and a huge sheet cake. Its white icing was decorated with blue waves and leaping salmon. Large red letters said: FREE ORVILLE SALWISH.

Some of the women had laid out jewelry on the scrubbed tables — earrings, necklaces, watchbands, bracelets. Danny admired the craftwork of a few Klickitat baskets. Examining the jewelry, he picked up a blue and red watchband with yellow crosses.

"That one's twenty dollars," a young girl said. She was wearing a pair of black glasses, taped across the bridge, and her left eye drifted a little to the side.

"It's good work, but I don't have a watch." Danny set the watchband on the table. Glancing up, he saw a flicker of disappointment cross the girl's face. "How long did you work on this, anyway?"

She shrugged. "I don't know exactly. A long time. My grandmother showed me how to do those crosses."

Danny touched his billfold. "Will you take fifteen? Maybe I'll buy a watch pretty soon."

"It's been kind of slow," she said. "Otherwise I'd stick to twenty."

He took out a ten and a five, and she tucked the money into her pants pocket. "I've been saving up for a Walkman. Got almost enough now, if I buy it in Portland." She helped him strap the band on his wrist. "It looks pretty good. Sort of like a bracelet."

Willis had come out and was talking to some of the women cooking the salmon. The oldest was Etta Salwish, Orville's wife. After conferring with the cooks, Willis turned on a Port-a-Mike and started talking.

"I want to thank all of you here today for coming," he said. "We got some friends here that aren't Indians, and they're welcome, too."

Danny glanced at the white people. Except for the lawyer, who wore a light suit and yellow tie, they all resembled hippies or retired schoolteachers.

"You know they got my son Orville in prison for catching them salmon, and we're trying to raise some money to help him out. They stuck him way down in Lompoc, and when his wife, Etta, drove south to see him, her car engine blew up, so there's some more expense. Seems like trouble piles on trouble." Willis shifted his gaze so he was looking over the heads of the people and off toward the river. "Some of you knew Jimmy pretty well. The Old Man took him two weeks ago, and they wouldn't even let Orville out for his service. They won't let him take traditional foods, either, just the prison food. Some of you remember what that's like."

Most of the old men sat stone-faced, but a few young men smirked. Danny saw the anguished look on Etta's face.

Willis continued. "We got us a good lawyer here working on bringing Orville back to Yakima Court, where he can be tried by his own people. They know why Orville was fishing and how it's part of his religion. As far as we're concerned, that federal court trial wasn't even legal. He should be tried in Yakima Court because we got us a treaty that says we're a sovereign nation. But the U.S. government's not honoring that treaty they signed."

Willis pointed at the river and the shoreline, moving his hands so they indicated all of the site. "You know our treaty guarantees we can fish in all the usual and accustomed places. Well, they took away some of the best places when they built Bonneville Dam and flooded them. They promised to give us four hundred acres in lieu sites, but more than fifty years later, we still got only forty. When they built The Dalles Dam, drowning Celilo Falls, we got rooked on that deal, too. Not to mention Hanford and all the radioactive crap it's dumping in our river. Over the years, a lot of our people been pushed off the river, and they're still trying to push us."

He held up a sheet of paper. "This is the Bureau of Indian Affairs Eviction Notice. Another one's tacked onto Orville's place down at Cook's. I guess they'll try bulldozing these houses again, but not without a fight this time."

A few of the younger people whistled and someone banged a drum.

Willis held up his hand. "When they get us all pushed off the river, maybe they can build more places for the tourists and windsurfers. Maybe they can put up a nice little museum here with statues and pictures, so the gawkers can see what Indians once were like. They'll have to carve wooden salmon, too, because the Creator said when the old-timers quit catching His fish, He'll quit sending them."

Everybody nodded at that and Willis smiled. "Now I've been going on too long here, and Etta keeps signaling for me to quit because the fish is cooked. First, though, the lawyer wants to say a few words about legal stuff. Then we can eat."

The lawyer talked about broken promises, Orville's arrest, and finally the BIA notices, but Danny wasn't listening to him. Instead, he heard water sounds that reminded him of voices the wind carried through the high Wallowa timber. After mountain elk hunts, the old men gathered around the campfires, their faces bright with the flames' glow. Passing the bottle, they told stories. But when the wind blew, tossing the pines' high, dark branches, they listened, for the wind told stories. Now, Danny knew the water carried stories, too, tales that started high in the mountains with the spring snow-melt. He listened, but not to the lawyer's words, because the white men changed their words or claimed they meant something differ-ent from what they signed in the treaties. But the voices of wind and water never changed, so Danny listened to the waves lapping shore rocks.

◈ 9 ◈

FISHING

WILLIS POINTED AT A submerged sandbar a hundred yards off the Columbia's Washington side. The shallow water over the bar appeared a milky light blue-green. From his vantage on the basalt bluff of Preacher's Point, Danny strained his eyes, wondering if he could see the salmon resting in the quiet water above the sandbar. He blinked from the brightness of the light, and when his eyes filled, he wiped them with his shirtsleeve.

"Maybe with Polaroids," Willis said, "but even then you'd have to have good eyes. My brother Oscar had eyes like that. He flew dive bombers out of Pearl Harbor in the Second World War. All day long he stared into the ocean looking for subs. Jap Steelhead, he called them. His eyes were brown when he left for the air force, but hazel when he came back. I guess staring at the bright water changed them."

"Where is he now?" Danny asked. He had never known anyone whose eyes had changed colors, and he wondered if he could meet Oscar sometime.

Willis picked a blade of coarse grass that grew on the bluff and stuck it between his teeth. "That's one the Old Man kept. He was drinking and running nets one night off Preacher's Point. A Tidewater barge ran over his boat, but we never found him."

The wind blew harder, and Danny tugged on his cap to keep it from blowing away. "We use a four-hundred-foot net on this set,"

Willis said. "Big Smokey. It takes a long time to run, but it's worth it. Coming off that sandbar, the fish cluster up. Sometimes that net gets so heavy you can hardly work it over the bow."

Danny nodded. His arms and back ached just thinking about the work.

"You hook the net to that cable." Willis pointed to a steel cable anchored in the basalt. One end had a hook and eye for attaching the net. "Put a couple of thirty-pound rocks on the lead line. Sixty pounds should hold the net down the right depth."

"Where do I get them?"

"Anywhere along the river," Willis said. "Or walk the track. And when you make the night run, it doesn't hurt to race the boat over that sandbar a couple of times. I think it spooks the fish toward the net."

"They move pretty good at night?" Danny asked.

"Around ten or eleven, they start moving upstream again, I don't know why."

The east wind started blowing stronger and a few whitecaps appeared on the water. Danny gripped his cap.

Willis found a little depression on top of the bluff and motioned for Danny to sit. "On the water, you'll lose that cap. Maybe you should wrap a bandanna around your head. I've got gum boots, rubber gloves, and a slicker. The buttons are taped over, so nothing catches the net. Don't wear rings or watchbands."

Willis leaned back and folded his hands behind his head. "Out of the wind, that sun feels good. I could fall asleep, just like an old cat." He rolled over and opened one eye. "When my old man fished here, I used to sleep right in this spot. All kinds of flowers bloom in the spring. Rock lilies and bluebells come first. Later on, the balsam root and lupine. It smells so good. Back then, I'd watch the boats on the river, the people fishing. Sometimes I'd practice braiding. Made my first belt right here."

"Why do they call it Preacher's Point?" Danny asked.

Willis got a crafty look. "Missionaries preached here. They used this bluff as a pulpit to spout off to the Indians gathered below. The River People knew this was a spiritual place, but the missionaries claimed the devil worked here, and they preached to frighten him off."

"So what do you know about it?" Danny asked.

Willis chewed the grassblade a moment longer while he thought. "When I came out of the armed service, this was a disputed site. A Warm Springs guy claimed it, too, and he kept trying to crowd out my dad. So I netwatched — slept on the bluff overlooking the river with a sleeping bag and a .30-.30. I was still drinking back then — I said it was because of Oscar — but I never got so drunk I couldn't keep track of the nets. The first night I heard voices down by the nets, I thought somebody was renegading — you know, stealing fish. So I crept to the edge of the bluff, ready to fire a couple of warning shots over their heads. Snapping on the flashlight, I pointed it right toward those voices. Nothing. I played the light all over the water, looking for a boat. Still nothing. After that, I realized what it was — the Old People. I crawled back in my sleeping bag and stayed put. In twenty minutes or so I heard them murmuring again, but I just pretended to ignore them."

"I'll bet they camped all along this river," Danny said.

Willis nodded. "My father said they drew pictures on the basalt cliffs, like at Wakemap. Before the water covered them, he copied a lot of those pictures. He showed me once: fish, animals, Water Devils. After the spring floods, he'd find stuff the Old People had left — pipestone, whalebone clubs, trinkets, some of those special speartips they used for fishing. At night they'd spear fish by torchlight." He shook his head. "A few times when I'd hear those voices coming from way down in the water, I'd see lights down there, pretty deep. But maybe it was the reflections of shore lights. Lights on water do funny things, especially at night."

"Did your father hear the voices too?" Danny said.

"Sure. When that happened, he went on to a different net and came back later to check this one. Once he said he heard Oscar. That's the only time he let this net wait overnight. And the next morning it was so full of fish, they filled the boat."

Danny shook his head. "No kidding."

"Those voices keep talking, but they don't usually mean any harm. People been living on this river a long time. Some of us plan to keep living here."

Danny knew that for the River People time was indistinct, so the past and present blurred. In the Wallowa Mountains, the Old

Dreamers performed the ceremonies to establish continuity. On the Columbia River, the people had their ceremonies, too. For the Dreamers, the elk held things together; here it was the salmon.

"When I was a kid, we lived at Celilo," Willis said. "The Old Ones there were plenty scary. They'd come near the camp at night, and it wasn't their voices I feared. It was the sound of their shoes. Wet shoes with water sloshing when they walked. So many people had fallen into the water and drowned. The bad ones came back and tried to lure the young people down to the river. You can bet I stayed right by the fire, with my arms tucked around my knees. Whenever I acted up or got out of hand, my mother used to point to me and say, 'Wet Shoes,' and that's all I needed to straighten out real quick." He shook his head. "Some young people made fun of the Wet Shoes or went down to the water too soon after they'd come around. Those people didn't last too long — car wrecks, drowning, suicide."

Danny knew the kind of young people he meant. In the Washat service they always danced too fast, ahead of the leader's bell. "Red Shirt scared me with Sasquatch," Danny said. "Sometimes when he'd show me one of those big cornhusk bags the old Nez Perce women made, he said it was a Sasquatch bag — just the right size for children. He had a bunch of Sasquatch stories but always told one about the big ugly sisters who carried children way off into the woods and ate them. That's why those bags were big enough to carry a child. You can bet I didn't go wandering off much."

Danny was quiet then, and he half expected Willis to say more about the river spirits or Water Devils, but he didn't. Willis could be like an old cat sometimes, cautious and secretive. He'd never tell Danny everything, just enough to keep him curious.

A couple of sportfishermen passed the point and then they saw a fast boat on the far side of the river. It was the Oregon Fish and Game Department's Jet-Sled, the fastest boat on the Columbia. The wardens were coming down from Memaloose Island toward Mosier and every so often they stopped.

"Checking the nets, I guess," Willis said. "Making sure everybody's got his net tagged right." The boat left the site and roared downriver toward the next net. "They probably started at The Dalles and are checking the pool down to Bonneville. That sled's sure fast. It'll outrun any other boat."

"You could give them a run with your new Evinrude," Danny said.

Willis laughed. "For about twenty yards. I put that little Evinrude on because those big old Mercs were keeping me broke. The big motors always go clunk, and they cost more to fix. Damn gashogs, too. I used a tank and a half just to run the nets. The harder I worked, the behinder I got."

"Your old boat seems solid."

"Those tri-hulls they made on the reservation were darn good," Willis said. "I don't know why that plant went broke. Poor management, I guess. It's a good thing a few of them are still around, though. Stablest boat on the river. The Yakimas got the original design from the Lummis. Puget Sound gets mighty rough."

A couple of windsurfers came into view, their bright sailboards skimming the water like paper boats.

"They're not paying any attention to those nets," Willis said. "They'll hit the cork line and foul it up — jiggle the net just when a fish is about to go in. Sometimes I'd like to sit up here with a rifle and make it hot for them."

"I can loan you my .30-.06," Danny said. "You could sink them with that."

"I think a varmint rifle is about right for those pests."

As Danny and Willis watched, the windsurfers tacked so they were approaching the small island on the Oregon side, just downstream from Mosier.

"That was my grandfather's island once," Willis said. "He was chased off in the early thirties. Shotgun deed. Now the people who live there actually think they inherited it fair and square from their relatives. Same with those people who planted their orchards on Indian land. Short memories."

He tossed a loose rock into the water. "I've talked with those island people a few times. They stand on the dock and try buying fish off me. Let 'em catch their own. But I wish I had that island now — it's nice and secluded. The wardens couldn't keep such close tabs on my place. Since they put Orville in jail, it seems like they're watching me all the time."

"How do you think that's going to turn out?"

"The feds had no jurisdiction, really. If we get him into tribal court, he's got a chance." Willis smiled a little. "I heard the cops spent a quarter-million dollars catching Orville. They even practiced raiding an old fish hatchery up near Mount Saint Helens. Different ones took turns pretending to be Orville. When they finally got it right, they busted into his place with twelve cop cars and a seaplane. They arrested Orville, and they terrorized his family. The government sure knows where to spend money."

Danny shook his head. "Twelve cop cars and a seaplane. You'd think he was selling bomb secrets to the Russians."

Willis held three fingers. "Three years just for selling a few salmon. They only gave that Rajneeshee woman five years for trying to poison the whole town of The Dalles. Anyway, it's Orville's religion to fish. The Creator sends the fish and Orville keeps catching them. He will keep sending more as long as Orville stays faithful and practices the old ways."

"Do you really think the Creator sends fish because Orville and some of the other old-timers catch them according to the old ways?"

Willis squinted at Danny, as if surprised he had even asked the question. "When the first fish comes up the river every spring, you have to treat it right — say some words over it and lay it on the rocks with its head pointing upstream so others can follow. It's always been that way on this river. In the old days, the men got their spears and nets and waited on the platforms. Some listened to the old singing river channel because its voice changed pitch when the fish came upriver. My father said they'd first see the fish way off downriver. Gulls wheeled overhead, and in the water, the salmon gleamed like ribbons of light."

"Put Big Smokey just above Preacher's Point," Willis said. "It's a killer net because the Japs make the webbing out of supercrystal, like Trilene. It just about disappears when it hits the water, and the fish swim in like churchgoers on Sunday."

Danny nodded. Taking its name from the gray tint of the six-strand nylon webbing, Big Smokey was four hundred feet long with nine-inch mesh, sixty units deep. Willis gave all his nets nicknames: Big Smokey, Little Smokey, Backstop, Blondie and Little Blondie, Frog (named for its green tint), and the Sub. While the others were floaters, with their cork lines visible above the water, the Sub was a diving net, designed to lie close to the riverbottom.

Its "floats" were made from hard black rubber so the water pressure a hundred feet beneath the surface wouldn't collapse them. When the water temperature rose or the surface chop calmed over several days, the salmon tended to congregate near the bottom, and the diving net caught more fish than all the floating nets combined. In addition, it was difficult to detect, so the fish and game officers never knew exactly how many nets Willis had out or their exact locations. Willis told Danny that he planned to buy some more divers with the season's profits.

Danny and Jack were standing in the boat, folding the nets onto the bottom. Willis and Velrae worked beside the boat, unfolding the nets from the blue plastic tarps the fishermen favored and handing the lead line to Jack, the float line to Danny. Now and again, Willis stopped to untangle the mesh or pick out seaweed strands that might scare off the wary salmon. Since this was a calm day, they could load all seven nets at once, separating them in the boat's bottom with the bright plastic tarps. When the water turned rough, they would carry four nets the first load, three the second.

Once the boat was loaded, Danny and Jack took the nets to the designated fishing sites and attached the cork lines to the wire cables sunk in shore rocks or to the white Styrofoam blocks that served as buoys. After attaching one end of a float line, Danny slowly backed the boat toward another buoy while Jack played out the net, taking care not to cross the float line with the lead line. In the water, the heavy lead line sank, stretching the mesh net to its full depth. With calm weather, it took between twenty minutes and half an hour to set each net. When whitecaps knuckled the surface, it might take twice that long.

"Great work," Danny said after they put out three nets. "Just taking a little boat ride while the salmon swim into our nets. That's easy money."

"Easy for you, maybe," Jack said. "My arm feels like it's made of rubber. I must have put out a quarter mile of lead line."

"Before long, your hands will hang below your knees," Danny said.

They laid out Big Smokey at the bluff where Willis had talked about the Wet Shoes, and Danny's neck tingled a little, thinking about Willis's stories. He watched the basalt rock column disappear into the gray-green water and he wondered how deep the Old

People's pictures were. Even in the daytime the place gave him an eerie feeling.

"What are you gawking at?" Jack said. "You look like you're about to fall out of the boat."

Danny made a note to pick up the fish here in twilight. He didn't like the idea of being around the site in the dark. If he mentioned the old stories to Jack, the boy would just laugh and call him superstitious.

Jack was halfway through playing out the Frog by the Dynamite Shack when he turned to Danny. "I think you're going to have to take over. My arms are cramping."

Danny put the motor in neutral. "Let's not trip over the net while we swap places." He and Jack moved carefully past one another in the boat, and Danny slipped on the soft rubber fisherman's gloves they used to handle the nets. "Go slow, now."

When Jack put the motor in reverse, he gunned it, and Danny tipped against the front of the boat, catching his arm in the webbing. "For Christ's sakes. You trying to drown me on a milk run?"

"Sorry." Jack looked sheepish. "I didn't realize it had this much power."

"That's a two-thousand-dollar motor," Danny said. "But when this boat's loaded with fish and we're nose into the wind, it'll seem powered by a rubber band."

After putting out Frog, they set Blondie and Little Blondie near the Spring Creek Fish Hatchery. Even though the tule fish caught nearby would bring low prices, Willis said some upriver brights followed the spawning tules, so it was still a good place.

On the way back to camp, Danny had time to study the sides of the Columbia Gorge. Some of the scrub oaks had started to turn doe-brown and a few vine maples were already tipped with crimson. He liked the fall's cool days and crisp nights because he seemed to get another burst of energy. September always signaled the Round-Up, and after that he enjoyed hunting along the reservation ridges, where the fallen leaves' earthy smell lingered on the cool air and startled coveys of mountain quail exploded from the thickets. He'd get out Red Shirt's old pump shotgun, he decided, and fry up some quail in the cast-iron skillet.

· · ·

The catch seemed to always depend on the light. They would run the nets just before daybreak each morning and again after dark, usually finishing past midnight. During the day, the swimming fish might detect the nets and avoid them, but after dark they could no longer discern the webbing. Danny quickly learned that a gray day meant better fishing and a bright moon signaled a poor catch.

For most of the runs, Danny drove the boat while Jack pulled in the lead line and float line together, drawing them across the center of the boat and disentangling the salmon. Usually, the mesh strands had snagged their gills, so they suffocated without damaging the net, but some of the smaller fish struggled through the mesh, weaving sections in and out until they became hopelessly tangled and broke nylon squares as Jack struggled to free them.

Cursing and complaining, Jack and Danny would flop the lead line over the cork line, trying to free the trapped fish. Their efforts popped nylon strands, ruining sections of the net, but the salmon were running heavy, leaving no time for repair, so they tried to minimize the damage and get the torn nets back in the water.

When a salmon was barely hooked, perhaps caught by its teeth or a fin, they gaffed it before it slipped free, the dead fish sliding from the net toward the riverbottom. A lost fish meant as much as a fifty-dollar waste, and Danny took satisfaction in knowing they didn't miss many. They gaffed the tangled sturgeon, too, sometimes out of quick anger, because these sharp-buttoned fish shredded the nets. Less than half the ones they caught were legal — four to six feet — and Danny thought dealing with sturgeon was a waste of time when the salmon were running. Moreover, it unnerved him to see how long the sturgeons lived out of water, their primitive slitted mouths opening and closing hours after they had been weighed at the fish buyers' scale and packed in ice. Danny had heard stories about gutted sturgeons somehow managing to swim off into deep water, leaving their entrails on the banks for the gulls and swarming flies.

If the river was calm, Danny helped Jack pull in the nets, but when the wind stirred whitecaps, he stayed at the wheel, keeping the boat steady while Jack struggled to keep his balance and preserve the catch. On a bad night, they might lose a gaff or spotlight, so they carried spares.

With the wind whipping stinging water into his face, Jack often avoided picking the net clean of seaweed and river gunk, but a dirty net meant a sparse catch the following day, so Danny had to shout sharp reminders into the blow.

Jack would cast furious glances over his shoulder and mutter words the wind snatched away. Looking sullen, the boy kicked his gumboots at the big Chinooks underfoot and flung strands of seaweed over the gunwales.

Danny couldn't complain about the money they made from commercial fishing, but it was hard work. Sometimes, as they approached the nets, the floats were bobbing with the struggles of a recently netted salmon. Most of the time, the corks were still; the salmon had already drowned and become dead weights, dragging at the float line. Danny preferred sportfishing with a spinning pole and lures, giving the fish a chance to fight and spit the hook. Now he avoided looking at the salmon opening and closing their gills, suffocating on the boat's bottom.

The best fishing he had ever seen had been in the Deschutes, during August, when they used molting crawdads for bait. Delbert Nooksak, who had moved from Warm Springs to Pendleton his sophomore year, showed Danny how. He had a special way of rigging the soft-shelled crawdads on their spinning outfits, then fishing them deep so they bumped along the bottom of the long drifts. He and Danny caught the thick, rainbow-sided Deschutes trout and cooked them along the river after rolling them in cornmeal. Fish had never tasted better. After they ate, they sat in the shade of junipers while Delbert bragged about the women he had known. He combed his long hair so a spitcurl lay across his forehead, and he smiled in a smirky way the women thought was sexy. Everyone said he looked like Fabian.

Delbert, Henry, and Danny played basketball together their senior year — the only Indians left on the Pendleton team. Delbert had an uncanny two-handed set shot, and he sunk six in a row at the district tournament. After each shot he'd run down the court, holding one arm in the air and smiling at the opposing cheerleaders.

The spring of their senior year, Delbert built a platform at Shearer's Bridge and dipnetted. One night he fell into the water. They spread a net for him at the Boxcar Hole, just below Sinamox. When Danny and Henry learned Delbert was in the water, they drove over from Pendleton and kept a vigil by the net. One watched while the other drove to the Tygh Valley General Store for sodas and supplies. They talked quietly about Delbert's basketball talent and his luck with women. When Henry got bored, he tied pieces of bologna on strings and fished for crawdads. After they seized the meat with their claws, Henry slowly pulled them onto land, then tormented them awhile, finally squeezing off their pincers and tossing them back in the river.

The sheriff from Sherman County showed up each evening to see if Delbert had come to the net. He'd pull on it a little, but it was too light. The fourth evening, it was heavy. "I think we've got our boy," the sheriff said, so they dragged in the net. Delbert had one arm tangled and he seemed to be waving. Danny expected to see the smile, but the crawdads had eaten away Delbert's face, and he could have been anybody. Henry puked in the sagebrush while Danny helped the sheriff get Delbert zipped into the rubber body bag. Danny took shallow breaths, trying to ignore the stench of fetid water that ran from Delbert's clothes and shoes. The letterman's jacket seemed too small for the bloated body.

Now, as Danny pulled in the nets and saw the white flash of salmon bellies, he closed his eyes, fearful they would catch a drowned windsurfer or another fisherman.

After Danny and Jack ran the nets each morning, three different fish buyers waited for them near the boat landing. Some of the fishermen had been selling to Neptune for years, but an Indian corporation, Grizzly Spirit Seafoods, was starting to compete with them. They had installed a fish-buying station at Celilo, where the volume was heavier, but were late getting to the Wind River site because one of their refrigerator trucks had broken down.

Velrae wanted to do business with Indians, and Danny hoped they were paying a good price. Most fishermen wouldn't sell to their own mothers if someone else paid a nickel more per pound. As Willis said, "During fish season, there are no blood relatives." When it turned out that Grizzly Spirit was paying two dollars a pound for bright Chinooks, everyone was pleased — except the Neptune buyer, who stood at one-ninety.

Danny and Jack would put on rubber gloves to help grip the slippery fish they unloaded, carrying them two at a time up the boat ramp to the scale. Each time, the buyer's boy helped them. A lean, freckled kid with the reddish-brown hair of a mixed-blood, he wore a Black Sabbath T-shirt that smelled ranker as the season progressed. The smaller fish he carried without flinching, but whenever he lifted one of the forty-pound Chinooks, he grunted, "Hell-bent for hernias."

They would pile the brights in a white plastic tub suspended from a two-thousand-pound Salter scale with a dial resembling a clock's face. When the tub was full — twenty fish or so — the weight was around five hundred pounds. If the buyer suspected one of the salmon of being an inferior tule, with the extended jaw and drab color of a spawner, he'd nod at the boy, and the kid would unsheath his hunting knife, first slitting the flesh just in front of the tail, then checking to see if the meat was red. The gills turned gray if the fish had been in the net a long time, but the red meat indicated a choice fish still, while white meat meant the fish was old, suitable only for smoking or catfood.

Danny was surprised the boy cut behind the backbone, thus ruining a filet, rather than under the fish by the tail, and each time he did it Willis shook his head, but the buyer didn't seem to pay attention.

Willis always watched the fish count carefully, correcting the boy if he missed the correct number of salmon, because he wanted the fish tickets made out right. On weight, the buyer was never off, and he bumped up partial pounds as a gesture of goodwill. He used a pocket calculator to add the totals. Steelhead were paying a dollar-ten a pound and sturgeon a dollar-sixty. Willis doublechecked every figure with a pencil and yellow legal paper.

Danny liked dealing with the Grizzly Spirit buyers because all their equipment was new. Their totes were dazzling white, and the orange Toyota forklift they used to hoist the loaded totes onto the refrigerator trucks was brand-new, too. The scoop shovels had unnicked hickory handles and smooth gray plastic heads.

Best of all, Danny liked the money. The buyer paid in crisp

hundreds and fifties, so new they stuck together, and Willis always counted twice. Strips of yellow paper bound the packets of ten hundreds. Blue paper marked the fifties' packets. After a good day and the split with Willis, Danny and Jack might each pocket between three and four hundred dollars.

"Easy money," Jack said. "Not like orchard work. These fish smell like cash."

Danny was only sorry it wouldn't last. "What are you figuring to pay next week?" he asked the buyer when he heard that gill netting season was opening below Bonneville Dam for the whites. As soon as they dropped their nets and swept the river, prices would plummet. It wasn't a shortage of fish; plenty of salmon remained in the pools above the dam. The problem was market glut.

The buyer squinted at Danny. "I'm trying to hold it at a dollar-fifty, but it could drop lower."

Willis nodded. "I've seen it go below a dollar when there are this many fish."

Jack whistled softly. "Even for brights?"

"Tules might bring a quarter," Willis said.

"I got a good market," the man said, "so I think my prices will stay fair. What I buy here today is halfway around the world day after tomorrow."

Two men pulled up in a green Dodge SportsVan. Danny had seen them the last few days. Even though they looked white and had aqua blue eyes, they had Yakima fishing numbers. The fish they unloaded had wrinkled skins in spite of the soaked gunny sacks used to cover them. They had driven down from the McNary pool, losing time and gas money, because they thought the Grizzly Spirit prices were worth it.

The kid took one of their big Chinooks out of the plastic tub and turned it so his father could see the deep gash in its side. He frowned. "Can't use it."

"Maybe a prop caught it," Blue Eyes said.

The buyer took a closer look. "Sea lion, I think. It's a wound. Anyway, I won't take it."

"Shit," Blue Eyes said. "That stinks like your wife." He ran his forefinger under his nose, and the other man punched his shoulder. They wrestled around for a moment, stirring the dust.

It was too bad about the fish. Danny guessed it weighed thirty pounds, so that gash cost them sixty dollars. He peered in the driver's window on the van and saw two fancy beaded roach clips hanging from the visor. "Where'd you get those?"

"Toppenish," Blue Eyes said. "Tribal heritage museum. Don't you know anything about your Indian culture? Someday an anthropologist will get his damn degree cataloguing roach clips."

After the midnight run, Danny's fatigue often seemed to sharpen his senses, although he also knew that could be the mind's trick. His night vision was remarkably good, as Red Shirt's had been before drinking dulled it, and he had learned to read the river by its buoys and lights as well as by the illuminated landmarks along the shore. During the calm days, he had run both sides of the river, memorizing the sites and the placement of other fishermen's nets so he could avoid their float lines in the dark.

At first he made the night runs with the running lights on, but one trip they shorted out, and Danny was surprised at how much better he could read the river without their interference. However, it was also more dangerous, and he listened carefully for the sound of other motors and watched for shadows on the water that might indicate other boats running without lights.

The shore lights near Bingen and Hood River almost dazed him after running in the dark, so he switched on the running lights until he saw he was approaching Wind River, when he turned them off again. Sometimes he'd cut the motor early and slip in quietly, just to check Willis's reactions, but Willis always knew his approach and came out to help unload the fish.

On the bluff overlooking their fish camp was a blue and white trailer occupied by Marvin Tenino and his grandson. They were Yakimas from White Swan, and Willis said they had been using the in lieu site for as long as he had. Marvin had thin white braids that he tied together with leather shoelaces while his son sported a lawn mower GI cut. Their fishing sites were farther downriver, near the Broughton Lumber Company.

Marvin and his grandson always returned earlier than Danny and Jack, and sometimes, as he docked the boat, Danny saw a light burning in each end of their trailer. The middle windows would be dark. Those lights and the dark space in between made him remember coming home from basketball road trips his sophomore year and seeing his father's trailer lit in much the same way.

The semifinals for the state tournament had been in Vale and the team got back very late. After hamburgers and pizza, Danny caught a ride to Mission and walked the rest of the way home. It struck him as odd to see lights burning in both ends of the trailer, and he checked his watch to see if it was past three. It wasn't like Red Shirt to wait up.

His father was asleep at the kitchen table, clutching a foil roll of Tums in his battered fist, a half-drunk pot of coffee beside him. He had a flashlight on the table, but it didn't work because he had let the batteries corrode. His mouth was half open, and Danny saw the chalky flecks that coated his mouth and tongue. At first Danny was surprised not to see a bottle, but when he checked the bathroom, it was there. All the lights in the bedroom were on, too, including the little reading light over the bed. Another empty bottle was beside the bed.

Danny couldn't wake his father completely, but he managed to get him on his feet, and he half carried, half dragged him toward the bedroom. In the middle of the darkened front room, Red Shirt went rigid and started screaming about Night Ghosts. By the time Danny dragged him to the bedroom, his father's eyes were wide with terror. He kept yelling and pointing a shaking finger toward the darkened front room.

Danny slept in his father's bedroom that night on a torn recliner chair. He had had to shove the bed over some to get the chair into the room. From time to time he awakened to his father's shouts.

This Night Ghost business went on for more than a week, and Danny got so jumpy from fatigue that familiar objects began to spook him, too. A jacket thrown over a living room chair seemed ominous. A hat perched on the useless lamp made his flesh crawl.

Finally, Danny sprinkled some rosewater around the trailer, and this calmed Red Shirt a little.

But Red Shirt's health became worse every day. Although Danny forced him to stop drinking, he took on the puffy, bloated look people get when their liver's shot. Looking at his pale reflection in the bathroom mirror one morning, Red Shirt remarked, "Gonna be a white man yet," and when he cut himself shaving, he didn't try to staunch the blood, but let it drip into the sink. "Maybe my eyes will bleed out," he muttered.

Everything Red Shirt ate was white. He drank milk and spooned cottage cheese into his tortured stomach. Danny went to the health food store and got him a special Springfield yogurt made with acidopholus. He ate puffed wheat and rice with milk and sugar.

One time when Danny got home from school, the old man was gone. He had taken all the money he could find, including some cash Danny had saved to buy new track shoes. Danny figured his father had slipped away for one last drunk, and he expected to hear from the state cops anytime. He wondered whether they'd call or show up at the trailer, hats in hand.

After the third week, Red Shirt returned wearing a new red cowboy shirt with coffee stains slopped down the front. "Fucking reservation roads," he said. His color was good and his health seemed much improved. He raved about a Black Face Healer from one of the coast tribes who specialized in curing alcoholics, although he refused to tell Danny anything specific about the ceremonies. Later, Danny heard him chanting words he had never heard before in the back bedroom.

He thought his old man had beaten the devil, and he might have, too, if he hadn't gone back to drinking as soon as he was convinced it wasn't going to kill him just yet.

After his father had wrecked his pickup on a reservation back road and frozen to death, Danny kept all the trailer lights burning for weeks. But that darkened living room bothered him, because those who should have been the centers in his life were gone. Now, running the nets, Danny vowed he would get the lamp fixed when he got back.

He nosed the boat against the dock. Willis was already down and helping tie it up. He glanced at the dozing Jack. "These whippersnappers can't take it."

Danny shook the boy. "Got some fish to carry," he said.

When they were finished unloading the fish, they stumbled toward the trailer and the beds. Jack was so tired, he almost went inside without taking off the slimy fishgear, but he remembered just in time. It got very hot during the day, and Danny didn't want the stench of fishgear in the trailer.

Although he was exhausted, Danny was unable to fall asleep right away. He wandered outside and looked around the camp. By the dock, the goose was asleep, its head tucked under its wing. Glancing up, he saw Tenino's trailer, a light burning on both ends, and he thought again of his father.

◈ 10 ◈

FISHING TROUBLES

THE THIRD WEEK, Big Smokey at Preacher's Point stopped producing a high number of fish. There were fewer fish in the Backstop, too. However, the other nets still yielded good catches, and Danny checked the daily fish count going over Bonneville to make certain it remained high.

"Think some renegade's running the net?" he asked Willis after they had sold the morning's fish.

"Might be," Willis said as he poured himself a cup of coffee. "But the water's slow at the eddy, and if the nets get weedy, that spooks the fish. You boys picking the mesh good?"

"We do great work," Jack said. He was drinking a Pepsi and eating a box of Cracker Jack for breakfast. Now and again he shook the box, looking for the prize.

"When I pick the net, it's squeaky clean," Danny said. "This one" — he nodded at Jack — "doesn't do too bad for a kid."

"I'll bet it's the sportfishermen stealing," Velrae said. "They're always raising trouble. The prices will drop, too, as soon as the white gillnetters sweep the lower river."

Willis sipped his coffee and rubbed his chin. "A few years back I wasn't doing too well with that site, and I kept wondering why. Then one day I hauled in the net and there was a rubber fisherman's glove tangled in the mesh. The best part was, the damn renegade wrote his tribal number on it in waterproof marker, so I knew who'd been stealing my fish."

"The hell," Danny said.

"I thought that guy was a friend of mine, too," Willis said. "We knew each other in school."

"Who'd be dumb enough to put his tribal number on his gloves?" Jack asked. "Especially if he's raiding nets."

"Those gloves get pricey," Willis said. "I guess he didn't want anyone awiping his. Anyway, I kept the glove under the seat in the boat, just waiting for a good time to give it back. Maybe it was a week later, his motor conked out and he was drifting in a pretty bad chop. I tossed him a rope and hauled him to shore. After he said thanks, I reached under the seat and threw the glove at him. 'Here, buddy,' I said. 'I found this floating around.' You should have seen his face. He damn near turned white."

Danny poured himself a half a cup of coffee. He didn't want too much caffeine because he needed to sleep some this morning. "Maybe that guy's renegading again."

"Not him," Willis said. "The old pirate died last year. Coughed a few times like a cat hacking out a hairball and crumpled over. The doctors said cancer gobbled his stomach."

"Plenty more to take his place," Velrae said. "Some of these punks run the river but don't even own a net. You can catch them with your net stretched across their boat and they'll just look past you and say they didn't see your float line until their prop tangled. 'What about those salmon in your boat?' you say. 'We were just fixing to bring them to you,' they say. Not much you can do, unless Inter-Tribal is around."

"It's a big river," Willis said. "They got almost one hundred and fifty miles to patrol with only two boats."

"What do you think we should do?" Danny asked.

"Keep an eye out and ask Inter-Tribal to check around that net more often. If it gets too bad, I guess we'll stick somebody on the bluffs to netwatch at night."

"Some of the sportfishermen use scuba gear to raid," Velrae said. "They swim out from shore, so you don't see a boat or anything. When people think they see seals at night, it's those scuba guys doing a little nightfishing."

"Is that true?" Jack asked. He shook the prize out of the Cracker Jack box and held it up. "Hell, it's a plastic fish." He handed it to Velrae. "Don't say I never gave you anything."

"You hear all kinds of stories," Willis said.

Danny finished his coffee and put the cup in the sink. He stretched, then slapped his cheek a couple of times. "I've got to get some sleep, but I think I'll wash up first. I'm starting to stink so bad I can't stand it."

"You should do the world a favor, too," Velrae said to Jack. "Take a plunge."

. . .

Half a dozen squeezed lemons littered the ground near the river where they washed. Jack had gotten into the habit of squeezing fresh lemon juice on his hands and forearms, attempting to remove the fish smell before he went to town. He had bought some new shirts, too, and kept them wrapped in cellophane. "Everything around here stinks like fish," he said.

Danny had almost gotten used to the smell, although the constant presence of flies bothered him. "Watch out for bears," he kidded. "A near-sighted bear might think you were a big spawner, dark and stinky."

Jack sniffed the towel that hung from a post near the water's edge. "This stinks, too. Somebody ought to do a laundry pretty soon."

"That's right. Why don't you ask Velrae?" Danny was trying to nudge Jack into saying something about her, but the boy kept a poker face.

"Why don't you jam those dirty clothes in a suitcase and bus them up to Pudge?" Jack said. He stripped quickly, then dove into the water.

Danny undressed, ducking behind some gunny sacks they had stretched across a wire for privacy. The government had installed bathroom facilities at the site, but for reasons Danny didn't understand, the facilities were kept chained and padlocked. As a result, the fishermen bathed in the river and used the bright Bishop Port-a-Potties trucked in from Goldendale.

Danny took some soap from the apple box they used to hold toilet items and went into the river. He left his underwear on because he didn't want the sportfishermen and their families to see him naked. The sportfishermen also used the in lieu sites to launch their boats, and Danny resented the sleek boats and new motors, fancy four-wheel-drive rigs, expensive clothes and fishing gear. Some of them wore clothes so new they still had the creases. As they passed Danny and Jack bathing in the river, a few gave them halfhearted waves, but most just seemed to stare beyond them, their eyes hidden by dark aviator glasses.

Watching a few pieces of lemon rind bobbing in the wakes of the passing boats, Danny tried to remember the name of a woman he had known briefly in Alaska. Stella. No, that wasn't it. Estelle. He had called her Estelle Eskimo just to make her angry because she was proud of being Tlingkit. The summer after Loxie had taken off with Jack, Danny had gone to Alaska to seek his fortune and wound up a casual laborer in Sitka. He helped haul furniture for Sitka Freight, laid carpet, painted houses. A few times he was hired out of the longshoremen's hall, if he managed to drag himself there by six in the morning.

He had a room on the top floor of a tenement and shared a doorless hall bathroom with stray cats that sprayed urine on the walls. After a while Danny couldn't stand the stench, so he bought a .22 bolt action single-shot and killed three of the cats with .22 shorts. He sat for hours on the kitchen chair, the hall door propped open, then shot the cats when they went into the bathroom. If he missed, the shorts made dull gray pocks in the cast-iron bathtub, like raindrops falling onto alkali.

The crazy woman below Danny believed the cheap alarm clock he bought to awaken him for longshoremen's hall was actually a sonic weapon designed to coagulate her brain. One morning, clad only in a stained bathrobe, she confronted him on the steps as he stumbled down the dark stairs. She swung at him with a ceremonial fish club, and her screaming woke Estelle, who calmed her down long enough for Danny to pass.

Estelle lived below the crazy woman, sometimes watching out for her while her son was away fishing. She explained to Danny that if the woman's son institutionalized her, she would be placed in faraway Portland or Seattle, making it difficult for him to visit. As a favor, the neighbors kept track of her instead.

Estelle was deep-chested with short arms and legs; she had wide-set hazel eyes and a pretty face, especially when she smiled. Danny never figured out who had fathered her four children, because the men didn't visit. She worked sporadically in the canneries, and while she was gone the older children watched the younger, although sometimes an elderly woman came to help out. Danny understood she was Estelle's aunt, but she never talked to him. Mumbling to herself, she read copies of *The Watchtower* while the kids scrambled through the house and yard.

Estelle's unflagging good nature attracted Danny; she had none of Loxie's aloofness or hostility. After the kids were asleep, Estelle dumped capfuls of lemon-fresh Joy into her bathtub and rinsed ReaLemon through her hair, trying to get rid of the fish smell. Fresh lemons were better, she explained to Danny, but they were so expensive in Sitka, she couldn't afford them. When they made love, the cannery smell lingered under the lemon scent and the musky perfume she splashed on. Sometimes it made Danny sick.

When Estelle wasn't working at the cannery, she cut salmon cheeks from the fishheads in the slop bins or clammed along the rocky beaches. Deep-fried in Crisco, the seafood tasted all right, but the house always smelled of fish. Danny would sometimes awaken at night and sneak out onto the porch just to breathe fresh air.

He liked Estelle. Things were easy with her in spite of all the kids, but he didn't like her enough. Somehow, she couldn't replace Loxie and he resented her for it. One day while she was working he left, taking the ferry to Prince Rupert and hitchhiking south through Canada. A few times since, he had thought about sending her a card, but he never got around to it.

Now he washed and rewashed his arms and hands, working the soap into a fine white lather that clouded the water when he rinsed. He realized that he smelled of fish worse than Estelle ever had, and thinking of how he had treated her made him ashamed. At a store or restaurant, he kept his distance from the other customers, but even then he imagined they were wrinkling their noses at him.

While Danny was taking his time, Jack finished bathing and went up the bank to the trailer.

The next boat wasn't a sportfisherman but carried Marvin Tenino and his son Philbert. As soon as they docked, Philbert leaped out and double-timed up to their Silverado, then drove away quickly. Danny wondered why Marvin and Philbert were late this morning. No matter how early he and Jack ran the nets, the Teni-

nos usually beat them back by a good half hour. Danny came out
of the water and dressed, then splashed his arms and hands with
Aqua Velva he had bought at Bridge-Mart.

Marvin Tenino sold his fish to Neptune, even though Grizzly
Spirit was paying better prices. He had explained to Danny that
over the years, Neptune had treated him fairly, and he wasn't planning on switching now. Those times when he'd been down on his
luck, unable to get his nets in the water, Neptune had advanced
him webbing, lead line, and floats, letting him pay off his debt with
fish. "When my wife died, her funeral had me flat broke, and the
lower unit on my motor was shot. Those Neptune fellows gave me
over a thousand dollars to buy a good used motor. I tell you,
they've always treated me square," Marvin had said.

Danny was glad Willis kept his equipment in top order because
he and Jack came out better that way. But he appreciated the Neptune buyer's helping out River People whose nets were shot or
equipment broken. Many fishermen ran such shoestring outfits
that one good net could make a difference.

Danny stopped by the cleaning table where Marvin was butchering a couple of steelhead. "You boys are running a little behind
this morning," Danny said.

Marvin picked up the fishknife. "More trouble down at Cooks.
I stopped by when I saw the cop cars at the landing."

"What the hell now?"

Marvin raised the knife and brought it down quickly, chopping
off one of the fish heads. He lobbed it underhanded, like a softball,
toward the squawking seagulls. "'More evidence' is what they said.
Scared Orville's wife and grandkids half to death." He chopped off
another head and flung it toward the seagulls. "Cops."

"They'll probably all make detective by this afternoon," Danny
said.

Marvin laughed, but his laugh was bitter. "Philbert went down
to help out." He put the butchered fish in a small ice chest. "Me,
I'm tired of hassles."

"It's always one thing or another," Danny said. "Lately, we've
been coming up short on Backstop and Big Smokey. I figure someone is renegading."

Marvin washed off the stainless steel counter with water from a
green rubber hose. Fish scales and blood swirled down the drain.

"That used to be a disputed site, you know. A Warm Springs man had it for a long time, but Willis's father claimed it was his. The story goes he snuck out there one night and clubbed the netwatcher senseless. Kept beating him with a fish club while he was still zipped in his sleeping bag. Eventually, the man decided it belonged to Willis's father after all."

Danny nodded. Willis hadn't mentioned that incident, but he knew most of the good places along the river had been disputed at one time or another. "Just let me know if you see anything strange going on."

Marvin picked up the ice chest. "You got it."

On the way to his trailer, Danny passed the fish-drying shack. He liked the smoky smell of the salmon the women hung from poles suspended below the cedar beams. They dried only the tules because the upriver brights brought such high prices. The shed was made of plywood and screen to let the air circulate. On quiet days, the women turned on a small fan to circulate the air. An aluminum stepladder allowed them to hang fish from the high poles or take down a piece that was sufficiently dried. They also climbed the ladder to hang flypaper strips from the roof. In one corner, a blue buglight crackled when a fly entered.

Outside the shack, blue bachelor buttons sprang from the hard dry earth, the only place they grew in the fish camp. Darting yellow jackets slapped against the fine wire mesh, trying to get at the fish.

Danny tried napping in the trailer, but it became hot as an oven by ten and too noisy to sleep. Small driftwood sticks held open the windows for circulation, but the screens were knocked out and the black flies hummed relentlessly. Only a few sportfishermen launched their boats during the day — perhaps men who worked the night shifts and therefore missed the best fishing — but they were especially noisy and played their car radios at high volume. About noon, a Yakima tribal policeman parked his car outside the trailer, leaving the motor running for the air conditioning.

Danny lay propped on one elbow, his mind turning over the problems on the river. The prices would plummet when the white gillnetters swept the lower river, someone was renegading, and the consistent police harassment of Orville's family signaled worse times ahead.

So tired his eyes felt greasy, he dressed and drank a lukewarm Pepsi. Why couldn't everything be simple, the way it used to be. One afternoon as his grandfather Medicine Bird dipped fish from a platform on the Umatilla, he had let Danny help pull the struggling salmon from the water. Danny still remembered the safety rope tied around his waist and how Red Shirt tugged it from time to time, teasing him and keeping him off balance. For helping his grandfather, Danny received a quarter and squandered it at the closest store. Pop was only a nickel, so he bought a Nehi strawberry in a long-necked bottle, two candy bars, and a comic book. Money was easy and life never seemed so grand.

He had helped his grandfather all that week, and just before the Fourth of July, the old man slipped him two silver dollars, coins so large that Danny couldn't close his five-year-old fist. He spent them at the fireworks stand just off the reservation, staring wide-eyed as the freckle-handed man stuffed a paper sack with Black Cat firecrackers, cherry bombs, Roman Candles, and Red Devils. That night, he set them off by the river. Danny still recalled the quick spurts of kitchen matches and the sawdusty smoke from the glowing punks. The Roman Candles arced green and red fireballs over the river, and if he held them low, he heard the gulp and hiss as the flaming balls dipped into quiet water, black and smooth as obsidian.

That night, when Danny and Jack had just finished running Blondie and Little Blondie near the Spring Creek Fish Hatchery, Danny heard a fast boat approaching. After it turned on its spotlight, Danny knew it belonged to Inter-Tribal and they would want to check the fish catch, so he cut his motor.

Jack threw up his hands as the boat approached. "Turn off the light," he shouted. "I give up."

The spotlight went off, and when the boat nosed over, Danny recognized Stoney Kiwash in the running lights' glow. Stoney was Silitz — not from one of the four reservations that fished the river — so he was supposed to remain impartial in any disputes. Of course, there was no telling what axe his wife or sister-in-law might want to grind.

"I confess. I'm sick of fish," Jack said. "Haul me in."

Stoney grinned. "I thought by now you'd be rich enough to retire."

"That'll be about the time you quit taking those two-hour coffee breaks," Danny said.

"You should have been along for the ride earlier today," Stoney said. "That wind kicked up and blew a bunch of windsurfers right off their boards. I picked up a dozen or so — finally lost count. One was missing her bikini top and wouldn't get out of the water until I pretended to look the other way. Hell, I've seen bigger scoops at the Dairy Queen."

Danny knew Stoney was just blowing smoke, because all the windsurfers wore wetsuits, but he wanted to humor him along, so he said, "You guys get all the good breaks. Must be the badge and gun. We're stuck out here chasing fish."

"How you been doing, anyway?" Stoney dropped his good-humor voice.

Danny looked at Jack. "What's the count?"

"Sixteen brights and three tules. A couple steelhead. One old sturgeon."

Stoney switched on a flashlight and played it over the fish in their boat. "How big's that sturgeon? I don't see him."

Jack kicked aside a couple of Chinooks with his gumboots, revealing the sturgeon's buttoned tail. "He's not quite legal, but we'll stretch him as soon as we hit the docks."

"Ha. That's a good joke. I just gave a ticket yesterday because some boys brought in a couple of sturgeon without the tails. We better look at this one." He took a tapemeasure from his pocket.

Jack grumbled as he moved aside enough salmon so he could lift the sturgeon. Grunting with the effort, he hoisted it from the bottom of the boat. "Damn near five feet. Good and legal."

Stoney ran the light the length of the fish and nodded. "I can see that." He switched off the light. "By the way, I'm checking net mesh. You guys are using nine-inch, aren't you — about the length of my dick?"

"We got one seven and a half," Danny said, thinking of the Backstop. "Most are nine." He wanted to add that Stoney's dick was probably closer to shad net — four and a half inches. But he didn't.

"Some guys are still dropping tight mesh into the water. We keep picking those up. Got quite a collection going at the Inter-Tribal office."

"While you're checking nets, we're coming up short on the ones over by Preacher's Point. Looks like somebody's renegading."

"I'll check it out," Stoney said. "Oh, before I forget, let's see those fishing permits."

The fishermen were required to keep their tribal fishing permits with them at all times. Danny took off his gloves and dug his bill-fold out of his back pocket, carefully unfolding the permit. It had been creased so many times, the permit was nearly torn, and it was smeared with dried moss and slime from showing it to other officers.

Stoney read their names and numbers, then handed back the paper. Suddenly he stared past them, whistling softly. "Look at that!"

Danny saw the running lights of a big tug pushing a barge upriver. The lights on the barge were hooded, so it appeared to be a dark mass against a darker background. A black circular object rested on the deck, and something about it caused Danny's flesh to goose-bump. "Looks like a damn big hockey puck. It must be fifty feet across."

Stoney laughed. "Don't plan on firing off any kids for a while. That's the core of a nuclear sub and you've just been zapped. Your kids might have six eyes now."

"The core of a sub?" Danny asked. "Heading for Hanford?"

"You bet." Stoney nodded. "We got radioed that one was coming through, but it was delayed. They had to anchor below Portland until the damn protesters gave up and went home." He gunned the motor and turned on the spotlights. "I'm wearing my lead jock, boys, so I'm swooping in for a closer look."

Stoney caught up with the barge, leaving the fishing boat rocking in his wash. "There's one genuine goofball," Jack said. "Chasing after a radioactive core."

Danny shook his head. Something about the unlit barge moving upriver sent chills along his backbone, as if someone had stepped on his grave.

"I don't see the float line," Jack called from the front of the boat as they approached Big Smokey.

"Stop looking with your ass." Danny was angry with himself because he'd allowed the wind to carry the boat into Frog net, and in the dark it had taken them almost an hour to work the tangled prop free. A few times, the brisk chop had nearly swamped their boat.

"No kidding," Jack said. "Look for yourself." He played the flashlight's beam over the dark water.

Danny couldn't see the float line, either. More puzzling, he didn't see the white Styrofoam buoys, and he double-checked the shore lights to make certain he had the right location. "If Inter-Tribal confiscated the nets, they wouldn't touch the buoys," he muttered. "Anyway, Stoney would have mentioned it."

"Maybe a barge," Jack said.

When the pilots got sleepy or careless and ran out of their marked channels, the barges frequently wiped out nets, but it was unlikely they'd sweep away both buoys.

"Let's take a look along the shore," Danny said. He drove the boat closer and peered through the darkness while Jack swept the beam along the rocks until it illuminated a cluster of white specks dotting the dark gray tumble of beach.

Danny hoped the specks would turn out to be seagulls or dumped motor oil containers, but he knew otherwise. "Damn," he muttered when they were close enough to determine that the white specks were the floats marking the tangled, smoky-colored net.

After the boat nudged against the shore, Jack stepped out to inspect the net briefly. Turning to Danny, he made a quick slashing motion across his throat with his forefinger.

The expensive monofilament webbing had been slashed beyond repair. The lead line had been cut loose, too, and was no doubt lying somewhere on the riverbottom. They could save only the float line. Whoever had slashed the net wanted them to find it and had left the white floats for markers.

"Let's get it into the boat," Danny said, dragging a section of net toward the water. "We'll show it to Inter-Tribal."

"That'll do a lot of good," Jack said as he picked up another slashed section. "Willis is going to have a shit fit."

"This is only half the fun," Danny said. "There's still the Back-stop."

·   ·   ·

"It might be that Warm Springs man or some of his people," Willis said. He was sipping coffee from a white porcelain mug with a jumping deer decoration. "That dispute goes back a long time."

Velrae was cooking pork chops and she banged the pan on the glowing front burner. "You know it was sportfishermen," she insisted, glancing out the window at a couple of men loading a sleek boat onto an EZ Loader trailer. "Those dumbasses blame us for their bad luck, but it's not our fault if they're too stupid to catch fish." She speared the sizzling chops with a fork and quickly turned them. "White guys did it. No Indian is going to slash your nets to ribbons."

"Maybe it was windsurfers," Jack offered. "They're always complaining about hitting the nets. Of course, they'd have to bring a boat over to take them out."

"Those rich guys wouldn't take a chance of getting busted," Velrae said. "They just strut around in their fancy gear and buy nice houses on the bluffs so they can watch us sweat."

Willis stood and stared out the window at the slashed nets. Danny and Jack had left them by the broken boat. "I don't have time to make up more nets right now. Even if I could get more good webbing from Seattle."

"You got friends," Velrae said. "Borrow one from Tenino."

"I don't want his nets to get slashed," Willis said. "So somebody's going to have to netwatch. Grab a rifle and sleep out by Preacher's Point. Remember 1965? There were more bullets on the river than boats."

Velrae took the pan off the stove and put a couple of pork chops on Danny's plate, two more on Jack's. "It was sportfishermen that caused all the trouble then," she said, "and it's true now."

"You got one right, anyway," Willis said.

Danny's chops were black on the outside, but the meat was pink when he cut into them. He preferred his pork cooked so the meat was white, because Red Shirt used to talk about a German friend of his that got trichinosis at a sausage festival. Danny had mentioned it once to Velrae and now suspected her of undercooking his meat on purpose. "I don't think Jack and I can sleep by the nets," Danny said. "We're stretched mighty tight already."

"I don't mind sleeping out," Willis said. "And Velrae can help."

"I hadn't thought of that," Danny said. He wasn't anxious to be anywhere around Velrae, especially if she had a rifle.

"Before we hatch any more big plans, I better see if Tenino's got a net to loan," Willis said.

After finishing their late supper, Jack and Danny went out by the water and waited for Willis to return.

"You ever hear the story of Salmon Boy?" Danny asked.

Jack shook his head.

Danny gazed at the moonlight dancing off the water and tried to remember the words and tone his grandfather had used to tell the story. "Winter lasted a long time that year," Danny's grandfather would say, "and the River People were hungry. After the snowmelt, the Chief built his scaffold and went to the river every day, taking with him Salmon Boy, his son and the most beautiful child in the village. Every day they prayed for First Salmon to return, because some of their people were near starvation.

"When First Salmon came, he had to be treated right, according to what the Maker had instructed. That way, he would return through the raging whitewater, leading all the Salmon People upriver to the hungry tribe. When the Chief found First Salmon in his hoopnet, he thanked its spirit and pointed its head upriver, toward the rising sun.

"The women prepared a big feast and cooked that salmon slowly over the alder coals after butchering it with knives made from the finest bones. The Chief invited all the hungry people to the feast, and after the Washat service, they ate that salmon along with roots and berries — the way the Maker had instructed.

"When they finished eating, the Chief returned First Salmon's bones to the river so it could swim back and lead the others upriver, but the Chief noticed it was having trouble swimming right, and he was afraid some of the bones were missing.

"Coyote, that old trickster, was jealous of the people. Every spring he caught a few salmon, but he was so greedy he devoured them bones and all, so no more salmon returned to him. He had tried carving some fish from sticks and throwing them into the water, but they never returned, either. They just floated out to sea. Coyote grew so hungry that he tried eating some of the stick salmon, but all he got was a mouth full of splinters.

"So he had disguised himself as a guest and eaten with the people. When he saw them saving the salmon bones, he kept his, too, but instead of returning them to the Chief, he hid them in his mouth. He thought maybe if he glued those bones on his wooden salmon, they could swim back.

"Coyote tried sneaking away from the feast before it finished, but the Chief wouldn't let him go. That evening Salmon Boy performed for the guests. He juggled and did acrobatic tricks. After it grew dark, they lit a fire, and Salmon Boy danced and sang the Salmon Song, making shadowy movements against the tent's walls to trick Coyote. His hands and arms rippled like salmon swimming upriver.

"Greedy Coyote had grown so hungry again, he opened his mouth to devour Salmon Boy. When he did, Salmon Boy snatched the bones from Coyote's mouth. Quick as a flash, Salmon Boy jumped into the Great Falls so he could return the bones to First Salmon.

"Coyote wanted to dive in after him, but he was afraid of the water, so he ran along the bank, calling out for the bones, but the river just kept sweeping Salmon Boy downstream, keeping him out of angry Coyote's reach.

"First Salmon was trying hard to lead the Salmon People upriver, but without his missing bones he didn't have the strength to leap all the falls or fight the whitewater in the old rushing river's channel. When Salmon Boy gave First Salmon the bones, he was once more complete and strong enough to lead the Salmon People upriver.

"Because of Salmon Boy's courage, they made him one of the Salmon People, too, and when First Salmon grew too old and tired to swim upriver, Salmon Boy inherited his duties.

"The Chief was sorry to lose his son, but he waited anxiously for him every spring, and when his son returned, the Chief treated him as a special guest and there was much rejoicing in the village."

When Danny finished telling his grandfather's story, Jack was silent. Willis cleared his throat, and Danny was surprised to know he had been sitting behind them, listening.

"That's an old story," Willis said. "I remember my father telling me about Salmon Boy."

"I heard it from Medicine Bird," Danny said. "Left Hand told him. What did you find out about the nets?"

"I've got to fix them up a little, replace some floats. They'll be ready to go by the night run tomorrow. The webbing's the wrong color, but we may catch a few dumb ones."

When Danny and Jack came in with the next morning's catch, they discovered that the Grizzly Spirit refrigerator truck hadn't shown up and no buyer was at the scales. Most of the Indians were selling to Pete Larson, a bald, freckled man from Neptune, but they were grumbling because he was paying only a dollar-thirty a pound.

"Those Grizzly Spirit fellows promised a dollar-fifty this week," Danny said.

Pete shrugged. "I could tell you I was paying three dollars a pound, then not show up. What I'm paying is a dollar-thirty. Cold cash for fresh fish. Now you going to unload your boat or what? My customers are lining up."

"Maybe we'll wait a little while," Danny said, wondering if mechanical problems had delayed the Grizzly buyers again.

Pete squinted at the sun burning off the river fog. "Going to be hot today. The radio said ninety or ninety-five. Won't pay to wait too long."

"I hear you," Danny said.

Willis came in from fixing Tenino's net and they held a conference in the trailer. Velrae was testier than usual because she'd stayed up half the night helping Willis. "We shouldn't take a dollar-thirty," she said. "Didn't the Grizzly buyer promise he'd stand at a dollar and a half?"

"That's what he said," Danny replied. His head felt fuzzy. Glancing at the coffeepot, he saw that only a black residue remained. "When you making coffee?"

"Fix some yourself," Velrae said. "I don't see my name inscribed on that Mr. Coffee."

Danny didn't move. As he watched Velrae's mouth open and close, he felt like popping her one.

"Figure it out," Velrae said. "This Neptune jerk thinks we're stuck with his prices, so he's screwing us. It's the same with stores on the rez. They charge skyrocket prices for rotten meat and lousy vegetables just because they think the people can't go anywhere else. I say we ice those fish good and take them into Portland ourselves."

"Not me," Danny said. "By the time you buy ice and gas, you're going to lose money. Anyway, I'm tired, and this afternoon I've got to put Tenino's nets out." He glanced at the coffeepot again, but Velrae ignored his hint, so he scraped back his chair and filled a quart container at the sink, then measured out the coffee.

"Let me use the truck, then," she said. "I can drive to Portland in two hours and the fish will still be fresh. You agree with me, don't you?" She reached out and touched Jack's arm.

Jack was spreading some strawberry jam on a piece of white bread, but he looked up when Velrae touched him. "Sure. We're working too hard for some white guy to gouge us."

Danny glared at Jack, but the boy missed it. He poured some of the coffee into his cup, but his hands were shaking and he spilled some onto the coffeemaker's hot plate. "Damn!"

"Give me a shot of that, would you?" Willis said. "Try getting mine in the cup." After Danny had poured the coffee, Willis added two tablespoons of sugar and stirred it with a wooden stick. "Bum's breakfast," he said, grinning.

"You're going to get diabetes," Velrae said. "Remember your sister? Ulcers ate up half her leg and they chopped it off just below the knee."

"What do you think?" Danny asked Willis.

"I'm not going to Portland," Willis said. "All those freeways confuse me. As long as I can remember, people on this river keep saying there's big money in Portland if you go to this buyer or that one. But nothing ever works out."

"Our people should have their own market right on the reservation," Velrae said. "Then the fishermen could deal directly with their own people."

"Already tried it," Willis said. "Some federal boondoggle. Went bust after a year. A few of our people stole the rest blind."

Danny laughed. "Velrae should have been in charge."

"She couldn't have done much worse," Willis said. "The operation was so poor, they didn't even supply the fishermen with ice, so we drove rotting dog salmon to the reservation and they paid us eighty cents a pound for fertilizer. Our pickups stunk all the way to the bank."

"How about your truck?" she said to Danny. "Jack can help me load and ice the fish."

"The gas and ice come out of your share if you lose on the deal,"

Danny said. "Otherwise, no go." He figured it might be worth letting her try. If she fouled up, he could have the satisfaction of reminding her whenever it came in handy.

It was almost an hour before they could get ice because the Neptune man had to finish buying from his regular customers first. "You can borrow one of my totes," he said, "but I've got to charge you twenty-five dollars for ice."

"It's worth it," Velrae said, counting out the money.

"She hasn't bought gas yet or figured her time," Danny said to Willis, "and we're already twenty-five in the hole. At this rate, I'll be panhandling on Burnside tomorrow."

Jack and Velrae loaded the tote, alternating a layer of fish with a layer of ice. When they were almost finished, Pete came over. "Look," he said, "I hate to see you make a long drive for nothing. The boss just called and told me to start paying a dollar-twenty. They're catching so many fish on the lower river, the market's plunging." He slapped his rubber gloves against his thigh. "I'll still go a buck-thirty and save you some grief."

"You just got a call on the radio, right now? That's real convenient," Velrae said. "Can you drive that forklift?" she asked Jack. "Those Grizzly guys leave the key in it."

"Sure," he said. "On the farm, I learned to drive all kinds of stuff." He climbed onto the orange Toyota lift and started it.

Danny was surprised at how easily Jack loaded the tote into the pickup bed, but he was concerned when he saw the melting ice start leaking out. It was getting to be a hot one.

Velrae climbed into the pickup and turned on the ignition.

"Put the pedal to the metal," Jack said, slapping the door.

The three men stood and watched as Velrae drove the pickup up the hill. With the fully loaded tote riding the springs, it bottomed out in a couple of places.

"I ought to have my head examined," Danny said.

"You got to admire her style," Jack said.

"My first wife was like that." Pete winked at Danny. "Maybe you'll be lucky enough to have Velrae for your daughter-in-law."

"How lucky can I get?" Danny followed Pete back to the little trailer he had parked beside the refrigerator truck.

Inside, Pete had a small fan turned on. "I wasn't kidding about that call," Pete said. "Business is business, and if the Grizzly guys just blew away quick, that would suit me fine, but I wasn't making anything up. I got my reputation to think about. On this river, word gets around."

"I hear you," Danny said. He was staring at the Snap-On Tool calendar, which featured a brunette with large breasts holding a box wrench.

"I been here a long time and always treat people square." Pete took out a bottle of Cornhusker's Lotion and started rubbing it on his hands. "That Grizzly outfit has Nevada money behind it. Maybe the Mob."

"What would they want with fish?" Danny asked.

"Don't you watch TV? Before they rub somebody out, the Mob sends them a dead fish wrapped in newspaper. The victim is fish-food. Get it?" Pete chuckled.

Danny managed a smile to stay on Pete's good side. "If things don't work out in Portland, we'll be seeing you."

"Sure. I'm always right here."

"Velrae's back," Jack said as he and Danny were coming in from the night run.

"Like a bad penny," Danny said, but his spirits were high because they had caught twelve fish in the replacement nets and he knew there would be no renegading with Willis on guard. He had found a good watchplace on a bluff overlooking both nets.

As he drove the boat closer to shore, Danny expected to see his pickup parked near the trailer, but it was backed up close to the fish cleaning table. The tailgate was down, and as he watched, Velrae climbed up on the tailgate and reached into the Neptune tote, bringing out a big salmon that she threw on the table. Her rubber-gloved right hand, holding a butcher knife, flashed above her head, then struck down against the fish. The dull thunk carried over the water.

Puzzled, Jack turned to Danny. "What's going on?"

"She's cleaning fish," Danny explained, and as he did, he realized that Velrae hadn't sold their catch in Portland. "I hope you haven't spent all your money yet, Hotshot."

They docked the boat, and Jack jumped out without waiting for

Danny. "Maybe I better talk to her. That is, if you can handle the fish."

Danny didn't want to talk with Velrae. He lifted a couple of the big Chinooks and started up the ramp toward the Neptune fish-buying station. Glancing toward the drying shack, he saw that the door was open and the light on. Velrae had moved the stepladder from the corner, and it was now positioned so she could hang the butchered fish from the cedar poles. As he passed the cleaning table, he didn't look at Velrae, but the night breeze carried the stench of rotting fish. He doubted those fish could be salvaged and suspected they'd taste putrid, even when dried. The waste of upriver brights made him sick.

Pete came out of his trailer to weigh Danny's fresh fish. He smelled of fried food and Cornhusker's Lotion. Slipping on his rubber gloves, he asked Danny, "You need some help toting fish? Seems like the boy's busy."

"Why not," Danny said, throwing the Chinooks onto the scale.

Pete slipped on his gumboots. "You know, I would've bought those fish when she came back, but the way they were smelling, I couldn't chance it. The boss would take my hide."

"Driving to Portland was a dumb stunt," Danny said. "I shouldn't have let her use my pickup."

"I guess she drove all over looking for a good price, but the market's shot. I can't blame her for trying to do a little better. Fact is, I feel sorry for her. She was blubbering like a baby when she started butchering those fish."

"How long's she been here?"

"Hour. Maybe a little longer."

"She must have stopped for a picnic," Danny said. He was still too angry to feel sorry for Velrae.

After Pete had finished weighing the salmon, sturgeon, and steelhead, he added the totals with his pocket calculator and wrote out the fish ticket. "Eight hundred and fifty-four dollars. Things are picking up a little."

Danny nodded. "No one's renegading — at least for now. Figure me out fifteen percent of that, would you? The same for the boy."

Pete punched the calculator again. "That's one twenty-eight apiece. Want me to divvy it up?"

"All right." As Pete counted the money and clipped each roll, Danny noticed how terrible his hands looked. The skin was split, forming angry red cracks similar to those in the garish advertisements for athlete's foot cures.

Pete saw him looking. "Contact allergies, the doctor says. Every damn thing I touch. Cornhusker's seems about the only thing that helps."

"Maybe when fishing season's over," Danny said.

"It can't hurt. These damn gloves and fish slime really set it off."

At the cleaning station, things were moving faster because Jack carried the butchered salmon to the drying shack and hung them while Velrae belly-cut the fish and chopped off their heads.

"Geez, you stink," Danny said as Jack stepped out of the shack. "Don't go crawling into your sleeping bag without washing." He tucked Jack's money into the boy's pocket. "Buy some clothespins for your nose."

"Don't go messing with Velrae," Jack said quietly. "She's on the edge."

"What else is new," Danny said as he watched Velrae scramble up on the tailgate again. "Why don't you take the forklift and get that tote out of the truckbed for her?"

"I tried," Jack said. "It won't start."

"Borrow Pete's. He's our man now."

Danny couldn't find anything ready to eat in the trailer's icebox, so he fried four hamburgers, taking two for himself and leaving the others for Jack. He made coffee, adding three fingers of whiskey to his cup. Drinking it, he felt a littler better. He fixed a cup for Jack and, after hesitating a moment, decided to make one for Velrae, splashing some extra whiskey into her coffee. He was sure her muscles ached and figured a stiff drink would help punch out the kinks. After carrying the coffee outside and setting the two cups on the bloody counter, he nudged one toward Velrae. "Looks like overtime," he said.

"It's going faster now." She picked up the cup with her rubber-gloved hand, and Danny thought the coffee must taste like rotting fish guts. But when she sipped it, her mouth twitched and a little smile played on her lips. "Coffee plus."

"Keeps you going down the road straight," Danny said. He wondered why the tote was still in the pickup.

Jack came out of the shack and paused when he saw Danny and Velrae together. He started to climb on the tailgate, but Danny shook his head. "Coffee break. Union rules."

"Thanks," Jack said, and joined them at the counter.

"I left some hamburgers up there, too. When you're ready. What's the story on this tote? I want it moved so I can drive."

"Pete's forklift is out of propane. They're bringing him another bottle tomorrow."

"Great," Danny said. "I'm not going anywhere until that tote's out." He was feeling a little restless and thought he might drive to the White Horse in Bingen for a couple of drinks.

Velrae set down her cup and chopped the head off another salmon. "I tried," she said, and gave a little laugh. "The Portland market was shot, and I drove three places before someone mentioned that Jake's out on Swan Island always pays good money. That's when I got lost. Those freeways were a nightmare."

"Didn't Willis say something about that?"

She didn't seem to hear Danny. "I hurried back to Neptune, but by then the ice was melted."

She could have bought ice in Portland, Danny thought. Every plant had plenty.

"I think these will be okay when they dry. Not great, but okay," she said.

"Sure they will," Jack said.

"Maybe tourists will buy them," Danny said.

Velrae looked at Danny. "That's an idea."

"Here's Willis's share." Danny put the bills on the counter and laid a small rock on top.

"I let us down," she said.

Danny didn't answer. He figured that was as close to an apology as she could manage.

"Don't worry about it," Jack said. "Without Big Smokey and the Backstop, we weren't getting sensational hauls. Things are picking up now."

"Bad luck comes in threes," she said. "The renegades, the slashed nets, and now this."

Danny closed his eyes, wishing she hadn't said anything. He

rapped his fist against a wooden leg of the counter. When he opened his eyes, he was looking at the sheen of salmon slime twinkling in his pickup bed. The truck reeked, but cleaning it would have to wait until the next day. Velrae ought to do it, even though she had been through enough for right now. He started to walk away.

Jack followed him a few steps, until they were out of Velrae's earshot. "You were almost decent to her," he said.

"Moment of weakness."

"Right."

Danny stopped. "Look at that fish stuff on your gloves."

"Gross, huh? We got to wash our clothes, anyway, before they stiffen up. You turning in?"

"Taking a little stroll first. Thinking some things over."

"Taverns will be closed. It's late."

Danny nodded. He followed the highway until he was a good distance from Wind River and could no longer hear the traffic on the interstate bridge. It felt good to walk away from the fish camp for a while. The night was warm, but somebody was burning wood, and the smoke streaked the sky above the evergreen-shrouded cliffs.

He passed the Broughton Lumber Company and turned onto the little river road that led to the Spring Creek Fish Hatchery. He passed two or three gravel pullouts. One held a Camaro. Danny figured it was a young man's car and that a couple of lovers had come down to gaze at the water.

Crossbars blocked the road at the hatchery entrance, where a sign warned it was federal property and trespassers would be prosecuted. Just outside the gates were a small dumpster and a basketball backboard and rim. Someone had tied fishnet below the rim. Danny picked up a few small rocks and tried a jump shot at the basket. The first two rocks clanked off the backboard — high and right — but the third sailed through the rim. Danny jammed his hands in his pockets and started walking back.

The Camaro was gone, and Danny followed a small trail through the scrub oak and dry grass until he was at the rocks along the river. He smelled cigarette smoke and found two smoldering butts on a little strip of damp sand.

Across the river, the bright lights of the Columbia Gorge Hotel stood out against the sheer dark bluff below it. Downriver, the arced span of lights revealed the bridge,

Kneeling, Danny dipped his hand in the water and was surprised at how warm it felt. He took off his clothes and waded in. He tugged at the medicine bundle but decided it was firmly fastened, so he left it on. When he had waded in up to his waist, he started swimming, measuring his strokes until he was some distance from shore. Then he turned over and floated on his back, resting.

He was still on his back when he heard the drone of a plane and saw the lights pass overhead. Something splashed not far from where he floated. Curious, he rolled over. Treading water and searching the river's surface, he heard the splash again and saw a black head not fifty feet away. Thinking of the visions, he squeezed his eyes tight and counted to three. As he opened them, he yelled, "Hey!"

The head remained motionless, as if watching Danny. Then it began swimming away from him, trailing a V on the water's surface. Danny swam after the V, but he couldn't gain on it. When he reached midchannel, he was winded, and the swimmer was nearly to the other side. Danny let the current carry him to a red navigational buoy, and he hung on there until he regained his breath. The pulsing red light was disorienting and he was unable to see the swimmer again.

When he was confident he could make the shore, Danny swam back, resting now and again, so the current carried him toward the hatchery until he reached the place he had left his clothes.

After shaking himself off and stripping away the water with his hands, Danny dressed. He wondered what he had seen swimming. It had seemed to be another man — one of Velrae's scuba divers, perhaps — but it could have been a seal.

11

PUDGE

PUDGE POKED HER NOSE into one of the Neptune totes the fish camp used for garbage. It contained oil cans, empty Pepsi bottles, Mountain Dew and Slice cans, and fast-food boxes from McDonald's and Kentucky Fried Chicken. Among the articles of clothing were worn-out tennis shoes, waterlogged life vests, and cheap polyester jackets ripped at the shoulders. "You might think about cleaning this place up," she said.

Danny hadn't been paying much attention to Pudge until she spoke. He had been watching a yellow minivan parked on the Wind River road overlooking the fish camp. A man was working on the engine, but he couldn't get it started.

Danny finished his Pepsi and made a hook shot about thirty feet from the tote. The bottle hit the edge and bounced in. "Two points. Pendleton wins the state championship."

She laughed. "Don't peddle me that. You guys lost to Grant. Everyone said Henry shaved points. For all I know, you were in on it, too."

"Come on, Pudge. That's old news." The loss had always bothered Danny because he never knew if Henry had shaved points or not. It could have been nerves.

Pudge surveyed the fish camp with a wary eye. "I thought that pickers' shack in Hood River was bad, but you've actually slid downhill."

Danny looked at the papers scattered over the camp. One of the sportfishermen had left a Sunday edition of *The Oregonian,* and the wind had blown pieces everywhere. "Another good wind should help clean this up."

"Noah's flood might."

Danny hadn't been too pleased to see Pudge show up because he didn't like her picking at him. He had been working hard for almost a month, making good money and helping Willis out at the same time. He figured he deserved some credit.

Pudge took a quick glance inside his trailer. "Jesus."

"It could stand a woman's touch, all right."

"Not mine. What's that green thing that looks kind of like a sofa?"

"A whoopee cushion," Danny said. "Back seat of a 1953 Buick. I thought you'd recognize it right away because there's no substitute for experience."

Pudge glared at him. "You better cover that thing before you catch something that eats penicillin." She walked back to her car. "That reminds me, I brought this blanket for you."

Danny recognized the blanket as a Pendleton Loxie had slashed years before. Pudge had mended it with strips of wool that almost matched. "Thanks. Some nights, I freeze my ass on the river and just can't get warm again."

He carried the blanket into the trailer and spread it across the green seat. He had to admit the place looked a little better. The blanket had been a raffle prize from the Rock Creek Powwow twenty years earlier. Danny was cashy with rodeo winnings then and tried to impress Shila Sam by buying fifty raffle tickets from her. She was the prettiest princess and became queen by selling the most tickets. One evening they made love in a willow thicket along the creek. Danny stayed sweet on Shila for a long time, but she married Iggy Two Medicine. Once Loxie caught Shila making eyes at Danny during an Owl Dance, and later that night she went after the blanket with Danny's hunting knife.

"Where'd you say Jack was?"

"Preacher's Point. That's about the closest he'll ever get to church. Velrae's out there netwatching, and he decided to keep her company."

Pudge thought it over for a minute. "So they going steady?"

"No chance." Danny knew they were but didn't want to admit it.

"If my nephew's sweet on somebody, I should know what she's like."

"Like crossing a pig with a pirate." Then Danny told Pudge the story of the fish Velrae had taken to Portland.

"Maybe you're too hard on her," Pudge said when he finished. "You've been working too much. I've been working hard, too. That's why I decided to come see you guys." A little light came into her eyes. "I passed my LPN exam. Flying colors."

"Hey, that's great. I should have remembered you were studying hard. What with running the nets morning and night, replacing lost equipment, and worrying about everything, I flat out forgot."

"I thought I'd take you and Jack to dinner. My treat." She glanced at her watch. "What time do you make the night run?"

"Right after dark," Danny said. "If we scare up Jack now, that's going to crowd us for time."

She thought it over. "We'll go by ourselves tonight, then. I can take Jack somewhere else tomorrow." She folded her arms and looked Danny up and down. "By the way, you're looking a little wilted. Got anything else to wear?"

Danny studied his denim shirt. Slime streaked the sleeves and chest, and bits of moss clung to the buttons. "I got a couple new shirts in there," he said, nodding toward the trailer. He figured one of Jack's would fit him okay, although it would be snug around the middle.

"Right now, the cat wouldn't drag you." She paused. "I better freshen up a bit, too, much as I hate to go inside that trailer."

When Pudge took her suitcase out of the Vega, the gray goose waddled up from the riverbank and hissed at her. Pudge returned the hiss. "He won't last through Thanksgiving," she said, making a wringing motion with her hands. "I'll soak him in Gallo and pop him in a pan."

"Lay off," Danny said. "That's the official camp watch goose. He chases off the bozos. That reminds me, what's Que up to now?"

"I've never seen him so mournful. He's lost his best friend."

"Percy died?"

She shook her head. "They're closing down the Outlaw Club."

"I don't believe it. One fight too many?"

"The old man died and his daughters got religion. Neither one touches a drink, so they boarded the place up."

"What happened to all of Que's girlfriends?"

Pudge chuckled. "You got to stretch your imagination a bit to think of them as girls. I heard they're working the migrant camps out of trailers. Que is all busted up about it. He stays half bagged and lurches around town like Percy used to before the street cleaner got his legs."

Following Pudge's directions, Danny pulled into the parking lot of the Columbia Gorge Hotel. "They must get a barber to cut that lawn," Danny said. "I don't feel comfortable about this place."

"I said the treat was on me," Pudge said, "and I wanted to go somewhere dress-up."

"As long as you're paying," Danny said. "These jeans are kind of worn." He wished he had brought his blue cords down from Pendleton.

"You're fine," Pudge said. She was wearing a blue denim skirt with a white blouse. When she pulled a red shawl over her shoulders, she looked pretty classy, Danny thought.

As they entered the front door, Danny saw the two brass chandeliers in the foyer and a giant flower arrangement on an oak table. He paused.

"Can I help you?" the woman at the front desk asked.

"We're going to have dinner," Pudge said.

"It'll be just a few minutes," the woman said. "We're still setting up."

"You got a bar?" Danny asked. If he had a drink, he might feel more relaxed.

"The Valentino Lounge is straight ahead," the woman said. "You can order drinks and appetizers in there."

Danny tried hiding in the corner, but Pudge insisted they sit by the fireplace. "That'll be romantic if they start a fire later on," she said.

The fireplace was tile with brass trim. Above it hung a large painting depicting Lewis and Clark arriving at a fishing village on the Columbia. They had stepped out of their canoes and were offering presents. The Indians were naked above the waist, their faces smeared with paint.

Pudge ordered a champagne cocktail and Danny had a beer.

"You're living high on the hog," he said.

"I was number three in my class," she said. "That's something to celebrate."

"If it was rodeo, you'd still be in the money," Danny said. He was proud of Pudge, but he didn't know quite how to tell her. He raised his beer and they touched glasses. The bubbles rose from the sugar cube in the bottom of Pudge's cocktail.

The waitress had left the appetizer menu, which opened like a small book. "The salmon pâté sounds good," Pudge said.

Danny made a face. "I don't want anything to do with salmon. Here's a cheese and cracker plate." He squinted at the prices. "You must get to keep the plate."

"I got it covered," Pudge said. When the waitress came, Pudge asked her about the Gravlax, but after she explained it was marinated salmon, Pudge ordered the pâté.

Outside the window, a man about Danny's age in light blue slacks and a sweater accompanied a red-haired woman in a miniskirt. The couple walked on the rocky path that wound over the basalt outcroppings, then ended at a fenced enclosure overlooking Wah-Gwin-Gwin Falls. When they reached the overlook, they hugged and kissed each other like teenagers.

"Guess they're not married after all," Danny said.

"Maybe this place rekindled the flame," Pudge said. "But she's no spring chicken. That red hair's straight from the bottle."

"I don't know," Danny said. "How can you tell?"

"If she hiked her skirt any shorter, we could double-check," Pudge said. She sipped her drink. "Let them have fun. But I wouldn't prance around those rocks wearing her shoes." She settled back and looked around the room. "This reminds me of a place in Minneapolis."

"I never knew you were in Minneapolis," Danny said.

"There's a lot you don't know." Pudge tapped her champagne glass. "Three summers ago, I went there with Lucy Pretty Mink."

"The one that went through the car windshield?"

Pudge shook her head. "That was her cousin LaDonna."

Danny nodded. "Minneapolis. That's a long way." He couldn't understand why he hadn't heard about this. He must have been off rodeoing.

"Lucy had an almost-new Ranchero and a sometimes boyfriend in Fargo. I had Gypsy feet, so when she asked me to go along, I said sure. We cut a wide swath along the way. That darned Lucy — she flirted with every gas station attendant." Pudge batted her eyelashes.

When the waitress brought their appetizers, Pudge's pâté had little dark spots in it and was surrounded by a white sauce.

"What's that?" Danny said.

Pudge spread some of the pâté on a large cracker and popped it in her mouth. After she swallowed it, she said. "Heavenly." She offered some to Danny.

He took a small bite. "Not bad," he said. "It hardly tastes like salmon at all."

"Fargo was some place. Lucy's boyfriend was gone and we had to get a room, but all the motels were full. They had gambling there, so busloads of people came from Minnesota. Came to Fargo. Just think of it. You'd have to be desperate." Pudge ate some more of her salmon. "From Fargo, it's just a hop and jump to Minneapolis, so we went. Lucy had a cousin there, and we had a grand time."

"What'd you do?"

Pudge smiled a little. "Don't expect me to tell you *everything*, but one night we wound up at this fancy seafood place on the river. The Mississippi, or maybe the Missouri, goes right through there." She wrinkled her brow. "I can't think of the name, but it was real nice, like this. They had green matchboxes, I remember that. Anyway, we hung around awhile and three blond guys picked us up. That city is full of blonds — Norwegians, Swedes — take your pick. My guy's name was Oscar. That was a hoot. I told him Oscar was an Indian name, but he explained it was a Norwegian name, too. Some king was named Oscar. He worked at Pillsbury and he was divorced, separated actually, but we still had a good time." She lifted her glass. "To good times."

Danny touched her glass with his, but a little slowly. He didn't like the idea of Pudge in Minneapolis with some blond guy named Oscar.

The couple from outside came in and sat at a table. Pretty soon they were joined by a man in a cream-colored suit and pink tie that was loosened at the knot. His date wore a dark blue outfit with matching feather earrings. They were all smiling, and their rich tans looked as if they came from a swimming pool or golf course.

Danny stared a little too long at them, and when the woman in blue saw him looking, she flashed him a quick smile and took a cigarette out of a paisley case, then snapped it shut.

"What are you gawking at?" Pudge asked.

"I wonder where she got those earrings?"

"A pigeon died. And it wasn't worth it."

Danny chuckled. "You got a good sense of humor, Pudge."

The two men were talking low. The man in the suit took out a pocket calculator and was writing some figures down for the other man. The two women started talking about houses.

"Kristen spent the whole summer redecorating," the woman in blue said. She sipped her drink and stirred it with the black stick. "Now the kitchen. I know this sounds a bit bold, but it just shows what Kristen can do. The wallpaper's black with a red and white floral design. Here's the brilliance . . ." She paused, holding her cigarette for effect. "She's using black and white floor tile, and her kitchen furniture is cherry." She settled back and crossed her legs. "*Cherry!*"

The other woman nodded appreciatively. "It sounds gorgeous."

Pudge rolled her eyes at Danny. "Tschuush," she said. "Bullshit."

"She's a talker," Danny said.

"Actually, I was going to fix my place up like that," Pudge said. "But what's the point if everybody's doing it?"

The hostess came in to tell the foursome their table was ready. As they passed Danny and Pudge, the woman in blue gave them a quick smile. "Darling shawl," she told Pudge.

Pudge tugged the shawl tighter across her shoulders.

The hostess came back to Pudge and Danny. "Did you care for dinner this evening?"

"We'll be right there," Pudge said. "I want to finish this delicious pâté."

When they started into the dining room, Pudge paused by the table where the two couples had been sitting. One of the blue feather earrings was lying beside an upholstered chair. Pudge scooped up the earring and slipped it into her purse.

"We'd prefer to sit by the window," Pudge told the hostess.

"Of course," she said.

Their table had fresh flowers and a candle. After they sat down, Pudge spread her napkin in her lap and Danny did the same. "Great view," Pudge said, looking out toward the river.

The waitress brought the menu, but Danny didn't notice the prices at first because they were written out. When he saw them, he didn't believe them. "Roast saddle of venison for nineteen ninety-five?" he said. "I could buy a couple boxes of shells and shoot a freezer full."

"I wonder if they cook the sturgeon over alder," Pudge said, ignoring his remark.

"They can keep the sturgeon," Danny said. "The way they rip up the nets. My advice is to stay away from fish. Who knows what's coming down that river from Hanford." He looked at the menu again. "Twenty-one ninety-five for eastern Oregon lamb." He whistled softly.

"Is that what you want?" Pudge folded her menu.

Danny shook his head. "No mutton. It leaves a tallowy taste. For that price, I could start a herd."

"Don't spoil this," Pudge said. Her eyes flashed danger, and Danny quickly looked again at the menu.

At the next table, the waiter ignited the brandy covering one dish and it burned with a bright blue flame. "Fancy," Pudge said. When the waiter stopped at their table, she said "I'm just curious. Do you have this same menu for room service?"

"Some of it," he said. "We can't do any flambé in the rooms because of the fire danger. Don't want to burn the place down."

"It looks terrific," Pudge said. "I'll have the breast of pheasant with pear wine and hazelnuts."

"Excellent choice. And you, sir?"

"New York strip steak," Danny said. "Can you torch that, too, or do I have to sit by a fire extinguisher?"

"I can if you like," the waiter said. He seemed to be enjoying himself.

"Let's whoop it up then," Danny said. "I'll try one of those champagne cocktails while you're at it."

"Very good, sir."

"Who's high on the hog now?" Pudge asked.

Danny drank the champagne and stared out the window. As it grew dark outside, the lights from Wind River and White Salmon winked high on the opposite hillside, their reflection glazing the river so it shone like a wide silver ribbon. From this height, it was easy to forget the fish and the work. Pudge's reflection glowed in the window. She seemed happy.

The two couples were seated some distance away, but Danny could catch their conversation from time to time. Kristen's bathroom tub was Italian marble. At one point, the woman in blue stood up and started searching under her chair and around the table. The waitress helped her look for the earring and so did the hostess. After a few moments they checked the Valentino Lounge.

The woman returned to her table. "I just don't understand it," she said. "With one earring I feel absolutely . . . asymmetrical."

Pudge smiled and sipped her drink.

Danny had never eaten a better steak. The burned brandy left a heavy, smoky taste on the outside and the center was warm and pink, exactly right. He tasted Pudge's pheasant and it was delicious, too. After the main course they ordered dessert, and for once he passed up apple pie because Pudge insisted he try the hazelnut cheesecake.

Pudge picked up the bill without blinking an eye. Danny counted the money she left on the table. Four twenties and a ten. Before leaving, she looked out the window. Her eyes were wistful. "I could get used to this."

Danny stood and held Pudge's chair for her. "That was the best steak I ever ate," he said. "Thanks."

"Better than the chicken-fried at the Husky truck stop?" she asked.

Danny nodded. "Just a tad." He helped her straighten the shawl around her shoulders.

"Better than Swanson's salisbury steak dinner?"

"You bet."

When they strolled outside, it was as balmy as summer. The grounds were illuminated by opaque lights on tall slim lampposts.

"We better walk this off a little," Pudge said.

"I've got to check the nets pretty soon," Danny said. "Some of us are still working."

"Those fish aren't taking off on you. Anyway, you claim you've been working too hard. But all I've seen is you stuffing your gut."

They walked the pathway to the rocky point overlooking Wah-Gwin-Gwin Falls and the Columbia River. A Cyclone fence prevented anyone from slipping over the edge and falling three hundred feet.

The falls were illuminated by spotlights. "I hear that's how they do it at Niagara," Pudge said. "They have lights on the falls at night. Sometimes they make different colors."

"How do you know that?"

"My cousin Darcy went there once, on her honeymoon." Pudge opened her purse and took out the blue feather earring. She held it over the fence a moment, then turned it loose, and they watched as the blue feather twirled through the lighted mist.

"Why'd you take it?"

"Because I wanted to." Pudge laughed. "Anyway, that feather looked better on the pigeon."

The Columbia Gorge Hotel's cupola was ringed with small white lights, and Danny realized he had seen that circle of lights the night before from the fish hatchery across the river. He wondered about the seal — if it was a seal — he'd seen swimming.

He started to say something to Pudge, but she seemed lost in thought. He stared at the river and the lights on the opposite shore until he was practically hypnotized. Only another week of fishing to go. Maybe they could just drop some dynamite into the pools and collect the fish when they floated to the top, their air bladders burst. A Du Pont spinner. That would sure save a lot of time shaking out nets and releasing fish . . .

"Marry me."

He had been thinking so hard, he almost didn't hear Pudge. Now he turned toward her, his mouth open. "What?"

"I'm half drunk and I'm asking you, because I don't think you're ever going to get around to it." She tugged the corners of her shawl and glanced down. "I might not ask again."

Something about her tone made Danny realize she meant it. "You don't have to go and threaten me."

"I'm waiting."

He decided to say yes, knowing he could always change his mind later. Besides, a nurse would make good money. "All right."

"You're saying yes?"

"That's right," Danny said, and Pudge quickly signed a cross over his lips, then kissed them, sealing the promise. She tasted like brandy.

"Maybe we should go someplace," Danny said after he and Pudge had gazed at the lights a while longer.

"I thought those nets were waiting — just crammed with fish."

Danny pretended not to hear her. "I wonder how much the rooms are in this place."

"About a hundred dollars. I checked."

He whistled softly. "They provide a girl?"

"No way. A hundred dollars buys the room and their world-famous farm breakfast for two."

"I wouldn't have time to eat it," Danny said. "Too busy racing my check to the bank." He quit leaning on the fence and touched his pocket, checking the truck keys. "Time to run the nets, I guess."

Pudge didn't move. "Five more minutes. I want to remember this."

"Just five," Danny said, although he realized he could watch the river and lights for hours.

Downriver, a sliver of gray light hung above the dark rim of the Gorge. In that direction, the water still had a slight silver glitter. Upriver, the dark span of the interstate bridge arched over the water. On the water, the running lights of boats indicated that some of the fishermen had already gone out to check their catch. Half closing his eyes, Danny imagined the dark shadow of the Tidewater barge coming upstream, and it made him uneasy.

Midriver, the buoy's light winked red, casting a crimson hue on the dark water. It winked again. Upriver, a spurt of red, like a lit flare, caught Danny's attention. At first he thought the Burlington Northern's signal lights had come on, indicating a train in the block, but the red spurt geysered until it was higher than the railroad bridge. Danny knew it was an explosion even before he heard the boom rumble across the water. Two more quick explosions followed the first, and Danny saw burning debris carried skyward, like burning shingles spinning off a roof, caught in the fire's up-draft.

"It's the fish camp!" Danny shouted and started for the truck.

He raced across the lawn, hurdling the low hedges. Pudge stayed with him until they reached the truck. She jumped in and slammed her door shut in unison with his. Danny started the engine and tore out of the parking lot, fishtailing in the loose gravel, then straightening out when he hit the asphalt on Westcliff Road.

"How'd you get so fast?" he asked Pudge, amazed that she had been able to keep up with him.

"Wind sprints." Pudge looked worried. "Are you sure Jack's with Velrae?"

Danny nodded. "Pretty sure. He should still be at Preacher's Point. To tell you the truth, he's getting sweet on her." For once, he hoped Jack was with Willis's granddaughter.

Pudge relaxed a little, but she braced herself by placing one hand on the dash. She was breathing heavily. "It's worse than running the bases."

Danny nodded. "Must be I'm slowing down." He kept the speedometer at sixty until he hit the exit for the bridge. He paused at the toll booth just long enough to fling two quarters at the tender. When the light flashed green and the twenty-five mph sign winked on, Danny gunned the engine. He went fifty across the gridded bridge even though the tires chattered and he had to wrestle the steering wheel. After passing two cars, he nearly hit a third head-on. Horns blared at him, and Pudge's shoulder slammed against the passenger door.

"Where's the damn seat belt?"

"I've been meaning to put one in," Danny said.

As he neared the Washington end of the bridge, Danny saw the Bingen fire truck race by. "Outlaw," he said. The Outlaw truck covered fires beyond the city limit.

The fish camp glowed eerily in the light from the burning boats. Three were raging fiercely, the burning fiberglass sending spirals of smoke into the night sky. Reflected flames danced on the side of Danny's trailer and against the shimmering fish totes. A few of the garbage-filled totes had ignited and were burning like flarepots.

Danny drove as close to the fire as he could and jumped out.

Staring through the haze of smoke and ash, he thought he saw bodies floating in the water, and for a terrible moment it seemed that the haunting visions of men on the river had become real. "Jack," he whispered.

Pushing past some firemen, he raced to the river's edge. After blinking several times, Danny realized nothing was floating in the water except pieces of the burned boats and a bobbing gas can. Dizzy, he steadied himself against one of the empty fish totes.

Pudge came up beside him and touched his arm. "I thought you weren't worried."

Afraid his voice would crack, he didn't speak.

The firemen from the Outlaw sprayed water on Willis's shack, Danny's trailer, and the fish-drying shack. The boats couldn't be saved. The goose waddled among the fishermen, hissing and spreading his wings, making himself a general nuisance. A couple of the firemen kicked at him, and he pecked at their thick rubber boots with his orange beak.

"Look at the nets," Pudge said.

Danny hadn't seen them at first. All the nets had been piled in one of the boats and were melting. The plastic floats burned slowly and popped with the heat.

Willis arrived in his pickup. He left the door open, and he walked stiffly, back straight, until he stood a few feet from the burning boats. His gray hair was unbraided and winnowed in the heat draft.

Danny half expected Willis's hair or flannel shirt to burst into flames. After a while, one of the firemen in an asbestos coat took Willis's arm and led him a short distance away.

During the next half hour, pickup loads of sportfishermen and Indians arrived at the camp and separated into small knots, tight as fists. Standing with their hands thrust in pockets and their legs spread, the groups of men eyed each other menacingly.

Each pickup had a gun rack, and Danny was afraid some hothead might push things too hard. "Better go sit in your car," he told Pudge. "Watch for Jack."

"Be careful, now," she said.

After a while, the sportfishermen determined that their boats weren't burning, so they relaxed a little. The Indians grew grimmer, but they were outnumbered. Two Bingen police cars had arrived, but the policemen didn't approach the Indians. Eventually, two highway patrol cars showed up, and those officers conferred briefly with the local men, then began interviewing the sportfishermen and the Indians.

The state policeman who approached Willis began by saying, "I'm sorry about these boats burning up."

"That's my boat over there." Willis pointed to the broken red boat that sat some distance from the fire. "I lost my grandson in that wreck."

The trooper took off his Smokey hat and wiped his forehead.

"See that boat in the middle." Willis pointed to the green tri-hull that was being consumed by flames. "That's mine, too. And the slashed nets over there? Mine. The burning nets are Marvin Tenino's. He's a friend."

The policeman wrote something in his notebook. "Are you insured?"

Willis smiled slightly. "No one sells Indians insurance."

The officer wrote something else. "'Any idea how this got started?"

"Ask them guys," Willis said, pointing to a group of sportfishermen. "All their boats are still floating."

"Don't worry. My partner's covering them. Can you think of anyone who'd want to do this? Old enemy? Past grudge?"

Willis folded his arms. "You want a list? Try this: sportfishermen, the state cops, the federal wardens, the sheriff's department, the Bureau of Indian Affairs. They all want us off these sites."

The policeman's mouth had set in a firm line; he was listening politely but not writing anything.

"This is an act of war against a sovereign nation! Someone has declared war on the River People!"

Velrae's voice made Danny jump because he hadn't seen her approach. Now she stood so close beside him he could feel her breath as she spoke. Turning slightly, he saw the rage that twisted her face.

"Could I please have your name?" The officer tapped his pencil against the book.

"Figure it out yourself. My father's already in prison for no cause." Velrae turned to Willis. "Why don't you just order him off here. We might be willing to talk to federal people — nation to nation — but no local yokels."

The policeman flipped his notebook closed and faced Velrae. "If we find out the perpetrators are sportfishermen, then they still come under our jurisdiction."

Velrae put her hands on her hips and leaned forward until her face was almost in the policeman's. "Listen. They put my father in prison for three years just for selling a few fish. The white guys have been violating all kinds of laws, but nothing happens to them. Suspended sentences — at the worst. She touched his elbow and turned him slightly. "Let me make this easy so even you can figure it out. Those guys" — she thrust her chin at the tight knot of sportfishermen — "check their rigs for gas cans and explosives. Make yourself useful before somebody gets killed."

"Better keep a lid on," the policeman said. "We'll get to the bottom of this."

"You couldn't find your butt in the bathtub," Velrae said, and went into the house. Willis went over to talk with Marvin.

"She takes some getting used to," Danny said to the policeman.

"If everyone would cooperate, our job would be a lot easier," he said. "She your relative?"

Danny shook his head. "That pleasure is someone else's."

"I may as well get your statement."

Danny told him about leaving the fish camp and eating across the river. When he mentioned where he'd been, the policeman looked a little strange.

"You were at the hotel?" he asked. "Having dinner?"

"That's right. I saw the explosion from over there." Danny guessed the policeman found it odd that they had gone to such a spendy place.

"I'm just curious what you had."

"Indigestion, as soon as the bill came." Danny didn't know if the policeman was checking on his story or what. "I considered ordering the eastern Oregon lamb, but who wants to pay twenty-one ninety-five for mutton? I had the steak. It was good, too."

The officer tapped his pencil against the page of the book. "That's what I had. Took my wife there for our thirtieth. It was damn expensive, but you only go around once, the way I see it.

Can you think of anything else that might help, anything unusual?"

"Right up there." Danny pointed to the road overlooking the fish camp. "A yellow minivan was broken down — some guy tinkering with the engine. I didn't get the license number."

"A yellow van?" The officer frowned. "I wonder what it was doing there?"

"So do I," Danny said, "now that I think about it."

"All right," the officer said. "We'll be in touch as the investigation progresses."

After the policeman left, Jack came over and stood beside Danny. He seemed a little dazed. "Can you believe this shit?"

"Where you been, Hotshot?" Danny tried to seem casual.

"Talking to Pudge." Jack patted Danny's shoulder. "Great news. So you're going to do it, huh? Make it legal?"

In the fire's excitement, Danny had almost forgotten about his promise.

"You got a bargain, if you ask me." Jack's grin widened. "By the way, when you move in with her, maybe I can have the trailer."

Danny put his hands on Jack's shoulders. "What I sort of planned all along was sticking Pudge with you. No way are you getting the trailer."

Jack's smile half faded. "Just a thought. We can talk later." He swept his arm over the camp. "We're done fishing — that's for sure."

The Indian fishermen began heading back in their pickups, and as they drove up the steep hill, Danny saw their broad shoulders and heads through the cabs' rear windows. The road dust made the taillights appear to wink dim and bright.

A few old fishermen remained, huddled around the small table in Willis's kitchen. The window was open and Danny heard them discussing ways to protect the fish camps. Someone mentioned a Washat, the traditional Seven Drum service, and the old men started making plans.

"When we heading out?" Jack asked. "No more fish means the kid can get it down the road. I want to check out the used car lots in The Dalles. Last week they had a hot Camaro on special, but I was a little short. Maybe you'd loan me five hundred so I can take care of unfinished business.

"Get Pudge to cosign," Danny said. "I been thinking about buying a boat, going partners with Willis for next year."

"No way." Jack pointed at the charred hulls in the water. "He's lost two this season."

Danny squinted at the burned boats, and another scene appeared: the burning cabin and the dead men along the river. He shuddered, recalling the fish camp debris he had mistaken for bodies in the black water. He had to learn what the visions meant, and he remembered Wauna's instructions. He would go to the Wallowas, gather dirt for Loxie's grave, and see what he could find. He decided to leave the next day and return in time for the Washat.

As Pudge undressed for bed in the Wind River trailer, she said, "It's pretty cramped in here. Reminds me of the places my mother rented."

"My trailer back home's a lot bigger," Danny said.

"I figure you'll be moving into my house." Pudge found a bent hanger and hung up her blouse. "I know you don't think much of those BIA houses, but I remember how Mom dreamed of buying a house. She cut out pictures from magazines she got at the grocery. Filled two scrapbooks. Mom would have given a lot just for a chance to live in a place like mine."

She kept talking and Danny muttered occasionally, although he wasn't listening too carefully. Her voice reminded him of Loxie's, and he was thinking back to those times when they were first married and they lay awake talking far into the night.

After Pudge fell asleep, Danny stared at the ceiling for a long time because he realized suddenly that he actually was going to settle for Pudge.

He got up quietly and put on his coat. By the time he drove all the way to Preacher's Point, a few streaks of gray shone in the east. He sat at the bluff's edge, feet dangling over the basalt cliff, and watched the early light brighten the sky. The wind, still dry but now cold, blew from upriver.

A barge headed downstream carrying grain. He saw the shadowy barge moving on the water and the yellow cabin lights streaming from the tug's pilot house. Two men leaned against the tug's railing, their voices carrying across the still water. One tapped his pipe against the railing, showering glowing sparks into the water. The smell of pipe smoke drifted to Danny's perch.

Danny tossed loose pebbles into the black water. Although he couldn't see them hit, he heard quiet splashes and imagined the dark pebbles sinking past the carving of salmon and Water Devils. How deep were those old drawings? he wondered. He listened for any voices that might rise from the depths, but all he heard was the wash from the barge slapping against the basalt. "Still not talking, huh?" he muttered. Peering over the edge, he thought about the watery campfires Willis had described, but he saw only the reflections of the shore lights dancing on the surface.

◈ 12 ◈

DUG BAR

A WOODEN INDIAN painted blue and red stood outside the Imnaha General Store and Bar. About fifteen feet to the left of the store was a state marker explaining how Chief Joseph and his people had once inhabited the Wallowa country and Imnaha River Valley. They wintered in the lower valleys, away from the wind and snow, and spent the hot summers in high meadows closer to the timber, grazing their livestock in the lush grass.

Danny gazed over the bridge at the clear Imnaha River, one of the places the Nez Perce had crossed on their forced march from their homeland. Shadowy trout hovered over a gravel bar in a quiet pool downstream. It was difficult to imagine the shallow river as a spring torrent, the way it had been when his people had to cross.

Inside the store, a woman with a thick blond braid was playing with a little girl who seemed to be six or seven. The woman wore no bra, but she was wearing a beaded necklace and scuffed sandals. Danny figured she was a leftover hippie.

"Can I help you?"

"Maybe I better have a six-pack of Oly," Danny said. As she went to the cooler, he added, "Make that two. This is dry country." He looked around the store. They had groceries and picnic supplies, sundry items such as mouse traps and clothesline, sporting goods and camping equipment. The long dark bar was nicely polished and had a RAINIER sign behind it. The heads and antlers of trophy-sized animals decorated the walls. One elk's head sported dark sunglasses and had a cigar dangling from its mouth.

Danny was curious about a wooden salmon sculpture. Luhr-Jensen spinners, resembling fish scales, covered the stained-cedar body. The head was a mask with an elongated nose and sharp white teeth. Underneath, a little plaque read: ANXIOUS SALMON.

The woman noticed Danny looking at the fish. "What do you think? We got it from an artist in Portland."

Danny could tell she was proud of it, so he said, "I kind of like it."

"Yeah, we did, too, especially my husband, Rocky. He's a musician. If you come through on a weekend night, this place jumps. You like country-western?"

"What else?" Danny said.

"A long time ago, this bar was owned by one of the original Sons of the Pioneers."

"You're kidding!"

"Nope. Got their record on the wall."

Danny saw the album cover *Sons of the Pioneers' Golden Hits.* He squinted so he could read the song titles across the bar: "Tumblin' Tumbleweed," "Cool Water," "Ghost Riders in the Sky" . . . "That's pretty neat," he said, even though he thought Johnny Cash sang "Ghost Riders" better.

"Lot of history in this old place," she said.

"I believe it." Danny gave the woman the money and she put the beer in a sack. "What's that road like down the Imnaha?"

"How far you going, and what kind of rig you got?"

"Dug Bar." He nodded at the pickup outside. The bed contained three buckets of dirt.

"You should do all right, but it'll take you two or three hours yet."

"I thought it was only thirty miles."

"*Slow* miles," she said. "Pretty good road down to Fence Creek. After that, go real careful and don't goose it on the corners."

"Gumbo?"

She nodded. "Real slick, even though the Forest Service threw some gravel on top. And steep — all up and down. Some guy was coming out the other day after floating Hell's Canyon and he went off the side. Wrecked his boat and trailer. But he went off in a good place or he'd still be falling. In some spots, it's deeper than China."

"I'll watch it," Danny said. "The brakes are good, the tires are fair."

"One other thing. The news said a storm's coming. If that road slicks, let it dry a couple hours before you drive. Otherwise, the Wallowa County Search and Rescue will have to hunt for pieces."

Danny drank two beers between the Imnaha store and Stubblefield Creek, about ten miles downriver. The farmhouses scattered along the river were modest but well kept, and most had gardens and small orchards. Danny remembered that his people had grown apricots and peaches in the lower Imnaha after seedlings had been introduced by the missionaries.

Herefords grazed on the steep brown hillsides and in the alfalfa stubble along the water. A few places were running sheep. Two ring-necked pheasants strutted across the dusty road, then disappeared in a serviceberry thicket. It was good country, Danny thought, and he imagined how it must have pained his ancestors to leave.

At Stubblefield Creek he stopped the truck, getting out to inspect the small white gravestone for Tinie Stubblefield, an early settler's daughter who had died at age three. Someone had recently built a Sears mesh fence around the gravestone, but Danny couldn't imagine why. Dry stalks of balsam root rustled in the light breeze, and he pictured spring hillsides colored with bright yellow patches.

At Cow Creek Bridge, the road crossed the Imnaha. Here Danny could hike the Nimipu Trail overland, following the rock cairns. The Forest Service marked the trail with rock cairns because trees were scarce. But there was no shortage of rock in this basalt landscape. It was so barren and rugged, it made him think of the Stinker Station signs he had seen traveling across the Oregon Desert, where the ground was littered with rocks: DESERT WATER-MELONS. TAKE SOME HOME TO YOUR MOTHER-IN-LAW.

The road narrowed and twisted, first climbing steeply, then plunging into canyons. Danny gripped the steering wheel and kept his eyes on the road. He was glad he had stopped at two beers. The pickup clung to the side of Cactus Mountain, then headed down the road into China Gulch. Glancing quickly over the side, Danny guessed it was a quarter-mile dropoff in some places.

"Must have been a pack trail," he muttered, thinking of the old days, when supplies came by sure-footed mule. They dug their hooves into the scree to keep from sliding, but at times they lost their footing. One sliding mule had rolled over three times to stop itself. The animal was carrying crates of eggs for the gold miners and only six were broken. According to the story, the packer stopped on the spot to fix a quick omelette. In this country, eggs were once worth about as much as gold, ounce for ounce. So was a good mule.

Dug Bar was named for Thomas Douglass, a stockman who built a cabin on the Oregon side of the Snake River in 1880 and used the area for winter range. He was ambushed in 1883, his remains buried by neighbors who found the body between Dug Creek and Robinson Gulch, a few miles upstream from the cabin. Deep Creek, the next drainage above Robinson, was known as Dead Line Creek because Douglass refused to allow the Nez Perce to graze their horses north of it. If they crossed, he shot them.

The road ended at Dug Bar Ranch, and Danny stopped the pickup at the cluster of buildings just beyond the five-acre hayfield.

The main house and cowboys' bunkhouse sat some distance from the river, with older buildings scattered between the new ones and the water. The original house stood just beyond the bunkhouse. Two burned-through woodstoves had been dragged from the house. The first sat a hundred yards up the hill; the second was just off the front porch. By the time the second stove burned through, Danny thought, the folks must have been too old to drag it way up the hill, so they just pushed it off the porch.

"If I lived here, I'd be home," Danny said to himself. He got out of the pickup after parking in the slight shade of one of the squat hackberry trees close to the house. Someone was raising a little garden and had designed cedar shake tents to protect the tomato plants from the fierce sun.

Danny walked toward the river. He passed an old shop, a barn with a corrugated roof, and a sunken post corral with a loading chute. Upstream from the cluster of buildings was a weed-choked pasture. A broken Fairbanks-Morse engine at the river's edge had once been used to pump irrigation water. Danny didn't know if the place was making it, but it couldn't be by much.

By the river's backeddy, at the edge of the alfalfa field, Danny read the sign that told about the Nez Perce crossing the Snake after General Howard had ordered them to Lapwai.

The Nez Perce had no boats and tied their possessions in large bundles covered by tipi hides to form makeshift rafts. Strong young men, including Left Hand, had pulled the rafts across the flooded rivers from horseback while the women, children, and old people rode the bundles or hung on to the trailing ropes. Although the Snake was especially dangerous in spring, they crossed without losing a human life. But getting the animals across was more difficult, and they suffered heavy losses of their stock.

The Dug Bar crossing was later used by outlaws and horse thieves who trafficked between the Wallowas and the Salmon River country. Even in September the backeddy looked swollen and ominous, and Danny was glad he didn't have to cross, but he knew that Left Hand returned this way after the war ended, hiding out and traveling by night.

Glancing downriver, Danny saw a red-faced man with a badly crippled leg limping toward him. The man waved his fishing pole as a kind of greeting. When he got closer, Danny noticed that his green canvas creel was plumped out with fish.

"You'll be staying for lunch?" the man asked. He tapped the creel to indicate the menu. "I don't get much company."

"Sure," Danny said. "Got some trout there?"

"Bass. River's too warm for trout. These are sweeter tasting, anyway." The man stuck out his hand. "Howdy."

"Howdy, yourself," Danny said. He shook the man's hand.

The man chuckled. "Howdy. That's my moniker. Folks named me Herbert, but no one calls me that unless they want their ear chomped.

"I'm Danny."

"Let's get out of the sun."

Howdy took the creel from his shoulder and dumped the fish into a large metal sink that sat just outside the back door. There were five nice bass weighing from a pound to a pound and a half.

"What did you catch those on?" Danny asked.

Howdy squinted at him. "If I told every cuss who passed by here all my secrets, I wouldn't be much of a fisherman, would I?"

"I guess not. You want some help there?"

"Just keep back." Howdy started cleaning the fish. He had a fisherman's knife — blade and scaler — and Danny didn't think he'd ever seen anyone prepare fish so fast.

"How about a beer? They're not very cold," Danny said. "I bought them in Imnaha."

"Damn right. Long as it's wet. Some of the boys went into Joseph a couple of days ago. Drank all my beer before they left and promised to bring back a case. I expected them by now, but they probably found some women. Heard there was a dance at Toma's, there in Enterprise."

Danny went to the pickup and brought back the beer. He handed one to Howdy, who drained the can in two long gulps. "Try another," Danny said, handing him a second.

They went inside, and Danny was surprised at how clean the kitchen was. Howdy poured an inch of oil into a cast iron skillet and turned on the stove. Selecting a thin knife from a rack, he cut some filets from the bass. Reaching into the cupboard, he took out a box of Krusteaz pancake flour and poured three inches into the bowl. Then he dipped the fish in the flour.

"I'm not a cook by trade. I used to be a packer until a horse rolled over on me. Gave me this leg. It was all I could do to climb back on that horse and ride for help. The pain made me black out, and I had to tie my hands to the saddlehorn. That was five, no, six years back."

He spit into the skillet and seemed satisfied that the oil was the right temperature. After dropping six filets into the sizzling oil, he turned down the heat a notch.

"This your place now?" Danny asked.

"Not mine. Judge Tippet's. I work for wages. I'd be money ahead if I'd done that all my life, but I kept prospecting." He took a spatula and turned the fish. "Never been quite flat broke. I'm working up to it. Still, I enjoy my luxuries. Tobacco and tea. Think I'll fix us a cup. How about it?

Without waiting for Danny to reply, Howdy reached into the cupboard and took down two white mugs. He blew into each cup, then turned them upside down and shook them hard. "Damn spiders."

Danny grinned because he knew it was for show.

Howdy filled a teakettle with water and set it on the back burner. "You probably heard of Buckskin Billy, over on the Salmon River?"

Danny shook his head. The fish bubbling in the fat smelled almost ready, and his stomach growled.

"Billy had more kinds of tea than anybody in these parts. The tour boats always stopped there, and dudes dropped off special blends, whatever they might brew up in Seattle or Vancouver." He poked at some containers on the shelf. "You want English Breakfast, Orange Pekoe, Earl Grey, or Gunpowder?"

"I always drink Gunpowder myself," Danny said. He was enjoying this.

Howdy took a tea strainer and measured out some dark tea. It was about the color of old black powder.

"One of Billy's favorite tricks was to ask people if they wanted some pickles to go with the tea. If they said yes, he'd pull down some mason jars stinking of formaldehyde and show them the creatures he had preserved. Some weak bellies took off without even finishing their tea." Howdy laughed. "The craziest were some cougar fetuses. Somebody gutshot the mother, I guess, and Billy found those cubs dropped along the trail." His eyes softened in memory. "Yeah, old Billy knew how to rattle the dudes."

Howdy set a cup of steaming dark tea in front of Danny. "See this belt buckle?"

Danny nodded. On the buckle was TRUE WEST — 30TH ANNIVERSARY. He hadn't seen one like it. "Where'd you get that?"

"The magazine people sent it to me all the way from back east in Oklahoma. After Billy died, I sent them an article about his life — being a hermit there on the Salmon — and they spruced it up a little and printed it. Got a copy around here somewhere." He looked around, then shrugged. "I'll get it later. That bass is ready."

The fish was delicious. Inside the sweet crust, the white flesh was moist and flaky. "Hey, this is damn good."

Howdy smiled. "That Krusteaz works on chicken, too."

After the sweetness of the fish, Danny's tea seemed bitter. "Got some sugar?"

Howdy took a bowl out of the refrigerator and put it on the

table. "Damn ants. Can't leave anything out. They don't mess with the tea, though."

Danny pulled the sugar toward him. The yellowish-white bowl had an odd feeling to it, and at first Danny thought it was some kind of hippie pottery. He stirred two teaspoons of sugar into the tea, then sipped it. "That's better." He examined the sugar bowl again. Dark cracks ran along the sides and bottom, and he traced one with his forefinger. Suddenly, he dropped the sugar bowl and half rose from his chair. It wasn't a bowl but the bottom part of a skull.

Howdy grinned and wiped his mouth with his sleeve. "Don't worry. That's not one of your people."

"Shook me up," Danny said. He wiped his hands on his shirt, as if they were dirty.

"I'm no graverobber," Howdy said, "although we've had our share of those around here. Some people go messing wherever they find tipi rings or scatter. You know, the stuff the Indians chipped on. But let me introduce you right proper. Fong, this here's Danny. Danny, what's left of Fong."

Howdy picked up the skull, turning it around in his hands. "I met this old fellow at Robinson Gulch. Figured he's one of the Chinese that got himself massacred. A passel of miners. After lots of hard work, they come up even shorter than I did." He set the skull on the table and Danny picked it up.

"It's sure well preserved," he said.

"It's the dryness, I suppose. Most people don't even realize they're spooning sugar from a skull, but when they do, Fong catches their breath right short. It's a conversation stopper."

"They were killed?" Danny asked.

"Murdered."

Danny closed his eyes. "How many?"

"Thirty, maybe thirty-five. Settlers kept finding bloated bodies down the river for months. Nobody knows how many for sure. No one saw it happen but the guys that did it." He tipped back in his chair. "Of course, there never was much gold this far up the Snake. Copper. Lots of copper right downriver at Eureka Bar. But only a little float gold washed down from the springmelt.

"You know, a lot of China-boys came into this country after the big strikes in central Idaho. Well, they had the devil's own time. You have to feel sorry for them. The law said they could only buy claims that were already played out, so they just worked the tailings. If they found anything worthwhile, someone claimjumped them. And they got taxed for working those worthless spots, lots of times by thieves posing as deputies. Some got slaughtered by Indians. They thought the yellow skin was poison."

Danny opened his eyes. "Not Nez Perce. Some of them took in the Chinese. A few married them."

"I don't know. Indians. After the scalping and butchering, it was pretty hard to tell what brand Indian was doing the hacking. I heard over a hundred China-boys got slaughtered out in the desert somewhere."

"That was Snake Indians, for sure," Danny said.

"Maybe so. But it was white boys killed these fellows on the Snake. Horse thieves and gold robbers. They had a little hideout not far from where the miners were working, and somehow they thought those China-boys were rich. They killed them for pocket change, though, so if they were rich, that gold's still out there waiting."

Medicine Bird and Red Shirt had been through that country so much, Danny thought he knew every story. "I never heard of that massacre," he said.

Howdy shrugged. "No one put up markers or anything. Not much left but some crumbling cabin walls. A few prospectors think there still might be gold, so they keep quiet. Me, I've been over every inch of that country. Only found Fong."

"Maybe the outlaws spent the gold after they left prison." Danny said.

Howdy slapped his knee. "No one went to prison. Maybe they would have over killing that many whites. But by the time anyone got around to holding a trial, the ringleaders — or those they said was ringleaders — had left the territory. The others claimed they just watched the shooting."

Danny shook his head.

"No witnesses, and those cowboys stuck to their story. So they all walked away scot-free."

"How far is it?" Danny asked.

"What?"

"Robinson Gulch."

Howdy scratched his head. "Hell, I don't know. Maybe two, three hours' walk if you're in good shape. I haven't been up there since this leg went bust on me. The trail along the bench starts right behind the house, just at the edge of the upper pasture."

"Easy walking?"

Howdy squinted. "Nothing's easy in this country but heartbreak. I suppose it's four or five miles as the trail winds. There's no water until you hit the river, and the snakes are bad because they're still shedding — blind as hell. But the poison ivy's knocked down a little bit. You won't find any gold, though. Lots of folks have already looked. One time when I was back there, I even found an old tobacco can. Someone had scratched on it: 'I was skunked here, too. D.B. 1934.' Not much to see. Part of an old rock cabin and some weird rock pictures. You know, petroglyphs. Indian stuff. Someone doctored them up to make them look Chinese, but they're a lot older than that."

"I'd like to borrow a canteen if you can loan me one."

"Sure. It's a thirsty trip." Howdy glanced out the window. The sky had turned gray and the wind had picked up, swirling the dust. "Storm's brewing."

"It won't hurt to get a little wet."

"Wet brings trouble in this country. The gumbo gets slick as snot. Come spring, when the gumbo thaws a little, a cow might lose her footing and slide down the hillside, faster and faster. She bellows and bawls real pitiful, but there's no stopping until she plunges over a cliff and bounces a time or two. By then, the meat's so bloodshot from striking rock, it's no good except for buzzards."

"I'll watch my step," Danny said.

Howdy nodded. "You do that. I'll pack you a flashlight and some matches. Maybe toss in a little tarp. If you get caught out, you might want to hunker down and build a fire." He glanced at the sky. "I wouldn't go, but it's your neck." Shaking his head, Howdy stepped into a storeroom and starting gathering gear.

Danny went outside to the pickup and rustled around in the paper sack behind the seat until he found a clean pair of socks. Taking off his boots, he put the fresh socks next to his feet, the worn socks over those. Two pairs should keep the boots from slipping and giving him blisters. The clean socks felt so good, he reminded himself to wash them out more often.

When he got back to the house, Howdy had put a canteen, a small tarp, matches, and flashlight in a "kidney buster," the old army surplus backpack with a curved metal frame. He had also packed some sandwiches and an apple.

"This pack's a little big, but it leaves your hands free. There's places where the trail's dicey on the bluffs above the river. You might need to hang on."

"Thanks," Danny said. "Tell me again, how do I get there?"

"The trail climbs a thousand feet or so to a middle bench and then levels off for a while. It winds around a couple of smaller benches. You cross one drainage — that's Fence Gulch — and you'll see some old posts. Keep going. Then you come to a bigger drainage — Dug Creek. Upcanyon, you'll see scattered ponderosas. Right there, leave the bench trail and work down to the Snake. Once you hit the river, follow the game trails. A mile or so farther upstream, that's Robinson Gulch. You'll see the remains of a rock cabin — not much to it. Somebody might have a camp set up. Lots of rafters stop there."

"Okay," Danny said. "I've got it."

Howdy opened the back door and they stood outside for a minute. Low gray clouds scuttled across the sky. "Think it's a bad storm?" Danny asked.

"I'd bet on it. If you get caught out, hunker down, just like I say. I wouldn't walk that trail in the dark, flashlight or no flashlight. Maybe you should wait. Stay here and we'll catch some fish before the storm hits. There's not much to see up there, anyway."

"It's personal," Danny said. "But thanks."

Howdy shrugged. "Suit yourself, then. I'll save a couple beers for tonight. I can usually find a nudie movie with that satellite dish, so hurry back."

"Sure."

"One more thing," Howdy said, gripping Danny's shoulder. "If you stumble on that gold, we divvy it fair and square."

Danny grinned. "Fifty-fifty."

·　·　·

It was midafternoon by the time Danny reached the Dug Creek gulley that dropped toward the Snake. Above the benchland, scattered ponderosas grew in a spring-fed upper canyon. Howdy's directions had been easy enough to follow, but the trail was treacherous in places, and Danny's respect grew for the men who spent their lives along the Snake. He walked carefully so he wouldn't slip on the basalt scree or trip over the sagebrush roots. Once he glimpsed a snake writhing off the trail and disappearing in the yellow bunchgrass. He hoped it was a bull or king snake, not a rattler.

The descent into Dug Creek was very steep. He was worried about turning an ankle — or worse. He didn't want to wind up coyote bait or have Jack mock him if search and rescue teams had to drag him out by packhorse.

He found one flat place between the bench and the river. An old bedsprings and a burned-through coffeepot indicated where a cabin had stood. Not a scrap of precious lumber remained, and he figured the settlers had hauled it away to build another cabin. Sometimes, if they couldn't carry the lumber, the settlers burned their cabins to retrieve the nails.

When he reached the riverbank, he rested in the shade of a hackberry. Klamath weeds and serviceberries grew along the river, not to mention the thickets of poison ivy he carefully avoided. As he looked at the rocks, spiders seemed to be everywhere, and he had to brush three off that started crawling up his pants. He washed his hands in the river, then dipped his blue bandanna in the water and washed his face. The air was getting muggy, as if a storm were coming.

Danny found a game trail and followed it downriver until he came to a place where both sides of the canyon had collapsed, forming steep rockslides several hundred yards across. "Howdy didn't mention this," he grumbled. Between the rockslides, the river narrowed into a series of wild rapids. Danny started making his way across the jumbled basalt rocks, placing his hands and feet carefully. The last thing he needed was a snakebite.

Beyond the rockslide was Robinson Gulch. The good-size sandbar and riverbank offered enough flat land to set up several tents, although none was there now. He studied the land and water, becoming convinced that this was the place he had seen in his vision, although the sandbar looked different, probably because the dams along the Snake had changed the water levels.

The place seemed gloomy to him, oppressed by a mood darker than the one cast by the gray sky. He climbed off the rocks and examined the sandbar. The marks of recent rafts were evident, and along the riverbank the grass had been trampled.

The remains of an old rock cabin stood at the mouth of the gulch, tucked against the rock face, which served as the fourth wall. The sides had been constructed of dark basalt rocks, and there was no sign of chinking. It must have been damn cold in winter, Danny thought. The inside of the cabin was crawling with spiders. On the floor was an empty can of Vienna sausage, a granola bar wrapper, and some sort of foil pouch that had held soy milk. It struck Danny as odd that the rafters who stopped there didn't pack out their garbage.

A short distance from the cabin, he found the rocks with the petroglyph paintings that Howdy had mentioned. Traces of the original ocher coloring remained, but someone had painted over the Indian designs with white and doctored the drawings to make them look more Chinese.

Danny poked around the riverbank awhile but found nothing of interest. Then he walked up the gulch for a short distance. "Maybe I'll stumble over the treasure chest," he muttered. He found the jawbone of a sheep and some ribs. A few other bones lay scattered by the coyotes. The canyon was steep here and, glancing up, Danny wondered if the coyotes had chased the sheep until it fell to its death. He knew wild sheep had once been abundant in the canyon. During the years the winterkill diminished the elk and deer, sheep were still plentiful, a staple for the Indians. Although Danny thought of the old Nez Perce as big game hunters, he realized they ate more salmon and sheep than anything else.

Danny had never cared much for mutton. It left a rancid, tallowy taste in his mouth most of the time, and Red Shirt claimed it gave you "Basque breath," a phrase he used because there were so many Basque sheepherders in eastern Oregon.

At the powwows and festivals, they sometimes served mutton stew, but Danny usually passed or took only a very small portion, out of politeness. Glancing at the steep cliff again, Danny decided the sheep had fallen. He didn't see any other way it could have gotten to this stretch of the river. He felt uncomfortable suddenly, realizing that he was vulnerable, just as the miners had been. It was a silly thought, he knew, but it made him uneasy, and he decided to fill the canteen, then head out.

Danny walked back to the sandbar and knelt beside the water. It was clear enough to reflect the cloudy gray sky and his face. Watching the sky and water appear to merge in the river, Danny felt a little dizzy. He shook his head and blinked.

Tilting the canteen to one side allowed the air bubbles to rush out. Ducks landed across the river, and Danny glanced up. Canvasbacks — a drake and two hens. It reminded him that duck season was close, and once he returned to Mission, he could puddlejump ducks along the Umatilla.

The canteen was full, and Danny had started to lift it from the water when something swirled on the water's surface. At first he thought it was mud stirred from the riverbottom, but the surface calmed and another face was reflected beside Danny's. He stared at the image. The face was Indian and fierce, with a fury burning in the eyes. Dreamer style, the hair was brushed into a roll above the forehead.

Danny rose and whirled about, but no one stood behind him. His heart pounded. The canteen had dropped onto the sandbar, and most of the water had trickled out before Danny noticed. He knelt again to rinse the sand off the canteen and refill it. This time he did not stare into the water but glanced quickly from the river to the high bluffs. Before standing with the full canteen, he looked again at the water and saw his own face, tight with fear.

A steep, broken trail led to a basalt outcropping overlooking the river, and Danny decided to climb as quickly as possible to the bench trail rather than stay along the river. Glancing at the sky, he was surprised at how dark it had become. He must have spent more time in Robinson Gulch than he realized. But he wouldn't spend the night, no matter what.

He started scrambling up the trail, pulling himself along with his hands where necessary. Now and again, he paused to glance over his shoulder at the river and sandbar. After he had gone a hundred yards, he suddenly realized he wasn't bothering to check for snakes. "Don't panic," he told himself, and slowed down a little.

He rested on the basalt outcropping. The basalt flow had formed a natural ledge, and from that vantage, he recognized the lay of the river as the one he had seen in his dreams.

Sweating after the steep climb, Danny unbuttoned his shirt at the neck, but the wind chilled his throat, and he buttoned up again. He took a swig from the canteen. The water tasted bitter, and he spat it onto the ground. After the long walk back, he'd be more than ready for a beer, and he hoped Howdy had saved one.

He was almost ready to leave when something in the canyon below caught his eye. Light glinted from the smooth basalt wall, as if the glow from campfire flames reflected off the dark surface. Puzzled, Danny watched the shifting light and figured it must be on the rock wall just opposite the cabin. Some rafters or kayakers could have pulled in for the night and started a campfire with dry hackberry branches, but the sandbar was empty. No smoke came from the canyon, no smell of smoke.

Danny studied the sky to make certain the sun wasn't casting any ray of light into the canyon, but the sky remained a uniform dark gray. The wind smelled of rain.

Now the reflection glowed orange-red, and the pattern of light shifted as it does with fire. Danny shook his head. He hadn't started a fire. He knew that. And he wasn't going back down to investigate. No way.

He started walking along the trail, moving fast as darkness settled. He had hoped for moonlight, but the clouds lowered. He took the flashlight out of the backpack and switched it on. Good batteries, he noted with satisfaction. Occasionally, he paused to glance back. It felt good to be up on the benchland, high above the water. Within the chasm, it had been confining and spooky. Devil's Gorge, Hell's Canyon. Whoever named it knew what he was doing.

Large raindrops pocked the trail, and the first lightning bolt shot out of the sky across the river. A jagged white line like a scar, it split the gray-black sky and struck a tree on Bear Mountain.

Danny counted the seconds until he heard the thunder crack.

Only four. The wind was in his face, and he knew he wouldn't make the return trip to Dug Bar before the storm hit full force. He hated being on the exposed benchland, dodging the lightning, but his fear of whatever lay behind was greater than his concern for the storm. He pushed on.

He tried not to think of Red Shirt's horse, but of course he remembered. His father had tethered his best horse to a lone pine on a mountainside high in the Blues while he trailed a deer on foot. Red Shirt had followed the deer for about two miles before he had a killing shot. A storm had blown in while he was on the trail, so he dressed the deer quickly, packing out just its liver, heart, and hindquarters to make better time. He hurried back to the pine only to discover that the horse had been struck by lightning — the bark and hide were still smoldering.

In spite of the trail's treacherous sections, Danny decided to hurry. The first strikes against the hillside wouldn't get him, he decided. If the lightning got too close, he'd scramble into a depression and wait out the storm under Howdy's tarp. He was almost trotting now, his breathing heavy. Lightning flashed closer, the dagger strikes hitting the basalt walls above the bench and some distance ahead. After the growling of the thunder, he heard a continuing rumble and realized the strikes had sent some rocks tumbling.

The wind drove the stinging rain straight into his face and he sucked in some water, cooling his parched throat. "I'm too old for this crap," he muttered. The gumbo slickened and clung to his boots, making his feet weigh a ton. Twice he stopped to sit on a rock and dig away the gumbo with his hands, but twenty steps farther, his boots were again slick and heavy.

He crossed Fence Creek Gulch, only a mile or so from Howdy's ranch, and he could see the lights glowing in the distance. It was difficult to say exactly how far, because there were no trees or markers on the hillside to use as gauges. Then, in a lightning flash, Danny picked out the satellite dish beside the house. It seemed about the size of a paper plate. Less than a mile.

He wondered if Howdy had caught any fish. Right now he was probably snug inside the house, his belly stuffed with bass, drinking tea and watching a movie. The rain and wind had chilled

Danny, and he thought maybe a good nudie movie would help him thaw. He and Henry used to go to the Four Star in Portland, where they had live burlesque acts between the shows, and Henry got to know most of the girls by name.

As he stumbled toward the ranch, Danny was surprised to see someone on the trail coming toward him. The wind was so strong, the figure seemed pushed along — bent at a strange angle, his clothes flapping wildly. He thought it was Howdy, walking awkwardly because of his leg.

Danny raised his arms and waved. "Hey! Go on back!" he shouted, even though the wind whipped his words away. He was pleased Howdy had come out after him, but he was also afraid for his safety. He could take a nasty tumble with that leg or draw lightning. "Put some water on for tea!" Danny cried. Trust Gunpowder tea and whiskey to take away the chill. But this time the sugar could stay in the damn skull.

The trail circled a large basalt bluff and Danny lost sight of the ranch. Lightning struck the hillside behind him, shattering rock. The thunder roared and Danny ducked, covering his ears. When he looked up, dislodged boulders were bouncing downhill, striking sparks as they hit other rocks.

Through the driving rain, the ranch lights came into view for a few seconds, but then the trail led between a high cliff and a sheer drop toward the river. Earlier in the afternoon, this place had seemed narrow but fairly safe. Now Danny stopped to dig the gumbo from his boots. He didn't want to slip and plunge into the rapids. Facing the rock wall, he moved carefully, sliding his feet along the trail, gripping the wet basalt with his hands.

Once he was across the narrow stretch, Danny saw it was mostly downhill to the ranch. "Hey, Howdy," he called to the figure ahead, "thanks for coming out after me. Let's hustle back."

Lightning struck the hillside, turning everything a brilliant blue-white. Electricity crackled. Danny stared at the figure. It wasn't Howdy or anyone else Danny knew, but a large man in a wolfskin cloak. He carried a thick walking staff with a wolfhead totem. His deep-set eyes reflected the lightning, and his flesh seemed to glow.

Pointing his staff toward Danny, the man spoke, but it was old tongue, and Danny couldn't understand at first. Transfixed, he heard himself speaking, too, although his lips and tongue remained still. The man stepped toward him and touched his chest with the wolfhead staff. Danny suddenly felt hollow, and the wind entered him, filling his head and body with a thousand shrieks and whispers.

◈ 13 ◈

LEFT HAND

DANNY AWOKE TO FIND himself lying on the ground. The man in the wolf cloak slowly passed his staff over Danny's body, singing in a high-pitched voice. As the staff passed over his limbs, Danny felt warmth returning. After a while he sat up, propping himself on one elbow and pushing back a hide blanket. Beneath the blanket he was naked. His drying clothes hung on bone pegs along the wall of the small hut. He checked himself with his fingertips and decided he was okay, although there was a dark mark on his chest where the man had touched him with the staff.

The hut was circular, perhaps seven feet in diameter, and made of elkhide stretched over bent pine poles. It resembled the temporary shelters the old Nez Perce hunters built.

A small fire in the center provided heat and some light, although not enough for Danny to study the large man's features. In the dimness, Danny could see that his head was covered with a cap of dark fur and his shoulder-length hair was as white as ermine. This surprised Danny a little, because the man seemed too large and powerful to be old.

Taking a horn cup from the fire's edge, the man in the wolf cloak handed it to Danny and motioned for him to drink. The thick liquid was hot and tasted strong but not unpleasant, and it reminded Danny of the smells from curing hides.

When Danny finished the drink, the man turned his face toward

Danny's, and his narrow eyes flickered yellow. Danny had seen those eyes before, during the first Wallowa hunt, and he had immediately been frightened, firing his rifle at the wolf before realizing it was his Wéyekin. Nevertheless, it had been a long time since he had seen his guardian, and never in this form. "Hímiin," Danny said, using the sacred word for wolf. "I know you, Grandfather."

Nodding, the old man took some green fir boughs from a pile near the door and passed them slowly over the fire, brushing the flame tips with the green needles until they glowed orange, flared brightly, then shriveled into black curls. The hut filled with pungent smudge.

He chanted a song Danny did not remember but knew as ancient. Now and again, he recognized a word or tone Medicine Bird had used in his chant. Listening carefully, Danny tried to catch hold of a few passages.

Passing his hands over the fire again, the large man burned more boughs, creating so much smudge that Danny could barely discern his hands moving over the fire. As the boughs crackled, it appeared as if the old man held his hands in the flames until they, too, glowed and smoked. He began to chant.

Staring into the fire, Danny saw the fierce face he had seen reflected at the river. The black hair was rolled above the forehead, Dreamer style, and he wore a red blanket-coat to show his bravery. On his belt were locks of hair shorn from his own head, which revealed he had hunted bison on the plains. A stone war club hung low at his side.

"Left Hand," Danny breathed.

The song changed pitch, and the large man moved his glowing hands over the fire until it seemed as if tongues of flames sprang from his fingertips, darting toward earth. Then Danny read his own face in the fire, surprised to learn how closely he resembled Left Hand.

He saw Left Hand standing beside a small warming fire made from hackberry branches. It was chilly in the twilight before dawn, and Left Hand blew on his cold hands. While his coffee water heated, he opened a tin of peaches he had brought from the Umatilla Reservation. Spearing one of the yellow halves with his hunting knife,

Left Hand bit off a chunk and wiped the juice from his chin. Remembering that Rose had packed biscuits, he took two from his cornhusk travel bag and crumbled them into the peaches, making a kind of trail cobbler. With the single spoon Rose had packed he ate, then carefully replaced the spoon in his jacket pocket. Rose would be annoyed if he lost it.

When the water was ready Left Hand made coffee, and as he drank, the coffee warmed his belly, and the cup, his hands. Feeling better, he smiled. Slick Bear, his old warmate, would show up today, tomorrow at the latest. Every year following the Nez Perce War, Slick Bear left Lapwai and came through the Salmon River country, crossing the Snake near the old Nimipu trail and meeting Left Hand at a safe place upriver.

Dug Bar, where the Nez Perce had crossed ten years earlier, had become a home for cowboys and drifters. The cabin was occupied by sullen-looking men who stole horses and pestered the more peaceful settlers. These outlaws still hung an Indian now and then, so Left Hand waited for Slick Bear farther downstream, in Fence Gulch. Here the slope was steep, with no flat place to build a cabin, no creek for fresh water, no reason to linger. Left Hand liked that.

He squatted at the river's edge, studying some of the heavy green stones that had washed down from the high mountains. They were stronger than the brittle gray stones and made good war clubs. Taking out his club, he pounded its stone head against some rocks he took from the river until they shattered. Nodding, he replaced the club, satisfied he had not found a stronger rock. His fingers paused at a large pock in the stone, where a bullet had struck the club at Big Hole. The stone had saved his leg, perhaps his life, and instead of being crippled at thirty-five he was stronger than ever, although the old shoulder wound still pained him.

The coffee tasted bitter and he flung it from the cup. Bad memories. After Left Hand's wife and daughter were killed at Big Hole, Slick Bear helped him carry his grief, even though they had no time to mourn during their escape and flight. Later, Slick Bear brought Left Hand a black ribbon shirt, and he grieved for a year. Following old trails and traveling at night to avoid hostile settlers, they journeyed back to their Wallowa homeland, stopping at the Medicine Tree so Left Hand could hang the shirt from the ram's horn.

Eventually, Slick Bear married a Christian woman in Lapwai, and even though Left Hand knew her heart was dead to the old ways, he never criticized her. But he regretted his friend's transformation as well as his own. For a disguise, they cut their hair short and wore store-bought clothes, blending in with reservation Indians. A few times they even attended church, mouthing the hymns and prayers.

But their hearts remained buried in the Wallowas, where they joined other Dreamers every fall for hunting and practicing the old ceremonies. And sometimes they secretly attended the January Medicine Dances, where the Wéyekins were revealed. Slick Bear's guardian spirit was very strong and he shared it with the young men, grabbing them in his powerful arms and carrying them around the dirt floor in an odd shuffle, like a dancing bear, while the old shamans nodded. Left Hand knew Hímiin was a powerful Wéyekin, too, but his bitterness would not let him share. Wearing some of the wolf claws he took into war, he watched the ceremonies, but he dreamed of power and revenge. Sometimes he thought of the few happy months he had spent with Swan Lighting and his daughter before the war. He gave little to Rose, a solid woman who bore him a son and saved him from imprisonment by swearing to the agent that he was no warrior but had lived with her during the war.

Rose was large, and she had grown much larger while carrying the baby, because her relatives had fattened her with oil-rich steelhead and salmon sugar. Even after eight years she remained big. When they made love, he closed his mind to the extra flesh on her belly and thighs, and sometimes in the dark, after Rose was asleep, his body was wracked with bitterness and longing.

Rose and her family stayed too close to the river, he thought, and adjusted their lives according to the seasons. He fished with them, helping to spear the bounty of salmon and steelhead, but his heart was never in it. The best part of his life was hunting the Montana buffalo with Slick Bear, Rainbow, and Five Wounds. They had to fight Blackfeet for the rights to the buffalo, and that had been adventure, too. He missed that.

Left Hand took some tanned leather strips from his bag and sat on a large basalt rock near the fire. He began braiding a new bridle for his horse. He wasn't accustomed to the work, and his fingers felt slow and clumsy.

When the sun appeared over the east canyon rim it took some of the chill from his bones, and he unbuttoned his red jacket. In the bright light, he saw a Snake-Biscuit blossom not far from the rock. Putting down his braiding, he knelt beside the flower, touching its delicate petals with his fingertips. The plant was difficult to find, and he thought about carrying this one back for Rose's garden. But that was a foolish idea, he decided. It was better to leave it here.

As he stood, he heard gunfire — many rounds — even if some had to be echoes off the basalt canyon walls. The shots came in flurries, the way they did in war, and he raced to his horse, slipping the rifle from the scabbard. He heard only a few shots now, spaced at wide intervals. Then they stopped altogether. He had heard many shots fired in the camps on certain holidays: Fourth of July, New Year's, even Christmas. But these seemed different. Left Hand thought of Big Hole, and his heart turned to ice.

He hid his horse and supplies under a rock overhang behind a hackberry thicket, and he kept a wary eye on the bluffs above. Although none of the shots seemed close, scouts or sentries could be on the benchland. When he felt it was safe for the moment, he quickly went to the river and scooped the campfire remains into the water, then covered the blackened ground with fresh damp sand. In twenty minutes, it would be dry. Walking backward to his horse, he swept away his footprints with a branch. Cradling the rifle in his arms, he watched and waited.

Hímiin's chant changed pitch as he added green moss to the fire. Through clouds of smoke, Danny saw a twisting river and a long gray sandbar where half a dozen men bathed or panned for gold. Two flat-bottomed boats were pulled onto the bar's lower end. A man wearing a loose blue shirt came out of the crude cabin nestled against the canyon's sidewall. He stretched, then dipped his hands into a sack, tossing handfuls of rice to caged chickens. Carrying a gold pan, he joined the others working on the sandbar.

Four cowboys spied on the miners from the basalt shelf overlooking the camp. The tallest one wore a dirty brown hat and chain-smoked. Cigarette butts and matches littered the ground near his feet.

In the early afternoon, when the sun's glare became intense, the tall cowboy rested his rifle on a boulder and nodded. At his signal, the shooting began. The miner in the blue shirt dropped first.

Danny's eyes widened at the scene. As the cowboys fired round after round, the panicked miners scrambled one way, then another, looking for safety. Three managed to shove off one of the boats, but they were killed before they could get beyond rifle range. Alarmed at the shooting, three more miners dashed out of the cabin; two ducked back inside when their companion fell.

The shooting became sporadic as the cowboys ran out of rifle ammunition. They climbed down the hill and shot the wounded miners on the sandbar with their pistols. That finished, the tall one walked over to the cabin and shot some of the caged chickens. He reloaded slowly as the others dragged the two remaining miners from the cabin. One was fat and so terrified, he had messed his pants.

The cowboys tied the fat miner to the wooden sluice box and questioned him about the hidden gold, but he couldn't answer: he spoke only Chinese. They broke his arm. The other miner ran toward the river, but they caught him in shallow water and brained him with a rock. Then they shot the fat man.

Two of the gang members started stripping the bodies and carrying them toward the river while the tall man and another ransacked the cabin, piling the bedrolls and extra clothing outside.

As they set fire to the cabin and clothing, Hímiin's hut filled with smoke, and Danny glanced up at the flickering yellow eyes. He realized that no one except the cowboys had witnessed the slaughter. Left Hand was waiting two miles downstream.

After an hour, shadows passed over his face, and Left Hand looked up and saw two buzzards circle, dark as razors against the pale blue sky. He gripped his rifle tighter and spat, trying to clear his mouth of the metal taste.

The first floating body resembled a black tree limb carried by the spring runoff. It was close to the Idaho shore — too far for a good look — but it rode high in the water — a fresh kill, because the lungs hadn't filled. The second body drifted close to his side and nudged against a small sandbar. The corpse wore black pants and a loose black shirt. The skin and hair color resembled those of an Indian. But the clothes were wrong, unless it was a whiskey Indian who hung around the mining camps. Another body appeared, this one naked, and bobbed in the quiet water near the second.

Left Hand stared at the dead, trying to figure out what had happened. Some ranchers might have cornered Indian horse thieves and shot them near the river. If they saw him, they would shoot him, too, and he was afraid that he would not see his family again. He remained snugged under the rock overhang. In case someone was watching from the bench above, he didn't want to be ambushed. When his horse snickered, he gave it a handful of corn from the saddlebag.

At midafternoon, three men floated downstream in a boat. Each carried a rifle and had a pistol strapped on as well. When they saw the bodies, the men rowed the boat over to shore. One man wearing a brown hat said something to the others and they all laughed. Brown Hat stepped out of the boat, grabbed one of the bodies by the hair, and splashed out to waist-deep water. He released the body, and the current swept it downstream. The others stayed in the boat, laughing and passing a bottle. Brown Hat grabbed the second body, but one of the others pointed at the circling birds and handed him the bottle. He let go of the corpse and drank, then splashed ashore to piss. Standing where the campfire had been, he took his time, glancing now and again at the bench above and at the hackberry thicket.

Left Hand covered the horse's nostrils with his hand so she couldn't make any noise. He studied the man carefully. If the man started walking toward him, Left Hand would kill him first, then try for the other two before they could scramble for cover. Even so, the odds weren't good. He had only a little ammunition, and they could wait him out.

Brown Hat finished, then took out his pistol and fired at the circling buzzards. One veered slightly. Brown Hat laughed, then climbed back into the boat, first pushing it off the sandbar.

After the men were around the bend, Left Hand quickly moved

down to examine the body. No one was watching from the bench or Brown Hat would have signaled. The dead man was a young Chinese wearing the laborer's loose black shirt and pantaloons. He had been shot in the shoulder and back. Left Hand pushed the body into the current with his rifle butt and let it float downstream.

He had no quarrel with the Chinese, although he didn't like them much, either. Their shuffling walk and constant jabbering annoyed him. Originally, they had worked for the railroads, but many were now trying mining. Sometimes, when he came across one of their camps, he traded them jerky or fresh venison for chickens and the hard sweet candy they favored.

He decided to risk traveling upstream, hoping that the killers had all moved out. He was positive the men in the boat had done the shooting because of the way they had acted. If they had cleared out, he'd find a crossing upstream and try to cut off Slick Bear along the Nimipu Trail before he tried crossing at Dug Bar. Most likely the boatmen would stay at the cabin there. He hated the idea of fording the river at night, but downstream at Dug Bar they would kill him quickly, especially if they thought he knew anything.

After tying cloth around his horse's hooves, Left Hand set out, following a game trail along the river rather than traveling above the river on the exposed bench. He recalled an old cabin in one of the gullies upstream that the cowboys might occupy, but he thought the noise of the river would cover any sound he made. There was some dense hackberry, too. Along the bench, bunchgrass and scattered rock provided little cover.

In midafternoon, when the sun dropped over the steep canyon's rim, Left Hand walked in long shadows, leading the horse and frequently stopping under hackberry cover to study the terrain. The settler's cabin seemed deserted, but he waited until past suppertime in case someone inside built a cooking fire. Around the next bend, he was preparing to cross a treacherous talus slope when he smelled smoke, but not the smell of cooking. The wind carried the bitter smell of burning villages. His stomach turned to stone as he remembered the slaughter at Big Hole.

Leaving the horse, he crawled through the jumbled rocks until he had a clear view of the next gulch. The river had deposited a long sandbar there and gravel washed in from a good-size creek. The bar held a placer mine with a central sluice box, gold pans, and shovels.

The smoke came from a crude cabin built against the steep side of the gulch. The walls were rock, but the wooden roof had been razed. A pile of partially burned clothing and blankets still smoldered outside the cabin. No one moved, but he heard something rustling. He listened carefully, finally deciding that the sounds came from caged chickens.

Tethering his horse, he moved quickly to the cabin for the cover it afforded and stepped inside, rifle cocked.

The floor was strewn with beans, rice, flour, and hard candies. Some smashed tobacco tins littered the ground, but he saw no tobacco. Bending to pick one up, he touched a thick amber substance, like molasses. Opium.

A few loose rocks had been pried from the walls by someone looking for a concealed cache. He counted the smashed rice bowls and tea cups, trying to determine the number of men who had occupied the cabin. Around a dozen, he decided. And he had seen four bodies. Had some escaped?

Stepping outside, he took a stick and turned the smoldering piles of clothes and blankets. Dragging a scrap of a photograph from the fire, he saw the faces of two young Chinese men. Their bodies had been burned away, the ash curling just below their necks, and he wondered if they were now alive or dead. Dead, he supposed, and he felt sad that they would not receive a Chinese burial. Left Hand had watched Chinese on their way to funerals. Behind the wagon carrying the body, they scattered scraps of paper punched with holes, believing the devil must crawl through all the holes before he could find the body. By the time the devil arrived, the body would be safely in the ground. Later, the bones would be dug up and sent home to China.

Squawking chickens scratched in makeshift cages. A few of them were dead, shot at close range. Pistol shells and bloody feathers littered the ground. Left Hand tossed a few handfuls of rice to the caged birds still alive, and their squawking lessened.

On the sandbar, the gold pans were scattered all over. One had a bullethole. There were bulletholes in the wooden sluice box, too, allowing the water to leak into the sand. He found more pistol shells and one flat Chinese sandal, crusted with blood. He scraped away some of the dried blood with his thumbnail. A piece of bloodsoaked rope dangled from one of the posts on the sluice box and there was a bloody hatchet. It had been a slaughter. Left Hand felt the old rage stir inside him. Ten years before, the whites had driven the Nez Perce from their homeland and hunted them like dogs all the way to the Bear Paws. Now they were murdering the Chinese.

Two hundred feet above the sandbar, a rimrock shelf held clusters of tall bunchgrass and a few scattered rocks. Left Hand climbed to the shelf and found cigarette butts and wooden matchsticks and almost thirty rifle shells as well as a few empty cans of chewing tobacco.

The men had spied from this post and ambushed the Chinese. It had to be for gold, but the only gold in the canyon was float gold that washed down from the hills. With hard work, a man might make a few dollars a week, so it wasn't likely the Chinese had much money.

He felt a sudden chill and scrambled down from the bench to retrieve his horse, hurrying now. But he stopped long enough to locate his paint pouch and streak his cheeks and forehead. If he was killed, he might not have time to chant, but Slick Bear knew his death chant. As warmates, they had learned each other's chant so if one died without a chance to sing, the other could do it for him later.

Near the cabin, the horse became skittish, and Left Hand talked quietly to calm her. He had traded for this horse after the war and she was not familiar with death. At the far edge of the sandbar, he suddenly remembered the chickens. Leaving them in the cages meant starvation, so he decided to free them for the hawks and coyotes. At least they would die quickly. He kept the biggest one for supper, tying its legs together and slipping it into the cornhusk saddlebag. The bird must have weighed four pounds and plumped out the bag nicely.

One of the cloth covers he had tied to the horse's hooves was loose and he bent to retie it. As his fingers fumbled at the string, the horse whinnied and shied. He cursed her and seized the hoof with his right hand. Suddenly, he was struck on the head and pitched face forward with a grunt.

He stayed semiconscious for only a few seconds before responding to the horse's whinnying. Kicked by my own damn horse, he thought. He opened his eyes but lay still, waiting for the throbbing to lessen. His ears rang and his head felt bigger than a pumpkin. He was almost ready to attempt sitting when he heard the crunch of a bootheel on dry sand. He prayed it was something else, another sound, but then he heard two more steps and he squeezed his eyes tight, hoping his head would clear.

He tried not to breathe. He remembered one of the Blackfeet lying as if dead for almost an hour. When Rainbow had finally gone near him, the Blackfeet leapt up, slashing at Rainbow with his knife, but Rainbow was faster.

This man approached slowly, two or three steps at a time. He paused, then spit some tobacco. "Where'd he come from?" he said. "God damn savage won't be needing that horse now. I thought those Indian bastards had all been chased off."

No one answered, and Left Hand almost smiled in spite of the pain, because the man was talking to himself. Against two he would have little chance, because his rifle was on the far side of the horse. Why didn't this man just shoot him again? he wondered, then knew the answer. This close, the noise might panic the horse, and he would have to chase her far up the canyon.

Left Hand smelled the man now, and the rancid odors of sour sweat and old tobacco rekindled his fury. He heard the man's quick breathing, but he wasn't close enough to grab. Leather creaked. A pistol clearing the holster? A knife unsheathed?

Left Hand shouted, quickly rolling under the horse and grabbing for his rifle. The horse reared, flinging the scabbard out of reach, and the man fired. The horse snorted and threw back her head as the bullet ripped into her side, and the man fired again as Left Hand dodged behind the crazed horse. The second bullet whined off the basalt.

Rearing back, the horse flailed the air and turned toward the man, her hooves flashing. Swinging his rifle toward the horse, he fired point-blank at her chest, and there was a *whuff* as the air rushed from the horse's collapsed lung. His rifle was beyond reach, so Left Hand hurled a rock at the man, then charged as he ducked and fired.

He tackled the man hard around the middle, driving him back a few steps as the man smashed the pistol against his back. Left Hand tried lifting the man off the ground, but he was too heavy. The rifle fell, and the man grabbed Left Hand around the middle; they wrestled like two bears. The man's small brown eyes were wild with hatred and he bit at Left Hand's nose, but Left Hand turned his head, sinking his teeth into the man's ear.

The man screamed and loosened his grip, breaking free suddenly to clutch at his bloody ear. He took out his knife with his free hand, and Left Hand wrapped his war club's thong around his wrist.

The man crouched, scooping sand and flinging it toward Left Hand's eyes. But Left Hand knew the trick and closed them. Still, he acted blinded and started digging at his eyes with his free hand.

The man sprang, slashing the knife toward Left Hand's belly, but Left Hand leaped aside and struck the war club against the man's wrist. The man gave a small cry of pain as the knife dropped, and he grabbed his smashed wrist. Taking a quick step forward, Left Hand swung the club hard against the man's side and felt the stone head break ribs. The man grunted but didn't fall; then he leaped forward, his good hand snatching like a claw for Left Hand's eyes.

Left Hand swung the club again, smashing the man's skull just behind the left ear. The man's hand dropped to Left Hand's shoulder and he gripped it firmly, as if in greeting. When his mouth opened, he coughed out bright blood, then made a small noise that sounded like bubbles rising in water. His knees gave way and he sank to the ground, pulling Left Hand down on top of him. Afraid the man was still alive, he raised his club again, but before he struck, he saw the man's eyes go dull and knew he was dead.

Left Hand rolled over, lying on his back, trying to catch his breath. He heard the horse cough, and knew he would have to deal with that soon. His head hurt again now, and he felt his scalp with his fingers, deciding it was just a crease. Stumbling to the river, he washed his face and head. The cold water on the wound made his teeth ache, and he nearly passed out. His reflection in the moonlit water was so filled with rage and grief that it frightened him.

After taking out his knife, Left Hand scalped the man, then sliced off his eyelids so he would have no rest among the dead. He dragged the body across the sandbar, stopping twice to rest. He weighted the body's pockets and boots with rocks, then towed it through the shallow water. The weight grew lighter in the water, and he gave the body a hard shove into the deeper current. It revolved twice as the current carried it toward the rapids, and after that Left Hand couldn't see what happened. He threw the man's knife and rifle into the water. The rifle was almost new, but to be caught with a dead man's gear meant hanging. The cowboy had no doubt tethered a horse somewhere close, and his friends would find it soon enough.

After much coaxing, Left Hand got his own horse to her feet. He pressed wet rags into the bulletholes, trying to staunch the blood, but it seeped around the cloth. He walked a quarter mile, perhaps a half, toward Fence Gulch before the horse collapsed, and he knew it would be pointless to coax her again. He rested with her awhile, speaking softly and stroking her muzzle. She hadn't been a warhorse, but he credited her with saving his life. Singing quietly, he praised the horse's spirit, and when she put her head down, he quickly slit her throat to hasten the dying. He couldn't risk firing a shot.

Left Hand took the saddle and cornhusk bags from the dead horse and started back toward Fence Gulch. If he could find Slick Bear, they would have a better chance. He felt weak and a little dizzy, but he would be fine after a rest. Every now and then he stopped to drink from the river, but his thirst persisted. When he looked at the chicken, it stared back with its unblinking eye. He was tempted to let it go, but Slick Bear would be pleased with a roasted bird.

He had traveled halfway back when he fell among the rocks and the breath rushed out of him. His gut ached from the fall, so he lay still until his wind returned. After a long time, he tried breathing, but began choking on his own blood. His head cleared for a moment, and he realized there was another rifleman somewhere. Touching the front of his shirt, his fingers came away sticky.

Turning his head slightly, he searched the basalt rimrock above him, but he saw nothing. The rifleman had concealed himself well, and unlike the eager cowboy Left Hand had just killed, this one was going to wait.

Left Hand heard scratching. The chicken was a short distance away, searching for bugs along the riverbank. How had it gotten untied? he wondered. Was he so confused he couldn't tie a chicken's legs? He thought he must get up now and catch the chicken as a surprise for Slick Bear. Still, he could not rise. Rest, he thought. Wait until dark.

He coughed, spitting blood, and he raised his head slightly until it rested on a flat rock. He wanted to make it to Fence Gulch, where Slick Bear could find him, perhaps heal him.

He lay quietly, listening to the river and his own ragged breathing. Maybe he had imagined being shot, after all. He touched his shirt again, and his hand came away wet. Opening his eyes, he believed he saw the glow from campfires and Swan Lighting baking camas roots by the river. His daughter had wandered from her mother and stood too close to the riverbank, but when he called to her, she would not leave the water's edge. He shook his head and the scene cleared. Sunset's light played on the river, and the shadows of small trees undulated across the glowing water.

He gazed at the water for a long time. Soon the salmon would be running, he thought, big ones, and he would travel with Rose and her people to the Columbia. Shadows flickered across the river, and he watched several ducks settle near the far shore. Remembering the chicken, he looked for it, but it had disappeared.

It took all his effort, but he unsheathed his knife and dug through loose rocks until he found some dirt. Dropping the knife, he sprinkled dirt across his chest and forehead. Taking the eagle feather from his hair, he gripped it in his hand. The light on the water had changed, and now he was certain it reflected campfires. As the evening wind cooled him, he began to sing . . .

"No!" Danny cried.

He tried to speak to Hímiin, but when he turned his gaze from the embers, the old man was gone. Danny blew on the coals and they brightened, but he could not conjure the vision.

Closing his eyes, he tried singing Left Hand's song. And he remembered every word.

> *I, Left Hand, have seen my people vanish,*
> *Blown into the wind like camp smoke.*

Hímiin, help Rose and my young son.
I travel to Swan Lighting and my daughter,
My old warmates, Rainbow and Five Wounds.
Nothing remains but the mountains and rivers.

Dressing quickly and taking his pack, Danny slipped out the door of the hut into the brushy canyon. Gray morning light angled off the basalt, and the earth smelled fresh and wet. Studying the canyon walls, Danny knew Left Hand had died close by.

A small stream ran through the canyon, and Danny knelt by the water's edge. Taking out his pocketknife, he slashed his palm and thrust the bleeding hand into the cold water until the aching palm numbed and his blood swirled downstream. The twisted face of his great-grandfather haunted him, and Danny knew that anger blazed in his own eyes.

◈ 14 ◈

ATTACK

"Is that sausage too hot?" Pudge asked. She put another cinnamon roll on Danny's breakfast plate. "It seems kind of spicy to me, but it's Jimmy Dean Regular, just what I always buy. Unless I made a mistake. I was pretty tired last week — working double shifts because some of the nurses called in sick. It's more likely they're hung over after the Round-Up."

She checked the sausage wrapper in the garbage can. She had folded the garbage sack so the corners were exactly square. "No, it's Regular, all right." She bit into another sausage from the frying pan. "Too spicy. I'm going to start buying the Mild. Who knows what they put in this stuff, anyway?"

"It tastes fine," Danny said. It was almost ten o'clock, and he was feeling better. On the long drive from Dug Bar to Pendleton, he had gotten so shaky he had to stop the truck a couple of times and calm down. His pounding had awakened Pudge in the middle of the night, and she had come to the door wide-eyed, afraid he or Jack had been seriously hurt. After she had put a clean bandage on Danny's hand, they had talked until dawn. He was concerned about spilling his guts, but he had to tell someone.

Pudge glanced at the clock.

"Get ready, if you have to."

She sat at the table and sipped her coffee. "I got a little time yet, but I can't be late. Every bed is full. Those Round-Up cowboys are made of softer stuff than when you rode."

Her table was crowded with piles of women's magazines featuring articles on weddings. On top was a recipe box filled with cards. But instead of recipes, the cards had brides' names and lists of presents Pudge had given them. Danny read one: "Parmelle Pretty Mink. Milk glass cake holder. Fondue pot. Walnut chopping block." He put the card back in the box. "She's been married four times. Didn't she invite you to her last wedding?"

Pudge held up her hand. "Five. I quit buying her presents. No way am I going to get back my investment on that one." She added some sugar to her coffee. "Who are you planning to invite, anyway?"

Danny thought of his old buddies. Most had moved to the cities, looking for jobs. Two were in jail unless they'd been paroled recently. The rest he couldn't stand. "Willis and a couple of guys from the fish camp, I guess." He chuckled. "So Parmelle got real fat, huh?"

"If she comes to the wedding, you'll see why they call her Jell-O. On second thought, maybe she shouldn't come. The last time they held a dance at the community center, she wore a pink boa and kept lassoing her partners. One was a little scrawny guy, and everyone said they looked like Jack Sprat and his wife. She's really gotten tacky."

"She used to be kind of a good time," Danny said.

Pudge made a face and stood. She walked over to the calendar above the stove. "I got four days coming in late October, so we can straighten out the Loxie business then. Think we can drive to Nebraska and back in four days?"

"As long as we take your car," Danny said. Pudge had helped carry the buckets of dirt into her garage. They'd put them on a high shelf, along with the laundry detergent, in case the washer flooded the garage again.

"What about late October, then? I want to put it on the calendar."

Danny didn't say anything.

Pudge looked at him. "So what about late October? I'll need some time to make out the invitations."

Danny tapped the recipe box with his fingers. She was going to need a lot of stamps. "I still have to go back down to Dug Bar and take care of Left Hand."

"You'll take Jack?"

Danny nodded. Billy Que, too. Even though Que could be a pest, Danny remembered how good his uncle had been after Red Shirt died. They had buried him up on Reservation Mountain, and the ground was so hard, they needed a pick and spudbar to dig. Que put some paint on Red Shirt's face and made certain no one touched his bundle. He lay an eagle feather across his chest and tossed in his Korean war medal, even though they thought he had bought it. As they were leaving, a wet snow washed their tracks clean, a good sign. Danny cut his hair short to show his grief, and Que quit drinking for two weeks, the longest time he ever stayed on the wagon.

"If you need the elk teeth, take them."

"It's all right," Danny said. He planned to take some dentalia and a ceremonial arrowhead. Que might have something else. He wondered if anything had been done for all the Chinese. Maybe back in their own country.

Pudge turned the calendar page. "I'm going to mark the first weekend in November. Any reason that won't work?" When Danny didn't answer, she circled a date. "That's settled, then." Glancing at the clock again, she poured half a cup of coffee and did the same for Danny.

"It seems funny in a way, driving all the way back to Nebraska," Pudge said. "Loxie never went in for the old ways much. When the first pedal pushers showed up in school, she went to Portland and bought three pairs."

"Except for dancing," Danny said, remembering how she looked in her doeskin dress and beaded sidepurse. "She always got into the finals."

Pudge chuckled. "She made eyes at the judges. Those eyes promised everything. I never danced past the first round, so I was proud of her and jealous at the same time." She stood and started clearing the dishes. "I'm glad we're getting it settled."

Danny scraped back his chair and rinsed his coffee cup in the sink. He was careful not to scald himself; Pudge kept the water hot enough to make instant coffee from the tap. "I got to get going, too," he said. "Help Willis set up for the Washat. Catch some fish."

She stopped putting the food away. "Seems like you're always running off. You be careful on those platforms. I think of that cute guy from high school, the one who looked like a rock 'n' roll singer. What was his name?"

"Delbert," Danny said.

"Tie your safety rope."

"Decided you can't get along without me now, huh?" Danny started to kiss her, but she ducked away.

"I've decided I need help with Jack," Pudge said. "He's chasing all over the country in that fancy car of his. When he's a pain in the ass, he's just like Loxie."

Upstream from Willis's fish camp, the Wind River roared through the Narrows, deep basalt cuts with almost vertical sides. The Indians had suspended flimsy platforms over the whitewater, from which they dipnetted fish. Since the flooding of Celilo Falls, this site and Shearer's Bridge on the Deschutes were the only places left where platform fishing resembled the traditional fishing at the Falls.

Danny was staying at the ancient fish camp where Silver Creek joined Wind River. Duff Whitecrow, an old Klickitat fisherman who had occupied this camp for over fifty years, had gone cataract blind and developed ulcerated teeth from eating dried, sandy fish. The way Willis told it, he wouldn't leave his camp for the comforts of a tribal rest home. Instead, he doctored himself with herbal potions and lived on food donated by other fishermen.

After he went blind, Whitecrow tied a rope tether to a large yellow pine between his fish camp and the river. This allowed him to wander the basalt terraces above the Narrows without falling. As he reached the end of his tether, he would stand on the basalt cliffs, only inches from death, listening to the water's song.

Willis told Danny that Duff knew by the river's song when the salmon ran. "One song for salmon, another one for steelhead," the blind old man had said. And he remembered the faint scent of each wildflower that grew on the grassy terraces and in the shrouded woods, according to Willis.

Danny had heard that sightless people developed their other senses to compensate, so while fishing from the platforms, he sometimes closed his eyes and listened to the rushing water. But all he heard was the whitewater's constant roar, and, growing dizzy after a while, he would open his eyes rather than risk a plunge. The different songs remained a mystery to him. Perhaps, Danny thought, to learn them would take half a century — the time Whitecrow had spent at his fish camp.

The first time Willis had shown Danny around Whitecrow's fish camp, he had pointed to the yellow pine's welt, a thick mark from the rope's rubbing. When Whitecrow knew his time had arrived, he paced to the tether's end, then sliced the rope with his whetted fishknife. No one saw him plunge off the basalt cliffs into the foaming whitewater, and although they spread one net for him below the Narrows and a second net where Wind River joins the Columbia, his body remained with the water.

Three wooden lean-tos and a rusted mini-trailer made up the temporary camp. During the fish run, a surplus Jeep had been parked near the trailer, but it was gone now, along with the transient fishermen who left when the salmon run stopped.

Old utensils lay scattered across the cedar picnic table, and a rusted-out coffeepot perched on the woodstove. Danny picked up an empty can of pine-scented insect repellant, concentrated enough for yellow jackets and hornets.

Two burn barrels overflowed with pop and beer cans, discarded clothing, and empty motor oil containers. Black and white commodity food cans with USDA labels were scattered across the camp. Special sections of the *Seattle Times* discussing the plight of contemporary Indians lay on a bare bedspring. The fishermen spread those sections, along with others, to make a thick newspaper blanket.

At first Danny wondered why the fishermen hadn't hauled away their camp trash. Then he smiled slightly as he realized he and Willis hadn't cleaned their camp, either.

Brakes squealed as someone drove down the twisting river road. Danny saw Marvin Tenino's Silverado stop beside the pickup. He waved as Marvin got out of the truck and walked to the Narrows bridge that overlooked the fishing platforms. He carried four Rainier tallboys with him.

"What's happening, Marvin?" Danny said after joining him on the bridge.

Marvin opened a beer and spray shot out, indicating the bumpy ride down the river road. He offered one of the cans to Danny. "Eye opener?"

Danny shook his head. "Still too early."

Upriver, someone started a chain saw. It was barely audible from the bridge. Marvin nodded. "Willis is fussing and clucking like an old hen. We still got plenty of time before the Washat service, but he's already got Philbert cutting poles for a longhouse. Too bad your boy's not around. We need to work those young bucks. Willis wants me to make some signs — give directions to this place. He keeps trying to get newspaper and TV people to come to the Washat and cover this river trouble. Yesterday, he kept calling reporters in the Dalles and Yakima." Marvin shook his head. "They don't jump at Indian stories."

Danny thought of the newspapers strewn about the fish camp. "Not unless they're getting thrown in jail."

"I hear you." Marvin finished his beer and tossed the empty can into the water. "Whoops. There goes a downriver bright. Some white guy can catch that silver." He grinned. "You been getting any from the platforms?"

Danny shook his head. "Not for a couple days now. Everybody else left camp when the run petered out."

Marvin opened another beer. This one didn't spray. "You like that scaffold fishing?"

Danny shrugged. "It's fine — after my knees quit shaking."

Marvin laughed. "I got to build me a platform next spring. The grandson — Philbert's boy — claims he wants to fish traditional. Some of these young people got to try the old ways." He spat into the water. "It's high danger and low money. Me, I like boats and a net."

"It's dangerous, all right," Danny said. "I nearly slipped in two days ago. Fish slime made that platform slick."

"The trick is not to get too tired," Marvin said. "You got to keep alert. That rushing water can lull you almost to sleep." He held up the beer can. "No drinking around the platforms, either. The Water Devils love drunks."

"I heard they lost a boy in here last spring."

"Epileptic kid." Marvin shook his head. "He picked a hell of a time to have a fit."

Both stared at the rushing water. The wind carried the faint sound of the chain saw, rattling and snarling. Danny imagined Philbert's broad back leaning over his work, sweet cedar chips flying from the chain. "Maybe I will have one of those beers." After he had drunk half, he asked Marvin, "You think the Washat will really help protect the River People?"

Marvin shrugged. "Who knows? My grandson thinks so, but he's pretty young. Me, I've seen too many people shoved off this river. It makes me bitter."

"Willis believes in it."

Marvin squinted at Danny. "That's right. But he's got Old Simtus coming, too. You know about him?"

"A medicine man, isn't he?"

Marvin nodded. "From up in the Wanapum country. Most people stay clear of him. Willis thought he was coming last night, but he never showed. Maybe tonight." Marvin tossed the can into the water and tugged at his cap. "Better get back to help them with that longhouse. So you're still fishing?"

One more day," Danny said. "Maybe I'll catch a straggler."

Danny sat on the wooden platform, watching the whitewater rush beneath him. His legs dangled over the side and his boots darkened from the soaking mist. He had tied the safety rope around his waist because it made him feel better, but no one else was fishing. If he fell, no one would rescue him from the fierce pull of the water.

One of the long hoopnets lay on the scaffold beside him. The hoop was four feet in diameter — too big to sweep the channels. A fisherman would brace this type of net against his shoulder and wait for the fish to enter. Danny had fished all morning and half the afternoon without success, so he had taken in his net and now just listened to the water.

Before, he had always been afraid of winding up like Delbert and had to choke back that clammy fear whenever he saw the scaffolds. But now he was no longer afraid. Although these Wind River Narrows weren't Celilo, they gave him a sense of traditional fishing, and he understood why his ancestors had come to the river. It made him sorry that Red Shirt had relinquished his fishing sites, and he vowed he would try to coax Jack onto the platforms next year.

Raising his gaze from the water, Danny was surprised to see a man fishing from one of the platforms downstream, across the Narrows. Lost in his thoughts, Danny hadn't seen him descend the swinging rope ladder along the basalt cliff. The man was barefoot and naked to the waist, with two grizzled braids hanging down his muscular back. A scar marked his right shoulder. Danny shivered a little, thinking the man must be cold; the basalt cliffs shadowed the platforms from the weak afternoon sun.

"They're not running," Danny said, even though the man couldn't possibly hear him. "You're wasting your time." Unlike Danny, who sat relaxed on the platform, the man stood poised, leaning slightly forward, arms tensed, with the net braced against his shoulder. Suddenly, the muscles on his back contracted and he began lifting the net, hand over hand, as a struggling fish threshed against the hoop's twine. After he brought the fish onto the platform, his arm flashed above his head, and he whacked the salmon with a white fish club.

When the man put his net back into the water, Danny felt compelled to do the same. "It was probably a straggler," he muttered, doubting if the river conditions had changed enough to start a fresh run. However, almost at once a salmon bumped into Danny's net with such force, it nearly tore the net from his hands. Grunting with surprise, he started bringing in the fish and had to redouble his efforts as the fish cleared the water and he felt its full weight.

By the time he had it on the scaffold, he was panting from the exertion. He had to kneel on the salmon to keep it from flopping off the platform. He brought the weighted fish club down on its head, feeling the thump of wood against the breaking cartilage. Three blows quieted its thrashing, and Danny caught his breath as the fish spasmed twice, then lay quiet.

He admired the bright silver markings — like new coins — along the fish's sides and the gunmetal gray of its back. This platform fishing was nothing like hauling in the deadweight of river nets, and Danny felt the exhilaration that follows a killing shot at a running buck or a flying bird.

Glancing toward the platform downstream, Danny was amazed to see the man pulling out another fish, which struggled like a thick black ribbon against the whitewater. As soon as Danny plunged his net into the water again, he had a second fish. On the scaffold, it seemed a twin of the first.

"*Huk-choot,*" he called downriver. "You brought me luck." But the fisherman didn't acknowledge Danny's greeting. He was bent forward, intent on hauling out another fish.

After he caught five fish, the man stopped. He crouched on the platform, his arm extended, fist closed. Opening his hand, he dropped something into the water. Beads or perhaps pebbles? Danny strained to see, but he was far away.

The fisherman strung his salmon together with a long piece of rawhide and, leaving the hoopnet on the scaffold, began climbing the crude ladder, all five fish hanging from his back like silver pelts. Danny couldn't believe his strength.

Danny put his two biggest fish in a gunny sack and started up his ladder. At the top he was panting, and he knew what Willis meant when he said the ladders became taller each year. Once he reached the basalt bluff, Danny expected to see the man's rig parked beside his own, at the narrow pulloff by the bridge. But his pickup stood alone. Danny searched the road, but there was no sign of a man walking. Throwing the gunny sack into his truckbed, he took another look.

Crossing the bridge to the opposite side of the Narrows, Danny followed the bluffs downstream, thinking the man might have returned to the platform, but it was empty except for the hoopnet. Danny descended the ladder and knelt on the damp boards. With his forefinger, he traced the outline of the salmon, where their slime remained, along with a few glinting scales. Examining the net, Danny didn't recognize the style; it was constructed of sapling and hemp, and the hoop had been fashioned from bent pieces of barrel stave.

When he glanced toward the bluffs above, Danny half expected to see the man until he suddenly realized why the figure had seemed familiar. Had the man looked at him earlier, Danny would have seen the yellow flicker in deep-set eyes.

Returning to his platform, Danny carried his remaining fish out in one load, strengthened by the near encounter. As he rested briefly on the tailgate of his pickup, Danny guessed he had a hundred and fifty pounds of fish, a good contribution for the upcoming feast and Washat.

As he started to get into the pickup, he noticed that the dusty road was pocked with water drops. Following the spots, he found more slime on the ground and a few fish scales brushed off against one of the scrub oak limbs. On the picnic table in the middle of the fish camp were five upriver brights, gill-strung by a braided leather thong. A few green flies circled the fish, settling on the bloody club marks. The club itself — an ancient one carved from elk antler — lay on the table along with five polished salmon vertebrae that shone like pieces of light.

Danny slipped the vertebrae into his medicine pouch and tied the club to his belt. He scanned the woods, but he saw no one, though he knew the yellow eyes watched from the dark green shadows.

Old Simtus broke some dried branches from the bushes along the riverbank and started digging in the dirt by the blackened remains of the burned boats. When he had a small pile of dirt, he scooped it into a cast-iron skillet from Willis's kitchen. While he dug, Simtus sang his power songs, and although Danny strained to hear, he couldn't make out the words.

Willis leaned against the front fender of Simtus's Buick and watched intently. Velrae sat on the front seat, talking to his granddaughter. The granddaughter had to drive the old man around because he was nearly blind, but his hearing was keen.

Simtus moved down by the river and scooped a handful of sand from the bank. Grains trickled through his fingers as he put the sand into the skillet. He swirled it like a miner panning for gold. He gathered earth from two more places: the steep road coming down to the fish camp and the timbered hillside behind Willis's shack. All the while he sang his power songs in a high-pitched, nasal tone.

The singing made Danny uneasy, but he was more uncomfortable with the old man's rattlesnake bracelets. He had the snake Wéyekin — powerful, but difficult to control. Except for those who handled sorcery and fire, most avoided the snake spirit.

"I should have gotten Simtus down here earlier," Willis said. "But he was up on Gable Mountain. No one follows him there."

Danny nodded. Gable Mountain was a sacred place for the Yakimas, but the government had seized it and included that land in the Hanford project. They had drilled deep holes in the mountain for their radioactive waste. Although it was on the federal reserve and off limits to Yakimas, some of the powerful elders still went there, believing their spirits were stronger than the radioactivity.

Willis had built a small open alder fire from the wood behind the shack. Once Simtus collected the dirt, he heated the skillet on the fire, his chant becoming louder and higher. He stirred the dirt with the sticks and circled the fire, pausing to stare at the four places he had dug.

His clouded eyes had the filmy, vacant look of a reptile, and Danny glanced away as Simtus stared past him. The old man held the skillet in his bare hands in spite of the heat. He stopped stirring and circled the fire again, this time pointing at the four places with the stick. He lifted the skillet from the flame and held it next to his ear, listening. The chanting became hushed.

Simtus carried the heated dirt to the first dig, by the blackened boats, and scattered some of the earth. Then he got down next to the ground and listened. After that, he lifted the skillet to his ear again. At the riverbank, he listened longer. Putting down the skillet, he lifted both arms toward the sky and shook his hands so the snake's rattles whirred with a dry sound that made Danny's flesh crawl.

Simtus scattered the remaining dirt by the road and behind the shack, and as he came back toward Willis, he seemed suddenly weaker. His granddaughter got out of the car to assist him. Velrae leaned against the roof, smoking a cigarette. Simtus said something to Willis that Danny couldn't understand. Then the old man took a rawhide bundle out of his pocket and handed it to Willis. In size and shape, it resembled the one that Wauna had given Danny. Willis put it in the pocket of his cowboy shirt and snapped it closed. While the granddaughter helped Simtus into the Buick, Willis got a Pendleton blanket box from inside the house. The granddaughter opened the car door so Willis could set it on the back seat.

Simtus jabbed his finger toward the river twice and made another gesture toward the camp. He seemed to be giving Willis instructions. Willis nodded, tapping the shirt pocket that held the bundle.

After Simtus left, Willis walked down by the dock and stood

there, looking at the water. Velrae went over by Danny. "That old guy gives me the creeps," she said.

"He's a strange one, all right."

"This is the first time I've seen him stick-read," she said. "But I've heard about him before."

After a while, Willis walked up to the two of them. Danny wanted to ask him about Simtus, but figured Willis would tell him when he was ready. Velrae didn't wait. "What did he say?" she asked.

"No one does that stick reading anymore," Willis said. "He didn't pass it on, although he says his granddaughter might know a little. He'd teach her more, but she won't quit drinking, and he's afraid she'll go bad, let the power get out of hand."

Danny nodded.

"When I was about your age" — Willis motioned toward Danny — "somebody stole my father's power bundle. Dug up his grave and stole it. I was sure it was his old enemy, the one with the fishing quarrels, but even though I confronted him about it, he said no. So Simtus and I went out to where my father was buried, and Simtus read the earth. That person who dug him up there left a little of his bad spirit. Simtus told me, 'You go to that man's house and tell him he's got that bundle he stole off your father behind the refrigerator, hidden by the motor. And he better give it back up to you, or I'll get into him and maybe his family, too, if they don't start doing right.'

"So I went and did like Simtus said. And that old enemy started shaking when I told him where the bundle was. And he got it for me quick, because he knew it could only be Simtus with that much power, and if Simtus was on my side, he wasn't going against me." Willis nodded. "I never had any more trouble with that man."

"What does Simtus say this time?" Danny asked.

"He said to get ready because they're coming back, and they're going to try to push us right off the river." Willis pointed toward the docks. "They're coming by boat."

"Sportfisherman," Velrae said. "Those bastards."

"They aren't Indians," Willis said, "so Simtus can't tell."

Danny was a little disappointed. He wanted to know who was coming and how many. That would make it easier to guard the camp. "When are they coming?"

"He didn't know," Willis said. "But they don't want us here, on these places, and they're going to get us off any way they can. So we got to get people organized to guard round the clock. Cooks and Lone Pine, too."

He turned to Velrae. "You go see Stubby. Shotguns are probably best, especially if they come at night."

"I'm not going to see that sleazebag by myself. He's like a slug. I don't trust him after the way he looked at me."

Willis shrugged. "I've got to warn the other camps. The sooner the better." He glanced at Danny.

"I'll go with her," Danny said, even though he wasn't crazy about spending more time with Velrae. Shotguns sounded pretty serious. "Look here," he said to Willis. "What about the bundle he gave you? That should offer some protection."

Willis tapped his pocket. "It's a war bundle," he said.

A week had passed since Simtus made his visit, and Danny was exhausted from pulling sentry duty every other night. Although it was his night off, he was too tired to rest. He got out of bed and drank a glass of water, then dressed quietly and went outside. It was cold and he reached back inside for his denim jacket. A few steps away from the shack, he turned toward the brushy hillside and waved. Velrae was concealed up there somewhere, but he couldn't see her. Maybe she had fallen asleep in spite of the chill, although he doubted it. Her anger kept her sharp.

In the past week, nothing much had happened. Most of the River People had little faith in the old shaman, in spite of Willis's belief. Now that the fishing season had passed, many of them were drifting away to go deer hunting or try the archery elk seasons on the reservation. Only a few remained to stand guard, and Danny was about ready to go home also. When the old man had been there, Danny was convinced his power was real, but now he, too, had started to doubt.

He passed by the burned boats and walked down the ramp to the dock. A slight chop made the waves slap against the steel girders. Danny gazed at the river. Now that he didn't have to break his back fishing, he could see how beautiful it was.

Small clouds dotted the moonlit sky; their shapes and movements reflected on the water. Toward the Oregon side, the water sparkled with the glow from Hood River's lights. It was spectacular, although it didn't quite hold the same mystery for him the Wallowas conjured. He preferred to be farther from civilization, and the Wallowas' remoteness, as well as their beauty, lured him. He had promised Jack — promised himself, too — elk camp this year, and now that the fall chill was in the air, he thought of the Wallowas, knowing that elk would be drifting down from the high timber as the snow began to pile.

A dark patch, a shadow of a drifting cloud, he thought, caught Danny's eye, and he remembered the night he had been swimming and saw the seal — if it was a seal. Now he knelt on the dock, dipping his hand into the water. Cold. No swimming tonight. The cold made him think of the faded wool coats they used in elk camp, the canvas cots and heavy sleeping bags he stored in the tack shed. As soon as he returned to Pendleton, he needed to check on the equipment to make certain the mice hadn't taken up residence.

Just thinking about elk camp made Danny feel good. He'd help guard fish camp until after the Washat, then head out. He and Jack had helped Willis when the old man needed it most, but now it was time to move on. Already he had missed the Round-Up and most of bird hunting. Pudge was mad as hell because he wasn't around to help with Jack, and each time she called, she badgered him about how much longer he planned to stay on the river.

As for Simtus, he was just a superstitious old coot. Danny figured he probably made a pretty good living off his dire predictions. Some of these old people needed to stop the mumbo-jumbo. Lawyers and courts were the new way. Maybe they'd whip the BIA's eviction notices in court.

He took some pebbles from the shore and tossed them into the water. Just for fun, he decided to see how far he could throw a couple of larger rocks. When he felt a sharp ache in his shoulder, he regretted not warming up first. He started throwing sidearm because it didn't hurt, and he was pleased with the distance. He imagined it was the bottom of the ninth and he had to fan the batter.

The exertion tired him a little and he stared at the reflected lights for five more minutes. Lights on the water could be hypnotic; he was starting to feel sleepy. If he crawled into bed now and thought of elk camp, that should do it.

He turned and walked halfway along the dock before he stopped. Something seemed wrong about the river, but he couldn't say just what. He watched the shadows and reflections. The old trick of looking indirectly didn't help either. Closing his eyes, he imagined everything he had seen on the river: the buoy, the reflections . . . He stopped when he remembered the dark patch. The shadows of the other clouds were drifting east, with the wind, but this one came downriver from Bingen. Was it a large piece of debris, the kind Orville salvaged from the river to build his shacks at Cooks?

Danny studied the river carefully, trying to determine where he first saw the patch. Now it was much closer, a dark oval hugging the timber-shadowed Washington shoreline. As it approached, Danny noticed knobs at both ends — men's heads. A black rubber raft was approaching the camp. He slipped behind one of the large steel girders supporting the dock so his shadow merged with the girders'.

If he shouted an alarm, the sound, carrying across water, would spook the rafters. He intended to surprise and capture them, finally ending this business. He dropped to his belly, keeping his head down, and started crawling along the dock. Halfway to the ramp he remembered his fish club and grabbed it, clutching the welcome weight in his fist. At the top of the wooden ramp he paused for a quick look, but the men in the raft hadn't seen him. He crouched behind one of the good boats, knowing that Velrae must have watched him crawling. The rafters had to cross fifty feet of moonlit water to reach the dock, and Danny was certain she would see them, too.

When the raft came out of the shadows, Danny expected moonlight to wink off oar blades or lighten an upturned face, but he saw nothing except the shadowy raft and dark figures of the men. He guessed they had smeared their faces.

They nudged the raft against the dock and got out quietly, then squatted beside the raft while one seemed to give the other directions. After a few moments, the stouter man started creeping along the dock with a satchel. The smaller man stayed on the dock, kneeling over something.

Danny stared first at one figure, then the other. Gripping the antler fish club, he began chanting his power song, and even though his lips moved slightly, only the smallest breath of air escaped his mouth. By springing from the shadows, he could disable the first man up the ramp, then let Velrae cover the second. He hoped she didn't lose her cool and open fire on the stout man, especially just as Danny approached. They had worked out strategies for such events and agreed that no one was to shoot unless lives were in danger. Danny just hoped Velrae kept it together.

The stout one started up the wooden ramp, and the moonlight winked off a pistol he carried. Danny hadn't seen it before because it was low and close to his hip. Anger swept over him and he hunkered lower, feeling foolish he hadn't brought a gun with him. Let Velrae cover him first, he decided. Then he could disarm him. He wasn't going to move against that pistol.

No alarm came from the hillside as the stout man reached the top of the ramp and crouched by the boats farthest from Danny. Remaining motionless, he appeared to be studying the fish camp — surveying the automobiles, the drying shacks, the trailer where Danny slept, Willis's shack. When he seemed satisfied, he took something out of the satchel, then quickly replaced it.

Explosives. Danny had contemplated someone's setting their place on fire, but he hadn't expected anything as devastating as explosives, especially at night while they slept. Where the hell was Velrae?

The man started for Willis's house, keeping close to the burned boats so he wouldn't be in the open quite yet. He would pass two steps away from Danny. Danny prayed he wasn't blessed with a sixth sense.

As the man slipped past him toward the shack, Danny moved, taking two quick steps and swinging the fish club. His eyes never left the man's pistol hand, and as he swung, he followed through, as if trying to hit a low pitch to deep center. The club cracked against the man's forearm, snapping bone, and the man screamed, dropping the pistol.

Danny lunged for the pistol, and the man karate-chopped him with his good hand, knocking him off balance. Then the man dropped to the ground, covering the pistol with his body. Cursing, Danny kicked him twice in the head, forcing him to defend himself with his good hand.

Cat-quick, he got to his feet again and aimed a karate chop at

Danny's gut, but Danny twisted so it caught him in the side. He stepped inside the next kick and swung the club for the man's head, but the man sidestepped, so Danny missed.

The man kicked him in the kidneys. Grunting with pain, Danny doubled over, then rolled under a boat before he could be kicked again. "Velrae!"

The man stepped back. "Kill the bastard!"

As Danny tried burrowing into the hard dirt, he heard gunfire from the raft. Gravel scratched his cheek, and chunks of the boat blew away.

A shotgun roared behind him, pumped, then roared again. Pellets clattered off the dock and clanged against the steel girders, striking sparks. The lean man jumped into the raft, using the dock to shield his body. He returned fire to cover his partner, who had started down the ramp, hanging on to his dangling wrist with his good hand.

Velrae stood behind the Neptune fish tote. She fired at the fleeing man, and pieces of ramp blew away in front of him. She fired again as he reached the dock, and he pitched forward, then crawled behind one of the girders. "I'm hit!" he yelled.

The door to the shack banged open and Willis started firing at the raft, but his aim was poor, and Danny heard the shot spray against water. The smaller man fired on the open doorway, but Willis had ducked back inside. Glass broke as the trailer's porchlight shattered. Velrae used the diversion to scramble behind the boats, where she had a better view of the dock. She crouched beside Danny, sucking air through her teeth. Her eyes were wide and fierce.

"You took your time," Danny said.

The smaller man fired again at the Neptune tote, apparently unaware that Velrae had moved. The wounded man kept slithering toward the boat.

"Check it in," Velrae murmured, taking aim with the shotgun. The buckshot struck the crawling man's legs, and he screamed again.

"You cocksucker," Velrae hissed. She pumped and pulled the trigger, but the shotgun was empty. As she started reloading, the shells jammed.

Danny peered out from under the boat.

The crawling man reached the end of the dock, and his partner pulled him over the side and into the raft.

Willis ran down the steps, braids flying. He was naked from the waist up, but had managed to put on shoes and pants.

"Keep down," Danny yelled when Willis started across the open space, then crumpled. He stayed down, but he wasn't hit. "Tripped," he shouted.

Having reloaded, Velrae was crawling along the line of boats, trying for a clear shot.

The raft moved away from the dock into open water. The smaller man paddled furiously while the wounded man slumped in the bottom.

Remembering the satchel, Danny scrambled to get it. The satchel was lighter than he expected, and he flung it so hard, it cleared the rock breakwater and landed in the river.

By the time Velrae began firing at the raft, the men were out of range. Finally, she put the shotgun down and held both hands aloft, giving them the fingers. With her legs spread and head thrown back, she reminded Danny of some warrior-priestess. He grinned. Velrae had her own style. He'd credit her with that.

The dock gave way suddenly, buckling in the middle as if rising from the water like a serpent. Planks broke away, carried skyward with a fountain of dark water. Danny felt the blast hit him, driving him under the boat, stunned. Pieces of the dock crashed against the boat, and river water rained down. When the junk quit falling, he crawled out.

Willis lay on the ground halfway between the boats and the shack. His eyes were closed and he clutched both hands to his groin. As Danny moved toward him, Willis's mouth opened as if he were laughing silently. Then Danny saw the dark wet stain covering the inside of his thighs.

He tried to pull Willis's hands away so he could see, but the old man clutched himself tighter. "Where's Velrae?" he whispered.

She was a hundred feet away, sitting on the ground, dazed but all right. She lurched to her feet.

"She's okay," Danny said. "Let me have a look at you."

Willis shook his head.

"How bad is it?"

"Pretty bad," Willis said. "I peed myself. Soon as I quit shaking, I got to get back in the house and change."

Danny slumped beside Willis and laughed. "You had me scared."

"They're getting away," Velrae called. She held the shotgun across her chest. "I was hoping that blast would swamp them."

"Help me in the house quick," Willis said. "It's hell getting old."

By the time they had finished answering questions and filling out police reports, it was almost four. No one had shown up at the hospital in The Dalles or Hood River, but Danny knew whoever had been in the raft would have to, sooner or later. One was hit bad, maybe dead.

He tried sleeping, leaving on the trailer light, but each time he closed his eyes he saw dark figures from the attack. As his mind replayed the action, his eyes popped open; he was afraid that in one replay the intruder would kill him before he could knock the pistol away.

After a while, he got up and poured himself some whiskey. Raising the glass to his lips, his hand shook, slopping the drink. Fatigue, he thought, and fear.

The whiskey had calmed him some, so he poured another half glass. Numbed, he crawled back into bed, leaving the light on, and he was almost asleep when he thought of Willis and the dark stain spreading across his thighs. Danny reached down, cupping his testicles with his hand, then dozed.

When the trailer door squeaked open, Danny lurched up in bed, his heart pounding. "Shit, Velrae. You scared me to death!"

"I saw your light." Closing the door, she sat on the edge of the bed. She tried lighting a cigarette, but her hands were shaking badly. "That was some night," she said.

"Take a dose of nerve medicine." Danny nodded toward the bottle.

She filled a glass half-way and took a drink, closing her eyes as she swallowed. "Think they'll find those guys?"

Her voice was husky, and Danny realized she was as tired as he. "They've got to show up at the hospital," he said. "Otherwise they'll get lead poisoning or gangrene." He propped himself on one elbow. "Maybe they drowned. The pellets might have ruptured the raft."

"Don't count on it," she said. "Shit floats." She finished her drink. "I wish I shot straighter. We'd have one less creep to worry about." Her hands had steadied a little, and Danny could read the tattoos as she tried lighting another cigarette. She almost made it, but the match burned her fingertips before she dropped it. She leaned forward slightly, hugging herself. "It feels cold as hell, doesn't it?"

"I could start the stove." Danny's pants were at the foot of the bed and he would need to slip them on under the covers.

"That's not it." Her teeth started chattering. Kicking off her shoes, she crawled in beside him. "I'm like ice," she said. "Just hold me."

He carefully put his arms around her, surprised at how thin she felt. Her ribs were sharp and hard under her shirt, and he suddenly missed Pudge's softness. For a while, Velrae shook like a frightened dog, but finally her trembling lessened until she lay quietly.

"Where's Willis?" Danny asked, but she was asleep.

He eased out of bed so he wouldn't awaken her and slipped on his pants and sweater. In sleep, her face had relaxed, losing most of its harshness. She's almost pretty, Danny thought.

He walked over to the window. His knees ached with fatigue, and he hurt where the intruder had kicked him. He was surprised to see that Willis was already up, walking around the ruined dock, poking at the debris with a shovel. The old man uncovered something, and Danny recognized the dead watch goose. Willis held it by one orange leg and seemed uncertain what to do next. Finally he carried it to the hillside behind his shack and started digging a hole.

◈ 15 ◈

WASHAT

WILLIS AND MARVIN had put up a temporary longhouse near Duff Whitecrow's fish camp on the Wind River. They'd used sturdy cedar posts and plywood sheets, with blue plastic tarps for a roof, but they had run short of tarps and filled in with opaque plastic sheets from Broughton's Lumber. The east end of the longhouse remained open as an entranceway. This old custom also enabled bad spirits to find their way out. To Danny, the entire longhouse looked a little flimsy, reminding him of the revival tents that traveling ministers threw together just off the reservation.

Danny, Jack, and Willis were unloading rolled carpet sections from a flatbed. After the attack, Danny had picked Jack up in Pendleton, insisting he come down for the Washat. Jack had agreed, although he seemed more interested in seeing Velrae than in the service. His car had blown its transmission, and Danny towed it to Milo's before they left. When Danny had complained to Pudge about cosigning for Jack, she ignored him.

The men carried the carpet sections into the longhouse and laid them on the dirt floor. The sections were odd shapes and sizes, so they spent a lot of time folding pieces under or rearranging sections until they more or less fit. Most of the carpet was lime green, although some was light orange with brown stripes, reminding Danny of tigers and the upholstery Henry had used on the bucket seats of his customized Ranchero. The colors clashed, but he figured it wouldn't matter much once they set up the benches.

They carried benches to the north side for the men. During the service, the women would sit on the south side facing them. Bare earth formed the middle section of the longhouse, allowing the people to dance and worship next to the land. Willis had borrowed the benches from Celilo; the letters CELILO-WY-AM were stenciled on the bottom. In a couple of places, partially buried rocks made the benches tippy, so Danny got a short-handled shovel to dig out the worst ones.

Willis kept glancing at his watch. "Where are the toilets?" he said. "That Bishop Sanitation guy from Goldendale is late. If he doesn't bring the honey houses soon, we're all in big trouble."

"Lots of trees," Danny said. "Anyway, he's probably running on Indian time."

They all chuckled.

"Let's get the firepit going while we wait," Willis said. "Marvin's back from town with the briquets."

Jack and Danny piled briquets and alder chips under the grill. Then Jack squirted two cans of lighter fluid over the fuel. After squirting a little extra in a coffee cup, he pretended to drink. "Firewater," he said, staggering around.

Willis struck a match on his pantleg and flipped it onto the coals. Danny stepped back as the fluid caught, the whooshing flames nearly touching the grill. "In half an hour, they can start cooking," Willis said.

The women were unloading boxes of food and equipment from the campers. Except for Velrae, they all wore pink caps with pompoms that said CHIEF COOK. The biggest one was named Zoots; Danny didn't know the others.

"Hey, handsome! Help us unload these coolers," Zoots called.

Jack handed Danny the cup. "Must be talking to me," he said.

Danny tossed the cup into the fire and helped carry the food.

Foil-wrapped salmon sections filled three big ice chests. They were too heavy for one man to carry, so Danny and Jack teamed up. Feeling the weight, Danny was proud he had caught some of the fish from the platforms. When Willis had asked Danny how he caught such big fish, Danny had said, "Beginner's luck."

While Danny and Jack carried the chests, Willis lugged four large buckets of eels to the grill. "This is going to be some feast," he said.

Jack helped Marvin set up a 35-horsepower generator to provide electricity for the coffeepots, Port-a-Mike, and strings of lights they needed to illuminate the longhouse after dark. Velrae moved among the workers, pouring coffee from a silver Thermique. She blew on Jack's before handing it to him.

"We're sure getting fancy," Willis muttered. "Used to be we had chipped coffeepots and tin cups. When the coffee was hot, you couldn't hang on to the handle without gloves."

After Velrae made certain everyone had coffee, she mixed Kool-Aid and Hawaiian Punch in a twenty-gallon galvanized container filled with river water, then sliced lemon sections into the mixture for more tang. Danny was surprised at how adept she was at setting up for the feast.

Wauna was the first religious leader to arrive. When she climbed out of her pickup, Danny saw she was already wearing a doeskin dress with porcupine quill designs. The emblems had originally been introduced to the River People by Smowhalla, the Wanapum Dreamer prophet. The yellow sun represented life; the white moon and stars were the throbs of the drumbeats. Down the left sleeve were six stars, the same number Smowhalla had worn, and seven stars trailed down the right sleeve. The seventh star indicated the seventh day, reserved for the sacred Washat service.

Wauna carried a small drum with a wolfhead emblem. Danny expected her to stop and say hello, but she walked directly to the longhouse. He watched from the open east end as she hung her drum on a nail. After studying the longhouse, getting its feel, she took a deerskin paint pouch from her belt and sprinkled white clay on the bare earth for the dancers. He was curious about the clay. The old Dreamers once collected it from White Bluffs, but that area was prohibited now, enclosed within the Hanford site and contaminated by radioactivity.

When Wauna finished sprinkling the clay, she noticed a lump in the carpet where green met tiger stripe. As she bent to straighten it, Danny approached.

"That carpet's not much, but we dug out most of the big rocks," he said.

"It'll do." She studied him for a few moments. "You seem to be in one piece. I stopped at the fish camp."

"We got some work to do before next season."

"I thought maybe you'd had enough fishing."

"I'm just getting started."

She smiled. "Willis said you went to the Wallowas before the attack."

"I got the dirt," Danny said, "and I found out about the visions."

When he finished telling her about the Chinese and Left Hand, Wauna said, "I've been down that canyon. Sometimes I feel our people so strong, I have to sing. And when I do, the old songs join mine."

"After I take the dirt to Loxie's grave, I'm going back to where Left Hand died to leave some ribbons and maybe an arrowhead." He chuckled. "If this keeps up, I'll be singing Seven Drums and braiding my hair."

She touched the side of his head. "Let it grow." Picking up the silver bell that summoned the people to the Washat, she began ringing. The Drummers entered and a few of the people followed, the men removing their hats. Most remained outside, visiting or drinking coffee. Danny left when he heard Willis shout.

"The cavalry is here!" Willis was pointing at a Bishop flatbed truck carrying four yellow port-a-potties chained to skids. Coming over the road, they bounced and tipped with the ruts, and if it hadn't been for the chains, they would have tumbled onto the ground.

The truck driver had a red face, and his left arm was deeply sunburned from hanging out the window. He took off his Seahawks cap and rubbed a lawn mower haircut. "Where do I drop these honey houses?"

Willis pointed. "Over by them trees in the shade so no one gets a hot seat." He stepped away from the truck as the man started backing up. "How come you're so late, anyway?"

"I couldn't find the damn turnoff. Finally I just followed some junker cars." The driver climbed out of the cab. He was big, maybe two-seventy, and he resembled a freezer chest stood on end. Pulling on work gloves, he climbed onto the flatbed and unchained the port-a-potties. When Danny offered to help, the man shook his head. "It's tricky. You got to learn the point of balance."

The ringing came louder from the longhouse and Danny headed

in that direction. Jack met him partway. He had been hauling wood to the firepit and now brushed sweet-smelling alder chips off his shirt. "You think any good's going to come from all this?"

Danny squinted at him. "Sure. Don't you?"

"It's a lot of damn hard work." Jack studied Danny. "You're staying, aren't you. No matter what."

Danny nodded.

"Is it really worth it? They'll lose anyway, won't they?"

Danny listened to the bell. "You coming inside?"

"Maybe later," Jack said. "I'm still helping Velrae."

The Seven Drummers stood at the west end of the longhouse, facing east. Each held a drum that contained his song, one inherited from his ancestors. Although five of the Drummers were elders from various river bands, two were young, and Danny felt a twinge of envy that their family songs had been preserved.

As Wauna stopped ringing her leader's bell, the first Drummer started his song, a light song for morning. He sang in a high, clear voice while pounding on a drum with a blazing sun design. As he sang, the worshippers stood, moving their right arms back and forth in arcs across their chests.

Three young men and three young women took positions facing the bare rectangle of earth. The boys stood at the east end, their backs to the Drummers, and the girls at the west end. The boys carried swan feathers, as Smowhalla had instructed, and the girls, eagle feathers. At the end of time, when the earth turned upside down, they would need the feathers to fly to heaven.

When the lead boy rang a bell, the dancers moved counterclockwise around the longhouse. Their moccasins tracked the white clay Wauna had spread.

Danny wished that Jack had been part of the dancing, but the boy had missed learning the ways during all those years he was in Nebraska. As Danny blamed Red Shirt for not passing down the songs, he now blamed himself for not teaching Jack about the longhouse.

When the first Drummer finished his song, the people raised their right hands, fingers spread, and offered an "aaahhh" of affirmation to the Creator. A second song began with a different singer and another set of dancers. This song was for the deer.

During the long service, Danny listened carefully to each of the sacred songs. When one Drummer, an old man with otter in his braids, sang the water song for salmon, Danny listened harder, hoping for a part he might recognize.

After the Seven Drum service, Danny and some of the other men began setting up benches and tables for the salmon feast. He worked with a big man in army camouflage clothes that had "Bruno" stitched on the shirt jacket. His hair was cut GI flattop, and when he turned, Danny could see the fat rolls on the back of his neck. Bruno smiled constantly and spoke in a low voice. "Look at those scummy kids," he said to Danny.

From the back of a Dodge pickup, several teenagers watched them working. The kids had been drinking beer, and their tape player groaned with loud music. One of the Drummers asked the boys to help with the tables, but they ignored him. "I'm no janitor," one kid said. He wore a Beastie Boys T-shirt over his jogging pants. When the old man returned to setting up tables, the kid laughed and told his friends, "My old man says Harvey there used to be the biggest boozer in White Swan. Now he's some kind of longhouse bigshot." The others laughed.

Bruno glanced over his shoulder at the kids a few more times. "Excuse me," he said to Danny. Arms folded, he walked over to the pickup and spoke to the kids, too low for Danny to hear. The Beastie Boy said something in return, and Bruno pulled up his shirt just a little, then pointed to the tables. One of the boys turned off the music, and the others jumped out of the truck to help set up. They worked quickly and quietly, casting sidelong glances at Bruno.

Bruno kept smiling and nodding until the boys were finished with the tables. Then he and Danny got cups of coffee and sat down.

"What did you tell them?" Danny asked.

Bruno held the Styrofoam cup to his lips and blew a little on the coffee. "I said if they didn't respect their elders I was going to cut out their tongues."

Danny set his coffee down. "What?"

Bruno half stood and lifted the front of his khaki shirt, revealing a sheathed combat knife. "In Nam I was an interrogation specialist," he said, still smiling. "You look at a prisoner awhile and realize there's nothing that won't come off. Ears, cocks, faces. Everything comes off." He dropped his shirtfront and sat down, sipping his coffee. "Sometimes I still see them. The doctors call it delayed stress syndrome and write it down in books, but they don't see faces every night."

"The white doctors don't know much about those things," Danny said. "Maybe you need a healing."

"I've been getting help," Bruno said. "You know Old Simtus?"

"I've seen him once," Danny said.

Bruno was nibbling the edges of his cup and watching Jack and Velrae working at the firepit. "Those two keep looking this way. I don't like people staring."

"That's my boy," Danny said.

"Not a bad-looking kid," Bruno said. He leaned closer. "I heard about the fish camp. Everyone has. You got to learn meanness. The enemy respects courage, but he fears meanness. You should have wasted those guys when you had the chance." He brushed the table with the heel of his hand. "Two players off the board."

"I'll keep that in mind," Danny said. He still didn't know who the attackers were or what had become of them.

Bruno stood, patting the bulge under his khaki shirt. "Think I'll check the perimeters. Maybe they got friends." He squeezed the back of Danny's neck. "Been good talking."

Drumbeats signaled the start of the salmon feast. Young women in ceremonial clothes carried traditional foods into the longhouse and to the extra tables outside, where Danny sat. Platters of grilled salmon came first, then steaming bowls of venison stew, bitterroot, and kaus. Tin buckets of huckleberries were last. Danny had hoped some of the older women would carry in the huckleberries, the woven baskets balanced on their heads, as they did at He He Butte in August, but the older women and Velrae were still cooking fish.

After the traditional foods had been placed on the tables, Willis walked through the longhouse, holding aloft a single eagle feather to bless the foods and the feast. Danny remembered seeing Chief Tommy Thompson bless the food in a similar way when Red Shirt took him to the Celilo Salmon Festival.

After Willis finished blessing the food, the young girls put small portions of the traditional foods on everyone's plates, using a community platter and bowls. Then they ladled a couple of fingers of river water into every cup from a bucket. Smowhalla had taught the River People to take the traditional foods together, as a communion, in order to ensure that the Creator would provide abundant food for the individual households.

Willis waited until everyone had been given water and the first foods. Then he raised the water glass to his lips. "*Choos!*" he pronounced, drinking.

"*Choos!*" everyone replied, drinking their water.

Willis pinched salmon between his thumb and forefinger. "*Nasau!*" He ate.

"*Nasau!*" Everyone repeated and ate.

Willis lifted the bitterroot to his mouth. "*Skoolkol!*"

The others followed. After the venison, kaus, and huckleberries had been taken together, everyone began loading their plates with large portions of the rich red salmon, savory stew, roots, and berries. As they began eating, the girls brought more: boiled potatoes, hominy, green salad, fruit ambrosia, pork and beans, fruit cocktail, corn bread, white bread, fruit punch, and coffee. One girl winked as she set a plate of grilled eels in front of Danny. "Velrae said you love these." Danny turned to glare at Velrae, but she was bending over the firepit. Rather than be impolite to others at the table, he tried a couple of eels, although they reminded him of a greasy boot tongue.

When everyone finished eating, the Drummers started again, and Wauna began ringing her bell. The people stood and made their way out of the longhouse, starting with the men in the east corner. Proceeding single file by the elders, Wauna, and Willis, the men were blessed with the eagle feather before walking to the longhouse's open end. As they neared the entrance, each man turned a full circle, his right hand raised to the Creator. Outside, they circled the longhouse — east to north to west to south — then formed a large semicircle near the river. Danny and the other men standing outside filed through the longhouse as well.

The women followed, repeating all the actions, until they formed a semicircle within the men's. The Drummers, Willis, and Wauna came last, with Wauna ringing her bell. Their backs to the river, they joined the semicircle, making it complete. Wauna struck her bell three final times and everyone turned full circle, hands raised, marking the feast's end.

Glancing toward the country road on the hillside high above the river, Danny noticed that a car had pulled over and someone was taking pictures. He wondered how the circle might appear from that perspective.

While the others moved away from the circle or broke into small groups, Danny remained, as if by staying he could make the circle last longer. But it was broken. Wauna, Willis, and the elders posed for photographers down by the river near the fishing scaffolds. Velrae had never joined the circle but remained at the firepit, cooking more salmon. Jack stood beside her, drinking a Coke. Danny remembered the last time he had stood in a circle with his father.

Following the Celilo Salmon Festival, the wind had blown so hard, Danny kept blinking to keep the sand from his eyes. He stood in the big circle between his father and Sammy Salwish. Sammy's long hair streamed in the wind and his head tilted slightly, as if he were listening to the water roaring through the basalt chutes. A reservation Indian joked that the river was angry because they were finishing the dam, and Sammy's face darkened. He was among the last to leave when the circle broke.

Danny had spent the late afternoon sliding down the steep, sandy hillsides with the other children. At dusk, he was cold and hungry, and he looked for Red Shirt, expecting to find him among the gamblers or in his pickup, drinking. Danny searched the entire camp before he saw two dark figures standing on the basalt cliffs overlooking the village and falls. Their blankets flapped in the wind, as if they might fly from the cliffs like dark birds, and Danny shivered. After nightfall, they left the perch, making their way slowly around the cliff face to the village. In the campfire's glow, Danny saw their eyes and believed the red was from the scouring sand.

Throughout the afternoon, Danny kept returning to the temporary kitchen for cups of strong coffee and handfuls of store-bought cookies. All the while, Velrae stayed close to the grill, turning the salmon with a long-handled spatula. The extra salmon and leftover food were for the elderly or those with trouble in their lives. As she cooked, Velrae kept up a good-natured banter with some of the older cooks, who took their breaks by sitting in aluminum folding chairs and placing their swollen feet on plastic coolers. The broken veins in their ankles looked like spiderwebs above their moccasin tops.

Danny never saw Velrae sit down. She was sweating with the heat of the firepit and had tied a red headband around her forehead. He couldn't have imagined her working this hard. Maybe she was trying to make up for the spoiled salmon, he thought, then put the harsh idea out of his mind because it was inappropriate for the feast.

It had grown colder outside, and people were drifting toward the longhouse in anticipation of the Giveaway. Danny had seen Willis carry in seven Pendleton blanket boxes, and he felt a little disappointed. He had hoped to receive a blanket himself for helping with the fishing, but he knew these blankets were for the seven Drummers.

As Danny refilled his coffee cup, he saw a young woman carrying an empty commodities box heading toward the grill. A couple of raggedy children tagged along.

The woman scuffed at the ground with her worn moccasins while Velrae filled her box with foil packets of salmon and containers of potatoes and corn. One of the children had a runny nose, and Velrae wiped it with a paper napkin, then tossed the napkin into the firepit, where it flared briefly. As the woman started toward her car, Velrae thumped Jack's arm with a spatula and pointed toward an empty box by the grill. Quickly he filled it with more salmon and two large cans of fruit cocktail as well as a couple of packages of cookies. He hurried after the woman, helping her load boxes and children in the car, a battered Buick with baby moccasins dangling from the mirror. The kids' faces pressed against grimy windows when the Buick drove off, the single taillight winking as the car jounced over the bumps.

Glancing toward Danny, Velrae saw him and quickly bent over the pit again, pretending to be busy, but no more salmon remained on the grill. Her spatula, half raised, twisted in her hand.

Danny drank some of the coffee, but it was too hot and made his eyes water. What the hell, he thought. Maybe Velrae had her good points, after all.

He had started for the longhouse when he heard Velrae yell. Jack had snuck up behind her and jammed one of the pink cook's caps on her head, smashing her spiked hair. She spun around, swinging the spatula, but he grabbed her wrists, twisting until the spatula fell to the ground.

Velrae shook her head vigorously, trying to loosen the cap, but it only slipped a little until it perched above one eye like a rakish sea captain's. "Let go of me!" she insisted.

Jack dragged Velrae toward Danny. Their struggling left heel marks in the dirt. "Found me a good cook," Jack said.

"I can tell by the hat," Danny said.

"Let me go, damn it." Velrae kicked back toward Jack's shins, but he stood too far behind her.

Jack grinned. "I catch the food and she cooks it. Just like old times."

"You pig. Let me go." Velrae laughed. "You'll eat it raw."

"Why don't you settle this?" Jack said to Danny.

"Do I look like a referee?"

"Give me the truck keys so I can take her away . . ." Jack released Velrae and made a sweeping gesture around the camp. "Away from all this."

Velrae grabbed the cap and tried to put it on Jack's head, but he sidestepped and caught her in a bear hug, pinning her arms against her sides. The cap dangled from her trapped hand.

"There's action in The Dalles," Jack said. "Movies. A rock band from Portland. All we need is keys."

"What about the Giveaway?" Danny asked. "You'll probably be getting something."

"I'll give him something," Velrae said, "soon as I get the chance."

"Enough celebrating," Jack said. "I was setting up camp before dawn and she damn near barbecued herself over that pit."

Danny took the keys from his pocket. "Here." He tossed them to Jack.

Jack released Velrae and grabbed the keys.

"Watch out for cops," Danny said. "They wait for Indians."

Velrae rubbed her arms. "Maybe I'll stick around here." She pretended to pout.

"Suit yourself," Jack said, heading for the pickup.

"Catch." She tossed Danny the pink cap, and instinctively he caught it in midair. "Hold down the fort," she said.

Turning the cap over and over in his hands, Danny watched them go. He realized that he had missed almost everything with Jack. In another year or two he'd move on to Velrae, or someone like her. Soon a young woman would be braiding his hair. The boy still had a lifetime, and Danny envied him that. Choking back a knot in his throat, he stepped inside the longhouse, glad for the bright lights and the action of the Giveaway.

Several of the women and young girls were still carrying goods into the longhouse. They placed them at the west end, where the Drummers had stood earlier. The presents were in bundled bedspreads, large green garbage sacks, Montgomery Ward shopping bags, and black and white commodities boxes.

Across from Danny, an older couple set up lawn chairs by the longhouse wall. The man was wearing a green and yellow John Deere cap, and she walked with a cane. They had difficulty with the chairs, and a couple of younger people helped them.

Willis had been off to one side, talking to reporters and answering their questions, but now he picked up the Port-a-Mike.

"Before the Giveaway starts, I got just a few things to say, while I got you all right here paying attention. The first thing I know is, we're going to be getting some respect along this river now." He paused for emphasis. "This land here is sacred land — holy land for us. The river that's running through it — that's the blood. The salmon here were given to us by the Creator, along with venison and roots."

Willis spread his arms a little to indicate the bigger river, the Columbia. "At one time there were longhouses and Indian people living all along the river. Those old houses were made of tule, which was sacred to the people, like the deer and the salmon. That's the reason the old people were buried in tule mats and deerskin, then put in plain pine boxes, so they could return quickly to the earth and the Creator."

"Now you know some of our people have been put in prison recently for fishing, even though that's what the Creator wants them to do. But that white man's law is no good for people like Orville, and he should have got a fair trial in tribal court by his own people, who understand the river and the old laws. We got a treaty that says we're a sovereign nation."

Willis held out one hand toward the reporters. "We'd especially like to thank those non-Indians here today, who came to witness our ceremonies and learn a little about our ways. On this religious day everyone is welcome, and there should be no anger or bitterness entering the longhouse. We got the Giveaway coming up real shortly now, and after that we've got lots of dancing . . ."

Willis looked as if he could talk on awhile, but Wauna stepped toward him and made a quick chopping motion with her hand.

"*Kitu! Kitu!* We got to hurry this along," she said.

"Before I turn over this mike, I just want to say to some of our veterans that a few of you have been asking how come you fought overseas for this white man's country." Willis tapped his foot on the bare earth. "You weren't fighting for this country but for this land right here."

A few people cheered, and one old man waved his cap.

Danny could tell Willis loved having the mike, but Wauna folded her arms and edged closer. Willis hesitated. "I guess it's time." Wauna took the mike from his hand and started the Giveaway.

As Danny expected, the blankets went to the Drummers who had performed the Washat. Each one received a blanket and fifty dollars for his help. The cooks received bright fringed shawls, blouses, and neckerchiefs. Two cooks had special gifts: a beaded bag with a red poppy design and a Virgin Mary shrine. Wauna called Velrae's name three times, but Willis had to accept the shawl and blouse. He seemed surprised Velrae wasn't there.

Wauna selected one of the commodities boxes. "We got special gifts now.'" The mike hummed, and she held it away from her mouth a little. "First, age before beauty. Danny Kachiah. Now where'd he go?" She spotted him. "He's just shy, hanging out in the back."

When he walked to the front, she opened the box and unfolded a red ribbon shirt with dark blue polka dots. He sucked in his breath at the beautiful gift.

"This isn't payment," Wauna told the crowd, "but just a little remembrance, a token of our appreciation for all the help you gave Willis and the other people along here." Reaching into the box again, she took out a beaded belt buckle with a leaping Chinook salmon. "This is yours, too. My mother made it."

Danny thought of Wauna's mother, in front of the flickering TV, working on the buckle. She had used expensive cut-glass beads, and light sparkled off the buckle. Both gifts were treasures.

Wauna called Jack's name three times, as was the custom, before Danny accepted a ribbon shirt for him. It resembled Danny's but was navy blue. Danny hoped the new shirt would take away some of the sting from his leaving the old shirt on the Medicine Tree.

Suddenly there was a crash, and across the way, a plywood section of the longhouse fell backward.

"Mose," Marvin said, and Danny saw the old man in the John Deere cap sprawled on his back, still sitting in his upended folding chair. Striking the ground with her cane, Mose's wife struggled to stand.

Two young boys had been drinking beer and smoking outside. They seemed startled at seeing the plywood section fall and the old man topple out of the longhouse, landing at their feet.

"Quit gawking, you two," Wauna scolded through the mike. "Help him up."

"I'll bet that's it for old Mose," Marvin said. "He's topped a hundred."

Everyone craned his neck to see as the two boys grabbed the folding chair by the arms and pushed it upright, old Mose clutching the armrests. "He's all right." The word passed around the longhouse. "Just fell asleep and tipped over."

The smell of marijuana drifted in the air as the two boys hastily lifted the plywood sheet back in place. One took off his shoe to pound in the nails.

Willis took the mike from Wauna. "Geez, that Marvin makes a good longhouse," he teased. "I hear he's going to be an inspector for BIA housing just any day now."

As Danny changed into his ribbon shirt by Willis's pickup, he heard the singers inside the longhouse warming up, their voices high and thin in the night air. He shivered with the cold. The falsetto songs reminded him of so many other dances — some with Loxie, some with Red Shirt and Medicine Bird.

He attached the new buckle to his belt, admiring the leaping salmon design and the flashing winks of the cut beads in the pale moonlight. Then he started for the longhouse.

Wauna stood beside her blue pickup. She had taken off her Washat clothes and now wore a patterned dress decorated with abalone and a blue fringed shawl draped over her shoulder. Danny felt a stir of interest as he approached her.

She didn't notice him at first.

"Hey."

"Oh, sorry. I was thinking," Wauna said. "Shirt looks good."

"Thanks," Danny said. "But maybe I butted in on something."

She touched his arm. "No, I'm glad you came along. I was slipping into a mood." She paused. "Every time there's dancing, I think of my kid brother, Virgil. His feet were wind."

"Virgil?"

She pulled the shawl tight. "He was some kid. Mom said he had the Nick in him." She smiled at the thought and fell silent for a moment. "After I went to San Francisco, he turned wild. Someone stabbed him outside a bar in Lewiston. No witnesses. I always wondered: Would it have been different if I had stayed close to home?"

"You can't blame yourself."

Wauna didn't seem to hear him. "He could dance, all right. Once in a while, if I squint my eyes while I'm watching the dancing, I can almost imagine that one of the young men is Virgil. But there's always something missing."

"I know how it is," Danny said, surprised because he didn't think anyone else did that. At every festival, he'd half close his eyes and gaze at any dancer who resembled Loxie. Sometimes — usually in August, when the dancers' feet raised dust in the dry circle — he didn't even need to squint to imagine her there.

They could hear the drums and Willis saying, "Hey, everybody. We're going to start tonight with the Greeting Dance, so everybody come on into the circle. Eagle Spirit Singers from Satus Pass got the first drum, so take it away."

Neither one moved toward the longhouse. Finally Danny asked, "Do you want to go for a walk?"

A crescent moon had risen above the dry hills, casting enough light so he could see quick gray puffs when he breathed. Neither spoke until they stood on the riverbank.

"How'd you wind up in San Francisco, anyway?" He had been there once with Henry, but couldn't remember anything except rolling a drunk in the men's room at the Condor Club.

"It's an old story." She laughed. "I followed a man. Married him, even. It's been over twenty years now since I heard from him." She watched the rushing water awhile. "Hard to believe."

"You ever think of marrying someone else?"

Wauna folded her arms and looked at Danny. "My work keeps me busy. Anyway, it's only a thrill the first time."

"I guess."

Wauna hugged her sides, then briskly rubbed her upper arms. "It's too cold out here. Time for me to head back to the longhouse."

Danny waited before saying, "I think I'll stay here a minute."

Danny could see Willis in the distance. He had come out of the longhouse and was standing by the kitchen tables, making more coffee. As he fiddled with the large coffeepot, a shower of sparks rained from the cord. The string of lights suspended from the long-house ceiling flickered, then dimmed to darkness.

"Willis, you sure do good work." Wauna's chiding remark carried to where Danny stood in the dark.

Shouts and whistles came from inside. After a few moments, matches and cigarette lighters flared in the darkness. Carrying a large flashlight with a dim yellow beam, Willis was inspecting the extension cords for the electrical system. He went back inside the longhouse and pronounced the cords shot.

"But this celebration isn't finished yet." His voice sounded faint without the Port-a-Mike. "We got to keep going, finish this dancing. We'll go all night, maybe. Wait for the sun, like in the old times."

As Danny watched, Marvin drove his Silverado to the east end of the longhouse and turned on the headlights to illuminate the dance floor. "Dim 'em, for Christ's sakes!" someone called, and Marvin switched them to low beam. "Good thing I just bought me a DieHard," he yelled, climbing out.

Squinting in the direct light, a couple of the drummers took dark glasses out of their shirt pockets and put them on. "Hollywood," one said. As the drumming and singing started again, Danny saw Wauna enter the longhouse.

"Take it away, Spirit Singers." Willis's voice sounded as if it were traveling a great distance, but Danny heard each word distinctly. "Let's have that Greeting Dance now. Watch your hands there, you guys. No taking advantage of the dark corners. You women there, kick high if they try anything funny. If they try again, kick higher."

Danny heard a low whistle upstream, then a quick answering whistle. Steah-hah? Holding his breath, he listened. A girl giggled, and dry brush rattled along the riverbank. Another, deeper voice calmed her. Tipi creeping, Danny thought, and he relaxed. Not Velrae and Jack. They would be making love somewhere else, perhaps on one of the grassy basalt bluffs overlooking the Columbia or in a small motel room just outside The Dalles.

He walked downstream, away from the voices, until he came to the empty fishing platforms. The wood appeared specter-white in the thin moonlight and reminded him of the bare tipi poles at Big Hole. Sometimes everything seemed so fragile, he thought it might all vanish before his eyes. He remembered Jack's question and answered it for himself. Yes, it was worth it. To believe in this life, to hold on, even if all that remained were faces carved in stone.

From the longhouse, the singing grew louder until Danny heard it clearly over the sounds of the rushing stream. Taking care to maintain his balance, he stepped onto one of the platforms. From there he saw the dark outline of the longhouse, the shadowy figures dancing. In the eerie glow, the place seemed unfamiliar, resembling the mysterious paintings of the ancient longhouses where thousands once had gathered for the river celebrations.

Water rushed beneath the platform. Untying the bundle from his neck, Danny loosened the leather thong and poured the five salmon vertebrae into his hand. They glowed like gems. One by one, he tossed them into the rushing water and saw them change to quicksilver ribbons.

Danny imagined all the waters pouring toward the Columbia. Clearwater and Snake, Deschutes and White, Klickitat and Wind . . . The salmon rode the swelling currents out to sea, then beat their flesh against water and rock, returning. Always returning.

As Danny listened, voices rose from the dark water. Many thousands of voices, old tongue and new, blended with the longhouse singing and echoed off the basalt hills until the valley seemed filled with their cries. They joined a deeper song borne downriver by the night wind, then fell to whispers. Stepping off the trembling platform, Danny started climbing toward the longhouse. Beneath the singing waters, Chinook glided among rocks, and campfires blazed.

ACKNOWLEDGMENTS

As with *Winterkill*, this novel places fictional characters in actual places and against some historical events. The Wind River of this book is invented and combines landmarks of the Klickitat, White Salmon, and Wind. The Chinese Massacre of 1887 did take place on the Snake River, and these pages contain my fictional version of its aftermath.

Some establishments exist as I describe them. However, I have felt free to invent details, such as the painting hanging above the fireplace in the Columbia Gorge Hotel.

I'd like to thank the following for their research facilities: the Oregon Historical Society; the Luna House in Lewiston, Idaho; the Yakima Indian Nation Cultural Center and Museum; the Nez Perce Tribal Visitors' Center; and The Dalles Library and Visitors' Center.

I am indebted to the River People, those contemporary Indians who live and fish along the Columbia River upstream from Bonneville Dam. I especially want to thank Johnny Jackson for his stories and tours of the fishing sites. Chief Howard Jim and the other people at Celilo Village provided generous hospitality during their salmon festivals.

Lillian Pitt, a friend and artist, knows the territory this book covers. Her Steah-hah masks and legends were valuable inspirations. Thanks also to Ed Edmo and Elizabeth Woody, friends and poets, who offered encouragement along the way.

Mari Watters was a vital source of Nez Perce history and anthropology. I also want to thank her for the invitation to participate in the Nez Perce Upward Bound Summer Program in 1987.

The pronunciation of Native American words such as *kaus kaus* and *p-tass-way* vary from band to band. The spellings here reflect the ideas of those individuals I consulted during my research. Some fishermen use the term "platforms" and others "scaffolds" when referring to the traditional salmon fishing places.

I am particularly grateful for Amanda Urban's skills as an agent and her insightful reading of the manuscript.

Katheryn Ann Stavrakis was essential in bringing this book to life. We worked side by side during the writing and revising processes. Fran Kiernan offered wonderful editorial suggestions and insights. Thanks to Luise Erdmann for her careful and helpful manuscript editing. And Gale Wall deserves credit for her helpful advice and many hours at the word processor.

Thanks to all who helped and encouraged along the way. Rich Wandschneider served as guide during a rugged trip to Dug Bar and Robinson Gulch. Philip Klindt offered research suggestions. My uncle Oscar Lange provided his recollections of the Mutton Mountain fire and Buckskin Billy. My good friends Ivan and Carol Doig offered seasoned advice, and I remain indebted to them both.

Finally, I'd like to thank the National Endowment for the Arts for its grant of a fiction fellowship for 1986. The selection panel included T. C. Boyle, Ernest Brawley, George Garret, Ivy Goodman, Robert Hemenway, Joyce Carol Oates, Elizabeth Tallent, and John Wideman.